LILY'S QUEST

BEYOND THE THIN VEIL OF **PARALLEL DIMENSIONS**

S.J. SAVAGE

CHAPTER 1

OCTOBER 1967

Awakened from a sound sleep, Lily opened her eyes to see a tall black shadowy figure standing over her bed. As she rubbed her eyes, more black shadowy figures came into focus. There were several. Terrified, Lily shut her eyes tightly and screamed at the top of her lungs. A few seconds later, the light switch was flipped and golden incandescent light filled the room.

"Lily, what's wrong?" Lily opened her eyes to witness the concerned expressions on her parent's faces. She looked around the room. The black shadowy figures were gone and her toys were scattered about. Everything looked the same as it had when she went to bed. As her mother felt her forehead, the mere loving touch of her mother's hand calmed her and she began to feel safe again.

"Did you have a bad dream Honey?" Her mother asked.

Lily had no words to describe what she saw, or at least what she *thought* she saw that caused her to cry out. "Scary black things were trying to get me." That was all she could say.

"It was just a bad dream sweetie." Her father said. He picked up her stuffed bunny off the floor and handed it to her. "Here's your bunny. Everything is ok, just close your eyes and go back to sleep. We'll leave the door open and we'll be right across the hall. You're safe." The comforting words of her father reassured her that all was well, but Lily knew it was real. It wasn't a dream. The shadowy figures were there and they wanted something. She could feel them and they would be back.

The sunlight shone brightly around the edges of Lily's bedroom window. It was morning. The black shadowy figures had not returned in the night and the atmosphere in her room felt quite normal. She crawled out of bed and slowly walked down the hall toward the kitchen to find her mother standing in front of the stove flipping pancakes, and her father sitting at the table with his coffee and the newspaper. "There she is!" Her mother said in her usual tone gushing with jubilant enthusiasm having just flipped the perfect pancake. "Are you hungry? I made your favorite—Pancakes!" Lily smiled and crawled up to the booth in the corner of their kitchen.

Her Father looked up from his newspaper with his reading glasses resting on his nose and gave her a loving smile. "Everything alright Pumpkin?"

"Uh huh." Lily mumbled. Everything *seemed* to be alright…For now. At only 4 years old, Lily was developing an understanding that was well beyond her years. She instinctively knew that last night's visit of the tall, black shadowy figures was the beginning of something that her limited vocabulary would not allow her to express properly. She knew it would happen again, all the time actually, and she was frightened by it. She also knew that even if her parents were sitting on her bed when the figures appeared, they would not see them. She knew this was an experience only she would have in their house. She knew her parents wouldn't understand. They couldn't.

How do you explain things that only you can see? How do you prove they are there? Have her brothers seen these things? Clearly her parents had not or they would have been able to offer a better explanation other than *'It was just a bad dream.'* The feeling of isolation on this subject was disheartening. A 4 year old child is supposed to have an imagination. They're supposed to be afraid of shadows in the dark. It's normal and in some ways, expected of them. Who will believe Lily if she talks about what she saw? Lily's mother set a plate of steaming hot pancakes with a partially melted pat of butter on top, and a moat of thick maple syrup surrounding the island of fluffy wonderfulness.

A strange phenomenon invariably occurs when eating anything with maple syrup. No matter how careful you are not to touch the syrup with your hands, the fork mysteriously gets sticky every time. Lily was an obsessively clean child. She didn't like getting her hands or clothes dirty and hated any knots in her hair. Yet, despite how consciously careful she was with her pancakes and maple syrup, her fork and her hands were now sticky. One of the benefits to having a dog in the family was that the dog was always ready, willing, and able to clean your hands off for you. This was no substitute for good old fashioned soap and water, but it saved a trip to the sink in the middle of breakfast.

"Lily…Don't feed the dog under the table." Lily's Mother said.

It was also uncanny how mothers were able to know what was happening in the room behind their backs. Do they really have eyes in the back of their heads??? You certainly couldn't see any. Still, she knew that Lily had quietly set her fork down and slipped her hands under the table to let Winnie lick the syrup off of her fingers.

"Momma? Can Winnie sleep with me tonight?" Lily asked as she recalled the scary shadowy figure experience she'd had the night before.

"I suppose that's okay." Her Mother said. "Now finish your breakfast and let's get you dressed. I see the neighbors are raking leaves into piles out there and the kids are jumping in them. Looks like fun!"

Leaves. Kids. Fun. Those 3 words were enough for Lily to stuff the last few bites of pancake in her mouth all at once and set her plate on the counter.

Outside, the neighborhood children were laughing and playing in the leaves. It was Lily's turn to jump in the leaf pile and as she backed up to take her running jump, she noticed a man standing across the street at the corner of her father's garage. She thought nothing of it. It must be a friend of her Father's who has come to visit. After diving into the pile of leaves a few seconds later, she lifted her head and spotted the same man, but he moved to a different place. In a few short seconds he repositioned from the garage across the street and was now standing next to the big Maple tree in the middle of the neighbor's yard—just 10 ft. from Lily. She sat in the leaves staring at the man. How did he get across the street so fast? Who was he? What did he want? She didn't recognize him but he looked at her with proud amusement just as her Father would watching his child play.

"Hello." Lily said as the man stared back at her. He said nothing and just smiled.

"Lily who are you talking to?" All of the neighbor kids stood quietly watching Lily engage with something, but they couldn't see what it was.

"The man by the tree. Right there." Lily pointed in that direction and all of the children looked that way.

"There's no man there Lily. Stop pretending. It's your turn to rake the leaves. C'mon it's David's turn to jump." Scottie said. He was the oldest at the ripe old age of 6 and tended to be the ringleader of the group. It was his yard they were playing in and he was positive that there was no man standing by the tree. As Lily stood up to grab a rake, she turned her back to the tree for only a split second. When she turned and looked back, she found the man had vanished. *He really was there a second ago... Wasn't he?* She thought to herself.

That evening after dinner, as the Carole Burnett Show was starting on the television, Lily's mother sat on the floor in the family room with a box of loose photographs and an empty photo album.

"I've found this box of photos in the back of the closet and thought I would sort through them. Do you want to help me Lily?" Her Mother asked. Lily happily joined her on the floor and began picking out all of the photos with Winnie in them and pictures of the Florida beaches where the family would often go to on vacation. She picked up an old yellowing black and white photograph with the corner bent of a man in a hat standing next to an old pick-up truck. Lily stared intently at the man in the photo. She had seen him before. She saw him today and she said hello but he didn't say anything back.

"That's my Dad—Your Grandpa Tom, Lily." Her mother said.

"I saw him today but I didn't know who he was. I said Hi but he didn't say anything." Lily couldn't take her eyes off the photo. She was absolutely positive that this was the man she saw.

"You saw *him* today?" Her Mother said as she reached for the old photograph from Lily's tiny hand and stared at it recalling the fond memories of her Father. "Honey it couldn't have been him. He died when I was a teenager many years ago." Her Mother said. She remembered what a kind, loving father he was and how much she'd missed him.

"No Momma, I'm sure it was him. I saw him in Scottie's yard today when we were playing in the leaves." Lily said.

"It was probably just somebody who looked like him. You say there was a man in Scottie's yard?" Lily's Mother said with concern.

"No Mom, I saw HIM." Lilly said as she pointed at the photo her Mother was holding in her hand. "First next to our garage, then he was standing next to Scottie's tree. It was him." There was no doubt in Lily's mind. This is the man she saw today, dead or not.

"Did anybody else see him?" Annie Campbell was a sensible woman. When your child says she's seen a mysterious man whom she recognizes as her dead Grandfather whom she's never met, it warrants a bit more investigation.

"No. They said they didn't. It was my turn to rake leaves and when looked back at the tree, he was gone. I don't know where he went." Lily said quietly.

Not knowing what more to ask at that moment, Annie carefully set the photo aside and proceeded to sort through the other photographs. She watched Lily as she happily picked out all of the photographs that appealed to her and wondered if there really was a man watching the children play today, which would be alarming and creepy, or if Lily just had a delightful imagination. Since Lily said that none of the other children saw the man, this made Annie believe that it was likely the latter.

CHAPTER 2

APRIL 1968

"Thank you for coming in to speak with me Mrs. Campbell. I have some concerns about Lily…" Mrs. Rosher was Lily's Kindergarten teacher and Annie was taken by surprise to receive a phone call from her requesting a meeting. Lily wasn't a disruptive child and she loved going to school every day, so Annie was a bit surprised to receive the invitation to come in and speak to the teacher.

"Oh, of course. What are your concerns Mrs. Rosher?" Annie asked.

"Well, I adore Lily. She's a very bright and imaginative child and she's always pleasant to have in class." Mrs. Rosher started. "But she seems to have a great deal of difficulty staying focused. She daydreams. A lot. It's almost like she's somewhere else and she's completely disengaged from what's going on in the class. I've moved her to the front row, but it doesn't seem to matter. She's often staring out the window or looking around the room at, well… nothing really." Mrs. Rosher was an older, attractive woman who seemed to be well experienced with children and came across as sincere in her observations.

"Well, Lily does have a vivid imagination. She plays for hours by herself. Sometimes with dolls, and sometimes she pretends she's a teacher at school. She arranges boxes like desks in a classroom and she passes out papers and occasionally scolds her imaginary students who aren't paying attention to their lessons. She also refers to herself as Mrs. Rosher so I know she admires you." Annie said.

Mrs. Rosher looked down at her desk for a brief moment in flattery, but quickly regained her composure and expressed her opinion further. "I certainly don't want to appear nosey, but, is everything alright at home? You know, sometimes children will internalize stressful situations which often presents as a detachment at school…" She said.

Annie was taken aback by the notion that trouble at home was even being implied. "No, no, everything at home is fine. She's a normal, happy child at home."

"Well, I was going to suggest that maybe Lily should talk to someone. You know, sometimes children will tune out when they feel like they can't keep up with the rest of the class…I must say though, we don't do a lot of testing at the Kindergarten level, but we do try to determine a student's aptitude for learning before they enter first grade. That said, Lily's test scores are very good—well above average." Mrs. Rosher said as she opened a file and pulled out Lily's test papers to show that she consistently scores between 86%-90%. "Most people think of Kindergarten as organized play time, but our curriculum is geared toward prepping the children for the school years ahead. We can test for indicators of strengths and weaknesses a child has in certain subjects so that we can better prepare them to do well in their elementary school years, which of course is the foundation of their entire education." Mrs. Rosher explained as she removed her reading glasses before continuing. "I have noticed that she squints sometimes to see the board. Perhaps you could take her to an optometrist and see if she needs glasses? That might help."

"Yes, yes I'll do that. I've actually noticed that she likes to sit close to the television. Thank you for letting me know. I'll make an appointment and have her eyes checked right away." Annie said as she stood and placed her purse strap on her shoulder. "Thank you for bringing this to my attention Mrs. Rosher. I appreciate all that you're doing for Lily."

Later that evening while Lily was playing with her toys in her room, Annie knocked on her door. "Can I come in?" She asked. As she opened the door, Winnie ran in between her legs and nearly knocked her over. Lily hugged Winnie while the furry Cocker Spaniel obsessively attempted to lick her face and knocked over a few of Lily's toys in the process.

"What are you playing with Lily?" Annie sat on the edge of Lily's bed as she scanned the room. The giant dollhouse that Lily's Father built for her was in the corner, and dolls and stuffed animals were arranged in a half circle facing Lily as if attending a lecture.

"Well, I'm a writer and I've just come to town to talk to people about my new book. They're listening to me read some of it." Lily pretended to read from one of her favorite *Amelia Bedelia* books as the dolls and stuffed animals looked on in a stoic state of awe.

"Lil, I was hoping I could talk to you about something. I met with your teacher today and she said you were having trouble concentrating at school." Annie thought she'd dive right in to the core of the problem. It would be bedtime soon and she didn't want to waste time with a lot of meaningless chit chat. "Mrs. Rosher thinks that you might have trouble seeing the chalkboard and she suggested that we take you to get your eyes checked. Maybe you need glasses to help you see a little better." Annie suggested.

Lily put her book down and stared up at her mother. "I don't need glasses. I can see the board just fine!" Lily said with a little agitation in her voice. "Especially since she moved me to the front row, which I don't like because everybody stares at me more there." Lily turned her head to the corner of the room. Her eyes seemed to be following something moving from right to left.

Annie looked the same direction but saw nothing. She recalled what Mrs. Rosher had said earlier about Lily *'looking around the room…at nothing at all.'*

"Lily, what are you looking at?"

"The balls of light. Don't you see them? They're right there." Lily pointed to the corner of the room near the ceiling.

"I don't see any balls of light Honey. There's nothing there." Now Annie was concerned that there might very well be a vision problem if her daughter was seeing balls of light that weren't there.

"There *is* Mom. They're always there. They follow me everywhere. I see them at school too." Lily said quite firmly. "Winnie sees them too."

Annie looked down at the family dog and indeed she was looking up at the same corner near the ceiling. Annie watched Lily and the dog intently. If Lily's head turned to the left, so did Winnie's. When Lily dropped her eyes closer to the floor, so did Winnie. Lily and the dog were completely in sync. They were seeing the same thing. How then, could this be a vision problem with Lily when the dog is reacting to the same invisible thing?

"Lily, what are these balls of light you see?" Annie asked.

"Spirits." Lily said very matter-of-factly. "They're around me all the time. Sometimes they talk to me. Sometimes they change to look like regular people. I was afraid at first, but I'm not afraid anymore. They won't hurt me. They mostly just like to talk. They want me to listen."

For the first time in a long time, Annie was speechless. Lily sees spirits?!? How? At that moment, Annie recalled the night several months prior when

Lily woke them up in the middle of the night screaming and talking about *'tall black shadowy figures standing around her bed.'* She also remembered Lily claiming to see her dead Father by the neighbor's tree when she was playing outside. Is my child psychic? How can this be? Annie was in shock and awe at the same time. She knew nothing about the spirit world. Is it dangerous? Can Lily be harmed? She had so many questions—questions that Lily herself probably did not have the answers to. This would be a subject that Annie needed to research. She needed to find help. Who can she turn to? It's not like she could call their family Doctor and talk about these things. He would think she was crazy. How could she find someone to help with this? Although she had never looked, it was doubtful that you could find a listing for *Spirit Help* in the Yellow Pages. Annie took a deep breath to calm herself and decided to explore this with Lily a little further. After all, Lily was in the center of it and she clearly knew more than Annie did about the subject.

"Lily? Do you remember when you saw your Grandfather by the tree that day?" Annie asked.

"Yes." Lily began rearranging her dolls on the floor into a different configuration. The *Amelia Bedelia* book was shut and it appeared that story time was over for her artificial audience.

"Have you seen him again since then?" Annie asked.

"Sometimes he watches me play at recess, but mostly I just see him sitting in that chair before I go to sleep at night." Lily said as she pointed to a wooden chair in the corner of the room that was once part of the dining room set that Annie's Mother used to have in the house where she grew up.

Annie looked over at the chair trying to imagine her Father sitting in it. It was a bittersweet moment to think that the one person who was so important to her in her younger years was now present in her daughter's life, yet she could not see him for herself.

"Does he say anything to you?" Annie asked.

"Sometimes. He's not really a talker. Mostly he just sits and smiles. He's there to protect me Momma. You shouldn't worry." Lily stood up and gave her Mother a hug. "He's here now and he says that he's proud of you Mom. He's always around us." Lily said.

Annie took a deep breath and hugged her daughter tightly. A tear came to her eye as she remembered the loving embrace of her Father—the man whom she could trust completely and had always protected her. The pain of her loss was still with her. He was removed from her life far too soon and she felt a hollow space inside her that was still lingering there. How wonderful that he was now protecting Lily, and even more wonderful that Lily could see and talk to him.

"He says to tell you that Roger Dodger is with him too." Lilly said as she pulled back from the hug to look into her Mother's eyes. "Who is Roger Dodger Mom?"

Annie's stomach dropped at that moment. She hadn't thought of Roger Dodger in several years and she did not remember mentioning that name to Lily, ever. How would she know that? "Roger Dodger was our dog. He was very attached to Grandpa and he went to work with him every day. After Grandpa passed away, Roger Dodger was so depressed that he stopped eating. He died a couple of weeks after Grandpa did. It was very sad." Annie explained.

"Well, he says not to be sad Momma. They're together again and they're both very happy." Lily said proudly.

"Lil, do you see spirits at school? Is that why you aren't paying attention in class?" Annie regained her composure and put her 'Mom hat' back on. It was time to be a mother again and solve the attention span issue she spent the afternoon speaking to Mrs. Rosher about.

"All the time." Lily said as she recalled her time at school. "Sometimes they bother me so much and I can't hear the teacher. The other kids make fun of me and call me a weirdo." She said. "One time a dead girl wouldn't stop talking. She wanted me to go outside and play with her but I couldn't. I said 'Stop it!' out loud and everyone laughed at me." Lily dropped her head down and sighed. "I don't like it when that happens."

"Did the girl leave you alone after you told her to stop?" Annie asked.

"Yeah, she did. But she just comes back again. I don't like playing with her Mom. She's very bossy." Lily reached down to pat Winnie's head.

"Well, I'm sorry that I don't know how to make her stop. I promise you though, I will see if I can find someone to help. You have a special gift that not many people have Lily. Most people will have trouble believing you, so let's just not talk about it to anyone else, okay?" Annie said.

"Ok Momma. But I'm glad that I can talk about it with you." Lily hugged her mother again and felt a new bond beginning to form. This was a secret that she was initially afraid to share with her Mother and she liked that her Mother seemed to be accepting of it. There was still much to learn, but now Lily did not have to navigate these phenomena alone.

CHAPTER 3

AUGUST, 1969

NASA had successfully launched the first moon landing and Neil Armstrong was now a household name. Woodstock was in full swing—At only 14, Lily's older Brother was determined to hitchhike to Bethel, NY from Chicago for the event. He got as far as Toledo, OH. One of his rides decided to rob him and leave him on the side of the road alone. He managed to walk to a nearby gas station where the attendant let him use the phone to call home. His Father promptly wired money for a bus ticket home and that was the end of his historic musical experience. He was grounded for a month. He would regret not making it all the way to Woodstock, but he now had a good story to share with his friends at school. It made him enormously popular and set the stage for many other outrageously fearless behaviors in the years ahead.

Lily was in awe of her Brother Vince, but she had troubles of her own. It had been 20 months since her first frightening encounter with the tall black shadowy figures looming over her bed, but it certainly was not the last. For a few months following the frightening encounter, this new gift of Lily's seemed to be a wonderful thing. Aside from the constant distraction at school, the spirits she interacted with daily were pleasant…Loving even. But that changed and not for the better. The night terrors and stream of shadowy black figures from her closet at night were becoming a regular thing. Things would move on their own, toys with batteries would turn on by themselves, and things would go missing. Winnie became a nightly inhabitant in Lily's room and she spent most of the night sitting straight up at the foot of Lily's bed staring at the closet…Growling. The vicious sounds of Winnie's defensive stance were loud enough to wake the house and ultimately, both Lily and Winnie began sleeping in her Parent's room.

Lily became withdrawn and irritable. Her Parents were terribly worried and although Lily's Father did not believe in the paranormal, he could find no explanation for the terrifying events taking place under his roof. The house felt cold—even in the middle of a hot, humid Chicago summer with no air conditioning on. In fact, it made no sense that they never seemed to need to turn it on at all.

Mark Campbell was a sensible man. He worked hard and kept his word when he made a promise. He was a fierce protector of his family, especially his little girl, but this paranormal phenomena that had plagued their home was beyond his understanding. It was one thing for his daughter to talk to 'happy ghosts' around the house, but it was entirely another for her to be terrorized by an unseen force. He felt powerless to protect her. As a truck driver, his job required him to travel quite a lot so he was very uneasy leaving his wife and family home alone. Annie was a fighter, but he had no idea how she would be able to defend herself against something you could not see. Only Lily seems to be able to see these things and she's just a petite 6 year old child. The odds didn't appear to be in favor of his family and Mark was desperate to find a solution that would get rid of whatever was in Lily's closet.

As Mark was preparing to depart the dispatch terminal, he signed off on his transport manifest and handed it back to the dock manager. Another driver and longtime friend, Ed MacKenzie approached Mark before he climbed into the cab of his truck.

"Are you doing your usual route today Mark?" Ed asked.

Mark snapped out of his perplexing daze and smiled at his friend. "Ah, yeah. The usual Quad-City turn. How about you?" He asked.

"Same. Wanna grab a bite later while they unload the trailers? We're unloading at the same dock this trip." Ed asked.

"Sure Ed, that sounds good. There's something I'd like to talk to you about anyway." Mark said. He had to talk to someone and Ed MacKenzie could be trusted with the keys to his home or full access to his bank account. He wasn't sure if Ed could help. It was risky to talk about the strange phenomena happening in his home and he was concerned that Ed might think he was losing his mind, but he had to talk to someone. Mark was truly at a loss as to what to do or where to go for help. All he knew was that he needed to make some sense of it and Ed was a good guy to help him sort through it without judgment.

Ed nodded his head in acknowledgement and walked over to the cab of his truck and climbed in. Both departed the terminal and headed down the highway toward their destination. The CB radio chatter kept them entertained on the road as well as informed of any "smoky bears" up ahead who might tag them for speeding. Truckers were a very tight knit group and they looked out for each other fiercely. Although you were alone in your cab, you were never really alone on the road. Some of the funniest jokes Mark had ever heard in his life were first heard on the CB radio. They kept each other thoroughly entertained, but more importantly, awake in the late night hours. They needed each other and a solid bond of loyalty and respect existed among each and every one of them.

Upon arrival to the loading dock, Mark found Ed waiting for him as he backed the semi-trailer into position. Mark handed the manifest to the loading dock manager and unlocked the cargo access door so the contents could be inspected before unloading. After signing off on the delivery manifest, Mark and Ed walked across the street to Betty's Diner and sat down in a booth in the corner of the restaurant. After a very pleasant waitress took their orders and brought them coffee, Mark silently pondered just how he was going to approach the paranormal topic with Ed.

Ed was the first to break the silence. "So what was it that you wanted to talk about Buddy?"

Mark took a deep breath and clutched his coffee cup. Here goes… "Have you ever had an experience that you can't explain Ed? I mean, things that happen that there is no reasonable explanation for?" Mark said hesitantly.

Ed took a long sip of his coffee and looked off to the side as if trying to decide whether or not to admit that he had. "You mean like an encounter with a ghost or something like that? Yeah, I actually have. Why do you ask?"

This was good—A wave of relief came over Mark to hear this. This was going to be a much easier conversation than he anticipated. Without hesitation Mark jumped right in with details. He talked about Lily and her ability to see and speak to ghosts. He talked about how she knew things about Annie's father that she could not possibly know—things that Annie had never mentioned and had herself long forgotten. He told Ed about the tall, dark, shadowy figures Lily claims to have seen standing over her bed that now seem to move in and out of her closet, and the toys that turn on and off by themselves. The things that go missing and then reappear in odd places. The bizarre drop in temperature in the house in the dead heat of Summer without turning on the air conditioner. Ed sat quietly, listening, and nodding occasionally but did not interrupt. Mark paused when the waitress came back to refill their coffee cups and deliver their plates of food.

"You probably think I'm crazy don't you Ed. I don't blame you. It sounds crazy, but it's real! It's real and I don't know how the Hell to fix it." Mark said as he lightly salted and peppered his mashed potatoes and took a bite.

Ed sat back on his side of the booth and sighed. "No, no, I don't think you're crazy. Your daughter is what they call a *Psychic Medium*. It's a real gift, but it can also be a curse. I know more about this than you might think. My Mother is a Psychic Medium. I've experienced things like that all my life. Psychics are magnets for ghostly encounters because they can communicate with spirits where others cannot." Ed explained quietly.

This revelation was a relief and very unexpected for Mark to hear. He had no idea! Mark knew Ed for over 30 years and he had never confided any of this to him before. As the two men ate their meals, Ed offered up a few more stories of similar experiences around his house growing up and how his Mother dealt with it as Mark listened intently. He was beginning to understand that there were different parallel dimensions that existed and that occasionally, beings who resided in one dimension had the ability to penetrate barriers into another. How and why was yet to be understood, but Mark now had an ally. Someone he could confide in and seek help from.

By the end of the meal, Mark had a better understanding of the paranormal and that there were unseen forces to contend with. Some good, like Lily's interaction with the spirit of her Grandfather, and some bad—like the dark, menacing shadowy figures that came out of her closet.

After paying the bill, Ed and Mark walked next door to the Best Western and checked into their rooms. Their trailers would be unloaded and reloaded with new cargo to transport by morning, and truck drivers needed their rest. After brushing his teeth and washing his face, Mark sat on the side of his bed, picked up the receiver on the rotary dial phone and called Annie.

On Tuesday evening Mark arrived back home from his trip. He was tired from driving but never too tired to spend quality time with his family. As he came through the door, Winnie ran to him with her usual excited body wiggle because her tail was just too short to wag the way she wanted to express her happiness to see Mark.

"Hi there Winnie! How are you girl?" Mark said as he knelt down to vigorously pet his wiggly dog.

"Daddy!" Lily squealed as she ran down the hall towards the back door to her Father. She held her arms up and her Father picked her up off the ground and gave her a big hug. Lily pulled her face back and looked her Father in the eye. "Did you bring me a treat?"

"A treat? I'm giving you a big hug. What kind of treat were you hoping for?" Mark teased her. "You know, Daddy…" Lily said.

It was a tradition. Whenever Mark was away from home on his 3 day route, which was about once per month, he always stopped at a vending machine at the terminal before coming home so he could bring Lily her favorite candy bar. Mark set her back down on the floor and she unzipped the side pocket on her Father's duffle bag sitting next to his feet. "Yummy!" Lily exclaimed as she pulled out her favorite—a Mars Bar. They never had candy or any sweets in the house, so this was a real treat for Lily. Annie stepped up just before Lily could open the wrapper and took it out of her hands.

"Not before dinner. Go wash your hands and sit at the table. You can have your Mars Bar for dessert." Annie said.

As Lilly ran off to the bathroom to wash her hands, Annie leaned in and kissed her husband. "I'm glad you're home. We missed you." She said. Mark kissed and hugged his wife tightly remembering how lucky he was to be blessed with his wonderful wife and family, and was grateful that he now had a friend to confide in and help him with the paranormal events happening in his home.

Lily…Come play with us, Lily…' Lily's body jerked her awake violently. She could feel large, cold hands wrapped around her ankles that were pulling her legs off the end of the bed. Lily struggled to kick herself free from the icy grip, but found herself powerless to do so. She opened her eyes to see the tall, dark shadowy figures surrounding her bed. She opened her mouth to scream but nothing came out. Winnie was backed up to the head of the bed as if she was being held there. Winnie let out a high pitched yelp as if she was in pain. Seconds later, the bedroom door flew open as Lily was being pulled off the end of her bed and her body fell to the floor. Her head made a loud *THUD* as it hit the hardwood floor.

"Lily!" Mark screamed as he witnessed his daughter being pulled off the bed by her feet. He stood in the doorway but could not cross the threshold. It was as if an invisible force field was thrown up to keep him out of the room.

Lily glanced over at her Father "Daddy!" She cried. At that moment, Lily felt a surge of energy that empowered her to sit straight up. She faced the direction of her closet which was where she was being pulled toward. Very calmly and sternly, she said "STOP. You do NOT have power over me. You do NOT have permission to touch me. GET OUT NOW."

All of a sudden, Mark felt the barrier lift and he ran to his Daughter and picked her up off the floor. Winnie was able to move from where she was held at the head of the bed, and Lily could breathe again.

Annie followed Mark into the room and helped pick Lilly up off the floor. "Are you alright Honey? Are you hurt?" Annie asked with great concern.

"No Momma. I'm not hurt." Lily hugged her Parents tightly.

"What the Hell just happened?" Mark said as he turned the light on and inspected the closet.

"The shadow figures Daddy. They came to get me. They wanted me to go with them." Lily said. She wasn't sure she knew what they were but she knew they weren't good. "They were trying to pull me into their hole in the closet but my Guardian Angel came and helped me send them away." Lily took a deep breath as she tried to make sense of what had just happened. Winnie ran to her and licked the tears from her face. She turned and made eye contact with her Father. "Daddy, it's not safe here. We have to find another house to live in. They are going to keep coming back. We have to go." She said as tears streamed down her face.

Mark heard his daughter's words and he knew she was right. He stood up and cautiously inspected the closet. It looked perfectly normal. There was no black hole in the wall or the floor. Lily's clothes were hanging on the rod and her shoes and a few toys were neatly arranged on the floor. It looked like an ordinary bedroom closet, but what existed there was a doorway to another dimension. He couldn't see it, but it was there and he had to seal it shut somehow.

It was shortly after 3:00 am and no one felt like sleeping. Mark tightly closed the closet door. He collected Annie, Lily, and the dog and took them into the living room at the front of the house.

He went downstairs to the Boy's bedrooms where Vince and Stephen were sleeping soundly in their beds. Apparently neither of them heard the commotion upstairs, but teenagers were known to be able to sleep through an explosion so this came as no surprise. Waking them for school in the morning was an hour long process and Mark didn't have the patience to deal with that. They were fine so he decided to let them sleep. Neither one of them had ever mentioned having a paranormal experience of any kind, and now didn't seem like a good time to interrogate them further. Let sleeping dogs lie…For now.

The morning came and as the sun shone through the split between the living room drapes, Annie stirred. Mark had been up all night and he sat vigilant next to his wife and daughter only getting up to make a pot of coffee a few minutes earlier. Annie opened her eyes to see her husband watching over them with a look of concern that she did not often see. "Good morning." Mark said.

"Morning. What time is it?" Annie said as she tried to sit up with a sleeping child snuggled up to her chest.

"It's a little after 7. I made some coffee. Would you like some?" Mark asked.

"Mmmm, yes please." Lily stirred as Annie pulled herself up to a sitting position. She gently moved the child so she could lay flat and continue sleeping as she covered her with a throw blanket. Winnie snuggled up to Lily and let out a sigh as she fell back asleep.

Mark returned with a hot cup of coffee and handed it to Annie. "Here you go." He said.

"Are the boys up?" Annie said as she took her first sip of coffee.

Mark smirked with a half grin on his face. "Nah, they're still hibernating. It's not noon yet."

"Hmmm, right." Annie looked around the room trying to put the events of the night before into perspective. There were just no words to describe what she had witnessed and she didn't know what they were going to do. They could not stay there—she knew that. But, she could not sell the house to another family knowing what occurred in Lily's room and what was coming out of her closet. There's no way Annie could do that to another family. She needed answers and she needed them now. "So, I think we should see if we can meet Ed's mother and talk to her about this. Is he working today?" She asked.

"He's been driving the same route with me all week. We're hauling freight to the same retailer so he's probably home today. I'll call him this morning and see what we can work out. I think that we should also find a place to stay for a while until we can figure out what to do next. I don't think it's safe to stay here anymore." Mark said as he stood up and opened the drapes just enough to let a little more light into the room, but not enough to wake Lily. He sat down with his coffee in hand and put his other arm around his wife. They sat quietly contemplating their next move while enjoying the peace and quiet the early morning provided, free from the melee that naturally occurs when the kids wake up looking for breakfast.

CHAPTER 4

Mark, Annie and Lily drove down the long gravel driveway to Edith MacKenzie's house. The Boys were content to stay at the neighbor's house for the day. They were building a go-cart in the Wilson's garage and it would take a couple more days to finish, so they would be occupied while Mark and Annie got some answers.

As they pulled up to the large white house with the circular driveway, Ed was standing on the front porch with a Coca-Cola in his hand. Mark came to a stop and put the car into park. Annie got out of the car and extended her greetings. "Ed, it's so nice to see you again. Thank you so much for arranging this meeting with your mother, we're really looking forward to meeting her." Lily emerged from the back seat and spotted a rocking chair on the porch. She smiled at Ed and asked very politely if she could sit on it.

"Of course you can Lily. Take it for a spin." Ed said as he grinned at the delighted little girl.

Mark extended his hand to his friend. "We really appreciate this Ed. We have no idea what to do here and we're very anxious to hear what your Mom suggests."

Edith McKenzie appeared in the doorway. She was a petite woman, a bit round in a well fed sort of way, with round rosy cheeks and an inviting smile. Her white hair was pulled up into a loose bun and small tendrils of hair framed her pleasant face. She was wearing a loose tunic top with matching palazzo pants and a colorful scarf with a flower print draped over her shoulders. "Welcome Campbells!" Edith said. She looked over to see Lily gleefully rocking in the chair on the porch. "And you must be Lily."

Lily glanced over at the nice lady without slowing her movement in the chair. "Hello. It's nice to meet you. Is this your chair?" She said in a sweet little voice.

"It is. I'm glad you are enjoying it. It's my favorite place to sit when the weather is nice." Edith replied. She turned her attention back to Mark and Annie. "Shall we come inside and talk? What can I get you to drink?" She asked.

"A Coke would be great." Annie said. "Lily, let's go inside now Honey." She extended her hand as Lily stopped rocking the chair and reluctantly stood up and took her Mother's hand.

"Do you have apple juice?" Lily asked as she looked up at Mrs. MacKenzie.

"Why yes I do. Come in and I'll get you some. Do you like butter cookies? I have some of those too." Edith said as she winked and looked at Annie for approval. Lily nodded and happily skipped into the house.

Edith's house was just what you'd expect a little old lady's home to look like. Very comfortable, full of picture frames full of family photos, flowery wallpaper on the walls, and crocheted throw blankets draped over the couch. All that was missing was an overweight fluffy cat sitting by the fire with a saucer of milk. Although it had that 'Grandma's house' feel, the house was updated with new doors, knobs, windows, trim, crown molding, and new hardwood flooring. The home smelled of fresh paint with a hint of banana bread. Edith led the group through the living room into the kitchen where she had a plate of Salerno Butter Cookies waiting on the kitchen table.

Lily immediately spotted the cookies and began stacking them on one of her tiny extended fingers through the hole in the middle that the flower shaped butter cookies were famous for. Annie gave a disapproving look to the little girl who immediately quit stacking the golden brown cookies on her finger, but certainly didn't put any of them back on the plate.

"Please, have a seat at the table and I'll get some drinks." Edith said as she walked around the kitchen peninsula counter to the large avacado green refrigerator on the other side.

Ed, Mark, Annie, and Lily pulled out chairs and sat down. "Mark," Ed began, "I told Mom a little about what you and your family have been experiencing, and as I told you, it's not that different from some of the things I've seen myself when I was growing up. My Mom thinks she can help and we're glad you were able to come over today." Ed said. Mark nodded and began to recap the conversation he had previously had with Ed at the Diner, then went into detail about the experience they had with Lily in her bedroom the night before.

Edith listened to the story as she served everyone their beverages, throwing in an occasional 'hmmm' while nodding that she understood what Mark was talking about. "May I ask when Lily's first encounter with the shadowy figures was? How many times has she seen them?"

"Um let's see…" Annie started. "I think it was almost 2 1/2 years ago when we first heard her talk about it. She woke up in the middle of the night screaming saying that there were scary black shadowy figures standing over her bed. She was terrified! But when we turned on the light and came in the room there was nothing there." Annie said as she looked down at Lily who was now staring past her Father sitting across the table from her with a pleasant grin on her face as if she just noticed a basket of kittens. Annie squeezed her hand to get her attention. "Lily, was that he first time you saw the shadowy figures?"

Lily was distracted by something but managed to answer the question. "Yeah. They were scary. I don't like them. They're bad." She responded without breaking her stare and redirected the conversation to what she was seeing. "Mrs. MacKenzie? Your Angel is so sparkly! How does she do that?" Lily asked.

Edith turned around to see what Lily was referring to, even though she already knew. "Yes, that's Aliana. She's beautiful isn't she?" Edith quickly turned her attention to Annie and Mark who were looking in the same direction as Lily but couldn't see anything remotely angelic or sparkly… Just flowery wallpaper. "Ed has told me a lot about Lily and the shadowy figures, and without seeing them firsthand, I can only guess what they are and more importantly, what their intentions are." She took a sip of her iced tea and continued. "If they're grabbing Lily by the ankles and dragging her off the bed, that's not a good sign. These figures are negative and powerful. They could be Shadow People, Demons, or just angry Dead People. We have to determine exactly what they are so we know how to deal with them." She explained.

"Demons? I don't like the sound of that!" Annie said as she stiffened up in her chair. "What are Shadow People? Are they some type of Demon?" She asked.

"No one knows exactly what Shadow People are," Edith explained, "but most people feel that they are not Demons. Most of us believe that they've never been human and that they come from another dimension. They're an alien being. Sometimes they just watch and sometimes they have physical interactions with the Living. It sounds like they are attracted to Lily and were trying to take her back to their dimension through their portal in the closet. If that's the case and they truly are Shadow People, I'm afraid we can't get rid of them. You'll have to move as far away as you can. They're not likely to follow you, but the farther away you go, the better." Edith said.

A wave of silence was cast over the kitchen table. Mark and Annie were lost for words. They knew what Demons were and knew that there were ways to get rid of them, but alien Shadow People from another dimension was something they were unprepared for and they did not know how to respond.

Lily broke the silence. "Grandpa told me that they're bad and they want me to go with them to where they come from, but I shouldn't go with them. I don't want to. They scare me." Lily said as she quickly lost interest in her butter cookies and apple juice and slumped in her chair with her head down.

Ed offered a solution. "Mark, my Mom has a guesthouse on the property. It's right behind the house here and we just finished the remodel. Mom was going to take on some tenants but we talked about it and she'd like to offer it to you and your family—Just until you can get your house sold and you can find another place." Ed said. Edith gave a warm approving smile at the suggestion, and offered to show it to them.

As the family walked out the patio door from the kitchen, you could see guesthouse. It was larger than they were expecting—It had 2 large bedrooms and 2 bathrooms, an ample sized kitchen and nook area, and a great room with a fireplace. There was no garage, but there was a single carport and enough parking space on the side for another vehicle. The guesthouse was so freshly remodeled that there were still small pieces of masking tape marking spots that needed touch up paint or caulking. "I know that you have 2 other children and 2 bedrooms might be a bit cramped, but it's yours to stay in for a while if you want it." Edith said as she showed them through the house room by room. "And there are no vortexes or portals here either. The property is clear of any of that." She assured them.

"Oh Edith, this is incredibly nice of you…" Annie said as she gave an approving look to her husband.

"Very nice of you Mrs. MacKenzie. Under the circumstances, I think we'd be fools to pass on this offer. But, I insist on paying you rent and we won't stay very long…Just until we can get our house sold and move to another one." Mark said.

"Agreed." Edith replied. "Having you all close by will give me the opportunity to work with Lily a little more as well. She needs to understand her abilities and how to deal with them. She's very young and she's seeing things that would frighten any grown adult. I can help her with some protective methods she will need to learn." She said.

Mark extended to his hand to Edith and then to Ed. "I can't thank you enough Ed. Last night I didn't know what to do next and you and your Mother came to our rescue. Thank you my friend. We'll never forget this kindness." Mark said with great sincerity.

"What are friends for?" Ed said as he pat his good friend on the back. "And Mark, I suggest that we take my truck over to the house right now and get your beds moved over here tonight. Lily is in danger and there's no need to spend another night there if you don't have to, you know?" He suggested.

"Thanks Ed. That's a great idea." Mark replied.

Edith reached down and took Lily by the hand. "Might I suggest that you leave Lily here with me while you and Annie go pack some things?" She gave a concerned, yet reassuring look to Lily's Parents that all would be well but she didn't think it was a good idea for Lily to return to the house. "Would that be okay with you, Lily? Would you like to stay here with me until your Mom and Dad return? That will give us a chance to talk a little more." Edith asked.

While Lily was not fond of being dumped off with strangers, she felt quite at home with Mrs. MacKenzie. Lily gave her an enthusiastic nod and began swinging the arm she was holding Edith's hand with. "Momma, please don't forget to bring Winnie back with you!" She yelled as her Mother opened the passenger door to the car to get in. Annie waved, gave her the 'okay' symbol with her hand, and got in the car. As her Parents drove away with Ed following in his oversized dually pick-up truck, Lily felt peaceful and safe. She looked up at Mrs. MacKenzie who was smiling down at her. "Can we go back and talk to Aliana again? I want to know how she makes herself so sparkly!" Lilly asked happily. Edith chuckled and they turned together to walk back into the house.

A few hours later Mark, Ed, and Annie returned with the second truck load of bedroom furniture and a few suitcases and boxes of things that they could pack quickly. Vince and Stephen were in the back seat of Annie's car—None too happy to be uprooted from their home and their friends, but curious to know about the series of events that prompted the disruption in their lives. Annie had tried to explain it to them on the drive back to the guesthouse, but it was difficult for them to wrap their heads around. They always knew their baby Sister was a little different, but she was a good kid and they loved her regardless. If there was something in the house that was threatening to Lily, then they were behind their Parent's decision to vacate immediately. Like all protective big brothers, they offered to stay behind and fight the bad ghosts but Annie was having none of that. She appreciated the solidarity but this was way over their heads and she really didn't want to go into detail and explain it now. She wasn't sure she knew enough about the situation herself yet, but she'd find out and explain everything to them later. For now she just needed them to be cooperative and helpful.

When the last bed was made and clothes were put away in the closets, Annie walked up to the main house to fetch Lily. The door was open and she could hear Lily talking through the screen door. "Knock knock!" Annie said as she peered through the screen.

"Come on in Annie. Lily was just telling me about the spirits she sees at school. I'm teaching her how to keep them from bothering her." Edith said.

"Oh, yes, they seem to distract her quite a bit. Her teacher has even noticed it. So, how can she do that?" Annie asked, grateful that she now had a source of information she could learn so much from and she was going to take full advantage of it.

"Well," Edith began, "there are some very basic *rules* if you will, that you should know about. In this plane, or realm, the Living dominate and hold higher power to the Dead. This is our world, not theirs. Although some of the Dead are able to learn how to manipulate physical things in our world, the Living have the power to stop it and send them away. There are many methods that can be used to do this, some that Lily can do herself and some things that will require your help too Annie." Edith explained. "For instance, by Lily stating with conviction that the Shadow People did not have permission to touch her, she was able to remove their power to drag her into the closet. Unfortunately, with Shadow People this is a very temporary fix. They learn very quickly how to bypass what would ordinarily work with the Dead or even Demons for that matter. It is very important that we establish exactly what these entities are. I'd like to go over to the house with you in the morning if I could." She said.

"Yes, yes of course. We are 100% behind you on this Edith and we will do whatever you think is best." Annie said as she collected Lily and stood up. "I'm going to get Lily to bed now. I'm sure she's tired. It's been a very big day.

Thank you so much Edith. Mark and I are so grateful for your help." She said as she gave the old woman a gentle hug around her shoulders.

"My pleasure." Edith smiled and unfolded her hands from her lap to stand. "You all should be able to sleep soundly tonight. If these are true Shadow People, and I believe they are, they will not follow you here. But, you can still expect the Dead to find Lily wherever she goes. She's like a little beacon in the darkness and the Dead will always be attracted to her. I can show her how to dim that light so she's not so bothered all the time. We'll go through that tomorrow. Get some rest...Do you have everything you need?" Edith asked as she opened the back door for Annie. "I know this move occurred rather suddenly and you probably didn't think to pack the coffee pot. I'm up early so come up for coffee and breakfast when you wake up. We'll talk more then." She said.

"Thank you Edith. We'll see you in the morning. Good night." Annie said quietly and walked down the path to the guesthouse holding her sleepy daughter. For the first time in several months, she felt safe and without fear. The guesthouse had a comfortable homey feel that was free of Shadow People, portals, and vortexes. This was the relief that Annie had longed for even if it was brief. They weren't done with this battle and she knew it. The worst was yet to come.

CHAPTER 5

The house was empty and completely still...Dark...Cold. The family had vacated quickly and most of the remaining furniture and boxes that were left behind were stacked in the garage. The closet door in Lily's old bedroom slowly opened by itself. A few moments later, a stream of tall, dark shadowy figures emerged and hovered in the hollow space of the empty bedroom. One by one, the shadowy figures drifted out into the hall and down the corridor to the living room.

Across the street, Patsy Sunderland was standing at her kitchen sink washing dishes. Her kitchen window offered a straight shot view of the Campbell's large picture window in their living room. Patsy saw some furniture being loaded into a truck earlier that day, but she never heard why her neighbors had abruptly moved out. When she finished stacking the last dish on the drying rack, she drained the sink and dried her hands. As she reached for the switch next to her window to turn the light off, she noticed movement in the Campbell's picture window. She stood quietly in the dark for a few minutes to let her eyes adjust. *Did she see someone standing in the window?*

Her husband, Don entered the room and thought it odd to see Patsy staring out the window in the dark.

"What are you doing Dear?" He asked.

"Well, it's rather odd." Patsy said as she cocked her head to one side. "I saw Mark and Annie loading a truck with some furniture earlier today and I haven't seen anyone over there all night. But I thought I saw someone standing in the front window just now. The drapes are open you know..." She said.

"Maybe they came back and they're packing stuff." Don said as he retrieved a small juice glass out of the upper cabinet. "Do we know why they're moving?

It's strange that they didn't tell us. Scottie and Lily were friends. He said he didn't know anything about it."

"No, nobody's home over there. There's no car in the driveway and I saw them stacking furniture and boxes in the garage so they couldn't pull the car in the garage." Patsy insisted.

Don stood behind his wife peering at the neighbor's house over her shoulder. "Are you sure you saw someone? It's pretty dark over there. If they came back to pack, surely there would be a few lights on." He said as he stepped aside and opened the refrigerator door to grab a pitcher of cranberry juice and poured some in his glass.

Just then, a car drove up the street and the headlights illuminated the Campbell's picture window. There, standing in the window were three tall, solid black figures—each clearly had a defined head and shoulders.

"What the heck?" Patsy gasped and grabbed a hold of Don's arm and pulled him closer to her so he could see.

"What is it?" Don said, trying to steady himself so he didn't completely spill his juice on the floor. Don squinted to see in the picture window. It was quite a distance away and it was dark. The car had passed so the light cast on the window from the headlights was gone. Don stared intently and could see only pitch black in the window, but not entirely sure he could make out anything other than just darkness. "What did you see Patsy? I don't see anything. Everything is pretty dark over there." He said.

"I could have sworn that I saw three people standing in the window. I mean, it was strange because there were no faces, just tall dark shapes that looked like people." Patsy dropped her eyes to the kitchen sink as she processed the images she thought she saw. "But...It's odd because they looked really tall...And all the same height." She remembered that Annie was about her height which was 5'7" and Mark was about 6'1". The kids were even shorter than that. Even Stephen who was the oldest at 16, was barely taller than Annie. The heads of these figures almost reached the top of the window. Patsy had been in the Campbell's living room many, many times and she recalled that the ceilings were about 8' high, and there was just enough room for a curtain rod above that picture window. That meant that these figures were about 7' in height!

Don glanced down at Patsy who was still contemplating what she saw. He put his arm around her and took a sip of his juice. "Well, Mark will be back for the rest of their things at some point. I'll walk over and talk to him about it when I see him. If they had intruders, there's nothing much left over there to steal anyway. I'm sure it was just a shadow from the tree or something." Don said as he patted his wife on the rear end and walked back to the den to watch television.

CHAPTER 6

The first night in the guesthouse was quiet and peaceful. This was the first full nights' sleep Mark, Annie, and Lily had had in a long time. Even Winnie seemed spunkier and well rested. Annie walked out to the kitchen to find Mark digging through boxes.

"I guess we left the coffee maker in one of the boxes in the garage. I've been through every one of these and we've got cups and we've got coffee, but no coffee maker." Mark said.

"That's okay. Edith invited us up to the house for breakfast this morning anyway." Annie said as she walked off to the bathroom, stopping along the way to stick her head into the bedroom where all three kids were still sleeping soundly. A short while later, Annie emerged in jeans and a T-shirt with her long brown hair pulled back onto a ponytail. "Have you seen my shoes? I thought I took them off by the front door last night." She asked.

"You did. I threw them in the closet. I almost tripped on them when I took Winnie out this morning." Mark said. He was stacking the empty boxes in the corner of the dining area as he unpacked. They would need to run back to the house and finish packing and the empty boxes would come in handy. "Why don't you get Lily up and we'll walk up to the house together. Don't worry about the boys—they're body clocks are still running on nocturnal time. They'll be fine sleeping in a little longer." Mark suggested.

Before Annie could turn and walk down the hall, Lily appeared in the hallway with messy hair and sleepy eyes. Her Scooby Do pajamas were well worn and she was starting to grow out of them. "Momma, is there breakfast?" She asked.

"Good morning Sweetie. We haven't gone to the grocery store yet so, no, there's no breakfast here. Remember that Mrs. MacKenzie invited us up to the house? Go get dressed and we'll walk up there and get some breakfast." Annie said as she gently turned her daughter around and walked her down the hall to the bedroom she now shared with her two Brothers.

This wasn't the most ideal situation, but with the help of a clever furniture arrangement, they would get by. This was only temporary until they could get their house sold and find a new home. The thought of returning to their house for more things was very unsettling for Annie. They had removed all of the bedroom furniture and packed toys and other items, but there were still clothes, shoes and toys in Lily's closet. Annie was terrified to open the closet door again and was even more fearful that they might be bringing some attachment back with them if they removed any of the items from the closet. She really didn't want to go and retrieve any of those things, but knew that it would be suspicious to potential buyers to leave such personal items behind. The beings in the closet had to be dealt with. They had to get rid of them before they could sell the house…But how? They didn't even know what they were or where they came from.

After Lily was dressed, Annie checked on the boys and left them to sleep a little longer. She scribbled a quick note and left it on the nightstand next to Stephen's bed.

As Mark, Annie and Lily walked up the path toward the house, Edith was standing in the kitchen window and she waved to them to come in through the back door. "Good morning!" Edith said in her cheerful Grandmotherly voice. "How was your first night in the guesthouse? Everything okay out there?" She asked.

"Perfect, thank you Edith." Mark said. "I think that was the best nights' sleep we've had in a very long time." He said as Edith poured two cups of coffee for Annie and Mark and set them on the table. She also had a large plate of pastries laid out with a large bowl of fruit and some yogurt.

"I can make some eggs if you'd like. I also have Raisin Bran if you'd prefer cereal. I wasn't sure what you'd be hungry for. I ran to the bakery this morning so the pastries are fresh baked." Edith said cheerfully.

"Oh my goodness Edith, thank you!" Annie said. "You didn't have to go to all of this trouble."

"No trouble at all. I'm glad to have some company for a change. Ed stops in once in a while, but most of the time it's just me so I enjoy having you here. What would you like Lily?" Edith said as she noticed that Lily had her eye on a great big glazed donut with chocolate icing. "Oh, good choice! Here, let me get you a plate and I'll cut it in half for you. That's a very big donut!" She said.

"Oh she can put that whole donut away, no problem." Mark said. "She's a bottomless pit when it comes to breakfast."

"True!" Annie added. "The Boys are going to kick themselves for missing out on this."

The four of them sat around the table talking about the guesthouse and how well it was working out for everyone. The kitchen appliances were new and Edith had not had a chance to go in and make sure everything was installed and operating properly. Mark, who worked as a carpenter for many years after high school could fix just about anything. He assured her that he would make sure everything was in good working order. He also assured her that if she needed anything repaired in the main house, he was more than happy to fix that too.

Lily finished her giant glazed donut and her glass of milk, and asked if she could be excused. Six year olds generally had the attention span of a gnat, and Lily was no different. The sugar rush induced by the donut was starting to take effect and she could no longer sit still. Annie was used to this and stood up to walk Lily to the sink so she could wash her sticky hands before touching anything.

"I assume that you will be going back to the house today to get a few more things?" Edith asked.

"Yes, that is the plan. I was going to meet Ed over there in an hour to get the rest of the furniture." Mark replied as he took a big gulp of his coffee.

"Well, I'd like to come along if you don't mind. I really need to see what you've got in that closet so we know what we're dealing with." Edith said. She stood up and asked if anyone wanted more coffee.

"Oh no more for me, thank you Edith. I'm afraid if I have any more coffee I won't be able to sit still." Annie said as she handed a towel to Lily so she could dry her hands. "I'm going to walk Lily back to the guesthouse and get the Boys up. I think it's best if she stays here with them rather than going back to the house." She said. Edith agreed and packed up the remaining pastries and some milk so Annie could take some breakfast to the Boys.

Although it was a bright, sunny, late summer day, the house looked dark even though all of the window shades were open. Annie dreaded going back into the house, but she knew she had to. Edith was quiet on the ride over, but forewarned them that it was necessary for her to get herself into a meditative state for what she called her 'opening.' It was a practice that Psychic Mediums engaged in prior to communicating with the Dead. It allowed for more clarity and awareness so that she could get as accurate a read as possible about what was going on and what type of entities she was dealing with. As Edith stepped out of the car, she paused and looked around the exterior of the house.

"There's a woman here. She's telling me that I shouldn't go inside the house. She says there's trouble in there. There's also a man. He calls himself the protector." Edith said. She finished her visual scan of the exterior and made eye contact with Annie. "I think this man is your Father Annie. Was his name Tom?" Annie nodded and smiled. She felt comforted that her Father was there. It would be just like him to watch over her and protect her.

Mark opened the garage door and unlocked the side door into the house with his keys. He very slowly opened the door and peered inside. Everything was still. Quiet. Eerily quiet. He continued inside and held the door open for Edith and Annie. The kitchen appeared exactly as they had left it and there, sitting on the counter was the coffee maker that they forgot to pack. Mark saw it and gestured to Annie as if to say *Ah hah! There it is—we forgot to pack it.*

After scanning the kitchen, Edith turned left into the living room and slowly walked to the front picture window. "Tom came in the house with us, but the woman outside won't come in here." She said as she turned to Annie with a clear look of extreme concern on her face. She took a deep breath and exhaled. "I was afraid of this…You have Shadow People here." Edith turned to look out the window. "And there are two of them standing in the hallway behind me right now."

Annie turned quickly to look down the hallway but she didn't see anything at all. "Where? I don't see them." She said anxiously.

"Oh they're there." Edith said as she took another deep cleansing breath. "Is Lily's room at the end of hallway?" She asked.

"Yes." Annie replied.

"That's where they're coming from. They are headed back that way now. They don't like us here. Tom says there are four more in that bedroom." Edith slowly turned and faced the hallway. "They're looking for Lily. They came to take her." She said quietly.

Tears welled up in Annie's eyes and her heart beat rapidly in her chest. She began to shake. Mark wrapped his arms around her and pulled her close. Edith turned and put her hand on the back of Annie's shoulder. "I'm sorry dear. This isn't good." Edith walked down the hall toward Lily's bedroom and opened the door. She stepped inside and turned to the closet door, which was already half way open. Annie collected herself and took Mark's hand as they followed Edith into their daughter's bedroom. Edith stood in front of the closet and turned to Mark. "There's a portal in here. This is their doorway into our realm. This cannot be closed completely." She reached into her pocket and took out a couple of black rough looking rocks, and another one that looked like a piece of green jagged glass. She turned to Mark as she handed him the black rocks first. "Mark, please put one of these on the top of the trim on either side of the closet door." Edith said.

"What is this?" Mark said as he examined the shiny, jagged edged stones. "That's Black Tourmaline. It protects against negativity." Edith explained.

Mark did as she said and placed one piece of the black tourmaline on top of the trim over both sides of the closet door. Then Edith handed him the other stone that looked like green glass. "This one is Moldavite. Please place this one on the inside of the closet next to the piece of Black Tourmaline you just put up there." She said.

"What is Moldavite and what does it do?" Mark asked.

"It's a type of tektite crystal formed by a meteorite impact millions of years ago. Because it's not naturally from the Earth, it will help the Black Tourmaline keep these beings from another dimension at bay." Edith explained.

Mark nodded and did as she said then stepped back. Then Edith pulled a lighter and a small tightly bound bundle of white sage out of her other pocket and lit the end of it. As soon as a strong flame appeared at the end of the sage stick, she gently blew it out and a stream of white smoke rose into the air. She gently waved it around so the smoke created a smoky curtain in front of the closet door opening. She began reciting: *All negativity must leave. You are not welcome here and you are banished from this home.* She turned to Annie and Mark. "Say it with me and say it with conviction. This is YOUR home. You have the power to cast this negativity out." She said.

Annie and Mark repeated the affirmation with Edith as she waved the stream of smoke around the room. Edith continued down the hall and smudged each room with her sage. After she finished, she stepped out the front door and extinguished the smoking sage stick, then came back into the house to find Annie and Mark standing in the living room wondering what they were supposed to do next.

"I've created a temporary barrier that won't allow them to come back through, but it won't hold for very long. They'll figure out how to get past it soon. I suggest you remove the rest of Lily's things from the closet while you can." Edith instructed.

Mark grabbed a big box and retrieved Lily's clothes, shoes, and toys that were left and folded the top flaps of the box together. He carried it out to the car and put it in the trunk as Ed was backing the truck into the driveway next to the parked car.

"Hey Buddy, sorry I'm late. The traffic was backed up on Plainfield Rd. Traffic light was out." Ed said as he stepped out of the cab of his truck.

"Not a problem Ed. Your Mom was just helping us cleanse the house with what she calls a smudge stick." Mark extended a hand to his friend.

"Ah, the sage. It's an herb that negative entities do not like and they can't stay in the presence of it. I've seen her do that a few times. It works, actually." Ed explained. "What did she say you have there?"

"A portal with Shadow People." Mark said.

"Shit. That ain't good. Let's get you of here as fast as we can. You can't get rid of those evil son-of-a-bitches. Best if we just get you the Hell out." Ed replied as he motioned Mark to pick up the other side of the living room couch in the garage.

Annie and Edith finished packing the remaining items in the house and carried them out to the garage as Patsy Sunderland was walking across the street towards them. Annie looked up and sighed. "Oh shit! It's Patsy. What am I going to tell her?" She mumbled.

Edith rested her hand on Annie's arm. "You tell her that you found a house that you fell in love with and you couldn't pass it up. Unless she's a close friend of yours who believes in the paranormal, I wouldn't go into detail." Edith suggested.

"Well, she's a nice neighbor but she's not really a close friend. I'm not sure she would understand. Patsy's also kind of a gossip so I want to tell her as little as possible." Annie said. As Patsy approached, both Annie and Edith greeted her with a smile.

"Annie Campbell, what on earth is going on over here? You didn't tell me you were moving!" Patsy said.

"I'm sorry Patsy, everything happened so fast and we didn't have time to tell anyone. We found another house that we just fell in love with, and well, we decided to relocate." That was the only thing Annie could think to say to her neighbor of 5 years.

"Well, where are you going? Is it far? Scottie was so surprised to hear that you were moving out. Lily didn't say anything to him about it." Patsy said. "And, I have to say, I'm surprised that you didn't tell me about it." She said sounding a little put out.

"It was *very* unexpected Patsy. It took us by surprise as well, but, you know, sometimes the best things present themselves very suddenly and you just have to pull the trigger!" Annie said enthusiastically. "We're not moving far, and we'll be able to see each other. The kids are still in the school district so Scottie will see Lily at school." Patsy smiled and glanced over at Edith standing next to them. "Oh, I'm sorry, this is Edith MacKenzie, Ed's Mother." Annie said.

Edith extended her hand to Patsy. "It's a pleasure to meet you Patsy."

"Same." Patsy said as she shook Edith's hand, then directed her attention immediately back to Annie. "Um, Annie, I need to tell you something."

"Oh?" Annie asked.

"Last night while I was doing the dishes, it looked like you had intruders in your house. I saw three very tall, well…how should I say this… solid black figures in your picture window." Patsy said as if she was very delicately delivering unpleasant news. "It was very strange. I don't know how else to explain it, but it just didn't look right."

"Hmmm." Annie said as she looked at Edith for some help explaining the Shadow People they had in the house. "That's strange Patsy. I'm not sure what it could have been. Probably just a shadow cast from the trees or something." She said.

Edith was guided by the dead woman standing among them who helped her very cleverly change the subject to something Patsy would be much more interested in talking about. "Do you have an Airedale Terrier? I see one jumping up and down in the window over there…" Edith pointed out.

Patsy's eyes lit up as she turned to see her pup trying to see where she went. "Yes I do! His name is Ladd and he's my baby!" She said very enthusiastically. "I probably should have put him on a leash and brought him with me, poor baby. He hates it when Mommy leaves without him."

Annie quickly picked up on the distraction that Edith created and jumped right into the conversation. "Oh Patsy, he's going crazy being separated from you. Look at the poor little guy! Hey, we'll let you get back to your adorable little pup and we're going to finish loading the truck. We'll be back to clean up in a couple of days, so how about if we get together and go out for pizza to catch up?" Annie said.

Patsy found herself needing to get back to her bouncy little terrier and started walking back toward the house. "That sounds great Annie—Just give me a jingle in a day or two and we'll work out the details. Nice to meet you Edith!" She said as she waved, then turned and walked briskly down the driveway.

Annie let out a sign and looked at Edith. "Whew! That was a close one. The dog thing was brilliant! How did you know to call attention to that? Patsy is a very persistent gossipy person. She's relentless when she's digging for information." Annie said.

Edith smiled and said "Oh, that's one of the nice things about being a Psychic Medium. I had a little help." She said as she winked at Annie and turned to help her with the smaller boxes.

As they drove back to the guesthouse, Edith explained what she did at the house. She explained the ancient use of burning sage for smudging and how the crystals she had Mark place above the closet door worked. She also explained that what they did was temporary. It would only last for a few weeks, because you can't ever really get rid of Shadow People. You can keep trying smudging and crystals one time, then salt and maybe tar water another time, etc... Anything you do will only have a brief effect so moving out was the safest action to take to protect Lily. She also explained that Shadow People are very mysterious and someone else could move in and not really notice them. No one knows much about them, but they do tend to target children, the elderly, and the most vulnerable. The end result is either death or they simply disappear.

Although this was terrifying for Annie and Mark to hear, they were relieved that they were no longer living there and that the Shadow People would not be following them.

CHAPTER 7

SEPTEMBER, 1969

Annie and Mark had the property listed for sale with a local Real Estate Agent, and the kids were all back in school. Life seemed to be getting back to normal. The guesthouse was working out very well, albeit a little cramped. Each of the kids were used to having their own bedrooms and now that they were all sharing the same bedroom, there were a few arguments here and there but nothing that couldn't be worked out quickly. Since Lily was in the habit of spreading her toys out when she played with her dollhouse or pretended to be a teacher at school, the Boys complained bitterly. Mark moved Lily's dollhouse out to the living room to solve that problem and it seemed to work out well. Stephen had just turned 16 over the Summer and got his driver's license. He got a part-time job at a local pizza place so he could save for a car. Vince was assigned the lawn mowing chore for the entire property. Edith paid him $10 a week and he was thrilled with that. All in all, things were calm and stable for now.

The Boys knew that Lily had abilities, but didn't thoroughly understand exactly what they were, only that she could see and talk to dead people. Stephen had a strong interest in Science and Chemistry and he was the more logical of the two. Everything could be proven mathematically. Although he couldn't see or hear who Lily was talking to at night, he witnessed the doors opening and closing by themselves and things moving on their own, and he could find no explanation for it. Lily was his baby Sister and he was fiercely protective of her. As long as these dead people weren't hurting her, he was content to let things be. Vince was the negotiator. If there was an opportunity to leverage Lily's gift for some benefit or advantage, he wasn't opposed to it. Like Stephen, he was also fiercely protective of his baby Sister, but he was a bit more accepting of her abilities. He often asked her to ask her dead friends to help him find things he lost, or help him understand the true motives of people he hung out with.

This was probably a good thing since Vince's trust radar would occasionally put him into situations that he should avoid. Hitchhiking to Woodstock by himself for instance, was probably a bad idea.

Lily started 1ˢᵗ Grade and didn't like her teacher quite as much as Mrs. Rosher last year, but she enjoyed school and was very excited to be attending the new Elementary School that was completed over the Summer. It was an open learning concept, so the classrooms were only separated by tall, movable cubicle walls. The library occupied the open space in the middle, so everyone had easy access to it. One side of the school was dedicated to the Art and Music classrooms, and a large school gym separated the two wings. After school every day, Lily would spend an hour with Edith learning how to control her abilities. She was still visited by the Dead quite frequently, but now she knew how to politely ask them to give her some space and come back another time when she could focus on helping them. Lily had learned how to keep the chatty dead girl who frequently showed up in her classroom from bothering her during class, but she would often talk to her during recess. Lily had also learned how to communicate with the Dead without verbalizing the conversation, which made it much easier to deal with—especially when she was around other kids.

Annie worked at the school as a teacher's aide in the 3ʳᵈ Grade classes and helped on Tuesdays in the lunchroom on Hot Dog Day. She enjoyed volunteering and Lily liked having her Mother under the same roof all day. Patsy Sunderland was also a school volunteer and mostly helped out in the attendance office, but would also assist in the lunchroom on Tuesdays with Annie. This made it difficult to avoid the topic of the new house the Campbell's supposedly rushed to buy since they loved it so much. Nearly every time Annie saw Patsy, a giant hint was dropped for the Sunderland's to be invited over to see the new house. Annie used the excuse that they were in the midst of renovations and they would invite them over when the work was finished. When pressed about the new neighborhood and where it was located, Annie did her best to be distracted by spilling something or rushing away because she was *late* for an appointment or to pick the kids up. This was only going to work for so long, and Annie knew it.

"Your Realtor has been showing the house quite a bit last week. There seems to be a lot of interest. Any offers yet?" Patsy asked. This was something she could keep Annie informed of while creating the perfect segue to her favorite topic—the wonderful new house that they fell in love with and couldn't wait to buy. It was driving Patsy absolutely crazy that she hadn't been invited over to see it yet.

"No offers yet, but there seems to be a lot of interest. I guess we just have to wait and see what happens. It's only been on the market for a couple of weeks." Annie said as she organized her kid sized bags of Jays Potato Chips and Fritos Corn Chips to take out to her table to work the lunch room.

"So, what kind of renovations are you doing at the new house? Kitchens and bathrooms or just paint, carpet, and light fixtures?" Patsy probed.

"Well, a little of everything really." Annie didn't get out of the kitchen fast enough to avoid being asked that question. "And quite honestly? It may take a couple of months to get everything finished. Money is a little tight until we sell our house, so we are doing it a little at a time." She said. *There, that should shut down the questions for a while*, she thought to herself.

Annie walked out to the table next to the wall at the far end of the gym while the janitors pulled the tables and bench seats down from the walls. The tables were very state-of-the-art and they folded up flat against the wall again when the lunch period was over. Another Mom was already sitting there organizing her cash box. Annie rushed over and sat next to her.

"Hi Janet. How are you?" Annie said as she set her chip box down and opened her cash box.

"Terrific, Annie. How about yourself?" Janet Castellino lived on the other side of their neighborhood and her daughter was in Lily's class.

"Oh, you know. Same stuff." Annie said, hoping that Brenda Olson, the other lunchroom Mom would sit down before Patsy did so Annie could have a little space from the interrogation her old neighbor from across the street was well known for.

Janet leaned in and said quietly: "I sense the tension between you and Patsy. Hopefully Brenda will be out next and Patsy will have to sit on the other end." She whispered.

Annie turned to Janet and gave her an appreciative smile. Janet respected everybody's space and never pried for information. She liked to keep to herself and never much cared for Patsy's busybody tendencies. This is one of the things that Annie liked most about Janet. "Thank you. Is it obvious?" She asked.

"Just a bit." Janet whispered.

The kitchen door swung open and Brenda emerged with her tray of chips and her cash box. She walked toward the table and Annie pulled out the chair next to her inviting Brenda to take a seat. "Oh thank you!" Brenda said. "Poor Patsy stepped on a ketchup packet on the floor and it squirted all over her shoe and up the leg of her pants. She's in there wiping it off." *Thank God for small miracles!* Annie thought to herself as Janet gave Annie a big wink.

After the lunch period was over, everyone packed up the remaining chips and took them back to the kitchen. The janitors were wiping down the tables and benches then released the kick-stop at the end of each table so they could be folded back up into the wall. This was a well-choreographed dance that occurred every school day between the hours of 11 and 1. Annie did her best to count out her cash box quickly so she could turn it in and get back to helping the students in Mr. Bishop's class, where she was assigned for the afternoon. She managed to avoid Patsy at lunch today, but when school was out, that was another story.

The bell rang at 2:50 pm sharp and the volume grew louder as the children chattered, yelled, and giggled on their way out of school. Lily waited at the usual rendezvous spot by the front office so she could go home with her Mother. Annie did her best to hurry out of her classroom when Patsy surprisingly emerged from behind one of the bookshelves in the open space library.

"Annie! Wait up. I need to tell you something…" Patsy hollered.

'Crap!' Annie thought to herself. Patsy's voice was loud and it carried in the open area. There was no way she could get away with pretending not to hear her. That would make things much, much worse. Annie bit her lip, put a superficial smile on her face and turned around.

"Hi Patsy!" She immediately drew her attention to the ketchup residue that was clearly smeared all over her light blue polyester pants. "What happened to your pants? Is that ketchup?" Annie asked. Nice try, but Patsy was on a mission and she would not allow the ketchup incident to dominate the conversation.

"Oh, yeah. It will come out in the laundry." Patsy continued on with what she really wanted to talk about. "I have to talk to you about something strange at your house." She said in a lower tone of voice.

"Strange? What do you mean?" Annie said as she tried her best to act clueless.

"Well, do you remember a couple of weeks ago when you were there moving furniture and I told you about the dark figures I saw in your window? Well, we saw them again last night and they are NOT shadows from the trees Annie. There's something else weird going on there!" Patsy said urgently.

Damn it! The Bulldog has latched on and she won't be shaken off easily. Annie tried her best to keep a confused expression but Patsy was skilled at spotting when someone was trying to fool her and she wasn't having any part of it—Especially from her neighbor who lived across the street whom she had known for several years. "Don and I walked over with a flashlight and we both saw something moving around in your house. We were going to call the police but since the house was empty and there were no cars around, Don thought it would be best just to let you know about it." Patsy said.

Annie thought carefully about what to say next. Patsy wasn't stupid and she was now an unknowing witness to the Shadow People in their house. She may not know what she saw, but that wouldn't stop her from finding out. *Should she just tell her the truth?* No, that would be a disaster. She'd tell the whole neighborhood and word would get out that we have a haunted house for sale that will never sell. She might go so far as to call the Channel 9 News crew out and they'd be screwed. Most of the money they had was in that house and they couldn't afford to lose everything because of Patsy's big mouth. Her only solution was to bring Patsy in as an ally, but she had to do it very delicately. While trying to think about what to say, Annie glance to the side and her eyes landed on a book titled *Fun with Science—A young investigator's guide to the world of science.* That's it. They would discover the strange phenomena in the empty house together. Patsy could keep a secret if she thought it would hurt her in any way, and if the house across the street is haunted? Annie was willing to bet that she'd silently list their house for sale and move away too.

"Patsy, I don't know what to say. I mean, what do you think you saw? Did someone break in?" Annie asked in an inquisitive way.

"I don't know, but I think we should get to the bottom of it. This is the second time I've seen something, and I'm not sure what it is, but we need to find out." Patsy said insistently.

"Well, yes, of course, but I…I don't know what to do. Um, Patsy, I have to meet Lily and go to the grocery store before heading home. Let me give you a call when I get home and we'll talk about this. I agree with you—if there's something weird going on over there, we need to find out what it is." Annie said. Patsy nodded in agreement and walked with Annie through the doors that opened to the front office area where Lily was standing there waiting.

"There's Lily." Annie pointed out. "Patsy, thank you for being such a good neighbor and letting me know. I'll call you when I get back home and we'll talk about what we should do next."

Emphasis on the 'we' Annie thought to herself. Since this was all very new to Annie and she was no expert on Shadow People, she decided to skip the grocery store and stop in to chat with Edith before calling Patsy back. Annie was relieved to solve the busybody gossipy neighbor issue for right now, but she had no idea what she would be facing going back into her house again. Patsy was a nosey pain in the ass sometimes, but she didn't want to see her harmed. Edith told her that Shadow People were capable of killing people or making them disappear. Annie needed to learn more so that she didn't do anything stupid where someone could get hurt. If Patsy was scared enough to move away, that was one thing, but Annie couldn't live with herself if anything were to happen to her neighbor. This was a bad situation all around and she had to find out how best to mitigate the danger as best she could.

As Annie pulled up in the circular driveway at the main house, Edith was out in her flower garden pulling weeds. She stood up when she saw the car and walked out to greet them. "Hello there! My, is it 3:30 already?" Edith said as she pulled her glove back so she could see her watch.

"Hello Edith! Your flower beds are gorgeous! You always tend to them so nicely." Annie complemented her. "I'm wondering if I could talk to you about something. Lily has a little homework to finish up anyway, so can we talk for a few minutes?" Annie asked.

"Of course dear. Nothing's wrong at the guesthouse I hope?" Edith asked.

"No, no. Everything is great there! This is something different. I need your advice." The three of them walked into the house and Lily pulled a chair out at the kitchen table. She opened her workbook to the page with the bent corner so she could find her assignment for today. She asked for a pencil, which Edith gladly provided, and she began to fill in the answers to the questions on the page.

Edith poured two glasses of iced tea and sat down at the table across from Annie. She scanned her and knew what Annie was troubled by, but waited for Annie to speak first.

"Patsy, my neighbor across the street, stopped me today and said that she and her husband saw something weird at our house last night. They went over with a flashlight and said they saw movement inside. She was pressing me for answers and I just acted like I didn't know what she was talking about, but she wasn't buying it." Annie explained.

"Yes, she's a persistent lady to be sure." Edith took a sip of her iced tea and let Annie continue with her story.

"I didn't know what to say, but I saw a book on the shelf next to us and I got an idea. I thought that if I brought Patsy over to investigate, she'd either see that there was nothing going on there, or she'd get a glimpse of the Shadow People and be so scared out of her wits that they would pack and move away too. That would be the only way that Patsy would keep her mouth shut about it because she wouldn't be able to sell her house if it was known to be directly across the street from a haunted house. She'd stay silent to protect her own interests. That was the only thing I could think of, so I planted the idea of investigating the house with me but I'm scared. I may have put my nosey neighbor in danger now and I am very troubled by that. What should I do?" Annie put her head down on the table and clasped her hands behind her head.

Since Lily was sitting at the table, she was listening to the whole conversation. She took a brief pause from her homework and made eye contact with Edith. "Mrs. MacKenzie? Didn't you say that the Shadow People are mostly interested in little kids and old people? Mrs. Sunderland isn't either one. Maybe they'll leave her alone." Lily said in her sweet little voice.

"Well, yes that's the way it usually is. They prefer to prey on those who are weaker than others, but they can go after anyone really. It's still dangerous to go back into the house. The barrier is no longer holding if she can see them through the window. We have to seal it again with some other method. It's probably a good idea anyway since you're trying to sell it. They'll take over the whole house if they're allowed to, and what we DON'T want to do is seal them in our dimension. That will only anger them." Edith said as she sat back in her chair and rested her hands in her lap. She took a deep breath and closed her eyes.

After a few minutes of sitting quietly, Edith explained that they should just sit down with Patsy and tell her the truth. This is too dangerous a situation to mess with, and she needs to know what she is walking into whether she believes what they tell her or not. Annie listens, and after a brief moment of reflection, she ultimately agrees.

CHAPTER 8

Early on Saturday morning, Annie and Edith pulled into the driveway of the empty house. Patsy was standing at her kitchen window sipping her coffee so she could see when they arrived. She took one final sip and set her coffee cup on the counter before walking out the door. Patsy loved a good intrigue and she was dying to get to the bottom of this mystery. The three women met in the driveway exchanging the usual pleasant greetings before entering the house. Edith had done her opening and both Tom and the dead woman were there standing amongst them. Edith looked at Patsy and felt that she should start by revealing her abilities to her.

"There's something I need to tell you before we go into the house, Patsy. I am what they call a Psychic Medium." Edith said. She cut to the chase. There was no dancing around the topic to be had. "Do you know what that is?"

Patsy stared in disbelief. She had heard of Psychics but had never actually met one. "You mean like a Fortune Teller?" She asked.

Edith smiled and glanced at Annie who pursed her lips and put her head down to keep from laughing. "Well, not exactly. It means that I have the ability to see and speak to the Dead." She paused for a minute to let that sink in.

"Are you telling me that my neighbor's house is haunted?" Patsy looked almost thrilled at the prospect of that. This was indeed a juicy tidbit of gossip that she could run with for a long time.

Annie regained her composure and decided to fill Patsy in on the events that caused them to pack up and move so quickly. "You know Patsy? Can we go over to your house and talk before we go in here? This might take a while to explain and I really think I need to fill you in from the beginning. It might take a while." Annie said.

"Of course! Don took Scottie to Eric's football game and Caroline is babysitting over at the Dickenson's house. We have the house to ourselves this morning. I'll make a pot of coffee. C'mon." The suspense was killing Patsy, but now she would finally get the whole scoop and there was nothing she loved more.

The three women sat at the kitchen table with their coffee and Annie shared every detail she could remember. She even disclosed that Lily had abilities, and she first became aware of it on the day the children were playing in piles of leaves in Patsy's front yard a couple of years ago. Patsy remembered that day and was slightly disappointed that it took so long for Annie to mention anything about Lily seeing a ghost man in her front yard. Edith gave the paranormal related explanations as they went, and after about an hour, Annie covered almost every detail she could recall. There was a moment of silence and all three women sipped their coffee at the same time. Patsy set her cup down, and looked out the window at the Campbell's house. She was not expecting to hear anything like this and for once, Patsy was speechless.

"I...I don't know what to say." Patsy said. "This is so surreal." Then, just as Annie thought that Patsy might back off and change her mind about going over to the house to investigate further, she says this: "I can't think of anything that has ever happened in my life more exciting than this!" Patsy exclaims gleefully. "We have to seal that portal once and for all!" Patsy sprang to her feet and disappeared behind the wall for a brief moment, then emerged with a large Crucifix of Jesus with a crown of thorns on his head hanging from the Cross. "Good ALWAYS triumphs over evil. Let's go ladies!" Edith's eyes were wide as she glanced over at Annie who was donning a similar expression. They both let out a subtle grunting sound as they held back their laughter. Even Tom and the dead woman who where were standing between Edith and Annie were giggling. But this was no laughing matter. What they were walking into was unpredictable and dangerous.

'*You must go carefully.*' The dead woman says in Edith's ear. '*They are dark and they are many.*' Edith took heed of the spirit's messages and urged Patsy to stay behind her and be watchful.

As Annie turned the key in the front door, she paused and took a deep breath. A feeling of dread and foreboding washed over her. She did NOT want to go in. Edith put her hand on Annie's shoulder and reminded her that fear is what these beings thrived on. If Annie entered the house with fear, she would empower them.

"Do you want to take a moment?" Edith asked. Annie took a couple of deep breaths and remembered that this was HER house and these beings invaded it without invitation to do so. She wanted them out and that's why she was there. This was no time to be weak and scared. Annie looked back at Edith and then at Patsy, who was standing behind them clutching the large crucifix she took off of her wall with both hands, ready to do battle. Annie thought of Lily and the night she witnessed her being dragged off her bed and nearly pulled into the closet. That was enough to instill enough courage to fight back.

"Here we go." Annie said. As she opened the door, a wave of strength and steady calm rushed through her. It was her Father's energy. He was here with her, protecting her. She could feel him and she was grateful for his strength and support.

The house was silent. As the three women stepped across the threshold, they scanned the room for shadows or signs of movement. Nothing. The drapes were closed and the air felt stale. Edith walked over and open the drapes of the big picture window and walked through the rest of the house, room by room, opening the blinds and any non-stationary window to let the fresh air flow through. Patsy cautiously followed Edith into each room, pausing to listen for the faintest sound. "Where are they?" She whispered to Edith as she clutched the crucifix tightly to her chest with eyes the size of saucers.

"In Lily's bedroom. They come out of the closet. That's where the portal is." Edith caught a glimpse of the look on Patsy's face and couldn't help but wonder if Patsy was now regretting participating in this, but could tell that she was also getting a thrill out of it. A few seconds after Edith spoke, a door slammed loudly down at the end of the hall. It was Lily's bedroom door.

Patsy jumped and Edith turned around quickly to catch the sight of the hall bathroom door slamming shut. Was it the wind? Possibly, but Edith knew better. Shadow People were mostly observers, but they have been known to interact in a very physical way. The entities that were in the Campbell house were definitely more aggressive than she had experienced in the past, and they were making it known that they were not going to go away without a fight. Edith began feeling terrible stomach pain. The wave of nausea came on so strong that she ran to the bathroom to vomit. Patsy called for Annie, who was standing in the middle of the living room unable to move.

"Annie! Edith is sick. What should we do?" Patsy called to her. No answer. Annie was frozen and couldn't move or speak. "Annie?" Patsy walked down the hall to find Annie standing completely still with a catatonic look on her face. "Annie? Are you alright?" Patsy began waving her crucifix around Annie as if to magically break the hold over her. "Annie! Answer me, please!" Annie broke her blank stare and tried to speak but only small moaning sounds came out. Patsy grabbed her by the arm and drug her outside the front door. As the fresh air hit her, Annie began to revive and was slowly able to get words out that made sense.

"I...I...can't talk." She was finally able to say.

"Just breathe." Patsy said as she proceeded to coax Annie to take deep breaths and exhale by doing it herself. After a few minutes of controlled breathing, Annie was able to snap out of the catatonic state she was in.

"Where's Edith?" Annie said.

"She was throwing up in the bathroom when I called to you. I think she's still in there." Patsy said. "I'll go check on her."

A couple minutes later, Patsy returned with Edith and helped her sit on the front step. Edith was very pale and frail looking all of a sudden. She was clearly under attack. Shadow People did tend to prey upon the elderly and although pretty healthy and spry for her age, Edith was in her 70's. The three women sat quietly for a few minutes and as they did, the color began to come back into Edith's cheeks and she was looking a little better.

"How many Shadow People did you say were tormenting Lily?" Edith asked.

"Um, she said four or five. I don't recall her mentioning any more than that." Annie replied.

"Well, one is enough to cause trouble but you definitely have more than four or five. I counted at least nine and there could be more than that." Edith said. "You have a large portal in there Annie and we have to close it somehow."

"Can you do it Edith? I mean, It's not worth you getting hurt." Annie was deeply concerned for her friend. She wanted to send Patsy home with a gag order and put Edith back in the car and call the whole thing off. This was turning into a much scarier thing than she had ever thought it would be and things were getting serious. Annie was feeling like they were in way over their heads.

Edith turned to Annie and looked her straight in the eye. "*WE* need to do it together. I cannot do it alone." Edith said. She turned to Patsy and said "We will need your help too Patsy. But you must be careful and do exactly as I say."

Patsy's eyes were wide and she nodded in absolute agreement. She was there to help and she was ready to face whatever came next. The danger was real and she was seeing it happen firsthand.

To her, this started as an innocent ghost hunt but having witnessed the physical attacks to both Edith and Annie, she was gaining a much different perspective. The paranormal phenomenon is real. It's here in this house. She had an opportunity to help and she was going to do just that. The three women stood up and huddled together to say a prayer. Annie's Father and the dead woman were there with them for strength and support, giving Edith clear direction about what she needed to do next. When the spirits directed her to do so, Edith broke the prayer circle and all three of them entered the house.

As Edith entered Lily's bedroom, the closet door was open and dark inside. The whole room was dark. Patsy paused in the hallway and peered into the room from a slight distance. Edith opened the blinds to both windows letting the sunlight stream in. She lifted the windows about 10 inches and a nice fresh breeze blew in and chased the dank stale air away. Patsy looked around the corner at Lily's closet. Now that the blinds were open, it didn't look so dark and it just looked like an ordinary empty closet. Edith walked to the center of the room and pulled out a plastic bag with salt a mixture of other ground up crystals in it that she acquired from a Voodoo Practitioner during her last trip to New Orleans. She motioned for Patsy and Annie to come to where she was standing, and once they were all together, she sprinkled the salt in a circle that surrounded them. "Stay in this circle. It offers protection." She said. Then Edith pulled out a stick of white sage that was wrapped with string and lit it. Once the flame was robust, she blew it out and the fragrant white smoke bellowed up into the room. Edith waved it around so that the smoke filled every corner of the room, lingering in front of the open closet. She asked Annie to repeat the affirmations she was verbalizing with conviction, and handed the sage stick to Patsy.

Patsy, who was thrilled to not only be witnessing a real cleansing ritual, but she was now an active participant of it! She waved the smoking sage stick all around them vigorously and took her role in this process very seriously. Edith reached into her plastic bag and grabbed a handful of the salt mixture. "You are BANISHED from this home and this portal is closed forever. You may never enter through it again." She said in concert with Annie. Then she tossed the handful of salt into the closet and made a big circle with her hand, followed by a big "X" and then gestured a tiny circle in the middle of the air X with her index finger. '*It is sealed now.*' Edith hears the dead woman whisper in her ear. She turned to Annie and Patsy who was still waving the sage stick around as if she was painting the ceiling with it, and smiled.

"Are we done?" Annie asked.

"Yes, we're done." Edith said. "We can step out of the protective circle now. Patsy, let's take that sage stick and finish cleansing the rest of the house. I'll show you what to do." Patsy was thrilled. She was now officially, in her mind, a Psychic Medium's Apprentice and this was one of the most exciting things she has ever done. She could see herself doing this as a part-time job.

As Edith and Patsy continued smudging the rest of the house, Annie retrieved a broom and a dustpan from the garage and swept up the salt circle they were standing in. She took it outside and scattered the salt by the front door, then returned the broom and dustpan to the garage where she found it. After smudging the entire house, Edith extinguished the sage and returned it to the plastic bag in her pocket. "Well, that was one of the most interesting things I have ever done before!" Patsy squealed. "Edith, is this what you do for a living?"

Edith chuckled. "Well, I have been asked to do this occasionally, but no, I wouldn't say it's what I do for a living." She said.

Patsy became even more inquisitive now and blasted Edith with a million questions. Where did she learn this? Can anyone learn to do it? How did Edith become a Psychic Medium? Is it something she could learn too? The questions were asked at such a rapid rate, Edith didn't even try to answer any of them. *'The dog is lonely...'* The dead woman whispers in Edith's ear giving her clear direction as to how to make the interrogation stop.

"Patsy, your poor dog is going crazy over there. You should go check on him." Edith said as she directed Patsy to the window where, sure enough, you could see that Ladd was springing up and down in a frenzy behind the window.

"Oh my goodness! Poor baby! I nearly forgot all about him." Patsy said as she rushed across the street to take care of the panicked pooch.

"We're just going to let the house air out a little and we'll be over in a little bit." Annie called out to Patsy, who waived and darted up her driveway. Annie sat down on the front step and breathed a sigh of relief. It felt like their mission was accomplished, and it was exhausting. She felt like she just burned 10,000 calories just like that.

"I think we closed it, but time will tell. Are you alright? Patsy said you couldn't speak." Edith said as she sat down next to Annie and patted her on the back.

"It was so strange." Annie said. "After that door slammed, I turned around and something rushed at me. I couldn't move. I was shrouded in darkness and I couldn't see or speak. It seemed like I was suspended in the center of a dense dark cloud, then all of a sudden I was outside with Patsy telling me to breathe." Annie recalled.

"You were being attacked. They were trying to stop us. They tried to inca-pacitate me by making me sick. That's what they do. They're very powerful." Edith sat quietly and reflected on what had just taken place.

"Why do you think Patsy wasn't affected by any of this? She didn't seem to be attacked." Annie asked.

"That's a good question. Maybe because they know who we are but Patsy was new. The likely didn't perceive her as a threat...But I'm glad she was here. I was not in a position to help you and you could have been drug off into the portal if Patsy didn't take you outside when she did." Edith explained. The two women looked at each other realizing that the one person whom Annie wanted to hide all of this from quite literally saved her life that day.

Just then, Phyllis Tipton drove up in her Pontiac Bonneville and got out of the car. "Hello Annie! I tried to call you and Mark, but no one answered. I was in the neighborhood so I thought I'd drive by and see if you might be here—And here you are! I'm so glad I found you!" She said.

Phyllis was their real estate agent. She was a tall, slim woman with red hair that was teased at the crown and pulled back with a paisley print headband. "I have some great news! I have an offer on your house. It's a couple with no children who want to basically tear it down and build a two story house right on top of it..." Phyllis said as she winced a little knowing that this might be upsetting for a seller to hear, since it was their home and someone basically wants to destroy it. What Phyllis didn't know was that Annie was just contem-plating setting it on fire after what they just experienced anyway.

"Phyllis, you don't know how good that sounds to me right now!" Annie said as she stood to give her a giant hug. "This is my friend Edith. She was helping me do a little cleaning this morning. It was smelling a little stuffy in there so we opened the windows to air it out a little."

"Well, you won't have to worry about the condition of the house. Like I said, it's a good offer and they're going to tear just about everything down and build on top of it anyway. Nice to meet you Edith." Phyllis shook Edith's hand and turned her attention back to Annie. "I will need you and Mark to sign it. Is he at home today or on the road?" Phyllis asked.

"He's expected home this afternoon. Can you come over around 5:00? He should be home by then." Annie ran her fingers through her hair and breathed a sigh of relief.

"Perfect. I'll prepare an estimate of your net proceeds after close of escrow and we'll go over everything this evening. I'll see you then." Phyllis waved good-bye, got back into her car, and drove away. This was the best news Annie could have ever hoped to receive. She was worried about another family moving into the house and possibly experiencing similar paranormal activity. There was no way to know if the portal was completely closed or not, but if the closet was demolished she assumed the portal would be too.

"Annie, I know what you're thinking but tearing down the house might open it back up again. There is a chance that it might." Edith cautioned her. There were certain 'rules' that applied when dealing with portals. Yes, they could be sealed, but certain events can just as easily open them back up again, or create new ones. The where and why of that phenomena was still relatively unknown. Only time would tell.

Annie was emotionally and physically exhausted and couldn't dwell on any 'what ifs' at the moment. She did all that was humanly possible to remedy the situation and she could not be responsible for it forever. This would no longer be her fight. Keeping Lily and her family safe was her objective and she had done all she could.

CHAPTER 9

DECEMBER, 1969

The house closed escrow quickly and it was demolished the following week. Only two original exterior walls were kept on the old house and they graded the lot to accommodate a larger first level footprint. From a permitting standpoint, Annie learned that if two existing walls remained, then the project could be permitted as a renovation rather than permitting a new home build, which was much more costly and a longer permitting process. The construction crew moved very quickly so that they could get the lot graded and the house framed and "dried in" before the heavy snow and below zero winter weather was in full swing. Patsy kept in touch every couple of days so they heard of all the progress in nearly real time. Mark and Annie were looking for a new home, but with the Holiday Season, there were fewer listings and Phyllis had shown them just about everything in their price range within the kid's school district boundaries. Although a little cramped, the guesthouse was working out pretty well. The kids got used to sharing a bedroom and didn't spend a whole lot of time in there except to sleep. Stephen saved enough money to buy an older Plymouth Barracuda and although it had a few spots around the fender that were poorly patched with Bondo, he was thrilled to have it and enjoyed the blissful independence it offered.

Despite the 8 year age difference, Vince and Lily were becoming closer and he would often accommodate Lily up to the main house when she visited Edith. He became more interested in her abilities and wanted to learn more about them. Edith determined that Vince was also a sensitive and could feel the presence of spirits, but did not have the clairvoyant and clairaudient abilities that Lily strongly possessed. That's not to say that he could not develop those abilities later. Edith was now training Lily to keep herself balanced through an exercise called Tai Chi and daily meditation. Tai Chi was not a familiar practice to most Americans, but Lily found it relaxing and kind of fun. Vince also enjoyed the fluid movement of the exercise and actually looked forward to this activity.

As the snow fell like fluttering butterflies in the breeze, Lily gazed out Edith's sliding glass door in the breakfast nook sipping her mug of hot cocoa with miniature marshmallows. She had just finished her training for the day and Edith treated her students to her special hot cocoa with a pinch of salt and cayenne pepper in it to bring out the natural flavor of the chocolate. Vince was asking Edith how he could develop the ability to see and talk to the Dead like Lily could, and she explained that she was naturally very open, but Vince could also learn to open over time.

Everyone has an intuitive sense, but she was always happy to work with anyone who really wanted to develop their abilities further. Her work with Lily had more to do with control and shutting it down so she could just focus on being a kid most of the time, but Lily's abilities were very strong and it was hard to dim the light at times.

As Lily watched the light snow fall, something caught her eye towards the back of the 5 acre lot along the tree line at the start of the woods behind the main house. It was peering at her from behind a big oak tree. It was solid black and it was staring right at her with red glowing eyes.

Lily nearly dropped her cup on the table and the harsh banging sound got the immediate attention of Vince and Edith. "Lily? What is it?" Edith asked.

Lily could only point. Edith and Vince stood up and ran to the sliding glass door to see what she was looking at. They could see nothing unusual, just the snow covered back yard and the sparse leafless trees towering along the back lot line. "What did you see Lil?" Vince asked. "I don't see anything."

"It was a Shadow Person! Like the ones that used to be in my room." Lily was instantly transported back to the memory of the night she was paralyzed and pulled from her bed by her ankles onto the floor.

Edith gazed out toward the wooded lot line. It was about 4:45 pm and it was just starting to get dark. She could not see anything out there, but thought it best to go investigate since Lily had just survived a terrifying experience. She didn't have any portals or vortexes on her land, but that's not to say that a new portal hadn't opened up now. There were Elementals in the woods. Edith knew of them and she often planted flowers back there as a peaceful offering to them. This kept harmony with the spiritual inhabitants of the woods that bordered her property.

and three glasses of French Burgundy for himself, Mark and Annie. "Merry Christmas everyone!" Ed said as he passed the tray around for everyone to take their drink.

"Merry Christmas to you too Ed." Mark said as he took a glass of wine.

Edith emerged from the kitchen in her apron with a glass of wine in her hand as she held it up to make a toast. "Merry Christmas to you all! We are so happy to have you here." She said as they all clinked their glasses together and took a sip.

"Oh my gosh Edith, your house is beautiful!" Annie said as she looked around the room and admired all of the garland, wreaths, candles, and the beautiful nativity scene set out on the tall, narrow console table behind the sofa. The tree was covered in colorful twinkling red and white lights, with golden glass ornaments on every branch, and the crystal star of Bethlehem on top gleamed as it reflected the lights from the tree.

"Why thank you! It's my favorite time of year you know. I use the same decorations every year and I never get tired of them. They're like old friends you only see at Christmas." Edith said as she admired the room with Annie. "Dinner is almost ready. Please make yourselves comfortable."

Annie followed Edith back to the kitchen to see if she could be of help, and Lily sat Indian style next to Winnie by the fireplace and sipped her hot apple cider. There, sitting next to her, was a dead boy chattering on about how lucky Lily was to have such a nice family to spend Christmas with and how he used to have a big family to spend the Holidays with but he couldn't find them anymore. Lily told him that he could find them and that she could help him. She visualized an opening on the wall behind the boy and bright white light poured through. Tiny orbs spilled out and surrounded the boy, who lifted his arms as he smiled. *'Go to the light. You'll find your family there.'* Lily said in her mind. The boy drifted up off of the ground and floated toward the light. He turned back to smile at Lily before passing through the opening she had created for him. *'Thank you.'* The boy said to her. Once he stepped through, she closed it just as effortlessly as she had opened it. This was a precious gift that Lily had—to be able to help the Dead who were lost or stuck here. She could help them cross over so they could be with their families and loved ones who had also passed away but didn't stick around. Sometimes spirits just get stuck. Sometimes they suffer very quick deaths and don't even realize that they are dead. Others know they're dead, but consciously remain here to attend to unfinished business or to look after a loved one who is still living. Some are

CHAPTER 10

CHRISTMAS, 1969

It was a MacKenzie tradition to cook a big meal for friends and family on Christmas Eve. Ed often came to spend the whole week with his mother and this year it was an opportunity to spend good quality time with Mark and his family as well. As the Campbell's walked up from the guesthouse in the dusky twilight, the snow glistened like diamond dust sprinkled across the ground. It had snowed heavily the night before and even though Ed had plowed the driveways, there were several inches of packed snow that crunched with every step the family took. The air was cold and crisp, and the sky was clear. It was a beautiful silent night, just like the song. Lily was happily skipping along singing *Rudolph the Red Nosed Reindeer* as Vince and Stephen ran through the deeper snow in the yard tossing handfuls of snow into each other's faces. Winnie ran out into the snowy covered yard after them, but found it difficult to move since the snow was deep enough to come up to her neck. She could barely move and she let out a whiney yelp calling for the Boys to come and rescue her.

When they arrived at the main house, Ed just put another log on the fire and Edith was happily cooking her famous Christmas Eve meal in the kitchen while singing along to Bing Crosby's *White Christmas* that was playing on the record player that was set up in the corner of the dining room. The whole house smelled of roasted prime rib with a background smell of fresh pine and sugar cookies. It smelled like Christmas at Grandma's house and that's essentially what it was.

Annie dusted the snow off of the Boy's coats before hanging them on the coat rack behind the front door. Everyone took their boots off and placed them neatly on the rug beneath the coat rack. Winnie quickly found her place on an old folded blanket next to the fireplace hearth as Ed emerged from the kitchen with a tray of hot apple cider with cinnamon sticks for the kids, put the family Christmas tree this year. "Momma? Can we put our Christmas tree up this weekend?" Lily asked in her sweet little voice.

"Actually, that was what your Father and I were planning to do on Saturday morning. I'm afraid I'm not sure where all of our Christmas ornaments are though, we'll have to go out to Ed's garage and look through our boxes." Annie said. Ed was kind enough to store some of their things in the corner of his garage. He had a separate heated 2 car garage with a large workbench in it and he often worked on old cars that he would collect, restore, and resell. It was a hobby that he was good at and it made him quite a lot of money on the side.

"Ed and I always go to the same tree farm to get our trees. They donate 30% to the food banks for the Holiday season, so we always go there. Would you like to come with us? They have some beautiful White Pines." Edith mentioned. Her family was small, just herself and Ed most of the time. The rest of her family was back in Scotland and they wrote often, but didn't see each other as much as they'd like to. Ed's Father, Ian MacKenzie, passed away over 30 years ago in an automobile accident when a truck skidded on a patch of black ice and crossed the highway hitting Ian head on. Ed was only 12 years old then, and Edith never remarried. She was content to raise Ed on her own and was very proud of her only son. Ian was a very good business man, and his smart investments took care of Edith and Ed very well after his death. They never felt that they lacked anything, and they took joy in the simple things in life.

Vince and Stephen walked Edith back to the main house after dinner and were amazed by how much snow had fallen in just a couple of hours. Once she was in her house and the lights were on, the boys walked back down the driveway to the guesthouse stopping only to pack snowballs to throw at each other along the way. Vince glanced over toward the edge of the woods where Lily saw the Shadow Person, but saw nothing but darkness. The guesthouse sat only 30 ft. from the woods and he sensed that something was out there waiting to cross that invisible barrier that Edith created when she first built the house. It wanted Lily and he needed to protect her... And a time would come when he would do just that.

"Well, we need to know what might be out there. It's getting dark, but light enough to go take a quick walk. Get your coats and boots on and we'll go out together." Edith said as she encouraged the children to finish their hot cocoa and get dressed in their winter gear.

The three of them got dressed and walked straight out to the place where Lily saw the shadow figure. Edith could neither see, hear, nor sense its presence, but this was not unusual since spiritual entities had the ability to move about quickly and could come and go as they pleased without a trace. Lily was tense and closed her eyes as she ran through her meditation to surround herself with Divine, white protective light. About 20 ft. away, a Fox appeared from behind a fallen tree. It paused to stare at them before running off deeper into the woods. A flock of crows cawed as they flew overhead. These were normal sounds and activities in the woods and this was reassuring to Edith. She knew that the time to be worried was when a silent, eerie, dead calm came over the grounds. That usually meant the presence of something evil.

"Lily? Do you sense anything now that we're standing out here where you saw the Shadow Person? Sometimes they leave an energetic footprint that can be felt." Edith asked.

Lily opened her eyes and looked around. She took a deep breath and let the cold, crisp air into her lungs. She didn't sense anything, but she knew what she saw. She could see three dead people standing nearby—people she hadn't encountered before. There was a man, a woman, and a girl around the age of 12. *'Evil was here Lily. You must be careful not to let it in.'* The dead man said to her. *'I know'.* Lily said telepathically. She turned to Edith and said "I think I should go in now. It's starting to get dark and I don't like to be outside in the dark."

"That's a good idea, dear." Edith said. Just as they turned to walk back toward the house, Annie approached with a flashlight.

"I was just going to walk up to the house to get you guys. Dinner is almost ready." Annie said. She tipped her head back to let the big fluffy snowflakes fall on her face. "It's supposed to snow all night tonight. We're expecting to get 9-10 inches by morning. Edith, I've made a pot roast with root vegetables. Would you like to join us for dinner?"

"Thank you Annie, that sounds delicious!" Edith replied.

After dinner, Lily sat on the floor in the corner and arranged the furniture in her dollhouse so that it could accommodate a Christmas tree. She sat back and looked around the living room and pondered where they were going to confused and don't understand that they should to go to the light when it comes for them, and instead they run from it not understanding what they're supposed to do. These are the spirits who visit Lily daily. They come because they see her light and want to ask her for help. Others hang around to serve and protect her, like her Grandpa Tom, who was also standing in the room next to the fireplace smiling proudly at his little granddaughter.

Edith called everyone to the dining room table that was so festively decorated with candles, pinecones, and sprigs of holly. The meal she made was impressive—Prime Rib with Au Jus and horseradish cream, fluffy garlic mashed potatoes, green beans, roasted carrots in brown butter, freshly baked dinner rolls, and a tossed green salad with apples and candied walnuts. Everyone stood in awe at the feast laid before them. Annie prided herself on being a good cook, but this was something right out of the center Holiday spread of Better Homes and Gardens Magazine.

Everyone took their seats and bowed their heads as Edith said a prayer in Gaelic that she and Ian used to say around the table in Scotland. Ed served the Prime Rib and plates were passed around. There was joyful conversation and laughter around the table. The meal was delicious, the room was filled with love, and the Campbells and MacKenzies were thankful to have each other in their lives.

After cleaning up dinner, everyone sat in the living room by the fireplace and sipped a hot after dinner drink that Edith made with Single Malt Scotch Whiskey, lemon, honey, cinnamon and cloves in a little hot water for the adults, and her special hot chocolate for the kids—this time with a peppermint stick. It warmed them from the inside out. Lily sat quietly beneath the tree petting Winnie. Everyone was warm, well fed, and growing sleepy. It was 9:45 pm and it was time to head home.

"We need to get going." Mark said as he stood up to collect empty cups and take them to the kitchen. "Santa comes tonight."

Lily sprang to her feet clapping her hands gleefully. Christmas morning was her favorite thing in the whole wide world and she knew that she would not have an easy time falling asleep tonight. It was the hardest thing for any kid to do, but it was necessary or Santa wouldn't come.

As the Campbell children put their winter clothes on, Mark and Annie hugged Ed and Edith and thanked them for the wonderful meal and wished them Merry Christmas. "Why don't the two of you come down to the guest-house for brunch tomorrow. Let's say, 11:30?" Annie said.

"Oh that would be lovely, we'd love to!" Edith said as the family went out the door. "We'll see you tomorrow then. Merry Christmas!" She said.

After Lily and the Boys brushed their teeth and were tucked into bed, Mark put his arm around Annie and they sat on the couch in front of their fireplace waiting for the kids to go to sleep so they could perform their annual Santa duties. "That was such a nice evening. And dinner? Oh my gosh! I had no idea Edith could cater a dinner like that. It was better than any restaurant I've ever been to." Annie said as she snuggled next to Mark.

"It was pretty impressive. Edith is full of surprises." Said Mark. As they sat quietly, they both reflected on the events of the past few months and how Ed and Edith had come to their rescue in more ways than one. It was funny how life played out and how certain people came into your life at precisely the right time when you needed that kind of person in your life. They were grateful that they had such good friends, a nice place to live, and that their family was safe and happy.

An hour later, Mark got up and quietly peeked in on the kids. All three were sound asleep and Winnie was curled up at the foot of Lily's bed in the corner. The coast was clear. Time to deliver Santa's gifts. They carefully retrieved the gifts hidden in the back of their bedroom closet and arranged all of the gifts under the tree. Stephen wanted a Chemistry set and seat covers for his car. Vince wanted a set of walkie talkies and a BB gun, and Lily wanted a Crissy doll and a LiteBrite set. Mark was happy that he was able to find the exact items on their wish lists.

Sometimes it was difficult if there was a particularly popular item in limited supply, but this year wasn't much of a challenge and he was glad for that. About a half hour later, Mark and Annie crawled into bed, closed their eyes, and easily drifted off to sleep.

Lily woke up and glanced out the partially opened blinds of her bedroom window. It was still dark, but she knew it was morning. The Boys were still asleep, but she couldn't stand it. She had to see if Santa had come. She sprang from her bed in her flannel onesie with a Pebbles and Bam Bam print from the Flintsones cartoon she loved so much, and squealed loudly to wake her Brothers—*accidentally* on purpose, of course. Vince stirred and slowly opened his eyes to see Lily jumping up and down in front of his bed. He smiled and looked over at Stephen, who was also stirring.

"Vince its Christmas! Let's go see what Santa brought!" Lily squealed.

The Boys both sat up in bed, rubbing their eyes. They both grabbed their hoodie sweatshirts and pulled them over their heads. Lily had a cute pink fuzzy bathrobe with matching slippers, but she didn't bother with those. She was too excited. As soon as her Brothers were on their feet, she bolted out the door and down the hall towards the living room. The blinds were open but the room was still kind of dark. The sun wouldn't begin to rise for another hour yet. There, in the corner of the room was the most glorious sight—The Christmas tree was lit and the tinsel was glistening on the tree making it truly a spectacle to behold. Beneath it and all around the floor below it were presents of various shapes and sizes, all beautifully wrapped in festive paper with colorful ribbons and bows. There were a few presents that were not wrapped, and those were the gifts from Santa. After all, he had SO many gifts to deliver to good children all over the world in only one night, so he simply did not have time to wrap each one you know...

The Boys emerged from the hallway and ran to the gifts they recognized from their wish list. The happy sounds from the front room echoed down the hall and woke Annie and Mark from their sound slumber. Mark rolled over and looked at the alarm clock on his nightstand. 6:22 am. "It's show time." Mark said as he sat up and stretched. Annie rolled out of bed and grabbed her bathrobe from the hook on the back of the bathroom door. They walked down the hall to see their three very happy kids playing with their gifts. It was a tradition in their household that they could play with the unwrapped gifts that Santa brought, but they had to wait until the whole Family was present before opening the wrapped gifts. Mark started the coffee pot and walked back to the living room to start a fire in the fireplace and enjoy the morning with his Family.

Stephen had the various parts of his chemistry set all laid out on the floor and he sat quietly reading the instruction manual as he routinely did with everything he was unfamiliar with. He was very smart and was interested in learning new things all the time. He retained nearly everything he read and had the potential to be a great Doctor someday. He also had a quick wit—so much so, that he would make a hilarious comment and it wouldn't register as funny until people had a minute to think about it. His gift of obvious humor was what made him so much fun to be around. Couple that with his high IQ and he could prompt belly rolling laughter in the most intellectual of adults.

Vince sat at the edge of the couch carefully pouring BBs into his new rifle, taking great care not to spill one. Lily had removed her Crissy doll from the package, pressed the button in the middle of her back that allowed her to pull her pony tail out to the longest length, and sat her doll next to her as she plugged in the colored pegs into the LiteBrite screen to form a backlit picture.

"Is everyone happy?" Annie said as she sat down with her cup of hot steaming coffee. A resounding "YES" was expressed by all. "Let's pass out the other gifts and unwrap them then."

After all of the gifts were unwrapped, Mark walked around the room and picked up the shredded wrapping paper and cardboard packaging and stuffed it into a large trash bag. After getting the brunch started Annie dismissed herself to go take a shower, and the kids were urged to go get dressed. They were hosting the MacKenzie's for Brunch and they had to put the guesthouse back in order before they arrived. "Dad, can I go out and shoot my gun in the woods before the MacKenzie's get here?" Vince asked as he held the rifle and peered down the scope through the window.

"Sure Son, I'll get dressed and go out with you. Let's bring the targets and see how good a shot you are." Mark said.

The sun was rising in the sky and it became lighter outside. The snow was deep as Mark and Vince trudged across the yard to the woods behind the house. The squirrels were scrambling through the woods gathering what acorns they could find at the base of a big oak tree, and the resident fox could be seen running off as they approached. Mark walked ahead and found a low hanging branch that he could easily hang the paper target from. He walked back to Vince and they took turns shooting at the target. Neither hit the bull-seye, but there were a couple of shots that Mark took that hit the second ring on the target. Vince hit the page several times, but needed more practice to actually hit the printed target. That was okay because he planned to practice with this gun every day.

They soon ran out of BBs and Mark walked out to retrieve what was left of the paper target from the tree. As he turned to walk back toward Vince, he caught a glimpse of a tall, black shadow out of the corner of his eye next to the big oak tree that the squirrels were foraging beneath earlier.

He stood still for a moment, staring at the place he saw it hoping to get a clearer picture of what he saw. Nothing. He looked back at Vince who was holding the gun up peering through the scope in another direction. Mark turned back to the oak tree and there it was again. This time it was staring back at him! It looked to be about 7 ft. tall with red eyes and it looked menacing.

Mark was frozen. He opened his mouth to speak but nothing came out.

"Dad! Let's go! Ed and Edith are here." Vince yelled to him. At that moment, Mark was able to break his stare and turned his head in Vince's direction. He turned back to the oak tree and the tall, dark shadow figure was gone. He found that he could move again and he ran toward Vince.

"Let's go Son. We're done here." He said. Mark knew that Vince had been spending time with Edith and Lily and that he was also a sensitive. He was debating whether or not he should say anything to Vince at that moment or if he should bring it up with Edith first. He didn't want to scare Vince, but this was exactly the thing that Lily described when she was terrorized in her bedroom at the old house. It was dangerous and he knew he would have to alert everyone to what he had seen for their safety.

The two families enjoyed their delicious Christmas Brunch. Annie made a honey cured ham and biscuits, with a platter of assorted cheeses and different types of mustard. She also made scrambled eggs, fruit, and fresh baked cinnamon rolls that she made from scratch earlier that morning. They exchanged a few gifts and relaxed around the table as Edith shared stories about her family and what it was like to grow up in Scotland. Vince and Stephen were testing out the walkie talkies from either ends of the house, while Lily sat on the floor playing with her new Lite Brite set. The fire crackled in the fireplace after Mark put a fresh log on, and Annie, Ed and Edith sat around the kitchen table with their Mimosas watching out the window as the snow started to fall again.

"Looks like I'll have to plow the driveway again if it keeps snowing like this." Ed said as he took a sip of his Mimosa. "Just one of the joys of living in the Chicago area in the winter." Everyone laughed and agreed. It was nice to live in a place that offered all four seasons, but the Winters in Chicago could be brutal. It was humid in the Summer, but it was also humid in the Winter too. This produced a bone chilling cold that took a while to warm up from. Still, the snow was beautiful and they were all mesmerized as the big fluffy snowflakes fell from the late morning sky.

Mark stood up after stoking the fire and walked toward the kitchen to pour himself a Mimosa and took his seat at the table. "There's something I need to tell you all." He started. "I think we may have problem with Shadow People again."

Annie nearly choked on her drink and Edith's eyes grew larger as she slowly set down her glass. Ed raised his eyebrows in surprise. "Why do you think that?" Ed asked.

Mark lowered his head for a moment to assemble the words he wanted to say then gazed out the window toward the tree line at the edge of the yard. "This morning, when Vince and I went out to the woods to shoot his new BB gun, I saw one. I saw a Shadow Person. It was standing next to the big oak tree by the creek and it stared right at me. I froze. It was tall…" He held his hand up high above his head to demonstrate, "…It had to be at least 7 ft. And it had red glowing eyes. I couldn't speak and I couldn't move. I don't know how long I was transfixed by this thing, but I was finally able to break my stare when Vince called to me. I was literally frozen in fear. This thing is bad…REALLY evil. I felt that."

Recalling what Lily had seen just a couple of weeks earlier, Edith took a deep breath and closed her eyes for a moment. '*They are here Edith. You must keep them out. Lily is in danger.*' Her guides said to her. She asked for their help in what she should do, and they told her that the barrier she laid prior to the Campbell's moving into the guest house was still holding, but they will figure out how to break through soon. She needed to reinforce it with something else.

"Mark, I'm not sure if Lily mentioned it or not, but she also saw it in the woods a couple of weeks ago. I laid a barrier of salt around the perimeter of the yard before you moved in, but it's time to reinforce that barrier. Shadow People are very clever and they'll find a way in somehow if they want to. We have to stay ahead of them." Edith explained.

Just then, Lily appeared next to the table and slid onto her mother's lap. "Momma? Grandpa Tom says I have to be careful when I go outside. He says there's danger in the woods." Annie gently kissed her daughter's head and hugged her.

"I know Baby. You shouldn't go in the woods anyway, not even with your Brothers." Annie looked to Edith for answers as to what they needed to do next. "Edith, I thought that Shadow People don't follow you when you move? Are these the same ones from our old house or are these different Shadow People?"

"Generally they don't follow you. They don't become attached to any one human being. They prey on whomever happens to be near their portal." Edith explained. "These are either new Shadow People, or they could also be the Dead who are showing themselves that way to be scary. Or…" She paused for a moment before continuing. "They could be Demons. Demons can follow you and they will attach themselves to a particular person. I just couldn't get a read on it when Lily saw it two weeks ago but I will investigate further." She told them.

Edith's property was large and well maintained. She made sure to keep it clear of debris and clutter, and she kept her flower beds weeded and her shrubs neatly trimmed. Not only did it look like an English garden in the Spring time, but it was equally as neat and tidy when covered in a blanket of Winter snow. She made regular offerings to the Elementals in the woods to keep peace and harmony on the grounds. She also created a barrier of protection around the perimeter to keep negative energies at bay. This was a ritual she grew accustomed to ever since she was a young girl growing up on her Family's sheep farm outside Inverness in Scotland. The Scots were a bit superstitious and believed in things such as Faeries and Banshees, but perhaps there was a reason for that. The Campbell's never dreamed that they would encounter anything out of the ordinary—certainly nothing paranormal, but they were wrong. Edith was their resident expert and she understood quite a lot about these things. She would guide them through it even if she was uncertain at times about what they were actually dealing with. They would figure it out and they would be prepared to win at all costs.

CHAPTER 11
LATE MARCH, 1970

The snow began to melt and the frozen ground began to thaw. The trees were beginning to wake from their Winter hibernation and were starting to bud. The birds were returning from their southern migration, and the morning light came a bit earlier now. The world was also changing a little. The legal voting age in the United States was lowered from 21 to 18, the new Concorde Aircraft made its first supersonic flight at 700 mph, and Ringo Starr released his first solo album entitled *Sentimental Journey*. Was this a clue that the Beatles were about to break up? Perhaps. It was a new decade and technology was changing rapidly. Stephen was feeling more like an adult and was thrilled that he could begin voting in less than 2 years. He didn't like the thought of being drafted in the Vietnam War and voting made him feel like it gave him a say in the matter.

Although it was comfortable and safe, the guesthouse was starting to feel very small. It was only 998 sq.ft, and with three kids spanning a 10 year age difference in the same bedroom, this living arrangement couldn't continue for much longer. Stephen worked very hard to maintain his 4.0 GPA, and there was no place quiet where he could study. Vince needed room to roam and found it too confining, so he never spent that much time in the house. He would often end up at a friend's house after school and stay there until Mark, Annie, or Stephen picked him up. Lily was a cheerful child who was happy just about anywhere she was, but even she missed having her own space to sit and talk to the Dead when they visited. It was really time to find a new home of their own and they were getting a little discouraged with the current Real Estate inventory available.

Phyllis Tipton called and insisted that the whole Campbell family meet her at a new listing in Brookridge—A subdivision that was located halfway between their old neighborhood and the guesthouse on Edith's property. The location was ideal. It offered easy access to the freeway for Mark to take to work, and it was within the boundaries of their existing school district. Annie wasn't sure they could afford a house in Brookridge because it was more expensive and therefore, out of their budget. The subdivision had its own private air strip for exclusive use by its residents, which meant some of them owned their own planes. The people who lived there were definitely considered the community's wealthier population. People such as successful business owners, Doctors, Dentists, and Lawyers lived there. Mark was a Truck Driver and Annie was a Housewife who volunteered at the local elementary school. Not quite the same income class, so she was concerned that this was a little out of their league. There was a boy in Lily's class whom she had a crush on who lived in Brookridge, and his father was a Scientist at Argon National Laboratories. No one quite knew what they did there, but it was evidently top secret government stuff because those who worked there were never able to talk about it.

They drove up to the lovely split level house that had a very rustic feel to it. The exterior of the house had Cedar siding that was stained a Mahogany brown color with river rock covered columns on either side of a portico entry to the front door from the circular driveway. The front of the lot was beautifully landscaped with mature maple trees and a few Birch trees clustered along the edge of the lot line. It looked like a house that would be in Aspen, Colorado, not that Annie had ever been there. The curb appeal was amazing and Annie instantly fell in love with it from the street.

The house had 4 bedrooms, 3 bathrooms, a formal dining room, large kitchen, and separate living and family rooms with beautiful stone fireplaces in each. It had a 2 car garage attached to the house and a separate single car garage to the rear of the house that the current owner used to store his boat. It sat on a large 3/4 acre lot with a babbling brook running along the far edge of the lot with a small wooden bridge arching over it that lead to the yard that belonged to the house behind it.

As they entered the house, the ceilings were very tall. There was a large coat closet immediately to the right and the living room was just to the left with a large picture window similar to the one in their old house. Just past the coat closet was a wide stairway leading to all 4 bedrooms and 2 of the bathrooms upstairs. Immediately past that stairway was a shorter stairway leading down to a nice family room with a large stone wood burning fireplace with a rustic wood mantle. To the right was the third bathroom tucked under the stairs, and next to that was the door to the garage.

On the other side of the wall from the front living room, was a spacious kitchen and breakfast area with big bright windows that exposed the grand view of the expansive back yard all the way past the creek. Through the kitchen to the other side was the formal dining room at the far end of the house—also with large windows facing the back yard with a large chandelier that hung from the center of the ceiling. You could walk in a big oval through the living room, breakfast area, kitchen, dining room, then back through the living room again. The flow was good. You didn't feel like there was a dead end destination anywhere in the house.

Mark and Annie really liked the house and could easily see themselves living there. Lily ran upstairs and carefully inspected each of the bedrooms before claiming the room with pale yellow walls at the top of the stairs that faced the front driveway for herself. It was right across the hall from the Master Bedroom, but more importantly, she could look out the window and see the house that her little boyfriend lived in, Joey Frasier, and that made her smile. Somehow she knew that was his house and she knew that this was meant to be her room.

Stephen and Vince both found the other 2 bedrooms more than suitable for their needs. Both bedrooms were nearly twice the size of the bedroom that the three of them were currently sharing. Stephen claimed the room at the end of the hall with the built in desk and bookshelves. It was perfect for him and he could see himself being quite comfortable there until he graduated from High School and got a place of his own. Vince liked the room situated between Stephen's and Lily's. It had a view out front and he had a great view of the airstrip to watch the planes take off and land. After the bedrooms upstairs were thoroughly inspected and claimed, the Family moved down to the main level. The Boys headed straight for the family room, plopped down on the big overstuffed sectional, and discussed how great it would be to have a place to watch TV without sharing the space with Lily's dollhouse.

Annie inspected the kitchen and liked what she saw, but as she began to visualize actually living there, she froze. She was terrified of the idea that they might be walking into another paranormal nightmare. After all, that's how it always happens, right? The house draws you in—perfect in every way, then you commit to it and the nightmares begin and you end up having to flee. She was a bit shell shocked by the experiences in her previous home and there was a little hesitation about moving into another house that might be vulnerable to the presence of portals and Shadow People. Lily instinctively knew what her mother was worried about and she rushed over to hug her. Annie knelt down to her level and whispered "What do you think Lily? Are there any bad things here?"

Lily looked her mother straight in the eye and smiled. She knew her mother had been put through Hell and she was scared. "It's okay Momma. This is a good house. Grandpa Tom says this is the one. He helped Phyllis find it for us. It's our house Mom." She smiled sweetly and squeezed her Mother's hand.

Annie smiled back at Lily and pinched her little nose. She stood up and made direct eye contact with Mark as she leaned across the island peninsula between the kitchen and the breakfast area that was open to the family room below. "What do you think? Can we afford this?" She asked. This was by far the nicest house they'd seen but it was also in a more upscale neighborhood and it was considerably larger than the other homes Phyllis had shown them.

"Well, it's at the very top of our price range for sure." Mark said as he tried to calculate how much the monthly payment would be in his head.

Phyllis walked back into the room. She could tell her clients loved the place and it was time to talk business. "What do you think? Nice, huh?" She said.

"I don't know if we can afford this Phyllis. It's a lot of house. I mean, I love this neighborhood. Always have. I just never thought we could afford it." Annie said. She really did love the house and could see herself living there forever, but she didn't want to get her hopes up. In a way, she was a little mad at Phyllis for showing it to them if it was beyond their reach because everything else they would see after this would be a huge disappointment by comparison.

"Actually, I think you're in luck. This house is not formally on the market yet. It's what we call a pocket listing. The seller called me out of the blue just the other day with an interesting proposition. He said that if I could bring him a buyer without having to list it, he would offer it for sale for only $90,000. It comps out at about $110,000 or better, but he feels it's worth saving the hassle of having people traipsing through all the time. He told me that if I could bring him a good offer this week, he'd consider taking it." Phyllis paused to get a read on what her clients might be thinking before she continued. "I know this is at the top of your price range and you'd rather not spend this much, but it's just too perfect for your Family—And in my opinion? DEFINITELY worth the splurge. These opportunities don't come along every day and it WILL sell fast even at the $110,000 price. This is a *very* desirable neighborhood." She said with a sense of urgency in her voice.

Mark stood quietly running the numbers through his head. "Annie, here's how it works out: We sold our house for $76,000 and after paying off the mortgage balance and closing costs we walked away with $54,500. If we put $50,000 down, our payment wouldn't be that much more than we paid before. You have to admit, this floorplan gives us a lot more living space and still gives everyone a place to retreat to if they want some peace and quiet." Mark said as he turned to look behind him. He could see that there was a straight shot view of the family room directly from the kitchen. "You can keep an eye on the kids from right here. It's perfect."

Annie looked around the room and then outside at the yard. It really was everything she wanted. As she turned back around she saw Lily standing next to the kitchen sink with her hands clasped together with that *pretty please?* look on her face. The Boys stood by the kitchen table also showing their approval of the home. She glanced at Phyllis whose expression clearly conveyed: *This is a once in a lifetime opportunity and you should jump on it!* Then she circled back to Mark and she knew what he was thinking. This was their new home and all she needed to do was just say yes. "Okay. Yes. Let's make an offer." Smiles and cheers broke out throughout the room and Lily began clapping her hands and jumping up and down.

"Fantastic! This is a very good decision. Let's lock up and you can follow me back to my office and we'll write it up." Phyllis said.

After signing their offer at the Real Estate office, Mark, Annie, Stephen, Vince, and Lily headed back to the guesthouse while Phyllis left to present the offer to the seller. Lily sat up on the edge of the back seat and leaned up against the back of the front seats with her arms crossed. "Momma? That's the right house for us. Grandpa Tom says so." Lily said.

"Oh he does? Well that's good. Now we just have to wait and see if the seller accepts our offer. It's not our home yet." Annie replied.

"Oh, it's our home all right. Grandpa Tom says the man is going to sign it. He's also going to leave his boat for us for free because he won't be able to take it with him where he's going and he won't have time to sell it… That's what he says." Lily said. She was hearing all sorts of good information from her spirit guides, but there was one bit of information that thrilled her the most and she wasn't going to tell anyone just yet. The boy she had a crush on lived right across the street. His Father was going to help them in a very big way sometime in the future, but she didn't understand how. Some things she just didn't get to know until the time was right, but this was all good to hear. Lily turned her head and watched the trees pass outside window of the car as they drove down the road. She would keep this information to herself for now.

Just shortly after 5pm, the phone rang. It was Phyllis. "Congratulations! The seller has accepted your offer!" Phyllis's voice came through the phone receiver so loud that Mark could hear her from across the room.

"That's wonderful Phyllis! Wow! This is fantastic news!" Annie could hardly believe what she was hearing, even though Lily previously predicted that this would be the case.

"There's just one thing that he's requesting…" Phyllis continued.

"Oh? What's that?" Annie said hoping that it wasn't a condition that they could not meet, but was somewhat reassured thinking back to what Lily had said earlier in the car.

"He's already made an offer on another house and he wants to close escrow by April 15th instead of the 30th. Since you have already closed escrow on your house, I didn't think that would be a problem…" Phyllis said.

Annie moved the receiver away from her mouth and relayed the information to Mark, who smiled and gave her a very enthusiastic thumbs up sign. "Tell him we're fine with that." Annie replied as she winked at her Husband.

"Perfect. I'll call him back and let him know. Well, congratulations you two! I'll open escrow in the morning and you guys will need to take a copy of the signed contract over to your bank tomorrow so they can get your loan started. If you can think of any questions for the seller, just let me know. Have a wonderful evening, Bye…" Phyllis hung up the phone.

"Wow. We're actually buying the Brookridge house." Annie said as she hung up the phone. "Am I dreaming this?"

Mark stood up, wrapped his arms around her, and gave her a big kiss. "It was meant to be Baby." He whispered to her. "Let's go tell the kids, then we have to let Edith and Ed know that we'll be moving."

CHAPTER 12

APRIL 17TH, 1970

Mark and Annie had closed escrow and the deed was recorded. Phyllis handed them the keys to their new house the day before and they spent the night packing up the last of their things in the guesthouse. It was a sunny Spring day and the temperature was a comfortable 70 degrees. Perfect moving weather. Annie stripped the beds and stuffed the bedding into large plastic bags. She'd wash it later at the new house once the washer and dryer were hooked up. The Boys carried their mattresses out to the front room and helped their Mother carry the clothes hanging in the closets out to the car. Ed backed his truck up the driveway and lowered the tailgate. Edith hopped out of the passenger side and came in to see if she could help.

"Morning All! What do we want to take over first?" Ed said as he came through the door. Edith followed him in. She was sad to see them go. She enjoyed having them close by and she was going to miss all of them, especially Lily.

"What can I do to help you Annie?" Edith said.

"Oh Edith, I think we're pretty well packed. I could definitely use a little help unpacking at the new house though." Annie said. It was kind of a bittersweet moment. They fully enjoyed living there and treasured their time spent with Edith. She helped them through so much and she was a part of their Family now. They would miss seeing her every day. But the guesthouse had served its purpose and it was time to move to their new home. This was a new chapter in their lives and Annie was ready to settle in somewhere more permanent...With a few more bedrooms.

"I think we should do a good cleanse of the new house before you move anything in. You know, just to clear out the old energy there so you and your family can have a clean start." Edith said.

Annie recalled how careful Edith was in laying a new protective barrier around the yard after Mark and Lily had seen the Shadow Person in the woods nearby. The barrier had worked and they never saw the Shadow Person again. Now that Annie had lived through the horrifying encounters with the Shadow People in Lily's old room and saw how Edith was able to fight back and keep them safe, it probably wasn't a bad idea.

"You know Edith? I think that is exactly what we should do. Let's put a few more boxes in the trunk of my car and head over there before Mark and Ed arrive with the furniture." Annie smiled and hugged Edith. She was so grateful to have her as a friend, and Edith was happy to be part of their extended Family.

While Mark, Ed, and Stephen stayed behind to finish loading the truck, Annie drove the short 2 ½ miles distance to the new house with Edith, Lily, Vince, and Winnie in the car. They pulled into their new driveway and Winnie began to bark and wiggle uncontrollably. "We're here Winnie! This is our new home girl!" Vince said to her as he pet her and stirred her excitement even more.

They all got out of the car and walked up to the house. Annie turned the key in the lock and opened the door. "Here we are!" She said as she opened the door wide. "Home." Annie took a deep breath and stepped across the threshold with a big smile. Lily grabbed Edith by the hand and led her inside.

"It's a good house Mrs. MacKenzie. There's good energy here. C'mon." Lily said as she stepped inside. Edith took a look around and she could sense that this was a happy home. The family who lived here before had loved the home and had created very happy memories in it.

Annie stood back to see Edith's reaction. She was relieved to see that Edith was smiling. "It's a good house Annie. You chose well." Edith said as she continued to look around. "Let's give it a good house blessing and make it yours."

After Edith and Annie completed their house blessing ritual, they went back out to the car to retrieve the clothes and the other boxes they brought. Lilly was in the front yard playing with Winnie when a young boy walked over from the house across the street to talk with her.

"Lily? Are you moving into the Miller's house?" The boy asked. It was her crush, Joey Frasier.

"Hi Joey. Yes, this is our new house now. Do you live across the street?" Lily already knew that he did but was nervous to be talking to him and didn't know what else to say. They didn't talk much in school. She mostly just admired him from afar.

"Yep. That's my house." Joey said. He always liked Lily and thought she was a pretty girl, but he had no intention of putting her in a *girlfriend* category. He was almost 7 and had no time for close relationships with girls. Joey had an older sister, Beth, who went to school with Vince. She saw Vince get out of the car earlier and she was curious if they were the people who were moving in. She also walked across the street to say hello.

"Hi!" Beth said. "Are you moving in today?" She asked Lily.

"Yes. My Mom and my Brother brought a few things over first and my Father is coming soon with the truck and the furniture." Lily explained.

From inside the house, Vince could see that Lily was talking to people but didn't recognize who it was at first. Unlike Joey, Vince was a little older and he *was* interested in girls. Especially Beth Frasier. She was one of the most popular girls at school. She was a cheerleader and everyone knew who she was. She had long blonde hair, big blue eyes, and long slim legs. Everyone adored her and the nice thing was, she didn't act like a snotty girl. She wasn't the least bit stuck up and from what Vince had heard, she was genuinely nice to everyone. He hadn't realized it before, but at this moment he felt his heart skip a beat when he looked at her. *Did he have a crush on Beth Frasier?* If he did, he never really acknowledged it until now. It would be very convenient if she lived across the street...Just in case anything did develop between them, of course.

As Beth, Joey, and Lily were chatting in the front yard, Ed pulled up and backed the dually into the driveway with the first load of furniture. Vince saw this as the perfect opportunity to casually stroll out to help move the heavy furniture into the house. He walked out and pretended not to notice Beth standing in the front yard.

"Vince? Vince Campbell?" Beth said.

Vince turned as if he didn't see her standing there, then walked toward her with his hand held up shielding his eyes from the sun. "Beth? Is that you?" He said.

"Yeah. Are you moving in here?" She asked.

"Um, yeah. We are. Do you live around here?" Vince asked her.

Beth giggled a little and put her hands in the back pockets of her jeans as she gently twisted her posture. "I live right there across the street. I guess we're going to be neighbors." She said.

"Oh, far out!" Vince said enthusiastically. *Score!* He thought to himself. The perfect opportunity to establish a close relationship to the most popular girl in school. *Don't blow it by being a jackass.* He was thankful is inner dialogue could not be heard by anyone else…although Lily was telepathic and he caught her rolling her eyes.

"Vince! We could use your help over here son." Mark called to him.

"Um, I gotta go. We'll hang out sometime, okay?" Vince said as he smiled and ran back to the truck.

"Yeah. I'm sure we'll see each other a lot." Beth said. She knew Vince Campbell from school, but didn't have any classes with him that year. They would occasionally pass each other in the halls but never spoke. There was something sincerely interesting about him and she looked forward to the next time they would meet.

It was a long day and the sun was starting to set in the sky. Annie had already made up all of the beds and unpacked most of the essentials, but there was no food in the house and everyone had worked up a pretty good appetite from moving all day. She and Edith ran out for pizza and beer to feed the moving crew, and they all sat down to the table to eat.

Mark handed a cold beer to Ed and grabbed one for himself. He pulled the tab to open the can and took a good long gulp. "Ahhhhhh. That's good stuff." He said before letting out a loud belch. "Oops. Sorry." He shrugged his shoulders and apologized for the loud burp in front of Edith.

"Well, you deserve it. You guys worked really hard today." Edith said as she sipped her own cold beer.

Annie's eyebrows raised and she pulled her head back as she looked at Edith. "Well, we did too! Look around. We put almost everything away already." She said.

"We all worked hard Mark. Here's to us!" Ed said as he raised his beer can for a toast.

There was a brief moment of silence as everyone took a bite of their pizza. In the time it took for Ed's toast, Vince had already eaten his first slice of pizza and slid the second slice onto his plate. Lily had already devoured her first piece of pizza, but didn't care much for the crust so she casually slipped it under the table where Winnie gladly took it from her hand and gobbled it up.

In all of the melee of the move, no one thought to get dog food or even put a bowl of water out for her.

"Lilly, don't feed Winnie under the table." Annie warned.

"But she's hungry Momma. Nobody gave her any dinner." Lily said unapologetically.

"Oh shit! Winnie I'm sorry." Annie said as the stood up to find a bowl for Winnie. She filled it with water and set it on the floor, and Winnie promptly lapped up half of it immediately. I guess since I haven't found the box with Winnie's dog food yet you can feed her your crust. But just this once." She said as she raised her index finger gesturing the number one.

"I think you have found yourselves a very nice home." Edith said as she took a bite of pizza. "The whole neighborhood has good energy. There is happiness here and good things are yet to come." She winked at Lily sitting across the table from her. "And I hope that you'll still come to visit me once in a while, Lily. I don't live far."

"Yes M'am. I will." Lily said as she took another bite of pizza. Winnie sat patiently under the table wagging her tail, waiting for another piece of pizza crust.

Just then, the doorbell rang. Mark stood up and motioned for everyone to stay seated and keep eating. He walked over, turned on the porch light and opened the front door. A man was standing there looking down at his feet with a Cubs baseball hat on. He looked up and smiled as he introduced himself.

"Hi Mark? I'm John Miller. I sold you the house." The man said as he extended his hand for a handshake.

"Oh yeah, John. Nice to finally meet you sir!" Mark said enthusiastically as he shook the man's hand. "Would you like to come in?"

"Oh no, I'm sure you're still getting settled in. I don't want to intrude." John said as Mark stepped outside and closed the door behind him so bugs wouldn't come in.

"What can I do for you John?" Mark asked.

"I'm wondering if you can help me out with something." John sighed a little bit before he continued. "I'm leaving town in the morning and I'm not going to be able to take my boat with me where I'm going. It's still in your garage out back…I apologize for dropping this on you last minute. I haven't taken it out since last summer and, well, quite frankly your offer to buy the house came so fast that I just forgot about it. Since I'm leaving in the morning,

I don't have time to find a place to move it to or even sell it for that matter. I was hoping you'd be interested in keeping it." The man said.

"Uhhhhhh, well, I've never owned a boat before. Wow. Um, how much do you want for it?" Mark asked. He just bought an expensive new house and wasn't sure he could justify buying a boat, but he didn't want to offend this nice gentleman who gave them a good deal on the house of their dreams.

"No, no, I don't want anything for it. I'll *give* it to you if you want it. Free of charge. I have the title right here." John reached in his pocket and pulled out a folded piece of paper. "It's a nice boat sitting on a nice new trailer. You and your family will certainly get more use out of it than I will. I'm moving to the Arizona desert. My arthritis has gotten really bad this past winter so I thought the hot dry desert would do me some good. Thought I'd take up golf instead."

For a brief moment Mark imagined taking his family out on the Kankakee River in the Summer and learning to water ski. Other truckers talked about it on the CB radio all the time and it was something he always wanted to do, but didn't know anyone with a boat and couldn't afford one himself. Mark was an honest man and didn't expect anyone to give him anything for free. He prided himself on being able to pay his own way in the world and wasn't accustomed to such generosity.

"Let's go take a look at it and see what you think. If you don't want it, I'll arrange for somebody to come and pick it up tomorrow. Again, I apologize for forgetting about it. I hope it's not in your way." John said as he motioned Mark to walk around back to the garage.

The two men opened the garage door and turned on the light. Mark was so preoccupied with getting the furniture moved into the house all day that he hadn't yet had time to look in the back garage. John peeled back the canvas cover and revealed a 1969 Glasspar Flying V with an inboard/outboard 175 hp motor. It looked brand new.

"Here she is. Ain't she a beaut? I only took it out a couple of times." John got a little sentimental as he continued his story. "My Wife passed away a few years back…"

"Gee I'm sorry to hear that John." Mark said. He could tell that John missed his Wife very much.

"Thank you. She was a lovely lady…Anyway, my Son and his Family got transferred to Tulsa, Oklahoma this past August and I haven't taken it out since. There's no place to go boating near my new home in Arizona so it seems stupid to drag it down there." John explained. The two men crawled up into the boat and sat in the front seats. John showed Mark how to operate the boat and pulled a complete instruction manual out of the glove compartment on the dash. Mark was speechless. He could not believe that this man was actually *giving him* this beautiful new boat.

As they rolled the canvas cover back over the boat, John pointed out three sets of water skis in varying sizes and six life preservers that were hanging on the wall in the garage. "You can have all of this stuff too. It all goes with the boat." John said.

"I...I don't know what to say John. This is incredibly generous of you! Are you sure I can't pay you something? I mean, I don't have a lot of money left after closing costs, but..." Mark said.

John shook his head and said: "No, no. Trust me, you're doing me a huge favor. I couldn't take any money from you. I feel like I'm inconveniencing you a great deal by forgetting about it and leaving it here. Please. Take it with my blessing and enjoy it with your Family." John reached into the pocket of his shirt and pulled out a pen. He unfolded the paper and signed his name, dated it, and handed it to Mark.

"I don't know what to say. This is...this is so very kind of you! Thank you. My Family and I will enjoy it and we'll think of you every time we take it out." Mark said as he shook John's hand.

They turned off the light and closed the garage door. John walked back to his car and before he got in, he turned back to Mark to say one more thing.

"You know, Mark? This is a good home. Lots of good memories. I'm really glad that you were the people who bought it." John looked down at the drive-way for a moment to collect his thoughts. He raised his head again and said: "It's almost like it was some kind of Divine intervention or something. I mean, you happened to be looking for a home at the exact time I needed to leave and it all worked out. I'm glad you own it now. You and your Family will be very happy here." And with that, John tipped his hat, got in his car, and drove away.

When Mark came back into the house, everyone had finished eating and were sitting around the table talking. They all looked up at Mark as he entered the room holding the title to a nearly brand new ski boat in his hand.

"Mark? What is it Honey? Is everything ok?" Annie asked. She could usu-ally read Mark's expressions pretty well but she was stumped this time. This was a look she hadn't seen before. He'd looked like he had just seen a ghost and she was starting to panic inside.

Mark turned his eyes to Annie and smiled. "You won't believe what just happened."

"What Dad?" Vince said. Something was up and the suspense was killing him.

"John Miller was just here. He just gave us his boat in the garage. Here's the title." Mark held up the title and started to laugh. "It's incredible! It's only a year old. He only used it twice."

"Oh my gosh!" Annie said as she glanced over at Lily who sat there with her head cocked and resting on her hand with her elbow on the table as she smiled.

"I told ya." Lily said very matter-of-factly. "Grandpa Tom told me he was going to do that. I told you that in the car, remember?"

"That's right, you did!" Annie said as she recalled that conversation. She was still getting used to her daughter being able to foretell future events.

"Wow! That's pretty damn nice of the guy. And you didn't invite him in for a beer? Man, what's wrong with you Buddy?" Ed joked. "Let's go take a look at this new boat." All of the Boys put their shoes on and went out to the garage to see the new boat they inherited. Edith and Lily remained at the table and Annie finished loading the plates in the dishwasher. She was a little in shock that they were now the proud owners of a new ski boat, but even more amazed by her daughter's ability to predict what just happened a few weeks before. Edith turned to Lily and smiled at her. They were having a little telepathic conversation between them, but it was now time to have that conversation verbally so Annie could be part of it.

"Lily has an amazing gift Annie. She is far advanced as Psychics go. As long as she stays true to herself and doesn't use her abilities deceptively, they will serve her well. It can be just as easy for bad spirits to feed her false information, so she will have to be very guarded with whom she allows to communicate with her." Edith explained.

"I'm shocked that she foresaw this happening." Annie said. "I don't have the abilities that Lily has. She didn't get it from me. I don't know anyone in Mark's Family who has abilities either. I'm not sure where she gets it from."

"Yes you do Momma." Lily said. "Your father had these abilities too." Edith nodded in agreement. She knew that Tom was the source of the inherited abilities, which meant that Annie likely had abilities too. She just hadn't realized it because she had lived her life so closed to the intuitive possibilities within her.

CHAPTER 13

It had been a week since the Campbells moved in and Mark was away on his monthly three day route. Annie rolled over and looked at the clock on her nightstand. 7:23 am. Normally she would be up by now, fully dressed and downstairs in the kitchen cleaning up the dishes from breakfast before the kids caught the bus for school. Today was Saturday and she could sleep in if she wanted, but she wasn't sleepy anymore. She laid there in her spacious new master bedroom thinking about how lucky they were to find this house. Was it luck? Maybe. Or was it something more? Everything just worked out too perfectly as if the whole process was carefully orchestrated by an unseen force in the Universe. "Thanks Daddy." She said to herself. Although she couldn't see him or talk to him like Lily could, she was becoming acutely aware of his presence and she was sure that he had a hand I the home purchase somehow. Annie could hear the laughter of a little girl downstairs and knew Lily was up and probably watching cartoons in the family room. She tossed her covers back, swung her legs around and planted her feet firmly on the carpeted floor. She went to the bathroom, then grabbed her bathrobe off the hook behind the door and as she put it on, she caught a glimpse of her messy long brown hair, dark circles under her eyes, and the pillow mark on the side of her face in the mirror. "Eeeesh." She said. "I'll have to do something about that later." Annie was a natural beauty and never needed much make up to look beautiful, but the stress and physical exertion from the move had taken its toll and she could tell she was in need of a little pampering.

As Annie walked down the wide carpeted stairs to the main level, she glanced over to the family room on her way to the kitchen. There was Vince—walking on his hands and Lily was right next to him trying to do the same, but kept falling over and when she did, she would break out in laughter.

"Vince? I'm surprised to see you up so early. Did you forget that today is Saturday?" Annie asked him.

Vince sprung off of his handstand back to an upright position and smiled at his mother. "No, I know its Saturday, I just didn't need to sleep anymore. I heard Lily get up so I came down to play with her." He said.

"Well, it's a very nice surprise to see you up and about. Thanks for keeping an eye on her." Annie noticed that they had already eaten breakfast. In typical fashion, they left their cereal bowls, the open gallon of milk, a banana peel, and an open box Rice Krispies on the kitchen table. "Thanks for taking care of breakfast!" She yelled to Vince as he and Lily resumed their morning gymnastics session. Annie put the milk and cereal away, then cleaned up the cereal bowls and put them in the dishwasher and wiped off the table with a wet dish rag. She poured a fresh cup of coffee and grabbed the stack of mail she had been meaning to get to all week, then sat at the table to go through it. Winnie's cold nose rubbed up against Annie's leg and she reached down to pet her. "Good morning Winnie girl! Did you have your breakfast this morning?"

"I fed her Mom." Vince said as he helped Lily stand on her hands by holding her ankles together.

"Momma! Look I'm doing it!" Lily hollered gleefully.

"You are! That's very good Lily!" Annie said in amusement. She loved to see Vince and Lily get along so well. It was unusual given the 8 year age difference between them, but they shared a bond that seemed to be deeply rooted. Could they have shared a past life together? Before meeting Edith this was something that would never even cross Annie's mind. The Universe was so much bigger and seemed to have many different layers. That was definitely a possibility and something she would be interested in learning more about.

As Annie separated the circulars and other pieces of junk mail, she came across a big envelope from Downers Grove High School South. Stephen would be entering his Junior year and Vince would be a Freshman in High School in the Fall. She opened the envelope and saw the usual final exam schedule for the end of this school year, information about Summer School classes to be offered, and try outs for the Football and Gymnastics teams were beginning after Memorial Day for the next school year. It was a requirement that all sports participants obtain a physical from their Doctor before they could try out for the teams. Annie appreciated that the School was giving them plenty of notice to be able to get that done before try outs began.

"Vince, do you have any interest in trying out for any sports next year at Downers South? Annie asked.

"Well, kinda. I'm not that interested in football, but I heard they have a gymnastics team that sounds really cool. I'd try out for that." Vince said.

Annie never considered that Vince would be interested in the gymnastics team, but it make a lot of sense. He was always doing handstands and back handsprings in the yard and she even caught him actually walking *up* the stairs on his hands the first day they moved into the house. He had an incredible sense of balance and the only thing he wanted for his birthday last summer was a Unicycle, which he quickly mastered in a couple of hours. Vince was a very talented young man. He was naturally inclined towards auto mechanics and could tear an engine apart and put it all back together again without hesitation. When Lily was 4 she got a tricycle for Christmas. Within days Vince mounted a sump pump motor on the back of it and had her racing around the basement on her modified electric powered trike. The front wheel spun around so fast, Lily kept hitting her knees on the handle bar and the top of her knees became bruised from keeping her feet on the petals. Vince solved the problem with Mark's soldering tools and modified her tricycle so it looked like a Chopper with a lower bar to rest her feet on so she wouldn't hit her knees anymore. Vince was smart. He could figure out how to make anything work and was able to cleverly improvise when the exact materials he needed to fix something were not available. He got that from Mark. He also had a bold, independent spirit and wasn't afraid of anything—Kind of a daredevil really. She had no idea where he acquired that trait from because no one on either side of the family was as fearless as he was.

Stephen came down the stairs, fully dressed, and headed to the refrigerator to pour a glass of orange juice. "Morning Mom." He said.

"Hi Honey. Why are you up so early?" Annie was pleasantly surprised that all three kids were up and moving before noon on a Saturday.

I'm going over to Wojick's. Dan and I built a rocket and we want to launch it to see if the parachute feature we built into it works." Stephen said. "The wind is always calmest in the morning so this is the best time to launch it."

"Oh, sounds exciting!" Annie replied. Stephen was her oldest son and very scientifically oriented. He was always studying how things worked and thought of creative ways to make them work better. It didn't matter if it was a biological organism, a chemical compound, or even quantum physics. He was interested in all things scientific and he had a natural aptitude for it. Although he was very 'hands on' with his experiments, he was a voracious reader and read a book start to finish about every other day. What's more, he seemed to retain everything he read. Stephen was full of interesting tidbits of information and 'fun facts' that you never really thought about, but it always made you go 'Hmmm' when he threw them out there in a conversation. Both Annie and Mark were very smart people, but Stephen was a genius and Annie wondered which side of the family he inherited his smarts from. Since both Annie and Mark lost their Fathers in their younger years, it was hard to say. Annie's Father, Tom, was clever but she never thought of him being in the same league as Albert Einstein. Mark was an only child and his father died when he was only 2 so he never really knew him. Since Mark had a natural propensity for problem solving himself, Annie assumed that Mark's Father was probably the source of the high IQ that was now ever present in her son. Either way, all of her children were gifted in one way or another, and she was extremely proud of every one of them.

"Are you working today Stephen?" Annie asked. She liked to know how many mouths she needed to feed at dinner time so she could plan accordingly.

"Yes. I have to be at work at 4:00 and I'm on the schedule to close so I won't see you until probably midnight. I'm taking my work shirt with me and I'll just leave from Dan's house." Stephen said.

"Close? They don't usually schedule you that late. You're only 16." If Stephen's grades were suffering she would be more concerned, but that wasn't a problem. She was just surprised they scheduled him to work so late. Usually he was home after the dinner rush and was upstairs with a book in his hand by 9:30 pm.

"They're shorthanded. They need to hire two more people in the kitchen and they haven't yet. I told them I would do it on the weekends if they were in a pinch, and they asked me, so..." He explained. "Besides, I'm trying to save money Mom. I'm not going to live upstairs forever." Annie shrugged her shoulders. It was hard to argue with a kid who was working hard to save money for something he really wanted. She emptied her coffee cup in the sink and put it in the dishwasher, then went back upstairs to take a shower and get dressed. About a half hour later, the doorbell rang. Annie opened the door and there was Ed standing there holding a big cardboard box.

"Hi Annie. I found this box sitting on my workbench. There's a helmet, motocross leathers, hockey skates, and other miscellaneous items that belong to the Boys. Somehow we forgot it when we moved your things over." Ed said.

"Oh, thank you Ed. C'mon in. Can I get you some coffee?" Annie asked as she held the door open for him.

"Yeah, I'd take a cup." Ed said as he stepped across the threshold and set the box down on the floor by the closet. "I guess Mark's doing his three day route this weekend?"

"Yes. He'll be back this evening though." Annie said. She paused and turned back around to give Ed an inquisitive look. "I thought you two were on the same schedule?"

"We were, but Bob Hoskins was out with the flu so I volunteered to pick up one of his trips last week and it threw us off schedule. We'll be running the same routes again next month." Ed glanced down at into the family room and saw Vince doing handstands with Lily. "So they're into gymnastics now?" He said as he took a seat at the kitchen table.

"Yeah. Well, Vince has always been walking on his hands, doing back flips in the yard, and things like that. He's been trying to teach Lily to do a handstand this morning. It's been pretty entertaining to watch." Annie said as she poured a cup of coffee and set it down in front of her guest.

"You know, I had to haul some sports equipment that was rejected by the destination terminal manager because a few crates fell off the truck when they were unloading and they got damaged. That was over a month ago and I saw that the crates were still sitting at the terminal the other day. I think there was a trampoline and one of those pommel horse things in the freight. They usually settle up with the insurance company and then just haul that stull off to the dump. If you're interested, I could call and see what's there. The kids might enjoy playing with that stuff. You certainly have a great back yard for it." Ed took a sip of his coffee and waited for Annie's response.

Annie glanced over at Vince who clearly had gymnastic abilities and would probably enjoy having his own gym equipment in the back yard. She looked out the window at the large relatively flat back yard and it was easy to visualize a trampoline back there. Annie always liked having her kids at home and that would definitely entice them to stick around. She liked the idea of having the one house in the neighborhood where all the kids liked to hang out. She snapped out of her daydream and looked back to Ed. "Sure Ed, if you wouldn't mind. I'd be interested in finding out what they have there...If it's still there." She said.

Ed stood up and walked over to the kitchen phone hanging on the wall. He dialed the dispatch terminal number and asked to be connected to the

Dock Manager on duty. After a quick conversation, Ed hung up the phone and sat back down at the table. "The Dock Manager says that it's all still sitting there. If you want it, we have to grab it tonight or tomorrow because they're hauling it off first Monday morning."

"Well Mark gets home this evening. I'll see what he thinks." Annie said.

"I'll do one better. Mark should be pulling in around 3:00, so I'll go in a little early this afternoon and show it to him. If he wants to bring it home I'll help him load it up." Ed offered.

"Deal. Thanks Ed. You're the best!" Annie grabbed his hand and squeezed it. Ed was always doing nice things for them and she was thankful to have him as a friend.

Annie walked out to the truck with Ed and asked about Edith. "I'm so used to seeing her every day and since we've moved out of the guesthouse, I'm afraid we won't see her much anymore. I think I'll give her a call and see if she'd like to come over this afternoon. Lily's been asking about her." She said.

"She'd like that I'm sure. She putters around in her garden and keeps busy, but she's grown rather attached to you all and I'm sure she'd take you up on the invitation." Ed said as he got in his truck.

As Ed pulled out of the drive way and drove down the street, Annie noticed a woman with wavy blonde hair pulled back in a clip walking towards her carrying what looked like a Bundt cake.

"Hello!" The woman said as she walked up the driveway.

"Hi!" Annie said as the woman approached. She was an attractive woman about Annie's age. A little taller than Annie, but she had a much curvier figure.

"I'm Cheryl Frasier. We live right across the street. I'm sorry it took so long to come over and introduce myself, I've been working extra shifts at the hospital this week and didn't have a chance until today." She said. "I baked you a cake to welcome you to the neighborhood."

"Why thank you Cheryl that was very sweet of you!" Annie held her hands out to receive the cake. "I'm Annie Campbell. Would you like to come in and have a cup of coffee? I just brewed a fresh pot." Annie said.

"Oh thank you. I'd love to." Cheryl replied as she followed Annie into the house.

Annie welcomed her neighbor in and poured a cup of coffee for Cheryl and herself, then sat at the kitchen table. Vince and Lily had already gone upstairs and for the first time all morning, the house was quiet. "So, you work at the hospital?" Annie asked.

"Yes. I'm a nurse. Maternity Ward. I help deliver babies all day and all night." Cheryl said as she bobbed her head back and forth. "My son said that he goes to school with your daughter, Lily, is it?"

"Yes, it's Lily. I think she kind of likes your son. She blushes a little bit when she sees him. I volunteer at the school so I get to see these things first hand. It's cute to watch." Annie said as she took a sip of coffee.

The two women hit it off pretty well. Before they knew it two hours had passed and they never stopped talking. They talked about their kids, their hobbies, who lived in the neighborhood, plans they had for the Summer with the kids, and things like that. Cheryl mentioned that her husband Chuck, was a Quantum Physicist at Argon National Laboratories. This piqued Annie's interest even further since she had never known anyone who worked there but had heard that it was a top secret government facility.

"Wow. My son Stephen would love to meet him! He's our brainy child. Very interested in all things science. So, what does he actually do there at Argon?" This was Annie's chance to get some real answers about this mysterious facility.

"Well, much of what he works on is classified. I mean, he never tells me anything about it. But, his area of expertise has to do with the study of the behavior of matter and energy at an atomic level." Cheryl explained.

"You mean like, black holes and stuff like that?" Annie asked.

"Oh yes. All of that. He's crazy about it. I married a super nerd." Cheryl said as she giggled. "But he's a very nice guy and a lot of fun to be around. You'd never know what he does for a living by looking at him. He's not one of those pocket protector kind of Scientists. He looks more like a tall Scottish surfer dude." She broke out laughing at her description of her husband. "You'll meet him and see what I mean."

Just then Lily came running through the front door followed by Vince, and then Joey and Beth Frasier. "Momma, can we have a snack? I'm hungry."

Cheryl was surprised to see her kids come through the door. "What are you two up to? I thought you were playing ping pong in the basement."

"We were, but Lily wanted to come over here." Beth said. Vince spotted the Bundt cake on the counter and asked if they could have a slice.

"Sure, it's okay with me." Annie said as she looked over at Cheryl. "Okay with you?"

"Sure, it's early enough that it won't spoil their dinner." Cheryl said.

Annie stood up and got a knife to cut the cake while Vince got some small plates down from the cupboard and a few forks from the silverware drawer. "Anyone want milk?" She asked.

Everyone nodded their heads and Vince grabbed four glasses and poured some milk in each one. The neighbors all sat around the table chatting and laughing. Everyone got along so well and Annie could see the start of some very close friendships growing around the table that day.

Mark arrived home from work around 5:00 and Annie had just put a meatloaf in the oven for dinner. He was immediately greeted by Winnie and her usual full body wiggle. He picked her up and hugged her, then set her back down on the floor. Lily heard him come in and rand down the stairs from her room. "Daddy!" She squealed.

As he picked her up he said: "There's my little Pussy Cat! Have you been good for your Mom while I was away?"

"Yes sir." Lily said with a cute little bashful smile. She gave him a big hug and he set her back down on the floor so she could retrieve her treat from the zipper pocket on his duffle bag. Annie came around the corner.

"Hi Honey. I'm glad you're home." Annie said as she draped her arms around him and kissed him. Then without breaking eye contact with her husband, she said "Lily, don't unwrap that candy bar now. Go wash your hands. You can have it for desert."

How does she do that? Lily thought as she handed the candy bar to her Mother and walked off to the bathroom to wash her hands.

"You should just hold off and give it to her after dinner you know. It saves me from having to be the bad guy." Annie said in her flirty voice.

"I know." Mark answered. "But it's kind of our thing. She so cute when she greets me and she looks forward to digging in that pocket of my bag."

"So, did you see Ed at the loading dock this afternoon? He said he was going in early so he could show you some damaged freight we might want." Annie continued. She thought about it all day and every time she looked outside in the back yard, she found herself convinced that it needed a trampoline back there.

"I did. I brought a couple of things home with me. Come take a look." He said as he led Annie outside to his pick-up truck. "We've got a Nissen Little

Giant Trampoline with a webbed mat. All we need to get are the pads to cover the springs so the kids don't fall through. I also got a Ring Tower with a spotting platform, rings, and an iron cross trainer."

"Ooooh, nice!" Annie said. "The kids are going to LOVE this! Especially Vince. He said earlier that he was interested in trying out for the boy's gymnastics team at Downers South."

"Well then, this is perfect." Mark said as he unhooked the bungee cords that held the crates in place. "Where are the boys? I'll need their help to unload this."

"Stephen is working tonight and Vince is over at the Frasier's playing ping pong." Annie said.

"And where do the Frasier's live?" Mark asked.

"Right across the street. The tan house with the red brick." She said as she pointed to the house across the street. "Cheryl Frasier came over earlier today and brought us a Bundt cake. She's a maternity ward nurse at Hinsdale Hospital, and her husband, Chuck, is a Physicist at Argon.

They have two kids, a boy Lily's age and a girl in Vince's class—Joey and Beth. The kids have all been playing together all day."

"Well it sounds like everybody's making new friends. That's good." Mark said. "I guess we can unload everything tomorrow then. I'll back the truck in the garage for tonight. What's for dinner?"

CHAPTER 14

JUNE 1970

School was out and Summer had officially arrived. The daylight hours were long and the Campbell's back yard became the preferred hang out for all the kids in the neighborhood just like Annie wanted. Vince made the Boy's Gymnastics team and had enrolled in a Gymnastics Camp at the University of Illinois Champagne for three weeks as recommended by his coach. All of the team members were attending the camp and Vince had a couple of weeks of free time before that session started the second week of July. They assembled the trampoline and the ring tower had been modified for yard use by planting the base in concrete in the ground. Vince worked with the iron cross trainer daily and his arms and shoulders were starting to show evidence of that. Annie could tell that Beth Frasier had noticed it too.

Lily was growing taller and she was becoming quite the acrobat on the trampoline. She spent hours out there, often by herself. Although, she was never really by herself. The Dead visited her every single day and she spent time listening and talking to all of them. Annie could tell that it was starting to exhaust her, and she was getting a little concerned. She invited Edith over to talk about it.

As Annie and Edith sat on the back deck in the shade with their iced tea, they cheered Lily every time she did a back flip, which was pretty often. After a while, Lily grew tired and came back in to the house to take a break and watch the Flintsones on television.

"So, we miss seeing you Edith. I know you don't live far, but we miss seeing you every day like we used to." Annie said.

"And I miss all of you too." Edith replied. "I'm glad you called me about Lily. Dead energy can be harmful to the Living if they are exposed to it all the time. I told Lily that she needed to limit her time with them to no more than two hours per week at the most. She's still very young and shouldn't be spending any more time than that."

"Well, I can guarantee you that she's not. I hear her talking to them in her room all the time. I make sure to interrupt when I catch it, but I'm sure she continues when I leave the room." Annie said. Edith could hear the concern in Annie's voice and agreed that some form of intervention was needed. She cared a great deal for Lily and although she didn't want to scare Annie, the constant exposure to dead energy would cause Lily's health to deteriorate over time.

"I'll work with her Annie. Don't you fret about it dear." Edith said.

Annie and Edith came back inside and went down to the family room to talk to Lily. The Flintstones cartoon was over, and Annie turned the television off.

"Hey Mom! I was watching that. The Jetson's come on next." Lily protested.

"Lil, you can watch TV later. Edith is here and we should spend some time with her." Annie replied.

"Alright." Lily said with a disappointed tone. She loved Edith, but wasn't really in the mood for a lecture.

Edith came down the stairs and sat on end of the sectional and put her feet up on the ottoman. "My, this is a very comfortable couch!" She said. "If I had this couch in my house, I might not ever leave it." Lily giggled at the thought of Edith becoming a couch potato.

"Lily, since we moved in here, do you find that the Dead visit you more often than they did when we lived at Edith's guesthouse?" Annie asked. She wasn't sure if that would be relevant or not, but it was a good way to start the conversation.

"Well, kind of. Now that I have my own room I guess I feel like I can talk to them more, so I do." Lily said as she shrugged her shoulders.

"Do you remember what we talked about? You can't keep your 'open for business' sign on all the time. It will begin to hurt you after a while." Edith explained to her.

"I know. There's just so many of them Mrs. MacKenzie and they need help. They're lost and confused and they miss their families." Lily said. She didn't mind helping the Dead—She wanted to…And she was really good at it. "Since we moved here, a lot more of them come to visit." Lily turned to Annie and said: "And Momma, did you know that Joey and Beth had a brother? His name is Jon-Jon. He's always around me. He's even here right now and he's afraid that you're not going to let me talk to him anymore." Annie was shocked to hear that. Cheryl never mentioned losing a child and they had become good friends. They spoke almost every day. She glanced over at Edith, who was clearly tapped into Lily and the Dead who were currently in the room.

"Oh, Jon-Jon doesn't need to worry. We're not saying that you have to stop talking to them, we're just saying that it's important that you protect yourself. Dead energy will cause you to become sick, Lily. They don't mean to, but they are existing on a higher vibrational plane than our physical bodies are equipped to handle. It will make you very sick if are exposed to it too much. Do you understand what we're trying to say to you dear?" Edith said. She was trying her best to explain the danger as best she could without scaring anyone, but she knew of Psychic Mediums who died from terminal illnesses from excessive exposure to the Dead. It never ends well.

"I understand Mrs. MacKenzie. That's why Grandpa Tom stays away sometimes. He only shows up when he needs to tell me something or to protect me from danger." Lily said.

"Yes, your Grandfather knows what can happen and he's trying to protect you. Are you still doing your Tai Chi exercises every day like I taught you?" Edith asked.

Lily put her head down in shame. She loved Edith and didn't want to disappoint her, but she stopped doing it the day they moved in and never gave it a second thought. "No." She let out a small sigh and turned her head toward the window hoping to find her Grandfather standing there to give her encouragement.

"Should we do some now?" Edith said as she stood up from the couch. "Come on Annie, I'll show you what we used to do. It's very relaxing. Let's go out into the back yard. It's best to do outside." She said.

Everyone stood up and walked back outside where they kicked their shoes off in the grass. Edith instructed Annie with the basics and told her to just follow along. After about 20 minutes of fluid movement and rhythmic breathing, Annie was shocked at how good it made her feel. "Why wasn't I included in these exercises when you were doing them before?" Annie said as she stretched her arms up toward the sky, and then slowly bent down to touch her toes. "This is great!"

Edith giggled and said: "Oh yes! This is an essential practice. I do it every day. It aligns your Chakras and keeps you balanced. People with abilities should make this part of their routine every single day. Especially you Lily"

Edith winked at her tiny pupil who was twirling around slowly in a circle like a dancer.

Lily put her arms down and stopped twirling. "I'm sorry Mrs. MacKenzie. I feel the difference now. I'll make sure I do this at least once every single day from now on. Vince will do it with me too." She said.

"I'd love to do this with you. Let's do it together!" Annie said as she put her arm around her daughter. Lily recently went through a little growth spurt and as Annie hugged her she could tell she was a little taller than she was even last week.

Edith sat with Lily on the deck for a little longer coaching her on techniques to shut down her spiritual communication with the Dead. She needed to take control of that so she could properly allocate time to getting enough rest, and just being a little girl. She explained that there were plenty of Psychic Mediums in the world who could also help the Dead and that Lily should never feel that she had to shoulder that burden by herself. Lily understood, and was relieved to hear it. She often became so involved with the Dead and their needs that she never thought about other Psychics out there helping them like she did.

"Tell me about the little boy who's here with you." Edith asked. Standing next to Lily's chair was a little boy who looked like he was no more than 3 years old. He was wearing brown shorts with a short sleeved plaid shirt, white socks and brown shoes, and a little bow tie. He looked very sweet, but there was a terrible sadness about him. He wasn't interested in talking to Edith at all. He just stood there and stared at her like a small child would if a stranger made faces at them in the check-out line at the grocery store. "Is this your friend Jon-Jon?" She asked.

Lily turned her head in the direction of the boy and smiled. "Yes, this is Jon-Jon. He's Beth Frasier's little Brother and Joey Frasier's big Brother. He fell down and hit his head and he died. He watches his family all the time. Sometimes he sits at the dinner table with them but he gets sad because they can't see him. He misses them very much." Lily said.

"Have you told Beth and Joey that he's with you?" Edith asked.

"Oh no. I don't know them well enough yet. Jon-Jon wants me to, but I told him that I didn't think it was a good idea. They would get scared and I don't want them to think I'm crazy." Lily said. She was demonstrating good common sense and Edith was glad to hear it. You can't just blurt something like that out to people. Some people don't believe in ghosts, and it would be even more disturbing for a new neighbor if she were to deliver news that their dead Brother is her friend and trying to communicate with them. Lily was using good judgment and this was reassuring to Edith.

"I agree with you Lily. That's not to say that there won't be a time in the future when you can tell them, but you're right to keep quiet for now." Edith said as she glanced over at Jon-Jon who was starting to cry. Edith and Lily began to console the little boy telepathically and promised to tell his family that he was always around them when the time was right. He nodded his head and very quietly said '*thank you.*'

This was going to be a challenge. This little boy has been hanging around for years since he died and he wasn't ready to cross over. He may never be ready—Especially if he has a method of communicating with his living Family through Lily. This is how attachments are formed and it can become dangerous for Lily. He could learn to jump her and take over her body so that he could live again through her and be with his Family again. Edith had seen it happen before and Lily wasn't an experienced Psychic enough to know how to prevent it from happening. Some spirits will take total control of a person's physical body and then it becomes a possession. The only way to rid the spirit of the physical body, is through an exorcism. This was not something Edith would be able to do herself and she hoped to never have to call upon a properly trained Priest or Demonologist to perform one. Since the boy was right there, it wasn't a good time for Edith to instruct her on how to keep from getting jumped by a spirit. She didn't want to inadvertently instruct the boy how to do it by teaching Lily how not to let him in. She would have to work with her off site and hope the boy doesn't figure out how to attach to her before then.

"Keep up with your Tai Chi Lily. It will help you to stay balanced." Edith said as she stood up to head home.

Lily smiled sweetly and promised that she would. Annie came back out to join them and saw that Edith was getting ready to leave. "Are you leaving, Edith?" She asked.

"Yes, I have some things to do at home before Ed comes over for dinner tonight. He's bringing a lady by to meet me." Edith winked at Annie.

"Yes, I heard he was seeing someone. Barbara is it?" Annie said. "Mark says that he's completely smitten. We haven't met her yet, so I'll be curious to hear what she's like."

"Oh, I'll call you tomorrow and tell you how it went." Edith said as she put her hands on Lily's head and kissed her forehead. "Bye Lily. Remember what we talked about."

"I will Mrs. MacKenzie. Thank you for coming to visit us." Lily said.

"C'mon Edith. I'll walk you out to your car." Annie said.

Annie opened the sliding glass door and they walked through the house to the front door where Edith's car was parked on the circular driveway under the portico. Once they were out of earshot from Lily and the dead boy, Edith told Annie of her concerns about Jon-Jon and what to look for if he figured out to jump her before Edith could teach her how to keep that from happening.

Annie was shocked to hear that this was even a possibility, but kept her composure and listened very carefully to Edith's advice.

"I think it's best if you bring her over to my house tomorrow. The boy will probably stay here to be close to his Family. I get the impression that he never goes far from them. He'd probably not even be over here if Lily couldn't communicate with him. Still, it's important that I work with her immediately. The longer he's with her, the more familiar he will become with her vibrational pattern and that will make it easy for him to jump her." Edith said. There was definitely concern in Edith's voice and Annie was taking it very seriously.

"I'll bring her over tomorrow afternoon. She's growing out of her shoes so I was going to go get her a new pair of tennies. We'll come over immediately afterward, say 1:30?" Annie said.

"That's perfect. I'll see you tomorrow." Edith said as she got in her car. Once the car door was closed, she rolled down her window to say one more thing. "And I'll let you know all about Barbara."

CHAPTER 15

The following morning, Annie and Lily made plans to go to K-Mart to look for new shoes and possibly some new clothes. Lily was growing fast and her clothes were fitting a little smaller than usual. Annie had hoped to get by without spending too much since she would be taking all of the kids shopping for school supplies and more clothes in the coming weeks, but Lily could no longer wait. K-Mart was Annie's "go to" store when she needed things but didn't want to blow the budget. Vince came down the stairs in his work-out clothes and stopped by the fridge before going out to his personal gymnasium in the back yard.

"Hi honey. Lily and I are going to K-Mart today. Do you need anything?" Annie asked him.

"I could use another tube of toothpaste…And maybe some first aid tape for my hands." Vince replied.

Annie took a look at his hands to see why he thought he needed first aid tape. "Are you hurt?"

"No, that's why I need the tape. To keep me from getting blisters. All of the gymnasts use it." He said very matter-of-factly.

"Oh. I guess that makes sense." Annie said. She continued to unload the clean dishes from the dishwasher when Lily came downstairs with Winnie.

"Does anyone want to do Tai Chi with me? I promised Mrs. MacKenzie I would do it every single day." Lily said. She dropped the ball once and she was determined not to forget about it again. She made a promise to Edith and she was going to keep it.

Annie and Vince enthusiastically joined her and they all went out to the back yard. Lily led the exercise, and after their 20 minute work-out, they all felt really good. Vince decided to warm up on the trampoline before practicing on the rings. He was determined to hold the iron cross for longer than 10 seconds. This would be a very impressive exercise to show his teammates at the upcoming gymnastics camp. He had been walking on his hands and doing handstands ever since he was 6 years old. That built up tremendous strength in his shoulders which was required in order to master the iron cross. He had a personal goal to be the best gymnast on the team and that meant discipline and lots of practice.

Annie backed her copper brown 1968 Olds Toronado out of the garage and Lily ran around to the passenger side and jumped in. As they drove down Brookridge Rd to the intersection at Plainfield, Annie asked if Lily had any of her dead friends along with her in the car. She said that she didn't, which was good. Annie remembered what Edith had said about not having Jon-Jon along when she worked with Lily today. Lily had to learn how to protect herself from being jumped.

After parking the car, mother and daughter held hands as they walked through the front doors of the store with the big red K. Annie got a shopping cart and the two of them headed for the children's shoe department where Lily quickly picked out a pair of white canvas slip on sneakers. Annie knelt down and pressed her thumb at the tip of the shoe to see where Lily's toe was. There was about an inch of space. "How do those feel Lil'? Too loose?"

Lilly marched and danced up the aisle and then walked back toward her Mother. "Nope. They feel pretty good Mom." She said.

"Ok, let's put them in the cart. You also need a couple of Summer tops and shorts. You've grown out of everything you were wearing from last year." Annie said as they headed toward the girls department.

As they were leaving, Annie thought it might be nice to take something over to Edith's, so they made a quick stop to Feinmann's Bakery. They made the best cherry pies anywhere on the planet. They were Mark's absolute favorite, so she got a second one to take home for him.

It was almost 1:30 as Annie and Lily pulled up to Edith's circular driveway. Her yard was always so neat and tidy. She had flower beds everywhere, filled with Zinnias, Daisies, Lavender, Peonies, Lilly of the Valley, Roses and other varieties of flowers that were carefully planted so that something was always in bloom throughout the Spring and Summer. Lily got out of the car and ran up to the front door while Annie retrieved the box containing the cherry pie from the floor behind her seat.

Edith emerged at the front screen door and greeted them enthusiastically. "Hello! Lily, did you get new shoes?" She asked.

"Yes I did! Aren't they nice? They fit me good too." Lily said as she admired her new white slip-ons. "And we brought you a surprise Mrs. MacKenzie—It's a cherry pie!"

"Oh my, that sounds tasty. Should we go in and have a piece?" Edith said as she held the screen door open for Annie who was carrying the delicious cherry pie.

Edith got some plates down from the cabinet and forks and a pie serving knife from the drawer, and brought them to the kitchen table. As Annie served the pie, Lily stared out the sliding glass door toward the tree line in the back yard where she saw the Shadow Person last December. She was wondering if it was still there or if it even figured out that she no longer lived in the guest-house. It was Summer and all of the trees were lush and thick with leaves so it was difficult to see the exact spot, but she sensed that there was something back there. Something that had never ever been human.

"So, how did dinner go last night with Ed and Barbara? What did you think of her?" Annie asked as she set a slice of pie in front of her Daughter. Lily quickly turned her attention to the golden brown flaky crust filled with sweet red cherries that was resting on her plate. She picked up her fork and took a bite. Mmmmmmm. She soon forgot all about the trees.

"Barbara seems very nice. You were right—Ed is VERY smitten. I haven't seen him like that with a girl since he was 18. She's very tall too, which is good because Ed is 6'4". I think it's a love match." Edith said as she scrunched up her nose and squinted her eyes.

"Does she live around here?" Annie asked as she took a bite of the world's best cherry pie.

"She lives in the city. She is an Assistant Curator of Egyptian Antiquities at the Field Museum. Ed met her at the dispatch terminal one afternoon. I guess her brother works on the loading dock and she was there to see him one day, when she bumped in to Ed...I mean, she physically bumped into him. They were both walking around the corner at the same time and he knocked her down on the floor. And when he helped her up, they're eyes met and that was it." Edith said as she took another bite of pie.

"Huh." Annie said. "Mark said they met at the terminal but I thought she worked there. See? I can never get the whole scoop out of Mark. We women have to keep each other informed or we'd never know anything!" They both laughed at that. "Egyptian Antiquities, huh? She sounds like she's really smart."

"She's very smart…And she seems to be equally as smitten with Ed." Edith turned her attention to Lily. She was very concerned about her developing relationship with the little dead boy whose family lived across the street. He really needed to be moved on, but you can't make a spirit go into the light if they are unwilling to go. He still had unfinished business here and Edith needed to help Lily find out what he needs for closure so she could help him cross over. If she didn't it could become a very dangerous situation and she was going to do everything she could to keep that from happening. This had to be done in baby steps and she was thankful that Lily was a quick learn.

"Now Lily, I'm glad to see that you came without your little friend today." Edith said. "I have something to teach you that I didn't want Jon-Jon to know."

Lily set her fork down on the empty pie plate in front of her. She was ready to learn what Edith had to teach her. She was young, but her abilities were very advanced and she was vulnerable. There was so much she needed to learn and she was grateful that she had Edith to teach her. "Is it alright if Grandpa Tom is here? He's watching over me right now." Lily said.

"Yes, I know. He's here to help you." Edith said.

As Edith worked with Lily using meditative techniques, Annie sat quietly and listened. She found herself looking around the room wondering where her Father was standing and whether she would ever be able to see him again. She closed her eyes and tried to envision her father's face. It was so long ago since she last saw him. She remembered that he lost his hair at a very early age, and he would often bump his bald head while he was doing things like fixing the leaky p-trap under the kitchen sink, or changing a manifold gasket under the hood of the car. When he'd lift his head up, he would bump it and it would start bleeding so he'd have to put a bandage on it. He was always bumping his head on something, but it never stopped him from taking care of all of the things that needed to be fixed. She remembered how determined he was to finish any job he started even if he didn't have the right tools or parts to properly fix it. He would improvise, and by golly it would work. As she sat there remembering her Father, she suddenly felt a tingly sensation on the back of her head kind of like static electricity. She opened her eyes to see that both Edith and Lily were staring at her.

"You feel him don't you Momma." Lily said.

"Feel who?" Annie said, even though she knew exactly who Lily was referring to.

"Grandpa. He's standing right behind you and he's petting your head." Lily gently said. She knew that her mother could feel him there. It was a powerful moment for Annie.

"Yes, I can feel him." Annie said with a sigh. "I miss him."

"He misses you to Mom. But you'll see him again someday. Until then, he says it's his job to keep watch over us and protect us. He will always come if you call him." Lily smiled sweetly at her Mother, and got off her chair and hugged her. Then she pulled back so she could see her Mother's face and said: "And he says to tell you that loves you very much and that he's very proud of you Mom."

A tear rolled down Annie's cheek. She missed her father so much and would give anything just to hear the sound of his voice again.

The phone rang and Edith got up to answer it. It was Stephen. She handed the phone to Annie, then cleaned up the dishes and put a piece of aluminum foil over the rest of the pie. After a very short conversation, Annie hung up the phone and walked back to the table.

"Stephen's car won't start and we have to go pick him up at the pizza restaurant. Edith, are you done working with Lily? If not, I can run and pick up Stephen and come back…" Annie said as she pulled the strap of her purse up on to her shoulder and dug her keys out of the side pocket.

Edith looked over at Lily. "Do you feel comfortable to be able to do what I showed you today on your own?"

"Yes M'am. I know what I have to do now. And Mrs. MacKenzie? I'm did my Tai Chi this morning and I will keep doing it every day like you said." Lily replied.

"Then I guess we're done for today." Edith smiled and gave her a hug.

Edith waived at the two of them as they drove away, then turned to her rocking chair on the porch that slowly began to rock. It was Tom who was sitting there. '*She felt that I was with her. She's beginning to open Edith.*' Tom said to her. "I know." Edith said. Then she turned to go back into the house and closed the door behind her.

CHAPTER 16

Early Saturday morning, Mark rolled over in bed and smiled as his wholesomely beautiful Wife slept quietly beside him. He was itching to take the boat out and today seemed like the perfect day to get the Family out on the water. Annie started to stir and Mark spooned up next to her and pulled her close. She tucked his arm under her and snuggled back down into her pillow.

"Good mornin' Darlin'." He said as he gently kissed her neck. "Mmmmm. Morning Honey." Annie cooed.

"I have an idea. Let's take the boat out for its Campbell maiden voyage today. What do you think?" Mark whispered.

Annie opened her eyes and looked at the clock. 8:36 am. She rolled over to face her husband. "That sounds like fun." She said.

Annie went downstairs and started the coffee brewing. She went to the fridge and took the bacon and a dozen eggs out, then she started frying the bacon in a pan on the stove. As the smell of maple cured bacon filled the house, Mark, Vince, and Lily came down the stairs into the kitchen.

"That smells SO good!" Vince said. Bacon was his favorite breakfast item. That smell would get him out of bed every time no matter how early it was.

As Annie broke eggs into a bowl, she looked up and noticed that there was one family member missing. "Where's Stephen?"

"He wanted to sleep. He said he had to work this afternoon so he couldn't go out on the boat anyway." Mark said as he poured a cup of coffee. "So if Stephen's not going, we've got room for two more. Shall we invite Ed and Barbara to come along?" He asked.

"Let's shall. It will give us an excuse to meet Barbara." Annie said as she winked at her Husband.

While Vince set the table, Mark picked up the phone and called Ed. Lily sat at the table swinging her legs as she pet Winnie, who was standing on her hind legs with her front paws on Lily's leg fully enjoying the affection. Vince put too slices of bread in the toaster and retrieved a butter knife out of the silverware drawer so he was ready to butter the toast as soon as it popped up.

As the Family sat down at the table for breakfast, Mark filled them in on the plans for the day. "Ed is going in to the city this morning to see Barbara, so he suggested that we take the boat out on Lake Michigan. I told him we'd pack a cooler full of sandwiches and he said he'd take us out for pizza later. What do you think?"

Lilly enthusiastically nodded her head up and down in perfect rhythm with chewing her bacon. Vince mimicked her, and then did the gross thing that all Brothers do at mealtime once in a while, he opened his mouth wide to reveal his chewed up bacon in his mouth. Lily saw that, began to gag, and threw up on the floor next to her chair.

"Vince! Knock it off!" Mark said sternly. "Go get a few paper towels."

"Oh Lily, come on Honey. Let's go to the bathroom and get you cleaned up." Annie got up from the table and took Lily to the bathroom, and Winnie went along with them. As Mark cleaned up the barf he managed to get it done only gagging once. He put the soiled paper towels in the trash can, then motioned for Vince to take the bag out to the trash cans outside. He got some new paper towels and some all-purpose cleaner, and thoroughly cleaned the spot on the floor where Lily had her mishap. After replacing the trash bag liner, Mark washed his hands in the sink and sat back down to the table, but found that he had completely lost his appetite. Annie returned to the table with Lily, but no one felt like eating.

"I'm sorry Daddy. That was disgusting." Lily said.

"It's not your fault Sweetie. Don't worry about it. I'll toss Vince overboard later for you and we'll call it even." Mark said as he exchanged smiles with his Daughter.

Vince came back in through the sliding glass door and sat down. "Is there anymore bacon Mom?" Vince asked. Everyone stared blankly at him.

"You have got to be kidding me!" Annie said.

"What? I'm still hungry." Vince said completely unaffected by what just happened.

"Tell you what Buddy, you can finish the whole plate of bacon if you want, and afterwards, you can clean up the breakfast dishes. How's that sound?" Mark said.

Vince thought that was a fair punishment for grossing Lily out, since it meant that he pretty much got to eat the entire plate of bacon. That sounded like a fair trade to him so he nodded in agreement.

Mark, Annie, and Lily went upstairs to get dressed and pack a bag with towels and a change of clothes. Annie went into Lily's room with her so that she could help her get dressed, explaining that she should put her swimming suit on under her shorts and T-shirt so she could go swimming without having to find a place to change. "Let's also bring another change of clothes and a sweatshirt in case it gets cooler this evening." Annie explained.

Mark and Annie got dressed and Annie went to the linen closet at the end of the hall to find some old towels for the trip. "You know? If we're going to own a boat, we need proper beach towels." Annie said.

"Well, next time you're at K-Mart you should get five or six of them." Mark said as he pawed through his dresser to find a polo shirt to wear later. "Annie? Make sure everyone packs a not-so-sloppy outfit for later. Ed's taking us out to Gino's East for Pizza after boating today."

"Got it. Should I make some sandwiches to bring along?" Annie asked.

"Definitely. But, please don't make any with bacon. I don't want a repeat from breakfast." He said.

Annie laughed and nodded her head. Once she had all of the bags packed with towels and a change of clothes for everyone, she handed them to Mark so he could pack the car and hitch up the boat while she made a few sandwiches for the cooler. She left a note on the table letting Stephen know that Winnie had been fed, and to remind him to let her out before he went to work. She rounded up Lily and Vince, and she locked the door behind her and put the keys in her purse. The kids crawled in the back seat of the 1969 Chevrolet Suburban, and Annie got in the front passenger seat. Mark gently pulled forward to make sure the boat was properly hitched to the back, then once he felt it was all good, he pulled out of the driveway on the way to the boat's maiden voyage on Lake Michigan with the Campbell Family.

As they drove down I-55 you could see the skyscrapers of the Chicago City Skyline in the distance ahead. *O-o-h Child* by the 5 Stairsteps was playing on the radio, and Annie and Lily were singing along while Vince sat reading the June copy of Popular Mechanics magazine. As they entered the city limits,

Mark exited to Columbus Parkway, which took him to Lake Shore Drive. As they drove along with the lake on the right hand side, Lilly was counting all of the boats she saw out on the water. It was a hot 95 degree day with 40% humidity—Perfect for a day on the water. Mark took the exit to Fullerton Avenue, and turned right toward the Marina. As he pulled up to look for the boat put-in, Ed was already there standing and waiving at him.

"Back it up right here Mark!" Ed said as he pointed to the boat ramp. "I'll direct you." As Mark backed the boat into the water, Ed jumped in so he could free it from the trailer and steer it next to the dock. Mark pulled forward and found a place to park, then Mark and Vince carried the cooler while Annie carried the bag with the towels. They walked out toward the end of the pier where Ed was sitting in the boat talking to a tall woman with light brown hair pulled back in a ponytail. She was wearing yellow shorts and a light blue tank top.

As the Campbell's approached Mark and Vince set the cooler down, and Mark extended his hand to the tall woman standing there. "You must be Barbara. I'm Mark Campbell." He said.

"I'm Barb Nedza. Ed has told me so much about you." The tall woman said. She was a pretty woman with big blue eyes, full lips, and a little turned up nose. She had extremely long legs that were nicely toned and she looked like she spent most of the Summer outside as evidenced by her golden tan.

"This is my son Vince." Mark said as he began to introduce his Family. "And this is my Wife Annie, and my Daughter Lily." He said.

Annie extended her hand. "It's a pleasure to finally meet you Barb. I've heard very nice things about you." Annie said.

Barb exchanged a pleasant greeting with Annie, then squatted down to Lily's level. "Any you must be Lily." She said. "Edith just adores you. She says you come to visit her all the time and you like to do exercises with her."

"Pleased to meet you." Lily glanced at her Mother for guidance as to how she should be addressing the new adult in her life.

"It's Barb." Annie bent down and whispered to her.

"Pleased to meet you Barb. Yes, I love visiting Mrs. MacKenzie. She makes the best hot cocoa! It's too hot for hot cocoa now, but I can't wait until it gets cold out so she'll make it again. It's yummy!" Lily chattered on nervously. She was a very polite little girl but often got nervous and didn't know what to say in front of strangers.

"Well, shall we get on the boat? This is our first time taking it out so bear with us." Annie said cheerfully.

"Oh it's nice! I'm honored to be one of the first people to ride in it." Barb said.

Everyone got in the boat and as Ed and Mark discussed how to operate the motor, Annie organized the cooler and towel bag and put a life jacket on Lily. She handed them out to everyone, but Ed and Mark stuffed theirs under the dash in the front of the boat. Mark put it in reverse and backed the boat away from the dock. They took a spin up and down the coastline to get the hang of it, and figured out the buoys indicating the traffic lanes for the boats. It was a very hot day and there were boaters everywhere. As they approach Oak Street Beach, Mark though that would be a good place to drop anchor, right outside the floating boundary line for swimmers. The water was deep there, about 20 ft., and pretty clear. You could almost see to the bottom.

It was lunch time, and as Annie opened the cooler to hand out sandwiches, Mark picked up Vince by the waist and threw him overboard. "Damn it Dad!" Vince yelled as he splashed in the water. "It's cold!"

Mark laughed. "That's just a little payback for that stunt you pulled this morning, Son."

"What did he do?" Ed asked.

"Trust me," Annie said. "You don't wanna know."

After having lunch, everyone took turns jumping over the side of the boat to cool off. The water was cold at first, but once you got used to it, it felt nice. Lily was having a hard time swimming with the life jacket on. It floated a little higher than her head and it was a little awkward, but she managed to maneuver around in perfect dog paddle form. Everyone had a great time swimming and when they were through, they all climbed back on the boat to sun themselves a little before heading back to the dock.

"So Barb, I hear you're a Curator at the Field Museum? That sounds so interesting." Annie said.

"Oh I'm not *the* Curator. I'm an Assistant Curator of Ancient Egyptian Antiquities. I've always found the Ancient Egyptians such a fascinating culture. They were very ingenious and modern in so many ways. Right now we're getting ready to receive two new mummies to the exhibit. We've been working very hard to expand the Ancient Egypt exhibit in hopes that SOMEDAY we will be able to host the treasures of King Tutankhamun. That is one of the most amazing collections of royal Egyptian artifacts ever found and it has been a dream of mine to be able to participate in curating that exhibit." Barb explained.

Annie knew very little about Ancient Egypt but was always interested in learning more about it. She could tell that Barb was extremely passionate about what she did for a living, and Annie was fascinated to hear her talk about it. "You know, it's been so long since I've been to the Field Museum, I can't even remember seeing the Ancient Egyptian exhibit. I think the last time I was there was when Vince was in 2nd grade and I went along as a parent volunteer on his field trip." Annie said.

"Really? Oh Annie that's just way too long. We've added so much to every exhibit in the museum since then. You really have to come out and see it again soon." Barb loved where she worked and always became very excited when she spoke about it. "Hey, I've got an idea. Why don't you come out sometime and I'll give you the behind-the-scenes tour? There's so much that the public doesn't get to see that is absolutely fascinating. Would you like to?" Barb asked.

"That would be great! Just say when. I'm always looking for interesting things to do with the kids during the Summer." Annie said.

After a day on the water, everyone was a bit worn out from the sun and the heat. Barb suggested that everyone go back to her place to shower and change before they went out for pizza. She had an apartment right on Fullerton Ave. and it was just a short distance away. Everyone agreed, and they all packed up their things while Mark went to get the Suburban with the trailer. Once the towels, cooler, and life jackets were stowed in the back of the car, Mark backed the trailer into the water and Ed drove the boat up on to the trailer. It was so smoothly done, you could tell that Mark was an experienced semi tractor-trailer driver. After the boat was secured on the trailer, Mark pulled ahead and found a place to park where no one would bother it while they went out for pizza.

Everyone piled into Ed's extended cab pick-up and they drove down Fullerton to Barb Nedza's apartment building. It was a tall modern building with a large portico covered circular driveway with a doorman who tipped his hat as he opened the door for them.

"Good after noon Miss Nedza." The doorman said.

"Hello Henry. How are you today?" Barb asked.

"Oh I'm doing well Miss Nedza. Thank you." Henry grinned and nodded his head as each person accompanying Barb came through the door.

The elevator opened on the 15ᵗʰ floor and everyone got out. Barb walked two doors down the hall and put her key into the lock and opened the door. Her apartment was very bright with tall floor to ceiling windows along the entire wall of the living room. "Come on in and make yourself at home." Barb said. The wall of windows offered the most amazing view of Downtown Chicago and a view of the Lake off to the left. Vince and Lilly ran to the big windows and they were in awe of the commanding view. "The bathroom is just to the right over there. There are fresh towels in the closet across the hall, and there's plenty of soap, shampoo, conditioner, etc… The nice thing about living in a big building like this is that there will be plenty of hot water for everyone." She said.

Barb walked over to the refrigerator in the galley kitchen and opened it. "Can I offer anyone a beer or a soda? Please, make yourselves at home." She said.

Everyone took turns showering and put on a fresh change of clothes. The sun was starting to set and the view of the City got even more spectacular as the lights were starting to turn on in all of the buildings. Annie sipped her beer and stood in the window taking in the view. "This view is amazing!" She said.

"Yes, it's what sold me on this place. The closet space is sparse and the bedroom is tiny, but the view more than makes up for it." Barb said as she brushed her long brown hair that she had just finished blowing dry.

Ed just finished showering and came back into the living room where everyone else was freshly showered and dressed. "Ok, everybody ready to go?" Ed asked as he looked at his watch. "It's 7:20 now. We should get going."

Shortly after arriving at the famous Gino's East Pizzeria, the group was seated at a large table in the back of the restaurant and after they placed their order, Lily took note of the writing covering the tables and the walls. People carved their names and wrote little messages everywhere. She looked over at Vince who was busy making his own contribution to the graffiti. Annie noticed Lily was getting a little antsy, so she dug down in the bottom of her purse and handed her a pen so she could scribble her name on the table.

"Thank you for such a fun Saturday." Barb said. "I had a terrific time and I'd really like to give you a tour of the museum after hours sometime. That's when we go out and set up the exhibits, you know, after all of the crowds have gone. It's the best time to enjoy the museum."

"That would be really cool." Mark said. "Just say when and we'll be there." Mark looked over at Annie who was very enthusiastically agreeing with her Husband's statement.

After stuffing themselves with the Chicago style Deep Dish Pizza the restaurant was famously known for, both Lily and Vince were starting to fade. Ed paid the check and he drove everyone back to Mark's Suburban parked at the marina. Everyone said their good-byes and Annie carried a very sleepy Lily to the car. On the drive home, Annie and Mark talked about how much fun they'd had and how much they liked Barb.

"I think that Ed found his match." Annie said in a low tone so she didn't wake the kids who were both sleeping in the back seat. "I really want to take Barb up on her after hours museum tour offer. That sounds incredible." She said.

"It does. We should take her up on that offer." Mark said.

By the time they turned onto the main street in their neighborhood, it was almost 11 pm. The neighborhood was quiet. There was a full moon so although it was dark, the moonlight made it easy to see so clearly, that Mark wondered if he could actually drive without any headlights. As they drove up their street, Mark was glancing at his neighbor's houses. There were barely any lights on in any of the windows which he thought was odd for a Saturday night. All of a sudden, Annie yelled "Mark watch out!"

Mark turned quickly and slammed on his brakes. There were three people standing in the road and he was about to hit them! The tires squealed and smoked as the Suburban came to a screeching stop and the boat trailer jerked hard on the rear hitch. Annie and Mark sat frozen.

Lilly began to cry in the back seat. She hit her head on Vince's knee as they were thrust forward off the seat. Annie sat up and pivoted herself to reach Lily. "Oh Baby, I'm sorry! Are you hurt?"

Vince sat up and winced as he held his knee. "She hit her head on my knee Mom. Owwww!" He said as he held his knee.

Mark stared out the windshield, terrified at the thought that he just hit people. He got out of the car and ran around to the front. Nothing. He walked around to the other side and looked in the ditch. Nothing there. He swallowed hard and knelt down to look *under* the car. Nothing. He could see all the way past the bottom of the trailer and there wasn't a trace of anyone. He stood up and scratched his head completely perplexed by what just happened. Annie got out and walked to the front of the car next to Mark.

"What just happened?" Mark asked.

Annie looked in the ditch then took a closer look at the front grill. Everything was intact. She looked at Mark and said: "Where are they? I saw three people Mark. We hit them. Where did they go?" She asked as she looked around.

"I...I don't know." Mark said. "I saw them too. But...They're gone. It's like it didn't even happen." He said.

Lily and Vince got out of the car, Vince was limping a little and Lily was rubbing her head which was now forming a large red bump. "What are you looking at Momma?" Lily asked.

Annie didn't know what to say to her because she wasn't sure if what she saw was real. But it had to be because Mark saw it too. She knelt down to Lily and looked her in the eye. "Daddy and I saw three people standing in the road and we really thought we hit them...But we can't find any trace of them now." She said.

Lily looked around and tried to get a read on the energy at the scene. "There's nobody here Momma." Lily said.

Annie stood up and looked at Mark. "I don't know how to explain that. We both saw them, right?"

Mark stood there scratching his head. "Well, let's get everyone home. We need to get come ice packs on Lily's head and Vince's knee. We'll figure it out tomorrow. It's late and we're all tired." He said as he gestured for everyone to get back in the car.

CHAPTER 17

The following morning Cheryl Frasier came over to take a look at Vince and Lily's injuries. Lily had a giant goose egg on the top right side of her forehead and Vince's knee was black and blue and very swollen. He had to leave for his gymnastics camp in less than two weeks and he was worried that the injury would force him to cancel. Annie was also a little concerned that one of the kids might accidentally let it slip *why* Mark had to slam on the brakes. She hoped they knew better.

Cheryl sat Lily up on the kitchen table and examined the bump. She also looked at her eyes and asked her some questions. "I don't think Lily has a concussion, but keep an eye on her. If she seems more sleepy than usual or if her pupils look dilated, you should call your Doctor. I think an ice pack will help keep the swelling down for now." She said. She lifted Lily off the table and set her back on the floor, then Lily ran off to watch TV in the family room.

Vince was already sitting on the couch in the family room with his knee elevated on a pillow. "Ok Vince let's take a look." Cheryl said. He raised the leg of his pajama pants to reveal an angry, swollen, black and blue knee. "That doesn't look good. Are you sure it was Lily's head you hit? How did this happen again?" Cheryl asked as she examined the knee.

"Mark saw something dart out in front of the car as we were coming home last night, and he slammed on his brakes to avoid hitting it. The kids were asleep in the back seat and they were thrown forward." *There. A completely plausible explanation…And not too far off from the truth.* Annie thought.

She raised his leg a little and as she slowly straightened his leg, he winced in pain. "On a scale from 1 to 10, 10 being absolutely intolerable, how much pain are you in?" Cheryl asked.

"About a 5." Vince said.

"Ok. Can you sit up and swing your leg around? Let's see if you can straighten your leg on your own while you're sitting." She sat down on the couch next to Vince and watched as he slowly straightened and bent his knee a few times. No grinding or popping sounds were heard. "Okay, put it back up here on the pillow. I don't think anything is broken, it just looks like a bad sprain. Keep it elevated and keep the ice on it for a couple of days." Cheryl stood up and removed the cellophane wrapping on the ACE bandage she brought. "I'm going to wrap it. This will make it feel a little more stable and it will also help keep the swelling down. I'll come back over in a couple of days and see how it looks. In the meantime, stay off of it and keep it elevated." She instructed as Vince nodded in agreement.

"Well Cheryl, he slept down here last night because he had a hard time going up the stairs." Annie said, then she turned to Vince. "I guess we'll just get you set up down here for a couple more days. It's perfect because there's no TV in your room, huh?" She patted Vince on the shoulder as she pointed that out. Mark could have carried him upstairs to his bedroom, instead Vince insisted on hopping downstairs to the family room. His true motivation had been revealed: Continued access to the TV all day and all night with no one to bother him.

As Annie walked Cheryl out, she asked "Do you think we should cancel the gymnastics camp? It starts in twelve days." Annie asked.

"I think it will be significantly better by next week. See how he does. You can give him Tylenol for pain if he needs it." Cheryl said. "I need to get back. Chuck's Family is coming over for dinner tonight and I still have to run to the store. Let me know if anything changes with either of them, but I think they'll both be fine." Cheryl waved good-bye and headed back home.

"Thank you Cheryl. I appreciate your help!" Annie said as Cheryl left.

When Annie went back into the house, she noticed Lily standing in front of the big window in the living room. She was waiving. Annie walked over to the window and stood behind her to see who she was waiving at. Cheryl had already crossed the street and had gone inside her house and there wasn't anyone else on the street. "Who are you waving at Lil?" Annie asked.

"The people standing in our driveway." Lily said as she dropped her arm to her side.

Annie could not see anyone, but that certainly didn't mean that there weren't any people standing there. She had grown accustomed to Lily seeing things that she could not. "What do they want?" Annie Asked.

"They're just staring at me. I'm asking them why they're here but they aren't talking. They look very sad too. I don't know what they want." Lily said in a tone that sounded like she was afraid.

"Lily? You sound concerned. Should we be afraid of these people?" Annie asked. Ever since she witnessed Lily being pulled off her bed by her feet in the old house, she was afraid that more evil would find her again.

"I…I'm not sure what they are Mom. I don't think they're dead people, but they want me to think that they are." Lily hesitated to say any more than that because she wasn't sure what kind of beings these were. According to Edith, Shadow People weren't known to show themselves as humans. They didn't care about that. Humans could show themselves as Shadow People to make themselves look scarier, and they often did. But these people looked like humans but didn't feel like dead humans to her. She wasn't sure what they were.

Annie put her hands on Lily's shoulders and stood behind her. This didn't sound like a good situation. There was so much to learn about other beings who penetrated our reality. What did they really want with us? As they stared out over the driveway, Annie had the image flash in her mind of the three people that stood in the road in front of them last night. They also looked sad. "Lily? How many people do you see standing in the driveway?" She asked.

"There are three. Two boys and a girl. They look older than Stephen, but younger than you and Daddy." Lily said.

Could these be the three people who appeared in front of the car last night? She remembered two boys and a young woman—all looked to be about 20-25 years of age. "Can you describe them a little more? What are they wearing? What color is their hair?" Annie asked.

"One boy has long wavy brown hair and he has kind of a beard, but no mustache. The other guy has short darker hair and no beard or mustache. The girl has long straight black hair with straight bangs. They are all wearing blue jeans and T-shirts, but their shirts are dirty and torn. The girl has a big tear in the knee of her jeans." Lily described the people that Annie and Mark saw EXACTLY, and she started to notice something else about the trio. She cocked her head to one side as she pondered why the boys were standing about 6 ft. behind the girl and about the same distance from each other. It was an odd formation. The Dead that Lily usually saw would stand around like normal people would—some side by side, others in clusters of small groups.

These three seemed to be standing in some sort of formation. There was also something strange about their eyes.

"Momma? When you saw the people in front of the car. How were they standing?" Lily asked.

"Um, the girl was standing in front of the boys, why?" Annie asked.

"Because they're standing that way now. The boys are standing far behind the girl, but also apart. It means something but I don't know what it means." Lily said.

The more Annie thought about it, the more she realized that they were standing exactly as Lily was describing. She didn't think anything of it before, but it was kind of odd that they were reappearing in the driveway in the exact same formation. Annie broke her gaze when Vince was calling to her from the family room. "Excuse me Lily. I need to go see what your Brother needs." Annie left Lily standing in the living room staring out the front window.

Usually when the Dead would visit Lily it was because they wanted to warn her of something or they wanted help. They never just stood there saying nothing at all, and they never ignored her when she talked to them. Who were they? What did they want from her? She wasn't sure. They just stood there. Staring at her…Until Stephen pulled into the driveway and they disappeared. She wondered if Stephen saw them. Probably not, or he would have slammed on his brakes like her Father did last night, but Stephen just drove right through them.

The phone rang and Annie answered it while she was in the kitchen getting a Coke for Vince. It was Barb calling to invite them to the museum tomorrow evening after close for that tour she promised.

"We would love to do that! Mark doesn't have to go back to work until Tuesday so tomorrow is perfect." Annie said.

"Ok, great!" Barb said. "The museum closes at 5:00, and it takes about 30 minutes for security to do their sweep to make sure everyone is gone. Why don't you meet me at the door on the East side of the building—That's the Lake side. There's a green door that says STAFF ONLY on it. Meet me at that door at 5:30 tomorrow and I'll give you the tour. We've got some new artifacts and we're setting up our display while the museum is empty. It's a fun process to take part in and I think you and the kids will really enjoy it." Barb said.

"Thank you Barb, I'm so excited! We'll see you then… Bye." Annie said and she hung up the phone.

Stephen came through the back door and stopped to see how Vince was doing on the couch. Winnie ran up to greet Stephen in her usual full body wiggle. Lily came down the stairs and plopped on the couch beside Vince. "How's your knee Bud?" Stephen asked.

"It hurts, but it's not broken or anything. I just want it to get better so I can go to my gymnastics camp." Vince said as he peeled back the blanket to show Stephen his bandaged knee.

Annie came down the short stairway with Vince's Coke and put her arms around Stephen. "Hi Sweetie! Are you going to be here for dinner?" She asked.

"Yeah. I don't have to work again until Wednesday, so I'll be around." Stephen said.

"Hey—I've got some exciting news! How would you guys like to go to the Field Museum after hours for a behind-the-scenes tour?" She asked.

"When?" All three kids asked in unison.

"Tomorrow at 5:30." Annie said. "Barb is giving us a private tour after the museum closes. Sounds cool, huh?"

Vince sighed and looked down at his injured leg. "Mom I can't even walk. I can't go to a museum tomorrow."

"We already thought of that. Barb will be there with a wheelchair." She said. Lily got very excited about that. She had never known anyone who needed to be pushed around in a wheelchair and she thought it sounded like a fun thing to do. "What do you say? Not everyone gets to do this. This is very special." Annie said.

"Really? That sounds cool." Stephen said. "But, who's Barb? Where do you know her from Mom?"

"She's Ed's new girlfriend. She works at the museum. She's an Assistant Curator and she works in the Egyptian exhibit." Annie said. "She was out on the boat with us yesterday. She's very nice."

Annie went back upstairs to see what she had in the fridge for dinner and Stephen went up to his room to put his rocket toolbox away. He had been launching rockets that morning at his friend Dan Wojick's house, and they decided to make a few modifications to one of their projects, but Stephen didn't feel like working on it today.

Jon-Jon appeared sitting on the couch next to Lily and was pestering her to walk across the street with him. *'Liddy, come with me to the house. Liddy I need you to tell them I'm still here.'* She heard him say. Lily wanted to help the small boy—He was so lost and missed his Family so much. She tried to cross him over but he refused to go.

'Jon-Jon, I can't go over there right now. You have to give me more time to tell them. I promise I will but not right now.' Lily said to him telepathically. The boy sat on the couch next to her sulking and Lily wasn't in the mood for that.

The doorbell rang and a few minutes later, Beth Frasier came walking down the stairs carrying a plate of chocolate chip cookies that she baked. Vince saw her and started blushing. He was still in pajamas and his hair was all messed up from lounging around. He straightened himself and sat up.

"Hi Vince. I heard you hurt your knee and couldn't walk on it so I made you some cookies to cheer you up." Beth said as she set the plate of cookies on the coffee table and took a seat on the floor.

"Thanks Beth. That was nice. It hurts, but your Mom wrapped it for me and it already feels a little better." Vince said.

"Can I have one of those cookies?" Lily asked.

Beth removed the plastic wrap covering the plate and offered one to Lily and then Vince, who gladly took one. Annie waived at Beth from the kitchen. "Hi Beth, how are you?" She said.

"I'm fine Mrs. Campbell. I just brought some cookies over for Vince." Beth said.

"That was nice of you. Thank you for thinking of him. So, your Mom says you have company coming over for dinner tonight?" Annie got a little chatty sometimes with the kid's friends and sometimes they wished she didn't engage. Vince kind of liked Beth and thought about how this visit might have gone differently if he was confined to his room upstairs.

"Yeah. My Grandparents, my Aunt and Uncle, and my Cousins are coming over. It's my Grandpa's Birthday today." Beth said.

That's why Jon-Jon wanted her to go over to the house today! Now it was all making sense to Lily. She turned her head to look at Jon-Jon but he had moved from the couch and was now standing behind Beth. He bent over and whispered in her ear, and when he did, she reacted by turning her head that direction and looked around behind her.

'She felt you Jon-Jon. You can go home with her and your Family will feel you too.' Lily said to him telepathically. He looked a little less sad since Beth arrived and Lily thought that going home with her would be a good way for him to get them used to his presence. That way, when Lily was finally able

to tell them that he was still around, like she promised, it would be easier for them to believe.

Beth got up off the floor and dismissed herself to go back home. Lily went up the stairs with her and walked her to the door. As Beth walked down the driveway, Lily could see Jon-Jon happily following behind her.

Later that evening, Lily went into Stephen's room to see if he had a book on Ancient Egypt. She was very excited about visiting the Field Museum and but she didn't know anything about Egyptians. As luck would have it, Stephen had a National Geographic Magazine featuring Ancient Egypt. Although this was a very adult magazine with lots of big words she could not pronounce, the photographs were top notch. She knew about the Pyramids. She had seen pictures of them before, but she didn't know what they were for or why they were built...Or *how* they were built without modern tools and equipment. As she turned the pages, she studied all of the pictures of artifacts and golden faces on the sarcophaguses. Why were they buried with so much stuff? She also thought that their writing was very unusual. It was all in pictures and symbols.

She would ask Barb about all of this tomorrow. For tonight, Lily was going to get some rest and hope her giant goose egg on her forehead was less pronounced in the morning.

Dead people were starting to line up in Lily's room waiting their turn for her to help cross them over. She had her "closed for business" sign on for the last few days as Edith had taught her, but she decided to open just for a little while. She was tired so she told them she could only help a few tonight, and as she did, she began to fall asleep.

CHAPTER 18

The parking lot of the Field Museum was almost empty. Only a few cars remained, likely belonging to the closing employees. Mark pulled the Toronado up to the Lake side of the Field Museum. It was 5:10 pm and they were a little early. Traffic at that time of day can be unpredictable, even if they were heading inbound to the city. Mark hated to be late so he made sure they left in plenty of time. Always better to be early than late.

The sun was shining and there was a little chop on the Lake that glistened in the sunlight as the waves rolled along. A few birds were singing happily in the trees amidst the backdrop of Chicago's rush hour traffic noise. Lily was sitting in the middle of the back seat prattling on about how excited she was to finally be going to the museum, and she felt so special because no one else would be there. They would have it all to themselves because they were special invited guests.

Ed pulled up next to them, turned off the ignition of his dually, and rolled down his passenger side window. "Traffic wasn't too bad tonight." He said.

"No it wasn't. It was a nice drive in." Mark said. "Have you been here at night before Ed?"

"Not yet. Between my schedule and hers, I only get to see her once or twice a week. She's been working on this exhibit for several weeks. I've heard all about it but I haven't seen it yet." Ed said.

At 5:30, the big green door with the EMPLOYEES ONLY sign opened and Barb appeared in the doorway. She waved, then she propped the door open with a wedge and carefully backed out with a wheelchair for Vince. Ed rolled up his window and locked up the truck. Stephen got out of the back seat and held Lily's hand as she was swinging her arm and dancing around like a typical little girl might after a big meal of cotton candy. "Get this all out of your system now Lily because you won't be able to dance around in there. Too many priceless items that can break." Stephen said.

Barb brought the wheelchair out to Mark, who wheeled it around to the passenger side of the back seat and helped Vince from the car to the chair. Ed grabbed Barb before she could say hello to anyone else and gave her a big kiss.

"Good evening everyone! How is everybody?" Barb asked with pure excitement in her voice.

"We're great! Thank you for inviting us Barb. This is really special." Annie said.

As they walked in through the green EMPLOYEES ONLY door, it was clearly different from the front entrance. They walked down a long beige hallway with industrial linoleum tiles on the floor that opened up into what looked like a giant rummage sale warehouse. There were lots of wooden crates stamped with the word "Fragile" with documents clipped to the front of them in clear plastic sleeves. In the center of the room were two rows of long tables covered in brown paper with pieces of Styrofoam holding various exposed artifacts. Barb turned around and set some ground rules.

"Okay, you are in the presence of priceless, irreplaceable ancient artifacts. Please DO NOT touch anything. You can look, but don't touch. These artifacts are thousands of years old and very delicate. In fact, I suggest that you either put your hands in your pockets or put them behind your back as you walk through here to examine our treasures." Barb explained. She sounded like she would make an excellent tour guide for fidgety young children in a candy factory. "This is what we call the Procurement Room. This is where we receive and inspect every shipment and validate each items' condition and authenticity. We keep very detailed records of everything—Who signed for the shipment, who validates the items according to the manifest, who authenticates them, and who prepares them for display. We have to document every step." She said. Barb went on to show them various pieces that they recently received and explained what they were, where they were found, and how old they were estimated to be. She knew just about everything there was to know about every item in the room. It was very impressive and Ed was very proud of his girlfriend.

"So, this is the area where you get a first look at everything. When you say authenticate, do you mean that you determine if it's real or not? Do you actually receive fake pieces?" Annie asked.

"Not so much fake, but misrepresented. Everything we receive is old, no question. Um…To give you an example, all of our exhibit pieces are acquired at an antiquities auction or they're on loan from another museum or a private collector. Someone from another museum may have thought that a piece was say, from 2,800 BC. When we receive it, our Archeologists may determine it to be from a much later period, like say 2,100 BC. So, it's not really fake, but there may be a vast difference of opinion about its authenticity in terms of how old it is." Barb explained.

"Fascinating." Mark said as he bent down to examine a tiny sarcophagus with the head of a Jackal as he held his hands dutifully behind his back. "Is there a baby mummy in here? It's so small."

Barb saw what he was looking at and got very excited. "No, no. That's not a baby. That contains some of the internal organs of a Pharaoh from the 19th Dynasty. Here, let me show you." Barb put a pair of white cotton gloves on and pointed to certain symbols and carvings on the small sarcophagus. "Do you see this here?" She pointed to a symbol in the center right below the Jackal mask. It was a picture of an oval with a vertical line on one side, and it had several symbols within it: Two circles with dots in the center, a staph with the head of a Jackal, a zig zag line, and a pharaoh holding the Ankh. "This is the name of Ramses II. He was the 3rd King of the 19st Dynasty. This particular piece dates back to about 1213 BC. He was known as the Great King, chosen of Ra. See here?" Barb explained as she pointed out the symbols.

"Why is there a Jackal mask on it?" Stephen asked.

"The Jackal represents Anubis, the God of death, the afterlife, and the protector of tombs. You'll see hieroglyphs of Anubis everywhere in Egyptian tombs." She explained. "Let's go out to the exhibit for a minute. We have a few things from Pharaoh Senusret I's reign in the 12th Dynasty out there. You'll see that all of the Ancient Egyptian Gods were represented the same way for thousands of years."

Barb removed her gloves and led everyone out through the door opposite from where they came in. Lily was doing her very best to keep her hands behind her back and she was looking forward to moving to an area where the hand restriction was no longer a rule. As they entered the exhibit, it was organized by Dynasty and in a chronological order. The oldest pieces were toward the front and it progressed to the newer pieces toward the back. Each exhibit displayed reproductions of hieroglyphs as a backdrop to the gilded sarcophaguses, mummies, jewelry, tools, furniture, figurines and jars that Barb called 'canopic jars' which were used to preserve the Pharaoh's internal organs after mummification.

As they walked through the exhibit, they stopped to see three mummies displayed behind the glass. Barb explained that the mummification process was very important to the Egyptians because they believed that there were certain preparations that needed to take place for the afterlife. The process took 70 days. They removed all of the internal organs except the heart because they believed it was tied to the soul and the soul lived on in the embalmed body. The body was dried with a salt called natron, then the body was wrapped in linen. The organs were preserved in the canopic jars or mini sarcophaguses like the one Mark examined in the procurement room, and placed in their tombs. They were also laid to rest with servant figurines for eternal assistance, and there would often be vessels of wine or beer for refreshment. Lily stood with her face very close to the glass and stared at the servant figurines on the floor next to the wall. There was something about them that looked familiar but she couldn't place what. Then she noticed a funny looking wooden sculpture with two women holding a curved piece of wood over their heads. "Barb? What's this thing?" Lily asked as she pointed to the strange object.

Barb walked over and squatted down next to her. "You mean this thing right here? This is a headrest." She said. "When the Pharaoh's would lay down to go to sleep, they would lay their heads on the headrest. Kind of like a pillow."

"THAT'S a pillow?" Lily could not believe that people used that hard wooden thing as a pillow. "Why didn't they just use a regular pillow? It's much softer."

Barb laughed at Lily's observation. "Well, that would be too close to the ground. Pharaohs never allowed their heads to touch the ground."

They continued on to the front of the exhibit where three other people were busy setting up displays. "Hi guys!" Barb said. "Everyone this is John, Ricky, and Cynthia. They're helping me with the 19th Dynasty exhibit."

Ed stepped up and shook each of their hands and introduced himself. "Ed is my Boyfriend. Barb said proudly. "And these are our friends—Mark and Annie and their children, Stephen, Vince, and Lily."

"It's a pleasure to meet you." They said.

"Hey Barb, we've got a lot of figurines in this exhibit. How do you want them arranged?" Ricky asked.

"Oh yes, I have a specific way I want you to display some of these." Barb said as she turned to face her guests for a moment. "Can you excuse me for a few minutes?"

"Of course. We'll just wander through the exhibit. Do what you need to do." Annie said.

Stephen was particularly interested in the hieroglyphs. He once read a book on the Egyptian writing system and was fascinated by it. It had about 1,000 distinct characters that combined logographic, syllabic, and alphabetic elements. He stood there mesmerized as he tried to decipher it.

Vince was not enjoying the wheelchair. Mark was pushing him around but often lingered too long in one spot, and Vince grew tired of looking at the same thing for too long. Lily could tell that Vince was bored, so she tried to distract him by explaining what the headrest was, but he had already heard Barb explain it to her earlier and he didn't really want to hear it a second time.

Annie was standing by the three mummies displayed in an upright position in a large glass cabinet. Lily ran over to her and held her hand. "Hi sweetie. Look at how carefully decorated these sarcophaguses are." Annie said.

"Why are some more decorated than others?" Lily asked.

"I think the more decorated they are, the more important the person was in life." Annie said. "That's why the Pharaoh's sarcophaguses are all done in bright colors and gilded in gold."

Barb came back into the area where Ed and the Campbell's were in the exhibit. "My apologies, I'm in charge tonight so I'll be bouncing back and forth." Barb said.

"So, how many Egyptian Dynasties were there?" Mark asked.

"Great question! Well, over the course of thousands of years, there were 27 Dynasties total. The first Pharaoh was Narmer in 3150 BC, and the last Pharaoh to rule was Cleopatra VII, who committed suicide when Rome invaded Egypt in 30 BC and that was the end of Pharaonic Egypt." Barb said.

"Do you have any artifacts from the 1st Dynasty?" Stephen asked.

"No, and, unfortunately…No one does. Tombs were raided by thieves and the artifacts were destroyed or lost forever. In fact, the Pyramids were built by the early Pharaohs as tombs. But later generations of Pharaohs stopped building them because they were basically giant billboards that screamed '*Find gold here!*' to thieves, so they made tombs that no one could see. This is why King Tutankhamun's tomb remained hidden for 3,000 years." Barb explained.

"This is so interesting!" Annie said. "I'm curious, we know about Cleopatra, but were there any other female Pharaohs?

"Excellent question Annie, and the answer is yes, but we don't exactly know how many. We have found evidence of at least 10—Nitocris, Twosret,

Merneith, Ahhotep I, Neferneferuaten, Khentkaus I, Sobekneferu, Hatshepsut, Nefertiti, and Cleopatra. Most did not reign for very long. They were installed as Pharaohs, but basically as placeholders in the line of succession because there was either no direct male heir, or the male heir was a very young child." Barb explained.

Ed could tell that Barb was thrilled to talk about ancient Egypt and loved when people were interested, but he could also tell that she needed to tend to the exhibit and he didn't want her to be there all night. "Barb, you've still got a long night ahead of you, so we'd better take off so you can get back to it. Thanks for giving us the grand tour and sharing these treasures with us."

"Yes Barb, thank you so much!" Annie said.

"My pleasure! Thank you for coming by." Barb said as she turned to Ed and gave him the key to her apartment as she whispered "I'll see you later—I won't be too late."

After leaving the museum, Mark took the family to one of his favorite drive-in restaurants, Dog 'n' Suds, for a bite to eat. As they sat in the car waiting for their food to be delivered to the driver's side window, they chatted about how interesting the museum tour was and they were amazed by how much Barb knew about Ancient Egypt.

"I couldn't believe she could list the names of 10 female Pharaohs off the top of her head like that." Annie recalled.

"That was pretty impressive." Mark said. "She has clearly studied this for a long time."

Stephen picked up some literature from the museum exhibit and he was in the back seat quietly reading through it. Vince was happy to be out of the wheelchair and he and Lily were starving.

They sat quietly gazing out the window waiting for the food tray to arrive at the driver's side window. "Hey, this is interesting…" Stephen found a curious bit of information that he wasn't aware of. "The Ancient Egyptians were a culture of Scientists and Mathematicians. They believed that everything in the Universe was animated by life forces, therefore, each particle is in constant movement and has interactions due to the effect of these life forces."

Mark and Annie looked at each other as if to say *'I have no idea what our genius child just said or what it means.'* They learned long ago that engaging in an intellectual conversation with Stephen means that you do a lot more listening than talking.

"The numbers 3, 4, and 5 were the formula of Pyramid construction. That's the basic Pythagorean triangle, which of course is the uniform angle of the Pyramids they built. Hmmm, it says that the number 1 is the whole structure itself. The triangular face represents the number 3. The square base is the number 4, and the four corners plus its apex complete the number 5." Stephen explained.

"That's interesting." Annie said, even though she had no idea what he was talking about.

"Yeah and they equate that with three of their Gods. The upright angle they associate with male and the God Osiris. The base they associate with female and the Goddess Isis, and the recipient as the perfect result, which is their son, Horus." Stephen explained. He was absolutely fascinated with all of it. Unfortunately, everyone else in the car was hungry, tired, and only half listening.

The food arrived and Mark handed the kids their food and drinks in the back seat first, then handed Annie her order. Everyone was so hungry that no one spoke until the last French fry was eaten. Annie collected all of the trash and got out of the car to return the window tray. As they drove the rest of the way home, Stephen continued to read aloud from the exhibit literature. "The Alchemists elaborated their theories using the same triangle. Osiris represented the 3 vital principles: Salt, Sulfur, and Mercury. Isis represented the 4 basic elements: Fire, Water, Air, and Earth. Horus represented the 5 stages of the development of life: Minerals, Plants, Animals, Humans, and Enlightened Ones."

As Stephen read, Lily began to correlate some of what he was saying with what she noticed about the three dead people who stood in her driveway. "Momma? The three people I saw in the driveway were standing in a Py-tha-gor-ean triangle." She said.

Annie thought about that for a moment. The three people who appeared in front of the car when they were driving home last Saturday were also standing in a triangle formation. She looked at Mark, who glanced back at her as if acknowledging that he had the same thought.

Lily also came to another realization but didn't verbalize it. All three of the dead people she saw standing in the triangle formation were all wearing heavy black eye make-up like the Ancient Egyptians.

CHAPTER 19

It had been two months since the Campbell family moved into their new home and they were pretty well settled in. Annie thought it was time to invite her old neighbor, Patsy, over to see the new house. Patsy had been calling trying to invite herself over for weeks, but Annie always had other things going on and it never worked out. She was interested in hearing what the owners of their old house did to the place and if they had any paranormal experiences. Patsy was the perfect person to ask about that.

By the end of the week Vince's knee looked and felt much better. He was able to walk on it normally now, and the bruising had faded leaving only a faint trace of yellowish green. He resumed his iron cross training on the rings in the back yard and was looking forward to attending his gymnastics camp the following week. Lily had become very interested in Ancient Egypt since their visit to the museum, and had been requesting to go to the Library so she could get some books on the subject that were suitable for young readers.

"Sweetie, Patsy and Scottie are on their way over for lunch, so we can't go today. I promise we'll go tomorrow morning and you can check out some books to bring home. Sound good?" Annie said as she bent down to pick up Winnie's water bowl so she could rinse it and fill it with fresh water.

"Scottie's coming over today?" Lily hadn't seen Scottie in a few weeks and was excited to show him their new trampoline. She agreed that going to the Library would be a better activity to save for tomorrow.

As Annie finished making the potato salad and sandwiches for lunch, she covered them in plastic wrap then put them in the refrigerator. She made a quick sweep through the house to make sure it was picked up and presentable before their guests arrived. She had to call Vince and Lily back inside so they could make their beds—a chore they were expected to do daily but were a little lax on since school was out for the Summer. Other than that, the house looked terrific and she was actually looking forward to seeing Patsy. Even though she was a bit of a busybody and a chronic neighborhood gossip, she was a good person at heart. Annie thought back to the day when Edith sealed the portal. It was Patsy who rescued her from potentially being drug down into the portal by the Shadow People. She had been told of the danger she was walking into before entering the house, and she still did it willingly and without hesitation. If Patsy wasn't there, the outcome might have been much different for both Annie and Edith.

As Annie stood in Lily's room inspecting the finished bed making task, she could see the Sunderland's white Olds Cutlass pull into the driveway through the window. "Oh, they're here Lily. Let's go down and greet them." She said.

Lily ran down the stairs, opened the front door, and ran outside. Annie followed her out. As Patsy and Scottie got out of their car, Lily ran up and grabbed Scottie by the hand to show him their new trampoline in the back yard.

Patsy stood with her mouth open as she gazed at the exterior of the house. "Oh Lordy! You really upgraded, Kid!" Patsy said as she gave her former neighbor a big hug. "So good to see you!"

"I'm so glad we could finally arrange this Patsy. I've missed you!" Annie said. "Come on in and I'll give you the tour."

As the two women went into the house Patsy marveled at the grand portico entry. The curb appeal of this house was far more impressive than their old house across the street from Patsy's. After giving Patsy the grand tour of the interior, Annie led her outside to the deck where they lounged on the patio furniture set in the shade, sipped iced tea, and watched Scottie and Lily jump on the trampoline.

"This house is amazing Annie. Your Realtor did a great job finding this one! It's perfect for you." Patsy said.

"Thanks Patsy. Everything just came together in the most perfect way." Annie said. "So, what does our old house look like now? I haven't been over there since we left."

Patsy's eyes grew bigger as Annie mentioned the old house. She took a sip of tea and began recounting each phase of the renovations. "You would not recognize the place Annie. It's now a two story Colonial style house with dormer windows in the roofline. It's very well done." Patsy said. "And the neighbors seem nice, but they sort of keep to themselves so I don't know them very well."

"So...No paranormal incidents?" Annie asked.

"Not that I've heard." Patsy said. "And I've made every effort to find out, believe me!" They both laughed at that since Annie knew how much of a gossip Patsy was, and Patsy sort of prided herself on that personality trait.

"Well, I'm glad if they haven't. I couldn't live with myself if I knew that we had passed that terrifying problem on to someone else. I wouldn't wish that on my worst enemy." Annie said as she recalled all of the frightening experiences they lived through.

"Like I said, I made it a point to go over and introduce myself and try to get to know them. They're nice people, but they don't participate in any of the neighborhood activities, and since they don't have any children I don't have the opportunity to see them at any of the school functions either…Curious though…" Patsy paused for a moment. "I don't really understand why they bought a house in our neighborhood in the first place."

"Why do you say that?" Annie asked.

"Think about it. He's an attorney and she's a VP at Rockwell I think. They're an executive couple. They have no children. Why would they want to live in a neighborhood full of families with children within walking distance to the Elementary and Jr. High schools? You never see them. They haven't attended the neighborhood Christmas Party, Easter Egg Hunt at the Park, or the annual Steak Fry. It just seems peculiar that they would pick our neighborhood. I mean, Brookridge with its private air strip and all seems more fitting." Patsy had that look in her eye that Annie knew so well. Something smelled fishy and Patsy needed to find out why.

"I can always ask Phyllis. She sold them our house so I would think that she would know why they chose it." Annie said as she took a sip of her iced tea. "Hungry? I made sandwiches and potato salad. I'll bring it out here. It's not too hot today and I don't think we're going to get the kids to come inside to eat." Annie said as she got up and went inside to retrieve the food while Patsy coaxed Lily, Scottie, and Vince to come to the table on the deck for some lunch.

After everyone ate, the kids started to head back toward the trampoline, but Annie stopped them. Jumping up and down didn't sound like a good idea immediately after lunch. "Lily, why don't you and Scottie play horseshoes for a while…Just until your lunch settles a little." Annie suggested. Lily nodded in agreement. Barfing on your friend while jumping on your new trampoline didn't sound like that much fun. Besides, Mark had recently made the perfect horseshoe area with sand and two large steel spikes stuck in the ground. Lily would be the first to play since it was built.

"So how is Edith? Do you still talk to her?" Patsy asked.

"Oh yes, we just saw her a week ago. She still works with Lily now and then so we keep in touch." Annie said.

"Works with Lily how?" Patsy asked as she looked Annie straight in the eye. Annie had just tipped her off and she was like a cadaver dog in a grave yard.

Shit! Why did I just say that? Annie thought to herself. She looked across the lawn at Lily trying to recall what Patsy was told about Lily's abilities. Did she tell her that Lily was a Psychic Medium? She couldn't remember.

"Oh, well Edith has been helping her cope with the trauma from her experiences with the Shadow People." Annie thought that was a good explanation since she wasn't really lying to Patsy by saying that. She just couldn't recall if they told her that Lily also had abilities. This was something that Annie was concerned about with Lily at school. If the other kids knew she had abilities, they would treat her differently and all Annie wanted for her Daughter was for her to have a normal childhood. She had some special gifts, but no one else needed to know about them.

"You know, I'd love to see Edith again. Perhaps we can all go to lunch sometime?" Patsy asked.

"I'm sure she would love that. Let's definitely do that." Annie said.

Just then, Beth and Joey Frasier came walking around the corner of the house from the driveway. "Hi Mrs. Campbell!" Beth said.

"Hello Beth, how are you?" Annie said.

"We're good, thank you." Beth said. "Is it okay if we hang out in your back yard?" Vince saw Beth and instantly jumped back on the rings and held a perfect iron cross for almost 10 seconds while acting the whole time like he was in deep concentration and he didn't notice her. Joey saw Lily and Scottie and ran straight toward them at the horseshoe pit.

"Where's your Mom today Beth?" Annie asked.

"She's on her way over here. She wanted to check Vince's knee." Beth said as she walked out toward the back of the yard to the ring frame.

"Oh good!" Annie said. She turned to Patsy and filled her in on who Cheryl was and how much she was going to like her. Patsy knew who Joey Frasier was from school, and she had spoken to Cheryl once or twice on the phone when Patsy worked in the attendance office, but had never met her.

"And Patsy, please don't say anything about our paranormal experiences or that Edith is a Psychic Medium. I haven't shared any of that with them yet. I thought I would wait until we got to know each other a little better, you know?" Annie asked.

Patsy pursed her lips tightly and made the '*my lips are sealed with a lock and throw away the key*' gesture. "Don't you worry, my lips are sealed." She said.

A few minutes later, Cheryl came around the corner. Annie greeted her and introduced her to Patsy. "Hi Patsy. It's nice to meet you." Cheryl said. "I hope I'm not interrupting, but I'm on the evening shift tonight and I thought I would just pop over and take a look at Vince's knee before I went to work. I know you were concerned about gymnastics camp next week."

"Oh thank you Cheryl, that was very thoughtful of you." Annie said. She called Vince over so Cheryl could examine his knee. "Can I offer you some iced tea?"

"Yes, that would be great. It never hurts to hydrate before I go in. There's no telling how busy it will be once I get there." Cheryl said.

"So you're a Nurse? Emergency room?" Patsy asked.

"Yes. I used to work in the ER as a triage Nurse, but I transferred to Labor and Delivery a few years ago and I love it. It's going to be a full moon tonight and most babies are born during a full moon. It's a strange phenomenon, but it's true. They schedule the nursing staff in the maternity ward around the lunar cycle." Cheryl said as she examined Vince's knee. "Well Vince? Your knee looks fantastic. How does it feel?"

"It feels good. Like normal again." Vince said.

"Well, I don't see any reason why you should miss out on your gymnastics camp then. I would suggest that you wrap it before doing any running, hand-springs, or anything like that just in case though, ok? I'll bring you another bandage that you can take with you to camp." Cheryl said.

Vince nodded and thanked her for taking such good care of him, then walked back out to the horseshoe pit with Beth.

"So Cheryl, how was the dinner party for Chuck's Dad?" Annie asked.

"It was good. They live in Naperville so they're fairly close, but we don't get to see them that often so any excuse to get together with them is always a good thing." Cheryl said with a little hesitation in her voice and then she quickly changed the subject. "So, any plans for the 4th of July?"

"I hadn't even thought about it." Annie said. "Is there anything going on in the neighborhood?"

"You mean a neighborhood party? Here? No. Nothing like Bruce Lake! Why do you think it gets so crowded in your park on the 4th? We all go over there!" Cheryl said as they all three broke out in laughter.

"That's where I've seen you before!" Patsy laughed. "I think that sounds like a great idea. Why don't you all come over to Bruce Lake's 4th of July celebration as my guests? Annie—you know how fun that is." Patsy said.

"It is fun. That sounds terrific." Annie said. "What do you think Cheryl?"

"Great! Count us in!" Cheryl said as they all raised and clinked their iced tea glasses. "Chuck will be thrilled that we actually have an invitation. He always felt a little guilty about crashing the party." She laughed.

"The fireworks are going to be spectacular this time too. Jim Zahlit is in charge of that this year and his brother is a Pyro Technics Engineer. We raised a few hundred dollars more than expected from the Steak Fry, so we put that into the fireworks fund. Jim and his brother are doing the show so it's going to be the best we've ever had." Patsy said.

"Annie, why did you ever move from Bruce Lake? I mean, we have an air strip but for those of us who do not own an airplane, it's useless. Your old neighborhood is always having parties. I would have stayed there. Why did you move?" Cheryl asked.

'Because our family was being terrorized by Shadow People from another dimension through a portal in my Daughter's closet…No wait…Don't say that…' Annie thought to herself. "We out-grew our old house and this one was such an incredible deal we couldn't pass it up." Annie said as she made eye contact with Patsy who winked at her.

As Lily stood by and waited for her turn to play the winner of the current horseshoe game, Jon-Jon appeared again. *'Are you going to tell them today Liddy?'* He asked her.

'No Jon-Jon, not yet. Be patient. I'll tell them when the time is right.' Lily said telepathically. She watched him drop his head in sorrow, and he walked up the yard to the deck and stood beside Cheryl. As he touched her hair, she reacted by putting her hand up to the back of her head and turned around to see what was touching her. Cheryl could feel his presence but Lily was sure that she didn't recognize it as Jon-Jon's touch. This was a very sad scene to witness—A lost little boy who longs for the loving embrace of his Mother. He kept stroking her hair and she kept shifting herself while frequently turning around to look behind her. Patsy noticed that Cheryl was bothered by something.

"What's wrong Cheryl? Is there a bug or something in your hair?" Patsy asked.

"I hope not!" She said. "Annie do you see anything?" Cheryl turned the back of her head to Annie so she could better see if there was an insect in her hair. As Annie inspected her hair, Jon-Jon flicked her hair and a piece of it moved in a swishing motion like a horse shaking its tail.

Annie witnessed that movement but could not see any logical reason for her hair to be moving like that on its own. She looked over at Lily who was standing in the yard facing them and she put two and two together. Lily made eye contact with her Mother and although Annie could not hear Lily's message telepathically, she knew of Jon-Jon and also knew that Lily was trying to tell her that Jon-Jon was playing with Cheryl's hair.

"Oh wait! There is a little bug." Annie said as she winked at Lily. "Nothing to worry about. It's a Lady Bug and those are good luck!" She said as she pretended to remove a bug from Cheryl's hair.

Cheryl looked down at her watch and it was almost 2 pm. "Oh gosh! I'd better go. I have to change into scrubs and get myself to the hospital by 3:00 for my shift." Cheryl stood and said: "It was a pleasure to meet you Patsy. I'm looking forward to spending the 4th of July with you. Thank you for inviting us."

"You're very welcome!" Patsy said. "It was so nice to meet you too."

"Annie? Is it okay if Beth and Joey hang around here for a couple of hours? Chuck will be home by 5:30 and although Beth is very responsible, I hate to leave them at home alone. Do you mind?" Cheryl asked.

"Don't you worry about it Cheryl. They're welcome here anytime." Annie said. Cheryl waved good-by to the kids and told them to be good, then she headed home to change into scrubs and go to work. As soon as Cheryl was out of earshot, Patsy shared her observation.

"Did you notice her response when you asked how her dinner with her in-laws went? That was clearly a sore subject." Patsy said.

"Yes I noticed that." Annie said. "But, Families are funny sometimes. Maybe her in-laws are just difficult to get along with. I'm sure that would be uncomfortable to talk about with someone she just met." She said, but Annie couldn't help but wonder if the tension between Cheryl and her in-laws had something to do with Jon-Jon's death. She would ask Lily about that later, but for now she didn't think it was appropriate to be discussing any of Cheryl's personal matters with Patsy.

The afternoon passed and Patsy had to get back home to let Ladd out. He had a limit to his bladder capacity and Patsy wanted to avoid a messy clean up when she got home. Annie walked her and Scottie to the car and she stood in the driveway and waved as they backed out. As soon as the car backed into the street, Annie saw that the three young dead people were beginning to manifest in the strange triangular formation in the driveway. She could see them! "Lily! Can you come here please? Right now sweetie!" She said.

Lily ran up to the driveway and immediately saw them. "You can see them Momma?" She asked.

"Yes, I can. They just appeared after Patsy pulled out of the driveway." Annie said. "Can you ask them what they want?"

Lily asked them but again, they said nothing. They just stood there, spaced apart in the formation of a triangle as they had the last time Lily saw them. This time Lily walked closer so that she could see their eyes in better detail. This was the one characteristic that was unusual about them compared to other dead people she saw on a regular basis. She stood just 4 feet from the young woman in the front and looked up at her. There was a sadness about her, but her energy also emanated the strength of a fierce tiger. Lily looked deeply into her eyes to see if she could feel the intention of this energy. Like before, they looked like dead people, but they weren't. They were different. In a flash, Lily got a glimpse of who they were. "Momma? We have to go to the Library tomorrow. I think I know who these people are."

CHAPTER 20

Auser, Auset, Heru… Auser, Auset, Heru…Auser, Auset, Heru…These words ran through Lily's head all night long as she slept. The sun was shining through the gaps in the venetian blinds hanging over her bedroom window. She slowly opened her eyes to see Winnie lying next to her, staring and wagging her short little tale. Lily pet Winnie and looked around the room. There, on the chair in the corner was Grandpa Tom. '*Time to get up little one. You have a big day ahead of you.'* Grandpa Tom said to her.

As Lily came downstairs to breakfast, her Parents were already up. Annie was making French toast and Mark was drinking his coffee and reading the newspaper like he did every Sunday morning. Lily rubbed her sleepy eyes as the bright sunlight burst through the large windows in the breakfast nook area. "Hi Daddy." She said as she gave him a big hug.

"Good morning Pumpkin. Did you sleep well?" Mark asked.

"Uh huh, but Momma said we might go to the Library today so I wanted to get up and get ready to go." Lily said as she crawled up into the chair next to Mark.

As Annie flipped the French toast over revealing the perfect golden brown crispiness on the upside, she turned around and smiled at Lily. "Do you still want to go to the Library today?" She asked.

"Yes I do. I want to find some books about Egypt that *I* can read…Books just for kids." Lily said.

Annie poured a glass of milk for Lily and set it in front of her. "Well, then I think that is exactly what we should do." She said. After setting the maple syrup on the table, Annie flipped the French toast over to check the other side. Perfectly golden brown like the first. She put one piece out on a plate, buttered it, and cut it up into small bite size pieces and set it in front of Lily. "You can put your own syrup on, but not too much." She said. Then she plated a couple of pieces for Mark and herself, turned the burner off and sat down.

"So you must have really liked the Ancient Egypt exhibit at the museum the other night if you want to go get some books on the subject." Mark said. "I thought it was pretty interesting too."

Lily glanced over at Annie. Did she tell him about the three people in the driveway? Annie knew exactly what Lily was thinking so she decided to bring him up to speed on what Annie witnessed herself in the driveway yesterday.

"Mark, do you remember the three people who appeared in front of the car when you slammed on the breaks to avoid hitting them on our way home from boating?" Annie asked.

"I do, why?" Mark said as he took a bite of French toast.

"Well, I saw them again yesterday. In our driveway…And Lily saw them a few days before, also in the driveway." She said.

Mark paused for a moment and looked at Lily, then at Annie. "Do you think it's the same people? Who are they?" He turned back to Lily for an answer to that question since he knew that she could not only see the Dead, but could also communicate with them. A skill that Annie did not have, as far as he knew.

"I'm not sure Daddy. I try to talk to them but they don't say anything at all." Lily said. The French toast was really good and she really wanted to finish eating before talking about it anymore.

"Well, this is why we're going to the Library today. We're trying to figure this out. Lily said that their eyes were painted like the Ancient Egyptian figurines in the exhibit. She thinks they're Egyptian." Annie said.

Mark set his fork down and took a sip of his coffee. "So, you think the people who appeared in front of the car that night were Egyptian?" Mark sat back in his chair to think this through. "That doesn't make any sense. First of all, I would have to wonder why Egyptians would be in suburban Illinois on a Saturday night…And second…That was two days before we went to the museum so they couldn't have come from there because we hadn't been there yet. This doesn't make any sense at all." Mark said. He looked to Lily for some clarity since she understood more about how these things worked.

"I don't know Daddy. They didn't feel like dead people to me. They're something else." Lily said.

"Something else??? Like what?" Mark was beginning to panic a little. A year ago he witnessed Lily being dragged from her bed by an unseen force who had the capability to paralyze her, hold the dog back, and put up a barrier in the door way that he could not punch through. He did not like hearing that the people who have been appearing might be something other than random dead people.

"Mom? Can we ask Mrs. MacKenzie if she wants to go with us to the Library today?" Lily asked.

"Edith? I suppose we could, but why do you want her to go?" Annie asked.

"Because we might need her help." Lily said. She was finished with her breakfast and quietly put her hands under the table so Winnie could lick the syrup off of her fingers.

Without looking in Lily's direction, Annie said: "Lily, stop feeding Winnie under the table. Go put your plate in the sink and wash your hands, then go upstairs and get dressed. I'll call Edith and see if she wants to come with us today."

Lily did what her Mother said and ran upstairs to get dressed as Winnie went running up the stairs alongside her.

"What do you think about this Annie? Should we be worried?" Mark asked.

"I don't know. Lily is unsure who or what these people are and it's nice that she can turn to Edith for help figuring it out." Annie said as she cleared the table and poured more coffee for both of them before sitting back down. "If they are Egyptian like we think, then we might have to call Barb too. I'm not sure if Barb knows that Edith's a Psychic Medium, but she may be finding that out very soon." Annie took a sip of coffee and gathered her thoughts.

"Well, if she doesn't know now, she'll find out at some point. I think Ed plans to ask her to marry him soon." Mark smiled as he took another sip of his coffee.

"Really? Wow. That's quick. It's only been a few months." Annie said.

Mark shrugged his shoulders. "I guess when you know, you know." He said as he reached over and held Annie's hand.

After spending nearly two hours in the Public Library, Annie and Lily checked out several books and carried their books to the car. Edith was unable to go with them to the Library, but invited them over afterward to see if she could help them figure out what they're dealing with. As Annie drove up the circular driveway, the fragrant smell of Edith's flower garden wafted through the windows of the car. It was a familiar smell and Annie had almost forgotten how beautiful Edith's flower beds were. She tended to them every day and it showed. Annie wished that she had Edith's green thumb, but she did not. It was all she could do to keep their two house plants alive let alone attempt to care for an entire flower bed. As they got out of the car, Edith was standing in the doorway waving. "Hello, hello! So good to see you!" She said as she opened the door to welcome them in.

"Hi Edith. So good to see you!" Annie gave her a little peck on the cheek since her arms were filled with books.

"Hi Mrs. MacKenzie. How are you?" Lily asked.

"I'm well Lily. Here, let me help you with those." Edith grabbed a few books from Lily. "Let's go out to the kitchen table shall we? There's lots of room to spread out there."

As they sat down, Annie explained the incident on their way home that night when the three people first appeared in front of their car, then about the two times since that Lily had seen them in their driveway. She told her about going out to the Field Museum to meet Barb and the neat behind-the-scenes tour they got of the Ancient Egypt exhibit.

"And you think they're Egyptian spirits?" Edith asked.

"Well, Lily does. She walked right up to the girl and looked in her eyes. She said they all three had their eyes painted like the Ancient Egyptians used to do." Annie said.

Edith looked over at Lily, who had opened one of her books to a page with a photograph of a hieroglyph showing the heavy eyeliner that was often depicted in Ancient Egyptian images. "Their eyes looked like this Mrs. MacKenzie." Lilly said as she pointed to the picture. "Even the boys had their eyes painted too."

"And did any of them say anything to you?" Edith asked.

"No. They wouldn't talk to me. They just stared at me, but they looked sad." Lily said before getting very serious. "They're not dead people Mrs. MacKenzie. They're something else but I don't know what they are." She said.

Edith closed her eyes and took a deep cleansing breath as she sat quietly for a few moments to get clarity. "No, they're not human...I'm hearing they're not human, but they mean you no harm." Edith said.

Annie sat back as a giant wave of relief came over her. She was not sure she was up for another battle with powerful paranormal enemy. "Well that's good to hear. But what do they want?" Annie asked.

"I'm not sure." Edith said. "Sometimes my guides can give me clues, but they don't tell me everything. We'll have to figure this out on our own."

"Edith…Does Barb know about your abilities?" Annie asked.

Edith looked at her and smiled. "Not unless Ed told her."

"Do you not want her to know?" Annie asked.

"It's not something we advertise. Mark and Ed have known each other for years and you didn't know until recently. I guess I like to keep it on a *need to know* basis." Edith said as she looked more closely at the picture of the hieroglyph in Lily's book. "But, given that you believe these entities are Ancient Egyptian and non-human, I think Barb may need to know." She concluded.

As Lily sat looking through her books, she recalled the three words that were repeated over and over in her head as she slept. Were those Egyptian words she heard? Auser, Auset, and Heru.

She carefully read each page searching for any mention of these words, but did not see them anywhere in her books. What did they mean? They had to be important or they would not have been repeated so much. "Mom? When I was sleeping last night I heard three words repeated over and over again until I woke up this morning."

"What three words did you hear?" Annie asked as she continued to browse through the books that were now spread out across the kitchen table.

"The three words were *Auser, Auset, and Heru*. Is that Egyptian?" Lily asked.

Edith paused for a moment and looked over at Lily. "Were the three people you saw in the driveway two men and a woman?" She asked.

"Yes." Lily replied.

Edith sat back in her chair and looked over at Annie. "I think we just solved the mystery."

"What do you mean?" Annie said as she looked up from the book she was browsing through.

Edith turned the open book she was looking at around so that Annie and Lilly could see the pictures. "Auser, Auset, and Heru are the Egyptian names for Osiris, Isis, and Horus. Lily, I think the three non-human entities you saw in your driveway are Ancient Egyptian Gods."

CHAPTER 21

JULY 4TH, 1970

The doorbell rang and Annie opened the door to see Cheryl and Joey Frasier standing on the front porch. "Hi Annie! I just wanted to let you know that we're ready to go when you are. I think we should take two cars in case someone needs to come home early, so we'll just follow you over to Patsy's." Cheryl said.

"That sounds perfect! We're just about ready to go, I just want to let Winnie out and grab some towels for the lake. The kids usually go swimming after the parade." Annie said.

"Oh, I hadn't thought about that. Thanks for reminding me. I'll have the kids grab their swimsuits and throw some towels in the car too. Just honk when you're ready and we'll follow you." Cheryl said as she turned to walk back over to her house with Joey in tow.

Mark appeared behind Annie with his keys in his hand. "Do you want me to throw in the inflatable raft? I could pump it up with the air compressor in the garage real quick."

"That's a good idea. I'm sure Vince and Beth would probably be more interested in that than playing in the sand on the beach." Annie said.

After taking Winnie out and tying the fully inflated raft on the top of the Suburban, Vince and Lily ran out of the house and got into the back seat of the car. "Where's Stephen?" Annie asked.

"He's already over there. He went to Dan's house about an hour ago and said he'd see us there." Vince said.

Cheryl and Chuck waived from across the street as they got in their car. "We'll follow you!" Chuck yelled.

Annie waved and Mark pulled out of the driveway with the Frasier's following behind. As they drove down Plainfield Rd., you could see the 4th of July festivities taking shape across Bruce Lake. There were balloons and

Happy 4th of July banners everywhere. You could see the smoke rising up from the giant neighborhood grills that were brought out to the park for just this occasion. As they turned on to Fairmount Drive, Annie realized how much she missed their old neighborhood. They drove past the McKay's, Beavin's, Lindahl's, Ellis's, Tilley's, Dickenson's, and all of the neighbors they knew and enjoyed living among. Since they moved to Brookridge, the Frasier's were the only people that they really knew, but they'd only been living there a couple of months so there was plenty of time to make new friends. Mark pulled as far forward in the Sunderland's driveway that he could so that Chuck had plenty of room to pull in behind him. There were cars lined up and down both sides of the street and Mark was thankful that Patsy and Don invited them to park in their driveway.

As everyone got out of the car, Patsy and Don came out their front door with a very energetic Airedale Terrier on a leash pulling Patsy down the sidewalk. "Hellooooo!" Patsy said very enthusiastically. "Welcome to our big 4th of July celebration at Bruce Lake!"

"Good to be back." Said Mark as he shook Don's hand and introduced him to Chuck and Cheryl. "Where are the kids?" Annie asked.

"Ladd, sit!" Patsy said as she was trying to get control of the little powerhouse in the end of the leash. "Oh they've been at the park for at least an hour. I told them we would be coming down as soon as you got here."

Cheryl glanced across the street at the stately Colonial style home. "Is that your old house?" She asked Annie.

"Oh my gosh no! Our house was a fraction of that size. They built on top of it. I'm afraid that our old house was reduced to just two walls, and frankly, I couldn't tell you which two walls they could possibly be." Annie laughed. This is the first time she had seen the new house since it was finished and it was substantially larger than she expected to see. She looked over toward the corner bedroom where Lily's room was and the image of Lily being pulled from her bed onto the floor by the Shadow People flashed in her mind.

"Geez Louise! Is that our old house?" Mark said. It was much more than he was expecting to see as well.

"Yeah, they built a big house." Don said. "Our house looks like Ladd's dog house compared to that one. It's nice inside too. They had us over for a glass of wine one evening and gave us a tour. I'm not sure why they need such a big house for only two people though."

"Well, maybe they'll be expanding their family someday." Mark said. "Hey, I'm hungry. Let's go grab a brat and a beer."

They all agreed that food sounded good and walked down to the park. Vince and Lily were shocked by the transformation of their childhood home and could hardly believe their eyes. Still, they did not miss the old house. Too many terrifying events occurred under that roof and neither one of them cared to revisit that.

As they walked down the street toward the park, they could see that the crowd was much larger than just the neighborhood resident population. Chuck and Cheryl recognized some faces from Brookridge and most of Beth and Vince's friends were there. "This is definitely the place to be today." Chuck said.

"Indeed it is." Said Mark.

As Lily, Joey, Vince and Beth carried the inflated raft to the beach, Don, Mark, and Chuck headed over to the grills to get some brats and beer. Annie, Patsy, and Cheryl walked toward the shaded grassy area near the beach where Patsy had previously laid out two large blankets for them to hang out on. "I came down here early and laid these out to save our spot." Patsy said proudly.

"That was great thinking Patsy!" Annie said. "It seems more crowded than usual. I guess the word got out that this is the best place to be on the 4th, huh?"

"No, I think since Jim Zahlit and his brother are doing the fireworks display this year, everyone heard about it. It's okay though—The extra money we make on concessions will be worth it." Patsy said. She was the Home Owner's Association Treasurer and she was very proud to be able to show a surplus in the coffers while she was in charge.

As they got situated on their blankets, Patsy tied Ladd's long leash to the basketball hoop pole next to their blanket set up. It was a hot, sunny, 92 degree day, and Lily and Joey were anxious to go swimming in the lake. Patsy managed to spread the blankets out in the best spot in the entire park. It was in the shade, on the grass, close to the water, and close enough to the concessions and the bathrooms. She must have come down very early this morning to secure it.

A few minutes later, Chuck walked over with a tray full of draught beers. "This should whet your whistles. Brats are on their way. Mark is getting hot dogs for the kids." Chuck said.

"Beautiful!" Cheryl said as she took a big gulp of cold beer. "Ahhhhhh. Good stuff. It's so nice not to have to work today."

"So, the other night when we had the full moon, were you busy at the hospital?" Patsy asked.

"It was a madhouse! We had 14 babies born that night. Our average is about 2-3 per day. The good thing about taking that shift is that the time really flies by. You get there and its heads down the whole time. All of a sudden you look back up again and you realize your shift is over and it's time to go home." Cheryl said.

Lily, Scotty, and Joey ran up asking if they could go get ice cream. In usual Mom style, all three Mothers told them they could after they ate their hot dogs and not before…Not that hot dogs were any more nutritious than ice cream, but it was a well-established mealtime habit not to have dessert before the meal.

The afternoon was spent laying around in the shade watching the kids play on the beach and swim in the lake. There was a giant slide out in the 6' deep part that the kids would swim out to, climb up the 20' ladder and slide down the long slide making a big splash in the lake. There was another slide set up on the beach that allowed the younger kids to slide down into much shallower water, but none of the Sunderland, Campbell, or Frasier children were interested in that. Lily was growing taller every day it seemed, and she was a fairly good swimmer. After a few trips down the big slide, Vince and Beth decided to drag the raft out and paddle around the lake. It wasn't his job to watch Lily today and he wanted to spend a little alone time with Beth. The raft offered the perfect escape. Mark and Chuck changed into their swimming trunks and waded out about waist deep where they took turns tossing the smaller kids into the water. The giggles and laughter emanating from the lake were intoxicating. The entire neighborhood was there and a good time was had by all.

As the sun was going down, the lightning bugs were starting to flash everywhere and the whole park took on a magical ambiance. The fireworks were set to start at 9 pm sharp and you could see Jim Zahlit and his brother setting up on the far side of the lake to get things ready for the evening's annual fireworks display. Vince and Beth had returned from their raft cruise around the lake and decided that they would watch the fireworks from the raft a little later. It was beginning to cool off a little and they came back to change into some dry clothes.

Cheryl stood up and offered to go get another round of beers for the ladies, to which both Annie and Patsy thanked her and off she went leaving the two of them alone on the blanket.

"So Annie, I've been meaning to tell you. There's something very strange about our new neighbors across the street. They don't ever seem to leave the house and they don't ever seem to sleep either. There are lights on at all hours of the night. I'm not sure they even leave to go to work. I never see them leave or come back from anywhere. It's very odd." Patsy said in her hyper gossipy voice.

"Well, maybe they like to sleep with the lights on. Haven't you been over there?" Annie asked.

"Yes, but only once. They invited us in for a glass of wine one evening after they moved in. We kept coming over to introduce ourselves, but they never answered the door until I saw them standing in the front window and waved." Patsy explained. "They were nice, but very odd people. Not very talkative. I still don't feel like they are the least bit interested in having a neighborly relationship. They just keep to themselves. I haven't seen them down here yet today and you know how this is the biggest neighborhood get together of the whole year." She said.

"Maybe they're just very private people." Annie said.

Then Patsy's eyes got very big and she grabbed Annie's forearm in a moment of epiphany. "You don't suppose that they're really Shadow People who have transformed themselves into looking human, do you?"

Annie was taken aback by that question. Such a thing had never occurred to her. "According to Edith, Shadow People never try to look human, so they're probably not Shadow People. And besides, we closed that portal. Remember?"

Patsy shrugged her shoulders but was clearly not convinced. There was something odd about her neighbors and she was going to find out what it was come Hell or high water. Cheryl returned with three cold draught beers and sat down on the blanket. "They're out of brats, but there are plenty of hamburgers and Italian Beef sandwiches. Is anyone hungry?" Cheryl asked.

"It's 7:20 now." Annie said as she looked at her watch. We had lunch late but I imagine everyone will want to eat again before the fireworks start. I'm getting a little hungry myself." She took a big gulp of her beer and set it back down on the tray. "I'll go see if anyone is ready to eat something. I imagine Lily is like a prune by now. She's been in the water all day and I want to get her into some dry clothes anyway. Be right back." Annie stood up and walked toward the beach where Chuck and Mark were still tossing kids in the water. A line had formed and they were tossing more than just their own children now. This would be an excuse to give them a break.

After everyone got out of their wet swimsuits and got something to eat, they all settled in for the fireworks display that was about to start. Cheryl and Chuck commented on how cute Beth and Vince were as they snuggled in the raft just a short distance from the big slide in the lake. "I think they kind of like each other." Cheryl whispered to Annie as she pointed out towards the raft.

"I think so too. Vince has had a crush on Beth since we moved in." Annie giggled.

"She's had a crush on him too. It's funny, they've been going to school together for years but this relationship really kicked into gear since you moved in across the street." Cheryl said.

"Good for them. They seem to get along very well." Chuck interrupted.

The 9:00 hour arrived and the fireworks display started right on time. A chorus of OOOHs and AAAHs was heard with each burst of bright glittery color that lit up the night sky. Cars were pulled over on Plainfield Rd. on the other side of the lake to watch this magnificent display.

Vince and Beth had the best seats in the house as they floated in their raft right below. After about 15 minutes of well-choreographed fireworks, Jim and his brother launched the finale, and what a finale it was! There were so many fireworks launched at once, it was hard to imagine that there could be any more room in the sky.

After the fireworks display ended, everyone packed up their things and headed back to the car. Chuck assisted Vince and Beth with the raft as Lily, Scottie, and Joey raced around playing tag with each other.

"It's hard to believe that these three have this much energy left after the big day they had, but I'm sure they'll be asleep in the back seat before we get home." Cheryl commented as the younger children darted in and out of the groups of people walking down the street to head home.

"Let's hope so!" Annie said.

As they arrived at the Sunderland's house, Mark and Chuck put the raft on top of the Suburban and tied it down. As Patsy was hugging Annie good-bye, she glanced across the street at the mysterious neighbor's house. "Annie look!" Patsy said as she pointed across the street. "There's our new neighbor right there."

Annie turned to look and there, sitting in a big chair by the window, was a dark haired woman with her head down reading a book. As if on cue, the woman slowly raised her head up from her book and stared through the window right at Annie. She froze. At that moment, Lily stopped playing tag and took her Mother's hand. Annie looked down at Lily who was staring straight at the neighbor, then looked back up at Annie.

"It's her Momma." Lily said. She was right. This was the woman who appeared in front of their car that night on the way back from their boating trip. This was also the woman who had been seen in their driveway…Twice. She was staring right back at them as if she had no difficulty seeing them from a lit room out into the darkness.

Annie was trying to recall what her name was, but couldn't remember the buyer's names on the purchase contract when they sold their house several months back. All she could recall was that it was an unusual foreign name. "Patsy? What's your neighbor's name again?" Annie asked.

"Auset. Her name is Auset." Patsy said.

CHAPTER 22

Now that the 4th of July celebrations were over and Vince was away at gymnastics camp, Annie felt it was a good time to get back to solving the mystery of the three Egyptian deities who were living in their old house and who would occasionally appear in their driveway. Ed and Barb were engaged to be married, and since Barb was about to become Edith's daughter-in-law, Edith thought it would be a good idea to disclose her psychic abilities. Edith had also filled her in on the three Egyptian deities who had recently made themselves known, and Barb was excited to be able to lend her expertise to help solve the mystery.

Annie had invited the MacKenzie's over for a BB-Q and as she began preparing the food, Lily came into the house holding a turtle in her hands. "Look Momma, I caught a turtle! Can I put him in a bowl and keep him in my room?" She said. Winnie was standing on her hind legs trying to get a good look at this strange new thing that Lily brought into the house.

"Oh nice! Where did you find him?" Annie said in slightly sarcastic tone of voice.

"At the pond. Joey tried to catch one too but his swam away. He's still at the pond trying to catch one. Can I keep him Mom?" Lily had been going down to the pond near the front entrance of their neighborhood with Joey and a few other neighbor kids almost daily. It was a popular Summer pastime to hang out by the pond and go fishing or just catch turtles and tadpoles. There were some interesting rock formations next to the pond that the kids liked to climb on, and there was also a small cave made by the large granite boulders that were clustered together. The neighbor kids would play for hours down there and it was the first place that Annie would look for Lily if she wasn't across the street playing at the Frasier's.

"We don't have a proper container to keep him in Lil. We need a fish tank or a terrarium and we don't have one. Why don't you see if Daddy can find something for you to put him in temporarily and we'll go get a fish tank from the pet store tomorrow." Annie suggested.

Lily took her turtle outside to Mark who suggested a bucket with a little water and some rocks from the creek behind their house. "We'll go get you a fish tank tomorrow. We have company coming soon so go get washed up before they get here." Mark told her as she said good bye to her turtle and went into the house to wash her hands and change her clothes that were slightly muddy from catching the turtle.

After changing her clothes, Lily came back downstairs into the kitchen. "Momma? I miss Vince. The house is quiet without him around." She said.

"I know, but he won't be gone long. Only one more week." Annie said as she sliced the fresh tomatoes that she just picked from her garden.

"When is Mrs. MacKenzie coming over?" Lily asked as she quietly snuck the end piece of a sliced tomato off the cutting board and stuffed it in her mouth.

"They'll be here any minute. Would you ask your Dad to start the Charcoal on the grill for me please?" Annie asked.

Lily nodded and ran off to the garage to give her Father the orders while Winnie stayed behind in the kitchen sitting nicely staring up at Annie hoping for a bite of something. Annie looked down at her and said: "Oh you don't like tomatoes." Winnie just wagged her tail as if to say: '*Yes I do!*' Annie gave her a small end piece of a tomato and as predicted, Winnie accepted it but promptly spit it out on the floor. "See?" She said. "You don't like tomatoes."

When Annie had everything prepared, she covered each platter in plastic wrap and brought it outside to the picnic table on the deck. She could hear the MacKenzie's car drive up, so she went back inside to meet them at the front door.

"Hello! I'm so glad you could come over today." Annie said as she walked out to greet them.

"Hi Annie!" Barb said as she walked up to give her a hug.

"Let me see this ring!" Annie said to her. Barb held out her left hand to show the sparkling half carat diamond with small sapphires mounted on either side. "Oh, that's beautiful. Congratulations!"

"Thank you." Barb said as she looked over at Ed with an amorous smile.

Annie hugged Edith and wrapped her arm around her as they walked inside. After giving Barb a quick tour of the house, she led everyone outside to the back deck and offered everyone something to drink. "Would you like iced tea? White wine? Or how about a Beer?" Annie asked.

"I would love a glass of white wine." Barb said.

"That sounds good to me too." Edith said.

"White wine it is." Annie went into the house and returned a few minutes later carrying three wine glasses and a chilled bottle of Chablis. She poured a little in each glass, set the bottle on the table and sat down.

"Annie, I've told Barb all about the Egyptian deities you saw and the three names that Lily heard spoken to her over and over again." Edith said as she looked to Barb to pick it up from there.

"Um, yes and I think I can explain who they might be, although I'm not quite sure why they would be here." Barb said as she took a sip of wine before continuing. "The names that Lily heard—Auser, Auset, Heru, are the Egyptian names for the Gods Osiris, Isis, and Horus. Isis is the pivotal deity. Her name means "Throne" in Ancient Egyptian. It was believed that the Pharaoh was given life and power by her. Isis was the Goddess of mothers and wives. She was the Goddess of nature and healing, but she was also known as the Goddess of magic or things that could not be explained. She married her brother, Osiris. He was the God of the Earth and the God of civilization. Horus was their son—He was regarded as the God of the sky, but also as the God of the living Pharaoh. He was the God of war and hunting. He is shown in hieroglyphs as having the head of a Falcon representing his dominion over the skies… Now, there are remarkably similar correlations between these three Ancient Egyptian deities and modern Christian beliefs…" Barb explained.

"What do you mean?" Annie asked.

"Well," Barb continued. "There are a few theories that the story of the immaculate conception of the Virgin Mary and the birth of Jesus, originated from the story of Osiris and the immaculate conception of Isis and birth of Horus. Horus was baptized in the river Nile, as Jesus was baptized in the river Jordan. Horus was tempted while alone in the desert, and so was Jesus. Horus healed the sick and the blind and he walked on water. And so did Jesus…" She said.

Edith sat quietly thinking about the similarities between the stories of the Egyptian Gods and Christianity. She had never heard of this before and it was comforting in a way that the Egyptian deities may not be threatening, but may instead be protectors sent for some reason.

"The Ancient Egyptians were a civilization of peaceful people." Barb continued. "They prided themselves on being true and just. For instance, many people believe that the Pyramids at Giza were built by slaves, hence the story of Moses. But we know that they were actually poor workers who were hired from the outlying villages to build the Pyramids and they were paid a good wage to support their families. Those workers were valued and respected. If any of them died during construction, and many of them did, they were buried with great care and were buried with gifts to assist them in the afterlife...Something they would not have received otherwise." Barb paused for a moment to regroup. Her enthusiasm for the ancient culture she was so fascinated with was causing her to get a little off track with the history lesson. She had to focus on possible attributes that pertained to the immediate situation. "Isis became very dominant and powerful. Her nature and powers to heal elevated her to a place of high stature. The Sun God, Ra was known as the creator of all things. Isis became so powerful that she ultimately became known as the Eye of Ra. I think it's a good thing that we may be dealing with Isis. She heals and protects. She's not threatening." Barb said.

"Why do you think they're here? What do they want?" Annie asked as she glanced at Barb and then turned to Edith for a more paranormal explanation. "Edith, something else happened on the 4th of July that I haven't told you about." Annie said.

"Oh?" Edith asked.

"We were at Patsy's house after the fireworks and as we were packing the car, I looked over at our old house...Which looks much different because they basically built a new house on top of it... But, I saw the lady who bought the house in the window." Annie said. "It was the same Egyptian woman who appeared to Lily and I in the driveway. She was sitting in a chair by the window. She was reading a book but when we were looking at her from across the street, she looked up and stared right at us. We were in the dark and she was in a brightly lit room. There's no way she could have seen us, yet, she made direct eye contact. It was very unnerving." Annie said as she recalled that experience.

Edith took a sip of wine and sat back. She glanced out over the back yard at the Dead who were there and she asked them for help in understanding what was happening.

"And Edith?" Annie said. "Patsy had met her after they moved in. She said her name was Auset."

Barbs eyes grew bigger. She didn't know what to think of that. *'Could a manifestation of Isis be here in this century? And for what purpose would that be?'* Barb thought to herself.

'She came to protect.' Edith heard in her ear. *'A doorway is open.'*

"Barb? Why would Ancient Egyptian Gods be visiting us? What do they want with us?" Annie asked.

"I'm not sure. I've never encountered anything like this before." Barb said. "But if this is a manifestation or reincarnation of Isis? I'm willing to bet that she is here to protect you from something dangerous."

After dinner, Ed and Mark excused themselves and went off to the garage to fix a broken headlight on the suburban. Lily helped bring the dishes into the kitchen and Barb loaded the dishwasher while Annie and Edith transferred the leftovers into smaller containers and put them away in the fridge.

"I have another bottle of wine chilling in the fridge. Shall I open it?" Annie asked.

"That was very good wine. I'd have another glass." Barb said.

After cleaning up from dinner, the ladies took their wine back outside to the deck and watched Lily do back flips and turntables on the trampoline. No one had an immediate explanation for the manifestation of Isis or what that was supposed to mean. Lily said that Auset didn't speak when she saw her. Without direct communication from the spirit entities, the purpose of their presence was anybody's guess. It was also odd that Auset was the new owner of Annie's old house. What was the point of that?

"Edith? Do you think that this might have something to do with the portal in our old house?" Annie asked.

"A portal is a doorway. I was told that a doorway is open and Isis, or Auset, is here to protect. You and I both know that you had a portal in your old house, but I don't understand the connection with Auset buying your house. Was the portal supposed to be protected and kept open so ancient entities could have access to our world? Is that why she bought the house? Is that what she is protecting? I really don't have an answer for you yet Annie." Edith said. This was a mystery unlike any she had encountered before. As she sat back in her chair contemplating these questions, Cheryl Frasier came walking around the corner of the house.

"Hi Annie, I'm so sorry to interrupt. I knocked on the front door but no one answered. I thought you might be out here." Cheryl looked concerned. This was a little out of character for her and Annie stood up see what was wrong.

"Cheryl? Is everything alright?" Annie could see the panic in Cheryl's eyes.

"I'm not sure. Joey hasn't come home yet and I don't know where he is." Cheryl saw Lily jumping on the trampoline, but Joey was not with her. "I was hoping he was here with Lily."

Annie called to Lily to stop jumping and come over to talk to them. "Lily? Do you know where Joey is?" she asked.

Lily shook her head. "No. We were at the pond catching turtles earlier and I caught mine and brought it home, but Joey's turtle got away so he was going to stay and try to catch it." She said.

"Was anyone else there with you today?" Cheryl asked.

"There were a couple of kids—One had red hair. I think his name was Pete. And there was another kid there too. His name was Trevor but I don't know where they live. They're older than me." Lily said.

"Ok, that would be Pete Tanner and Trevor Simms. Thanks Lily. Maybe Joey went to one of their houses. I'm going to go look for him." Cheryl said. "Annie, if Joey shows up will you please send him home? It's getting dark and he missed dinner."

"Sure thing Cheryl. I'm sure he'll be home soon. Kids lose track of time when they're playing sometimes." Annie tried to assure her.

After Cheryl left, the conversation resumed and Barb continued explaining everything she knew about the three Egyptian Gods. Edith was trying to make some sense of the purpose of the return of Egyptian Gods to suburban Chicago at this particular point in time. Annie was convinced that the portal in their old house was open again which is why Auset probably bought the house, although that seemed like an odd reason. The theories were moving in many different directions and not one made any logical sense. Barb volunteered to do more in-depth research on Isis and see if she could find any hieroglyphic indications of time travel or portals, and Edith would meditate and ask for more help from her spirit guides on the matter.

As Mark and Annie's guests were walking out to the car to leave, a police car pulled up in front of the Frasier's driveway. Two police officers got out of the car and walked up to the front door. Annie's stomach dropped. She knew something was wrong. Lily walked up behind her Mother and held her hand. "Momma?" Lily said in a quiet voice.

"What honey?" Annie said as she tried to stay calm.

"Jon-Jon says Joey is in trouble." Lily said. "He's missing."

A wave of panic came over Annie and she shut her eyes tightly as she tried to keep from crying. She knew something terrible had happened even before Lily said that. Edith stepped up next to Annie and put her hand on her shoulder.

"This has to do with the doorway Annie. Joey passed through the doorway. We have to find it." Edith said.

"Oh God." Annie said. "We have to help."

Ed stepped up behind Edith. "Mom? I think you, Annie, and Lily better go over there and help them. It's time to put your abilities to work for the sake of this little boy." He said. "Barb and I will wait right here for you... Go."

Cheryl answered the door and saw Edith, Annie, and Lilly standing there. "Can we come in?" Annie asked.

Cheryl was half hysterical, but invited them inside and introduced them to the police officers. "Um, this is my neighbor and her Daughter. Lily was playing with Joey earlier today." She said.

"And my name is Edith MacKenzie. I'd like to help." As Edith introduced herself, the older officer recognized her right away and stood up before she could explain just *how* she could help.

"I know who you are. You probably don't remember me—I'm Officer Clemmons." The officer stood up and removed his hat as he acknowledged her. Cheryl, Chuck, and the other officer all stood there in shock as Officer Clemmons explained how Edith had helped them many years ago. "Mrs. MacKenzie is one of the best Psychic Mediums the department has ever worked with. There was a case that had gone cold back in '58 and she led us right to the body. She also helped us find the killer. She's very good... Tell me M'am, can you help us find this little boy?" Officer Clemmons asked.

"Of course I'll do everything I can." Edith said. "Can we sit down? There are a few things that we need to tell the Frasier's first."

Cheryl brought everyone in to the living room and Chuck went and got a couple of the dining room chairs so everyone had a place to sit. Lily looked up at Annie and whispered "I'm going to tell them Momma." Annie nodded her head and began to preface what was about to be said by filling them in about Lily's abilities.

"Chuck, Cheryl, I know that you never told us anything about the other child you lost, but Lily has been having regular conversations with Jon-Jon." Annie started to say as Cheryl broke out in tears and Chuck hugged her tightly.

"How? How did you know about Jon-Jon?" Chuck asked.

Lily spoke up. "Mr. Frasier? Jon-Jon came to see me the first day we moved in. He knows I can see and talk to him and he wanted me to tell you that he's still here with you and that he misses you." Cheryl started sobbing harder as Lily paused for a moment. Jon-Jon was standing next to her but she was too upset to feel him there.

'Tell her not to cry Liddy. Tell her that I love her very much and it wasn't her fault.' Jon-Jon said. "Mrs. Frasier? Jon-Jon is standing right next to you and he's hugging you. He says not to cry and he loves you very much. He says to tell you that it wasn't your fault." Lily said.

"W…Where is he?" Cheryl stuttered.

"Right there. If you feel cold, that's him. Spirits feel cold when they touch you." Lily said as she pointed to Cheryl's left leg.

"I know this is a lot to take in, and we can talk about all of this later. Right now, we need to find Joey." Annie said.

"Do you have any information about the missing boy M'am?" Officer Clemmons asked.

"Well, what we can tell you is that the boy may have gone through a portal. I believe it's somewhere near the pond where the kids were playing today." Edith said.

"I'm sorry, what? A portal?" The other officer, Officer Rankin said.

"It's a doorway to another dimension. There's an open portal by the pond somewhere. That's where he went." Edith explained.

"Jon-Jon says that Joey went through the doorway. He said he tried to stop him but Joey couldn't hear him." Lily said.

Chuck, being an expert in Quantum Physics, knew what a portal was and he was terrified of it. Portals were just that—Doorways to other dimensions. A continuum that transcends time and space. His research at Argon National Laboratories recently was focused on portals and time travelers. There was so much more that he could add to this conversation, but his work was classified and he had to keep his mouth shut. His son was missing. He needed answers. And now he's told that his first boy, who died several years ago in a terrible accident, was now here in the room with them. Science and the Paranormal was about to converge for Dr. Frasier on a very personal level.

Chuck bent down to look Lily in the eye. "Lily? Can you ask Jon-Jon where Joey went? How can we find him?" Chuck asked.

Lily could see the pain in his eyes and she was going to do everything she could to help. She closed her eyes and took a deep breath. *'Where did Joey go, Jon-Jon?'* She asked telepathically.

'He went into the hole. I don't know where it goes to.' Jon-Jon replied. *'Come and I will show you where.'*

Lily opened her eyes to see Chuck still kneeling in front of her. "He says he went into the hole. He doesn't know where the hole goes to but he wants to show us where it is." Lily said.

Everyone got into their cars and they drove down to the pond at the entrance of the subdivision. Lily got out of the car and walked over to the rock formations next to the edge of the pond. She led Chuck and the Officers around to the other side where the opening of the cave was. "We were catching turtles over there, but Jon-Jon says that this is where the portal is." Lily said as she pointed directly inside the cave.

Officer Clemmons shined his flashlight into the cave and it was only about 5 ft. deep. He could see the back wall of the cave and it was empty. He scanned the sandy floor of the cave for footprints but saw that many people had clearly gone in there and there were just too many to be able to identify a clear path left by any one set of prints. There were also several different footprints in the sandy dirt in front of the cave indicating that more than one child had been there.

"This may sound like a dumb question but I don't see anything in there. Where's the portal?" Officer Clemmons asked.

Edith walked around to the other side of the rocks where the cave opening was. "You're not going to see it Officer Clemmons. Portals are invisible. You can't see them with the naked eye, but sometimes you can see light around them on film." Edith said. Officer Clemmons motioned for his partner to bring the camera and for everyone else to stay back.

"You can also detect electromagnetic energy around them too, but I wouldn't expect that you might have an EMF Instrument, would you?" Chuck asked.

"A what?" the Officers asked.

"It's an instrument used to measure Gauss and Milligauss to determine the strength of an electromagnetic field. If there's a portal the EMF will show an increase in electromagnetic energy." Chuck said.

"No, sorry. We don't have one of those." Officer Clemmons said as he directed his attention back to his investigation. "Alright. I'm going to need everybody to move back to the street. I need to tape this area off." He led everyone back to the squad car then got on his radio to request a forensics team.

Officer Rankin approached with a roll of crime scene tape and began marking the area. Edith felt that there was something unusual about Joey's disappearance. This wasn't a simple energy vortex where people felt a rush of unexplained emotion or became disoriented. This was a portal—a doorway to somewhere else. People who went missing through portals never came back, but Joey's life force could still be strongly felt. There were several Dead who were standing among them and their message to Edith was clear: *'The boy is alive. You must seek help from the Ancient ones.'*

CHAPTER 23

Word that Joey Frasier had gone missing spread quickly and there were several rumors starting to circulate throughout the neighborhood. All of the neighborhood children were on lockdown and parents were of the belief that a child abductor was on the loose. The Police Department was conducting their usual investigation when it came to a missing child. The details about Joey passing through a portal was not made public, and Edith's involvement in the investigation was kept confidential and only known to a select few at the top of the Police Department.

Annie had gotten up early and went to the Bakery to get some fresh cinnamon rolls to take over to the Frasier's house. She wanted Lily to come along to bridge the communication between Jon-Jon and his Parents, but she also wanted to comfort them in any way she could. It may be a little premature to disclose the Egyptian God connection since there was a chance that it may not be related. First and foremost she wanted to lend comfort and support to her neighbors who had become good friends and that was exactly what she was going to do.

After getting dressed, Lily came downstairs where her Mother was standing in the kitchen waiting. Annie made coffee for Mark and fed Winnie. She was ready to go. "Lil? Have you been able to get any more information about what happened to Joey?" Annie asked. She wanted to make sure that she was kept informed of anything new before they went to talk to the Frasier's.

"A little." Lily said. "Grandpa Tom says he's stuck. He's alive but just somewhere else and he doesn't understand what happened to him or how to get back. He's scared."

"How do we get him back? Does Grandpa Tom know how we do that?" Annie asked.

Lily looked over to the corner of the room where her Grandfather was standing. "He says somebody has to go get him. He can't find his way back by himself." She said.

"Somebody has to go get him? Well, who the Hell is going to do that?" Annie asked. She knew her Father meant well, but she was completely frustrated by this answer. Just then, the phone rang in the kitchen. "Who could be calling this early?" Annie mumbled.

Annie answered the phone. "Hello?"

"Mom? It's Vince." Vince sounded a little upset. He likely heard about Joey and wanted to know what was going on.

"Hi Honey, is everything okay? How's camp?" Annie tried to sound somewhat normal so she didn't alarm him too much. She wasn't sure how much he knew, if he knew anything at all.

"It's fine. Um, can I talk to Lily?" Vince asked.

Annie was a little surprised by that, but Vince and Lily were close so it wasn't an unusual request. "Sure, she's right here…" She handed to phone to Lily.

"Hello?" Lily said. "Uh huh…Ok. I'll tell her…Ok, here's Momma." Lily handed the phone back to Annie.

"Everything okay Honey?" Annie asked.

"I heard about Joey. Trevor Simms's Mom called him yesterday and told him what happened." Vince said.

"It's horrible. We're doing everything we can to find him. Edith and Lily are helping the police with their investigation." Annie said.

"I think I'm going to come home early. I sprained my wrist and I can't do much of anything here. Can you or Dad come and pick me up today?" Vince asked.

"Oh no! Yes, of course I'll come and get you. Dad's working today, but I can drive down. Get your stuff together and I'll be there as soon as I can." Annie said as she hung up the phone. "Well, so much for spending the morning with the Frasier's."

"Mom? We should take them breakfast before we go. Jon-Jon keeps telling me I need to go over there and talk to them." Lily said.

"Yes, that's a good idea Lil. Let's not stay too long though." Annie said as she grabbed the box of cinnamon rolls off the counter.

Beth opened the door and she looked exhausted. Her eyes were red and puffy and she looked like she had been up crying all night. She let Annie and Lily in and led them to the kitchen where Cheryl and Chuck were sitting at the table, also looking like they were up all night crying. How could they not?

Their son was missing and they were devastated. Annie couldn't imagine what it would be like to be faced with the loss of their second child.

"Good morning." Annie said, not quite knowing what else to say. "I brought some fresh cinnamon rolls. I know you probably don't feel like eating, but you should. You need to keep up your strength."

Chuck stood and took the box of rolls from Annie and set them on the table. "That was very thoughtful, thank you Annie." He said.

"Any news?" Annie asked.

"Nothing. Officer Clemmons said he would call later. They're doing a full forensic sweep at the pond today." Chuck said.

Beth brought a few small plates to the table and passed them out to everyone. "Can I get some coffee or something for you Mrs. Campbell?" She asked.

"No, thank you Beth, we can't stay long. I have to go pick Vince up early from camp today." Annie said.

Beth looked a little worried. "Is he okay? Did he get hurt?" Beth asked.

"Oh he's fine. He just sprained his wrist. I think he's more worried about what's going on here at home and he wants to get back." Annie said.

"He said to tell you that he will help with whatever you need." Lily said to her.

Beth blushed at that. She had a crush on Vince and that meant a lot to her. She was devastated about her brother and it was nice to hear that she had someone who cared about how she was feeling other than just her Parents.

Cheryl put her hands over her face and started crying. "Where is my boy? I don't understand what has happened to him!" She cried. Chuck put his arms around her and pulled her close. She was devastated and Annie knew that there wasn't going to be anything that she could say to ease her pain. Lily sat quietly with her eyes closed. Annie could tell that she was communicating with the Dead—probably Jon-Jon, and Annie wasn't sure that Cheryl was ready to deal with that.

"Momma? We need to go get Vince." Lily said. Annie did not expect her to say that, but decided to follow her lead.

"Yes, we need to get going. We have a long drive ahead of us." Annie said. She reached over to hold Cheryl's hand across the table. "Cheryl, we are here for you. Whatever you need, just ask."

Cheryl nodded her head as she sniffed and dried her tears with a tissue in her other hand. Then she looked over at Lily who was staring at her in a very sympathetic way. "Do you know how Jon-Jon died Lily?" She asked.

Lilly nodded that she had. "He told me that he fell and hit his head." She said quietly.

Cheryl looked down and folded her tissue. "Yes. He fell down the stairs to the basement. I thought I had closed the safety latch on the door, but I was tired when I got home from my shift and… I must have forgotten." Cheryl said as she sobbed thinking about that painful day. "It was about 9 years ago. He just turned 3 and he went downstairs by himself to get some cake out of the refrigerator down there. I…I…went to change my clothes and then…I…I…couldn't find him." She said as she was fighting to hold back the second wave of tears. "Then I opened the door and I saw him lying there…at the bottom of the stairs in a pool of blood…" Cheryl put her hands up over her face and started sobbing uncontrollably.

"It wasn't your fault Mrs. Frasier." Lily said. "You did latch the door. Jon-Jon pushed a chair up to it and unhooked it. He did it himself."

Cheryl stopped crying for a moment and stared at Lily. "Did he say that?"

Lily closed her eyes for a moment before continuing. "Yes. He said that he was wearing jammies that were too big and he tripped on them and fell down the stairs. It was an accident."

Chuck and Cheryl looked at each other, completely taken by surprise that Lilly knew that small detail. "It was an accident and he says he's sorry that he made you cry. He didn't mean to…But he's fine and he's here with you. He never left you." Lily said as she smiled sweetly at Jon-Jon's Parents.

This revelation seemed to make a difference and Annie was glad that Lily shared that information. Cheryl was carrying a tremendous amount of guilt and it seemed to help ease the pain a little. "He got a new pair of blue Roy Rogers pajamas for his birthday from his Grandparents. They were a little too big, but he loved them and insisted on wearing them anyway." Cheryl said. She took a deep breath and collected herself a little. "Thank you for telling me that Lily. It means a lot."

"Well, we should get going." Annie said. "I'll check in when I get back, ok?" She hugged Chuck, Cheryl, and Beth before she left and told them to hang in there and that they would do everything they could to find Joey. Edith and Lily were gifted with their abilities, and they would find a way to bring him back home she assured them.

When Annie and Lily got back to their house, Annie let Winnie out one more time, then got her purse and her keys and opened the garage door. Lily followed behind her and crawled into the passenger seat of the car. "Mom?" Lily said.

"Yes Lil?" Annie answered.

"Who's gonna go get Joey?" Lily asked.

"I don't know Baby girl… I just don't know." Annie said.

CHAPTER 24

It had been 1 week since Joey Frasier had vanished. The Police had reached a dead end. The trail stopped at the empty cave and there were no other clues to follow up with. Edith had told them everything she knew, which was that Joey had passed through a portal in the cave. He was still alive, but stuck and didn't know how to get back. The Police had no protocol for retrieving missing persons from portals, so they were at a loss as to how to proceed. Edith knew that she had to pay a visit to the new owners of Annie's old house. The *'Ancient Ones'* her guides told her about—*'Seek the Ancient Ones for help'* they told her. Edith called Annie and arranged to meet with her.

Edith pulled up to Annie's house and Lily was throwing a ball for Winnie in the front yard. Across the street, the Frasier's house looked gloomy and she would expect it not to look otherwise under the circumstances. Lily saw Edith and waved, then she took Winnie in the house and told her Mother that Edith had arrived. Annie grabbed her purse and locked the front door.

"Hello Edith!" Annie said as she walked around to the passenger side of the car. Lily hopped in the back seat.

"Hi Mrs. MacKenzie!" Lily said.

"Hello there." Edith put the car in park and turned around so that she could talk to Lily in the back seat. "Lily? When was the last time you saw the Egyptians?" She asked.

"Ummm, it was before the 4th of July." Lily recalled.

"So you've only seen them the two times you told me about?" Edith asked.

"Yes." Lily said. "But my Mom and Dad saw them in the road one night before that."

Edith sat back to think for a moment. "I'm wondering how we should approach this with Auset." Edith said.

"I think we should just go knock on the door and talk to her. If she acts like she has no idea what we're talking about, then we leave…Then we'll have to figure something else out." Annie suggested. Edith nodded her head in agreement. There really was nothing else to do if she knew nothing about it. Edith put the car in reverse, backed out of the driveway, and they headed over to the old house in Bruce Lake.

As Edith pulled in the driveway, she gasped at the magnificent transformation of the Campbell's old residence. "Oh my." She said. "Is this the right house?"

"I know! I never imagined that our little brick house would grow up to be such a beauty!" Annie said as she laughed at Edith's reaction to seeing the new house for the first time. "Shall we see if anyone is home?"

The three of them got out of the car and walked up the stone paver sidewalk to the front door. Edith rang the doorbell and it had a nice chime to it. They were about to ring the bell a second time when they heard the deadbolt on the door turn. The door opened slowly, and a young woman with straight dark hair with blunt bangs was standing in front of them. Lily's mouth dropped. It was her—the woman she had walked up to in her driveway a few weeks ago. There was a long pause before anyone spoke. The young woman finally broke the silence. "I have been expecting you…Please come in." She said with a slight Middle Eastern accent.

"Thank you." Edith said as they stepped inside.

The front room was light, bright, and airy. The ceilings were much higher than the old house and it made it feel very inviting. "Please, come this way." The young woman said as she led them down a hallway that opened up to a large sitting room with 20' high turret windows that overlooked a lavishly landscaped backyard. This was a slightly different view than Annie and Lily had remembered it. There were four wing back armchairs arranged around a round marble table. On the table was a tea set with four cups and a plate of cookies. It appeared that she was expecting company.

"Please sit. I made apple tea for us." The young woman said.

She made apple tea for us? She knew we were coming? Annie thought to herself. Edith looked at Annie with one eyebrow raised and nodded. She knew what Annie was thinking.

Lily hopped up on one of the chairs and sat with her hands folded nicely in her lap. "I've never had apple tea before but it sounds yummy." She said.

The young woman smiled at Lily as she poured tea in her cup. Her face was radiant like the sun when she smiled. She never smiled when Lily saw her before. She had presented herself looking sad in the driveway. Lily felt unthreatened and completely safe. This young woman was a different being. Although she was standing before her in human form, she was not human. She was a higher life force. Lily did not know what kind of higher being she was, but she radiated love and light and it felt wonderful to be in her presence.

"Um…We're sorry to drop in like this. It's just that, well, we need some help. My name is Annie, by the way. I used to live here. Well, it looked much different when I lived here—Wow! You've done an amazing job on this remodel…" Annie said with a nervous chatter.

"I know who you are. I have been expecting you." The young woman said. "I am Auset." She said as she made direct eye contact with Edith. "And I know that you have come for my help."

"Well, yes, we have." Annie said. She didn't quite know if she should be talking or if she should just turn it over to Edith. Annie was the only one in the room who could not communicate telepathically and felt as if an entire conversation was going on between the other three that she could not hear.

After pouring tea for everyone, Auset sat down and took a sip of tea. Everyone else did the same. The tea was unlike anything they had ever tasted before. It was sweet like an apple, but not in a sugary sort of way. It wasn't quite like apple cider either. After one sip of the delicious hot liquid, it warmed you from the inside and it almost made you feel…Enlightened.

"Mmmmmm." Lily said.

"Nectar of the Gods." Auset said as she smiled at the delightful little girl.

"Auset, if I may ask, we need your help. A boy is missing. He has gone through a portal and we don't know how to bring him back." Edith said.

Auset nodded and sat calmly. "The boy exists in another time. I have come to warn you of these doorways. There are many open that should not be." She looked directly at Annie. "The doorway that was opened in this house has been closed and will never open again. But there are many others that must be sealed." Then she directed her eyes to Lily. "You Lily, have been given a gift. You must develop this gift and when you do, you will use it to save others. But you must take heed—You will be hunted by the Dark Ones. They want to take your power and use it for death and destruction."

Although Lily had always known that there was something more within her than just having psychic abilities, she never thought that evil entities would hunt her down to take her power from her. In fact, she wasn't even exactly sure what her power actually was yet.

"These doorways…Are there more opening up at this time for some reason?" Edith asked. She knew that portals existed everywhere and always will, but Auset implied that there were more open than there usually would be and Edith wanted to find out why.

"Yes. They have been opened by accident and the people who have opened them know not what they did." Auset said. "If they are left open, there will be imbalance and chaos and destruction will plague this realm."

"Who opened these doorways?" Annie asked.

"The boy's Father knows." Auset said as she took another sip of her apple tea. "You seek my help to return the boy to this realm. I seek your help to close the doorways to this realm." Auset set her tea cup down on the table and placed her hands flat on her lap. "I will help you retrieve the boy. It must be done 3 minutes before Midnight on the night of the New Moon."

"How? Will he come back on his own at that time? What do we need to do?" Annie was relieved to hear that there was a way to bring Joey back and she was willing to do anything she could to help make that happen.

"We must wait until that night." Auset said as she stood up. "You will need to prepare. I will come to you with further instruction soon."

The conversation ended rather abruptly, almost like Auset had to get everyone out of her house before she turned into a pumpkin or something. Edith and Lily stood up when Auset did, but Annie remained seated not catching that that was the queue to leave. It seemed like there was so much more to discuss. Why were they leaving now? She had more questions, but clearly Auset was no longer in the mood to answer them. They thanked her for her time as she showed them to the front door.

"Thank you for the apple tea Mrs…Mrs…" Lily was in the habit of addressing adults in a respectful way but she had no idea what Auset's last name was.

"You may call me Auset, Lily." She said as she placed her hand lovingly on Lily's cheek.

"Thank you very much Auset. I really liked the apple tea…And I'm very pleased to meet you." Lily finished her sentence respectfully—Just like Annie had taught her to do. This made Annie very proud.

"Thank you for your help. We will await your direction." Edith said. Annie wondered what she meant by that, but figured that she would ask Edith about it once they got in the car.

As they drove away, Annie saw Patsy looking out her kitchen window with a surprised look on her face. Annie knew her phone would be ringing by the time she got home and she contemplated what she would tell her. Patsy knew about the portal in the house when Annie lived there, but she was not sure she knew that Joey Frasier was missing because he went through a portal. That fact was only known to a very select few for good reason and Patsy did not really need to know that at this point, if ever. Annie would think of something to tell her, but for now she needed a little more clarification about what just transpired in Auset's house.

"Would somebody please tell me what just happened in there? I don't feel like we got any clear direction about what to do at all." Annie said bearing a little frustration in her voice.

"She will help us get Joey back at a designated time. Annie, would you please open the glove compartment and see if there's a calendar in there? I got one from my bank last time I was there making a deposit and I think that's where I put it." Edith said. Annie opened the glovebox and there was a small pocket calendar laying on the top of a small pile of papers. "Ah, there it is. Look at July and August and tell me when the next New Moon is." She said.

Annie scanned July, but the New Moon date had passed, so she turned the page to August. "Saturday, August 1st is the next New Moon. That's…18 days away. How can we wait that long?" Annie asked. "How will Joey survive?"

"I don't know, but we have to trust Auset. We have no other choice." Edith said. "She knows more that we do so we have to do what she says."

"And what was the comment about 'the boy's Father knows.' Did she mean Chuck? Does she think Chuck has something to do with all of this?" Annie grew more upset by the minute. She could not imagine that Joey's Father would do anything to cause harm to his own son.

"I know what she means Momma." Lily said from the back seat. "She means that Mr. Frasier's work at Argon is causing the portals to open…But he doesn't know what's happening."

Annie pondered that for a moment. No one really knew what research was conducted at Argon. Everything was so hush-hush that went on there. Dr. Charles Frasier was a Quantum Physicist and they did study Black Holes and cosmic phenomena such as that. Could he be working on something that has opened up portals in the area? Portals that would cause people to just disappear? He did ask Officer Clemmons about an electromagnetic something or other when they were investigating the stones…Does Chuck know more than he's telling us? A million questions were running through Annie's head.

"Edith, I think that we need to talk to Chuck about his work at Argon. I think he has information that could help us get Joey back." Annie said.

"She also said *'they know not what they did.'* He may not know that they're opening portals." Edith said.

"Why did we leave so quickly? We should have stayed and asked more questions. I don't feel like we learned very much." Annie said.

"Annie, you have to consider *what* Auset is. She is not human. She is a higher being. She is only presenting herself as human so that we will feel more comfortable communicating with her." Edith explained.

This had not occurred to Annie. She thought Auset was a little odd, but she regarded her as a human being. "What do you mean *higher being*?" She asked while Lily sat quietly in the back seat. She knew exactly what Auset was but waited for Edith to describe it to her Mother.

"She functions at a much higher vibration level than we do. She had to slow that vibration level waaaaaay down to appear and speak to us. She is an ethereal body. She is a Seraphim. One of the highest order of Angels. A heavenly being that surrounds the throne of God." Edith said. After she heard herself verbalize it, she gasped. She was in complete awe that she would be allowed to be in the presence of such a Divine being.

They arrived back at Annie's house and Edith put the car in park and turned off the ignition. All three of them sat in the car for a few minutes in complete silence. Edith picked up the pocket calendar that was sitting in on the dashboard where Annie had put it. She opened it to July and counted the days to August 1st, the night of the next New Moon. As Annie said, it was 18 days away. Edith closed her eyes and took a couple of deep breaths. That always helped her to gain clarity and perspective when she was trying to figure out the next steps. Lily finally broke the silence.

"Mrs. MacKenzie?" Lily said. "Joey is safe. Heru is with him."

"Who is Heru?" Annie asked.

"Heru is the third entity you saw in the driveway. His Egyptian name is Heru but he is also known as Horus. He is the son of Isis, or Auset." Edith said.

"Auset sent him to protect Joey." Lily said.

"I don't understand. If Auset already sent Heru to be with Joey, why can't he just bring Joey back? I assume he is also a Seraphim Angel like Auset, isn't he?" Annie asked. She was having a little trouble following the logic of the paranormal.

"I'm not sure why, but we absolutely have to be involved in some way. This is our realm. Our world. Auset said she would give us direction soon. We will have to wait and see." Edith said as she looked back toward the back seat at Lily, who was nodding in agreement.

Annie turned to Edith and said: "We need to talk to Chuck. We need to find out what he's involved with at Argon before we go any further."

CHAPTER 25

Mark and Annie sat at the kitchen table paying bills and discussing their budget for school supplies. Mark had taken extra trips all Summer so that they wouldn't come up short. Lily and Vince were growing out of everything they had in their closets. Summer clothes were easy to accommodate. Shorts, tank tops, and flip flops didn't cost much, but winter coats, boots, sweaters, wool socks, jeans, and flannel shirts required a lot more cash. Luckily Stephen was still wearing the same size shoe, so he could get at least one more year out of his boots, but he would need a new pair of gym shoes since he trashed his other pair working at the pizza place.

"Too bad I never learned to sew." Annie said as she perused through the JC Penny Catalog. "Clothes seem to cost twice as much as I remembered last year."

"Your time is better spent doing other things Honey. Besides, the kids like their Levi's and you can't make those." Mark said. "We can cover it. Just get them what they need for now. We can get more as they need it."

"So Mark, has Chuck ever talked with you about what he does at Argon?" Annie decided to change the subject. She was hung up on what Auset had told them about Joey's father knowing something about the portals.

"Not really. He just explained what a Quantum Physicist studies and that's about it. He never talked about a specific project he was working on or anything." Mark said. "Why do you ask?"

"It was just something that Auset said. She said that he knows something about the portals." Annie replied.

"Well, you could always go ask him. I'm sure if you explained who Auset is and what she told you he might be more willing to talk. He'd do anything to get Joey back. Any parent would." Mark punched a few numbers on his calculator and balanced the check register before putting everything back in the box that he kept their checks and receipts in.

"I think I will. I'm just not sure how I'm going to explain that Auset is not human, but a higher being not from our world." Annie said as she stacked her catalogs on the table.

"Well, it seems to me that the two of you might have a lot to talk about. Both seem related in a cosmic sort of way, you know?" Mark had a way of chunking things down to their simplest form. Maybe the best thing to do was to just go talk to him and ask him about how and why they are opening portals everywhere. Even if it's top secret classified government information, surely he'd be interested in knowing that his work was impacting our world so negatively that an Angel had to come down from the Heavens to fix it.

"You might want to take Edith with you though. Chuck is going to have some questions about Auset and you may not know how to explain that. Edith seems to understand the paranormal pretty well." Mark said as he looked at her over his glasses that were sitting low on his nose.

"Mmmm, right. Good idea." Annie picked up the phone to call Edith to see what she thought. Annie was anxious to solve the mystery of Joey's disappearance but equally as anxious to know what actually did go on at Argon National Laboratories.

Edith picked up after the third ring. After a few minutes chatting, Annie said good-bye and hung up the phone. "Edith is on her way. Although she said it would be best to wait for further direction from Auset on how to get Joey back, we should probably find out what Chuck knows about opening new portals… Auset did say that she needed our help to close them." Annie said.

"Good. While you're doing that, how about if I take Lily, Vince and Beth out to Baskin Robbins. I'm sure Beth would like to get out of the house and get her mind off of this for a bit." Mark was always thinking of others. He was a very thoughtful and caring man and Annie thanked her lucky stars that he married her.

"That would be very nice Honey, thank you." Annie smiled and kissed him on the cheek as she tidied up the kitchen table from all of the papers scattered about.

It was mid-afternoon and it was a hot, sticky, humid suburban Chicago Summer day. It took no effort to convince the kids to go get ice cream. Beth was looking a little skinny. The stress of her little brother having gone missing was taking its toll. She had no appetite and it showed. Mark wanted to get a few calories in her and ice cream would help with that. Mark was a little surprised that Annie did not include Lily in her plans to speak with Chuck this afternoon, but he was thankful for that. Lily was like a ray of sunshine and she definitely lightened the mood. Her presence would help to cheer up Beth.

"Daddy? I want two scoops of Rocky Road in a cup. Can I have two scoops?" Lily said in her usual chipper voice.

"Two scoops huh? Well, I don't know…" Mark teased her. "What's your favorite kind of ice cream Beth?" Beth was half listening as she stared out the window of the Baskin Robbins ice cream store. "Beth?" He said again.

"Oh, um, I like Cookies 'n Cream. But Rocky Road is good too." Beth said.

"Well I think you should get a big scoop of each." Mark said. "Vince? Pick your poison Son."

"I'll take two scoops of Cookie Dough on a sugar cone." Vince said.

Mark got two scoops of Rum Raisin for himself and paid the cashier. Lily found a table in the corner of the store with four chairs and sat down with her cup of two scoops of Rocky Road. Beth and Vince sat down with her and Mark joined them. "This is SO yummy Daddy. Good idea to come here today!" Lily said.

"Yes, thank you Mr. Campbell. I haven't had ice cream in a while." Beth said. Mark was glad to see her eat something. She had dropped too much weight and was terribly thin.

"I'm glad you could join us Beth." Mark said as he thought about what he could say next to keep the conversation going without focusing on Joey. "So have you gotten your school schedule yet? Do you and Vince have any classes together this year?" He asked.

"Yeah, we got them but I'm not sure if we have any classes together." She said. She wasn't really in the mood to talk and it seemed like she would rather just be left alone.

"I've got Biology 4th period with labs on Tuesdays and Thursdays." Vince said in an effort to keep Beth talking.

"Um, I think I have Biology 4th period too. Do you have Mr. Wilhite or Mr. Dunbar?" Beth asked.

"I have Wilhite. Who do you have?" Vince said.

"I have Mr. Wilhite too." She said. It had been a while since anyone had seen Beth Frasier smile, but Vince managed to do it with a simple acknowledgement of being in the same Biology class together.

The conversation lulled shortly after that and everyone had nearly finished eating their ice cream. Mark had to find something else to do to keep them occupied for a while so Edith and Annie could talk with Chuck uninterrupted. As he looked outside at the other stores in the strip mall, he noticed a sporting goods store and decided that would be the next stop.

The inside of the Frasier's house was gloomy and dark. Cheryl kept the blinds closed all the time these days as if that would shelter her from the cruel world outside that had taken her son away from her. As Annie and Edith walked into the kitchen, Chuck offered them something to drink and brought a pitcher of iced tea and four glasses to the table.

"Cheryl? Do you mind if I open the blinds and let a little sunshine through?" Annie asked. "The light will help lift you up a little." Cheryl nodded okay so Annie went around the room and opened the blinds on every window she could. "There. That's better."

"Edith? Do you have any new information about Joey?" Cheryl asked. The desperation in her voice was heartbreaking to hear.

"I know that he is alive and he will be coming home soon." Edith told her.

Cheryl closed her eyes and felt a wave of relief come over her, but her apprehension intensified from hearing the word *soon*. She wanted him home now. *What were they waiting for? Why couldn't he be brought back right now?* "When is he coming home?" Cheryl asked as she tried to remain calm.

"We must wait for a specific time that will allow him to come back through the portal. We have to wait until the next New Moon." Edith explained. Cheryl did not like hearing that because it meant that she had to wait longer to get her Son back. Edith didn't want to say anything more on the subject of Joey's return until Auset gave them the additional information that she promised, and she did not know when that would be. But, she didn't want Cheryl to lose faith because they didn't have all of the answers yet. Edith looked over at Annie to urge her to start the conversation they came over to have with Chuck about what he was working on at Argon that was opening the portals.

"Chuck, there's something we need to ask you and I'm hoping that you can talk to us about it." Annie jumped right in. She wasn't going to pussyfoot around with small talk. She knew that he was going to be secretive. Everything that went on at Argon was handled on a need-to-know basis, and as far as they were concerned, this was just such an instance where that should apply.

"Anything Annie." Chuck said.

"What are you working on at Argon right now?" Annie got right to the point.

"Anything but that." Chuck replied.

"Chuck, I'll just be blunt. Whatever it is that you are working on in that Laboratory has opened portals everywhere. Your son fell through one of them. Why are you opening doorways to this world?" Annie asked.

Chuck expected her to be curious about the Lab. Everyone was. But it wasn't something he could talk about. Their work there was classified and not a word about what they were working on was allowed to be spoken outside of the building. "I'm sorry Annie. For one thing, I'm not sure what you're talking about, and second, I can't talk about it." Chuck said. "But can I ask you why you think our work at Argon is opening doorways?"

Annie sighed and looked down at the floor. She was afraid he'd ask that question and wasn't sure how she was going to explain why she thinks he has anything to do with portals being open.

Edith could see that Annie was stumped and decided it was her turn to jump in.

"Chuck, it's important that you share with us anything that you know about why portals are being opened. Your Lab is creating doorways to other dimensions and all kinds of terrible things can come through…And will. There will be tremendous chaos and destruction if we don't close them, but we need to know why they're being opened." Edith explained. She looked Chuck in the eye to convey that this was an urgent matter and that many lives depended upon it.

"Chuck, we respect that you are sworn to secrecy, but your Lab is doing tremendous harm to the community, possibly the world and they don't even realize it. Please, we have to work together on this." Annie pleaded.

Cheryl looked at her husband with tears in her eyes. "Please Chuck. Classified government projects be damned! This is our Son we're talking about!"

Chuck took a deep breath and looked out the window toward the airstrip just beyond the back yard. A Cessna was coming in for a landing and he envisioned the plane vanishing into a portal. There was so much out there that people didn't understand and it was his job as a scientist to research and explain these phenomena. Chuck had top security clearance at the Argon facility and it was important to him to keep the oath he took about confidentiality, but what about the oath he took to his Family? His Son was lost somewhere and he needed others to help him get Joey back. It was only fair that he do his part and if he could provide information that would help bring his Son back then he had to do it.

He sat down at the table, folded his hands together and brought them up to his chin. Then he looked up and said: "Ok. I'll tell you everything I know, but you HAVE TO promise me that you all will keep this to yourselves. This is highly classified information and I can get fired for this, but I have to get Joey back and I will need your help too. Can you all promise me that?"

"Yes, of course!" Edith, Annie, and Cheryl said almost in unison. They were relieved to hear that he was being reasonable about this.

"Ok. We *are* doing some research on the existence of parallel dimensions and time travel. BUT, I am not overseeing the project so there is very little that I know about how the experiments that are being conducted." Chuck turned to look at Edith. "I do know that there are naturally occurring portals all over the planet, and that we were able to open one in the Lab on our own, but I am unsure if the portal that Joey went through is one that we created or not. I have not been back to the Lab since Joey went missing."

Edith took a deep cleansing breath and opened herself to hear messages from the Dead who were now in the room with her. *'They have brought forth evil entities through their portal. They do not know what they have done.'* Edith's blood ran backwards. This is exactly what Auset had told them. Chuck's colleagues had no idea what they were dealing with and they were in danger. "Chuck, you have to return to work and find out *why* they are opening portals." Edith said.

"I just told you that they are researching the existence of a parallel dimension. That's why they're doing it. First to see if they can, and second to see if time travel is possible through the portal. But, like I said. I am not overseeing the project. They only come to me when they need validation of the precise composition of subatomic energy particles they've captured from a vortex." Chuck could tell that he lost them with that last comment. He needed to keep it simple or it would be too much like talking to someone in Mandarin Chinese who didn't understand Mandarin Chinese.

"I have no idea what you just said, but we're going to need you to go back to work and find out exactly what they've done. Can you do that?" Annie asked. She didn't fully understand what Chuck was talking about and didn't feel that she really needed to. What they needed to know was whether his co-workers in the Lab fully understood what they were doing and if they had seen any entities come through it.

Chuck looked at Cheryl. He could see the desperation in her eyes and there wasn't anything he wouldn't do for her and his Family. "I will go back to work tomorrow and find out whatever I can." He said.

"Good." Annie said. "We'll talk tomorrow then."

Annie and Edith gave them both hugs good-bye and reassured Cheryl that everything was going to be okay. As they walked across the street to Annie's house, they could hear shouting and laughter coming from the back yard which was in sharp contrast to the sounds they just heard inside the Frasier's household. As they walked up the driveway past the house, there was Mark playing volley ball with Vince, Beth, and Lily.

"I guess we own a volley ball net now." Annie said.

"Yes you do!" Edith replied. "How fun!"

"Hi Momma!" Lily said gleefully. "We're playing volley ball and Daddy and I are winning!"

Mark was a good man. He knew that Beth needed a day of fun to distract her and he seemed to have accomplished just that. Annie had not seen her smile in well over a week and he managed to make that happen. "Hey let's take a break for a minute. I want to talk to Mom." Mark said.

Vince went under the net to the opposite side so that he and Beth could continue to hit the ball back and forth, while Lily and Mark went to see how the conversation at the Frasier's went.

They went up on the deck and took a seat on the patio furniture, while Mark went into the kitchen to get something to drink.

"Hi Mrs. MacKenzie. It's good to see you." Lily said.

"It's good to see you too Lily. Have you been practicing your Tai Chi?" Edith asked. "Yes I have. But I didn't do it on the 4th of July. I kinda took a little break." Lily replied.

Mark returned to the table and sat down. "Well? Did Chuck tell you anything?" He asked.

"He didn't know very much. He says that he knows that they are doing research on parallel dimensions and time travel but he doesn't know much because he's not directly involved in the project. He's just sort of a guy who verifies their particle compositions or something to that effect." Annie explained.

"He is returning to work tomorrow so that he can find out more." Edith added. "They have accidentally brought an entity through and they just don't realize what they've brought into our world."

Lily got very quiet. "We need to go see Auset. She's telling me we have to go see her tomorrow..."

CHAPTER 26

As Dr. Charles Frasier drove up to the gate to the Laboratory, the security guard stepped out of the guard house to check his badge as he always did. "Good morning Dr. Frasier." The guard said.

"Good morning Stan. How are you today?" Chuck asked.

"Fine sir, thank you for asking." The guard said. "And, how are *you* Dr. Frasier? I'm surprised to see you back at work so soon after…Well, I'm just surprised to see you sir."

"Thank you Stan, I appreciate that. It's been difficult but I need to keep busy, you know? Too much time sitting at home can really get to you after a while." Chuck said.

The guard nodded and went back into the guard house to press the button that raised the gate. Chuck drove through and went around the building to the back entrance where he usually parked. Only a few people had a badge that would open the back door, and Chuck was one of them. He swiped his badge through the magnetic slot and the door clicked, then he grabbed the knob and pulled the heavy steel door open. He walked down the long well-lit corridor and turned left down another hallway that led to his office. Along the way he passed the office of John McMillan who was writing in a log book and looked up just in time to see Chuck passing by. "Chuck? Is that you?" He said as he stood up and walked around his desk.

"Hi John. Yeah, it's me. How are you?" Chuck asked.

"I'm fine Chuck. I'm just surprised to see you back." John wasn't sure what he should say. He could not imagine what it would be like to lose a child.

"I just had to get out of the house. The walls were starting to cave in. I need to keep busy." Chuck said.

"Yeah, sure. I understand. I'd probably be doing the same thing." John said. "Hey, we're making some progress on the PDTT project and there's some data I think that Lenny wants us to verify. I took a look at it but I'd like your opinion before I submit my report."

"Of course, yeah, ahh, let me put my stuff down and grab some coffee and I'll be right back." Chuck said.

Chuck set his briefcase down on his desk and went down the hall to the break room to grab a cup of coffee. There, standing in front of the coffee pot waiting for it to finish brewing, was Lt. Col. Leonard Kawalski. Lenny was the Parallel Dimension Time Travel (PDTT) project manager. He was a very intense sort of character who was determined to make a name for himself and was always seeking recognition for everything that was ever successfully done at Argon. He was a disciplined retired Lieutenant Colonel in the U.S. Airforce and everyone feared him, but respected him.

"Good morning Lenny." Chuck said as he retrieved a ceramic coffee cup out of the upper cabinet.

"Chuck? What are you doing here? I thought you'd be taking a longer leave of absence. How are you doing?" Lenny asked. He was surprised to see Chuck Frasier back at work, but was also very glad that he was.

"I'm hanging in there. Just needed to get back to normal a little bit I guess. I kind of missed this place." Chuck said as he managed to smile a little albeit very forced.

Lenny patted him on the shoulder. "I'm very sorry to hear about your Son. Please let me know if there's anything I can do for you." He said sympathetically.

Bingo! A perfect opportunity had just presented itself and Chuck wasn't about to pass it up. "Thank you Lenny. Actually, there is something you can do for me Lenny. I really need to keep busy, you know? I'm wondering if you might consider bringing me in a little more on the PDTT project. I need to throw myself into something to keep myself distracted…The data looks very compelling and I would love to become more involved." Chuck said.

Lenny raised one eyebrow as he thought about the proposition. "Actually Chuck, I could use another man on the job. We've made significant progress recently and I could use someone with your expertise to help me advance the project to the next phase." Lenny extended his hand to Chuck. "Welcome aboard." He said. "Why don't you come into the Lab room at 9:00 for the briefing and we'll bring you up to speed."

"I'll be there." Chuck said as he poured a cup of coffee.

Lily awoke with a gasp. She was completely open and had been visited by the Dead all night long, but there was one visitor who dominated her consciousness: Auset. She had visited Lily in her dreams and shared with her the vision of the death and destruction that was to come. The portals had to be closed and sealed and it had to be done soon. The evil that poured out through the doorways was like a deadly plague. Shadow People, grotesque Cryptids, and even Demons. They were feeding off of the fear of human beings and sucked the life force out of them. Their souls were what they wanted to take possession of and they had to be stopped. Auset also revealed to Lily what her higher purpose was and what her gifts actually were. With that revelation, Auset wrapped Lily in Divine white light and shielded her. She gave Lily a small glimpse of the immense army of Angels who were there to do battle on behalf of her and all of Humankind. Lily had much to learn in a very short period of time.

She got out of bed and got dressed after a quick visit to the bathroom. She could hear her Mother downstairs making breakfast. She went downstairs to find Winnie sitting next to her chair, waiting for Lily to sit and eat her breakfast and share a bite or two with her under the table as she usually did.

"Morning Momma." Lily said.

"Hi Sweetie. Did you sleep well? I'm making your favorite—Blueberry pancakes." Annie said as she flipped the first one over to expose a perfect golden brown color.

"Thank you Mom." Lily said as she opened the refrigerator door to get some milk. "Is Vince awake yet?"

Annie turned to give Lily that 'you've got to be kidding me' look. "It's way too early for Vince. It's only 8:30. I don't expect to see him until at least 10:00, so it's just you and me for breakfast kiddo." Annie said as she put a pat of butter on Lily's short stack of pancakes and set it on the table. "Here's your syrup. I trust that you won't put too much on. You can always add more if you need it. We don't want to waste it." She said.

Annie had a good handle on preventing wastefulness in the house. Mark worked very hard to provide for them and Annie took nothing for granted. She never bought more than they needed and used every last drop before buying more of something. She made sure that nothing went to waste and she was trying to teach the kids to be mindful of that as well.

As usual, Lily's fingers and her fork were all sticky before she could take a third bite. No matter how careful she was with the syrup, everything she touched was sticky. She quietly dropped her hands under the table so Winnie could lick the syrup off of them. It was Winnie's little job and she did it quite dutifully. After a thorough finger licking, Lily finished her breakfast and took her plate to the sink.

"Mom, I'm going outside to do Tai Chi. Do you want to do it with me?" Lily asked.

"Sure honey. Just let me finish cleaning up here and I'll be right there." Annie put the dirty dishes in the dishwasher, put plastic wrap over the remaining pancake batter and put it in the refrigerator. Winnie followed Lily outside where she stood in the usual Tai Chi spot and waited for Annie to join her.

When they were finished with their exercise, they sat down in the grass and talked for a while. Lily shared what Auset revealed to her in her dream and what she indicated that Lily's gifts would evolve into. Annie sat quietly. It was a lot to take in for an adult let alone a soon to be 7 year old.

"Lily, I've always known you were an old soul but I never imagined any of this." Annie finally said. "Do you still think that we need to go see Auset today?"

Lily pondered that question for a moment. Yesterday she thought that they should, but Auset came to her in her dreams and revealed so much she didn't think they needed to. "I don't think we need to today Momma. We can't do anything for Joey until the New Moon and she is going to help us with that. There's nothing more that she needs to tell us until then." Lily said.

"Hmm." Annie said. "I guess we need to see what Chuck finds out about the portals too. I'm sure she already knows though…She seems to know everything anyway."

Lilly giggled at that. Auset did know everything but she also understood why Auset wanted all of them to do their own investigative work. All of a sudden, Lily said something out loud that Annie thought was bizarrely off topic.

"In the refrigerator next to the milk in the red bowl." Lily said.

"What?" Annie was slightly confused by what Lily just said.

Lily laughed. "Sorry Momma. I'm talking to Vince. He's looking for the pancake batter."

That took Annie by surprise. One, because it was still too early for Vince to be up, and two, how could Lily know that he was up and looking for pancake batter and how could Vince possibly hear what Lily said from out here?

"Your welcome." Lily said.

Annie stood up and looked toward the house. There, in the kitchen window, was Vince. Waiving at her with a spatula in his hand. "What the heck?" Annie said as she walked quickly toward the house with Lily and Winnie following closely behind.

"Good morning Honey. I didn't expect to see you this early…Oh good. You found the pancake batter." Annie said as she looked down at Lily who was giggling.

"Sure did! Thanks Lil." Vince said as winked at his younger sister.

"Momma, Vince is also a Telepath. I knew he was, he just had to open to it." Lily said.

"You kids. Wow." Annie said as she sat down in her kitchen chair. "Well, this is going to make things around here a whole lot more interesting. Does anyone else know about this?" She asked.

"You're the first!" Vince said as he flipped his giant pancake that took up almost the entire surface of the pan.

"Well, I suppose that will be very helpful…In some ways." Annie was a bit overwhelmed by this news. She wondered if Stephen also had abilities that she wasn't aware of.

Vince plated his giant pancake, slathered it in butter and syrup, and sat at the table to eat. "Great pancake batter Mom. I actually think it's better if it sits in the fridge for an hour or two before you cook it. The pancakes turn out fluffier." Vince said.

"Well I'll remember that next time I decide to make pancakes." Annie said. "Hey, I'd like to take you two shopping for some school clothes today. What do you say?"

"Where to?" Vince asked.

"I was thinking Yorktown Mall. We can get everything done in one trip. We'll be done in no time." Annie said.

"Ok." Vince said with a mouthful of blueberry pancakes.

"Yeah! That sounds good Mom. I like Yorktown." Lily said.

"Can we ask Beth to come too?" Vince asked.

Annie thought about that for a moment. That might be a nice thing to do with Cheryl too. Cheryl hasn't stepped foot out of the house in two weeks and that might be the perfect thing for her. "I think that is a terrific idea. I'll see if Cheryl wants to come along too. You finish your breakfast and get dressed. I'm going to walk over and see if they want to come with us."

Annie walked across the street and knocked on the Frasier's front door. All the blinds were drawn again, which wasn't a good sign. She knocked a second time before Beth opened the door.

"Hi Beth. How are you?" Annie asked.

"I'm ok. Would you like to come in?" Beth said as she opened the door wider to let Annie in.

"Where's your Mom?" Annie asked.

"She's in the kitchen." Beth closed the door behind Annie and followed her down the hall to the kitchen.

"Hi Cheryl, how are you doing?" Annie said. Cheryl was dressed and washing the coffee pot in the sink. The kitchen was spotless indicating that she was throwing herself into cleaning the house, which was good. Last time she saw her she looked sad, tired and disheveled. It was nice to see her doing ordinary things again.

"Oh hello Annie. I'm just tidying up. I've been sitting around so much that things were looking pretty bad around here and I couldn't stand it anymore. What brings you by?" Cheryl asked in a much more cheerful voice than Annie had heard in a while.

"Well, I was going to go to Yorktown Mall to do some school shopping with Vince and Lily and we thought you and Beth might like to join us." Annie said. She looked over at Beth to see what she thought and Beth looked pleased about the proposal.

"Thank you Annie. That sounds nice." Cheryl said as she looked at her Daughter. "What do you think Beth, should we get out of the house for a little while?"

Beth smiled. "That sounds great. I would like that Mom." She said.

"Terrific! I've got the Suburban today so we can all drive together." Annie said.

"Let me grab my purse and lock up and we'll meet you in the driveway." Cheryl said. She sounded a lot more chipper than she had a few days before and Annie was very glad she thought to ask them to go shopping.

Several hours later, Annie, Cheryl and the kids returned back home with shopping bags full of stuff. Everyone got the essentials needed for school—Jeans, shirts, socks, school shoes and gym shoes for P.E. Annie made sure that they made a day of it to keep Cheryl and Beth out doing something other than sitting at home in a dark house. Cheryl had a brief weepy moment at the mall feeling bad about not buying anything for Joey, but Annie quickly reminded her that he would be back in a couple of weeks and Cheryl could take him shopping when he got back. She would want to spend some good one-on-one time with him and that would be another thing they could do together.

When they arrived back home, the three kids jumped out of the car and carried their bags inside their houses, then came right back out and headed toward the trampoline. Cheryl and Annie lingered in the driveway and talked a little longer.

"I know that sitting home and waiting for something to happen isn't good. Thank you for inviting us out today Annie. Beth and I really needed that." Cheryl said.

"My pleasure Cheryl. What are friends for?" Annie said.

Cheryl sighed. "I can't say that it hasn't been pure Hell, but it's different this time with Joey. I have hope that he'll come back to us…I never had that hope when we lost Jon-Jon."

"I'm so sorry for your loss Cheryl." Annie said not knowing what else to say. The loss of a child was unimaginable to her and she thought she needn't say anything more than that.

Cheryl looked up at Annie and shared a little more. "You know? I carried so much guilt with me for SO Long because I blamed myself." Tears started to well up in her eyes as she spoke. "I'm so thankful that Lily was able to tell me the truth about what really happened."

"Yes, Lily has a true gift. I'm glad she was able share that with you." Annie said.

"She truly does. Who does she get that from? Are either of your Boys gifted?" Cheryl asked a very good question.

"Actually? Yes. Vince is also a sensitive, and, we just found out this morning that he's also a Telepath. Let's hope my kids don't decide to gang up on me! I'll be in trouble!" Annie laughed.

"A Telepath? I'm not sure I know what that means. Or what it means to be a sensitive for that matter." Cheryl said.

"A Telepath has the ability to communicate non-verbally with other Telepaths. Lily also has Telepathic abilities, so the two of them can talk without saying a word. They were doing it this morning." Annie explained. "…And I have a feeling it's going to drive me nuts!" She laughed.

"That's amazing! Where does that come from? Is Mark Telepathic?" Cheryl asked. She was a maternity nurse and she was always fascinated by how some babies adopted traits and mannerisms from only one parent or sometimes they were a balanced blend of both parents.

"No, neither Mark nor I are Telepathic. My Father had abilities, and that's where we think they get it from. I'm afraid it skipped my generation though." Annie said.

At that moment, Cheryl's garage door went up and Chuck turned into the driveway and pulled his car into the garage. He saw that Cheryl was across the street talking to Annie and decided to walk over.

"Hello Ladies." He said as he grabbed Cheryl with one arm and gave her a kiss. "I'm happy to see you outside. And you've been shopping I see." He said to Cheryl.

"Don't get too curious. We just went school shopping for the kids. I bought nothing for myself." Cheryl said.

"Hmm. That's too bad." Chuck said. It was nice to see them interact in a loving way rather than in the crippling devastated manner that they have been recently.

"How was work today Chuck? Did you find out anything interesting?" Annie asked. She didn't mean to spoil the flirt that was going on, but she needed to know what was really going on in that Lab.

Chuck stood up straight and shared his news. "Actually, I did. I got myself on the PDTT team and off the advisory panel…And you were right Annie— They opened a portal and something very, very strange came through."

CHAPTER 27

JULY 29, 1970

There were only three days left to go before the night of the New Moon. This is the window when it would be possible for Joey Frasier to return home from wherever he had been for the last few weeks. Lily had been visited frequently by Auset in her dreams. She had been shown what would happen to this world if the portals were left open, and she had also been shown her special gifts, but Lily did not know how or when she would need to use them. Auset summoned Lily to visit her in the daytime when she woke.

Edith had also been visited by Auset in her dreams. She was also shown the chaos and destruction of the Earth if the portals remained open and told that they must be located and sealed. Edith knew how to seal the portals, she did it successfully many times in her life. This would be Edith's primary role to assist Auset. Upon waking, Edith felt compelled to go and visit her. She knew that Auset would give her further instruction about what she must do to assist with Joey's return, and then seal the open portals. She got dressed and headed over to see Annie and Lily. There was much to do today.

Annie sat at the kitchen table drinking her coffee and reading the paper. Lily came down the stairs and Winnie followed her. Winnie did the fully body wiggle at the sight of Annie. "Good morning Lil." Annie said.

"Morning Momma." Lily rubbed her sleepy eyes and yawned. "Is there breakfast?"

"There's always breakfast. What would you like this morning?" Annie asked. Usually Lily was a little more awake in the morning when she was ready to eat. "You look really tired Honey. Didn't you sleep well last night?"

Lily recalled the visit by Auset, which was extremely vivid, but also all of the Dead who visited her all night long. "No, not really. I'm 'zausted." Lily said as she slumped in her chair at the table. "Could I have scrambled eggs this morning?"

"Sure Honey. I'll make you some." Annie got up and opened the refrigerator to get some eggs. "Would you like some orange juice?" She asked.

"Yes please." Lily replied. "Thank you Momma."

Annie poured her a glass of juice and put it on the table in front of her, then walked back to the kitchen to scramble some eggs. "Did you help cross over too many people? Is that why you didn't sleep?"

"Yeah, there were a lot who needed help." Lilly said as she took a sip of her juice. "But it was Auset who kept me awake most of the night." She admitted.

Annie nearly dropped the bowl she was scrambling the eggs in. "I'm sorry, did you say *Auset* kept you awake?" Annie was a little annoyed that Auset was visiting Lily at night. Auset was a higher celestial being and all, but she would have preferred it if Auset communicated with her in a normal setting during the day. Lily was a small child and she needed her rest.

"She wants us to go visit her today. She has more to tell us about Joey." Lily said.

Annie finished making her eggs and was cleaning up the pan when the doorbell rang. She dried her hands with a towel and went to answer the front door. It was Edith.

"Good morning Annie. I'm sorry I didn't call first, I hope I'm not intruding." Edith said.

"No, not at all. Come in Edith." Annie said. Edith looked a little like Lily in that she looked like she hadn't slept much all night. "Would you like some coffee?"

"Oh that sounds wonderful. Yes, I'd love some." Edith said as she followed Annie into the kitchen. "Good morning Miss Lily. How are you today?" When Lily turned around, they both started laughing because they both looked terribly tired and they both knew why.

"Hi Mrs. MacKenzie. You didn't sleep either!" Lily giggled.

"Not a wink! There is a lot going on." Edith said. Annie set a cup of hot coffee down next to Edith and sat down on the other side of the table.

"Can I make you some eggs Edith?" Annie asked.

"Oh no dear. Coffee is fine, thank you." Edith said.

"So, I assume Auset visited you in your dreams too?" Annie asked.

"She did." Edith said as she took a sip of coffee. "We need to go see her today. She has more to tell us."

"That's what Lily said too." Annie replied. "Chuck Frasier also managed to get himself added to the research team that is creating the portals. He says they've opened one inside the facility and something very strange came through."

"Oh? What came through?" Edith was curious to know more about what came through. There were countless types of interdimensional beings that have the ability to manifest in countless different ways. She was curious if it was an entity that she had encountered before.

"He said that he hasn't seen anything himself, but that it was only described to him as an '*Ultraterrestrial*' being…Whatever that means." Annie said as she took another sip of her coffee. She glanced over at Lily who had just finished her plate of scrambled eggs and was tipping back the last little bit of juice in her glass. "He said that they were setting up a new camera system in the lab so that they could monitor it 24 hours a day from a different room. It seems that they haven't been able to interact with it yet and they are still observing until they understand more about what it is and where it came from." She explained.

"So they have this ultraterrestrial being contained?" Edith thought that this was interesting since things that came through portals were able to transport themselves anywhere. Containment sounded a little fishy to her.

"I'm not sure. Chuck is still trying to understand it himself. He hasn't seen it yet." Annie said.

"Well, we'll figure that out in due time. Right now we need to prepare for Joey Frasier's return. The New Moon is only three days away." Edith said.

"Right." Annie agreed. "Lil? Why don't you go upstairs and brush your teeth and get dressed."

Annie also dismissed herself and went upstairs to take a quick shower and get dressed while Edith waited in the kitchen with her coffee and the newspaper. Annie thought about what Chuck had said about the ultraterrestrial and that they were still observing it. She thought about Joey and wondered what kind of strange beings he might have encountered wherever he was. Did he go back in time? If so, where did he go and what time period was it? Or, could he have gone to the future? Annie had a million questions but realized that there were plenty of experienced experts who were working to bring Joey home so she didn't need to figure it out all by herself. She threw on a pair of faded jean shorts and a T-shirt, and pulled her hair back into a pony tail. This was her usual attire during the Summer. Then she paused for a moment wondering if she should dress a little better to go see Auset…She was after all, a higher being. After a few seconds of contemplation, she decided that she would not change her clothes but would dress it up a little instead with her brown leather sandals rather than tennis shoes or flip flops. At least the T-Shirt had a nice finished trim around the neck and sleeves and it didn't have a print of the Rolling Stones or Jimmy Hendrix on it.

When Annie came down the stairs, Lily was sitting with Edith chatting. They were comparing notes about their dreams with Auset and didn't seem to be the least bit surprised that the dreams were virtually identical. There were a few blanks that needed to be filled in though, and the only way to do that was to go see Auset together. Both Edith and Lily instinctively knew that they were both to play a very important role in the return of Joey Frasier. They were ready. It was time to visit Auset to make the mission clear.

"Ready to go?" Annie said as she came down the stairs and picked up her purse from the small desk area in the corner of the kitchen.

"Indeed we are." Edith said as she winked at Lily.

Annie paused for a moment. "I do feel like we need to call her first...You know, just to let her know we're coming." She said.

Lily and Edith giggled. "Oh, she already knows Momma." Lily said.

"Probably so." Annie said. She hadn't considered the telepathic construct of the Psychic Mediums in the room and the Diving Being who they were about to visit. "Edith? Would you like to drive or shall I?" She asked.

"I can drive. I'm parked behind you anyway." Edith paused for a moment. "Besides, Patsy doesn't know my car."

Patsy. Crapola! Annie didn't have a chance to talk to her since they visited Auset the last time when she saw Patsy looking out the window as they were leaving. They got away with it once, but she highly doubted that she would be able to get away with it a second time. "I kinda think she might figure it out." Annie said. Still, Edith's car was less obvious than Annie's Toronado so they decided that they should take Edith's car.

As they pulled up to the large white house, Annie felt a wave of intimidation come over her. She was the only one who did not have psychic abilities and this was a very important meeting they were about to have. This was when they would receive their specific instructions about how to bring Joey back and she was feeling a bit inadequate compared to Edith and Lily. All of a sudden, Lily sat forward on the back seat so that she could put her arm around her Mother's shoulders. "It's alright Momma. You have an important role to play in this too." Lily said. She knew what Annie was thinking and that was the best thing that Annie could hear at that moment. She put her hand on Lily's and turned and smiled at her.

They walked up the paved sidewalk to the front door and rang the doorbell. "It has such a pleasant chime sound. Almost like church bells." Edith said as she winked at Annie.

Seconds later, Auset appeared in the doorway and invited them in. Annie felt terrible showing up unannounced and empty handed, but Lily squeezed her hand reassuring her that it was unnecessary. This was not a social call.

Auset led them back to the same room with the tall turret windows and the same four wing back chairs arranged around the round marble table. On the table was the same tea set with four cups and a plate of sugared nuts and dried fruits. "Please sit." She said as she poured the tea.

"Miss Auset? Is that the yummy apple tea we had last time?" Lily asked. She loved it and hoped that it was.

"Yes Lily. I knew that you liked it so I made it again." Auset said as she smiled radiantly at the little girl.

After pouring four cups of apple tea, Auset sat down and took a few seconds to regard each one of them by making uninterrupted direct eye contact, one by one, for a few seconds each.

"The New Moon comes in three days' time. The boy will return unharmed." Auset began. "But we must prepare. It cannot be done without elements of this realm, unconditional love, and a retriever."

A retriever? Annie was not sure what she meant by that. Did she mean a dog? A Golden Retriever or a Labrador Retriever? And what were the '*elements of this realm?*' Annie glanced over at Edith who seemed to understand exactly what Auset was saying, so she decided to keep quiet and not ask any questions.

"The retriever should be strong and unafraid." Auset continued. "It cannot be a relative of the boy. The boy's Family must remain in this realm. They are the unconditional love force needed to pull and stabilize the boy's energy."

Edith knew exactly what she was describing. It needed to be a strong male figure who was not related to Joey. Someone who did not fear the unexplained. Her thoughts went Ed. He had grown up around the paranormal all of his life and was somewhat numbed to it. He would not be afraid to walk through the portal, and would trust that Edith would know what to do to bring him back if anything went wrong. He was a big, strong man and would be perfect for this role. "I have a retriever." Edith told her.

Annie was thinking of Mark, but she hadn't discussed that possibility with him because it was not proposed until now. She felt that Mark was a big, strong man who could swoop in and bring Joey back. She wasn't sure how he felt about it, but he was the first person who came to mind. She wondered if Edith was thinking the same thing.

"Auset?" Lily asked. "Who holds the elements?"

Annie was surprised that Lily seemed to know what Auset meant by '*elements*' and that someone had to hold them.

"Forgive me, but, what are the elements?" Annie asked. She was going to remain quiet but she couldn't help herself.

Auset turned her attention to Annie and smiled. "Of course." She said. "The elements are physical properties of this realm. Physical things that can be held in the human hand. They serve as protection and grounding to this realm." She explained.

"Ohhhh." Annie said, even though she had no idea what any of that meant.

"You will need pure Silver for the unconditional love. You will need Iron, Black Tourmaline, Blue Calcite, Quartz, and Moldavite for the retriever, and you will need religious talismans, Black Tourmaline, Selenite and candles for those around the unconditional love." Auset said as Edith nodded in agreement.

"I'm sorry, why do we need those things? What do they do?" Annie couldn't help herself. She needed to know why all of this was necessary.

Auset sat back in her wing backed chair and looked at Annie with a caring look that had an undeniable radiant glow. "Silver vibrates to the Moon. It enhances the awakening of tender affections that are untinged with self-interest. It is the pulling force. Joey's Parents should hold Silver in their hands. The Iron furnishes Humans with energy, courage, resistance, forcefulness, and aggressiveness. The Black Tourmaline protects from negative energies who might interfere. The Blue Calcite enables free movement into the astral plane and Quartz eases their travel. Moldavite is not from this world—it will allow safe passage." Auset explained with a calm, reassuring tone.

"I see." Annie said. This was all so new to her, but she was starting to see that there was some cosmic logic being applied and it made a little more sense.

"I know what to do." Edith said.

"So do I." Said Lily.

Wait, what? Lilly knows what to do? How? Annie thought. Lily was her Daughter and sometimes she had a difficult time not seeing her as anything other than a sweet little girl, but Lily was different and she had to remind herself of that.

Auset looked over at Edith and said: "After the boy and the retriever return through the doorway, you must seal it. For it is one of the doorways that the Government men opened without knowing they did so."

Edith nodded in agreement. This was her primary role in this mission and she took it very seriously. "How much time will pass before they return?" Edith asked.

"Not long." Auset said. "The boy will be near the doorway on the other side. He will not be hard to find. Heru will guide him at the appointed time."

Auset stood up indicating that the meeting was over, and as before, Lily and Edith stood up with her and Annie remained seated for a moment not realizing that the meeting was over. As they walked to the front door, they thanked Auset for her time and advice.

"Auset, will you be with us on the night of the New Moon?" Annie asked.

"Not as I am today." She said. "But I will be all around you."

"Um, could I ask one more question?" Annie said as Auset opened the front door to show them out. "You are clearly more powerful than any of us. Why couldn't you help us by bringing Joey back? Why do you need us less powerful Human Beings to do it?" Annie thought this was a very obvious question that deserved an answer.

Auset looked at her and smiled. "Because Human Beings have free will."

CHAPTER 28

It was late at Argon National Laboratory and Bill Wilcox settled in for his shift to monitor Laboratory 2C. He listened to Rod Serling's *The Twilight Zone* on his transistor radio in the small confined closet sized room where the monitor equipment had been set up. He used to be one of the security guards who walked the parking lot at night, but the Winters were bitter cold, the Summers were hot, humid and sticky, and the rain was miserable no matter how much waterproof clothing you had on. When the new position for a Night Shift Lab Monitor was posted, he applied for it immediately. His hours were the same, but the working conditions were much better. At least he'd be dry and would be able to work in an environment without extreme temperature variations.

Bill heard the sound of heavy footsteps coming down the hall toward him, and he rolled his chair backwards just enough to be able to peek out the doorway and down the hall in the direction that the sound was coming from. "Oh, it's you." Bill said. "Coming in for a piss Artie?"

"Yep. That coffee is moving through me like a hurricane in the Caribbean." Artie the outside Security Guard said. "I'd love to chat but nature calls in a big way." He cut the conversation short and hurried off to the Men's bathroom.

A few minutes later, Artie stuck his head in to the small room that was now Bill's nighttime post. "What choo doin' in here Billy? You got all kinds of surveillance equipment, huh?" Artie said.

"Yeah, this is all new. They're doing something in 2C that requires 24/7 monitoring for some reason. I have no idea what I'm supposed to be looking for. Nothin' going on in there. It's just an empty lab room." Bill said. "But at least I don't have to be outside all night in the rain."

"Ahh, that ain't nothin'. You just dress for it. I like the fresh air myself." Artie said.

"How's the new guy working out?" Bill asked. He was referring to the new Security Guard who took his old job.

"He's alright. He keeps talking about how he thinks his wife is cheatin' and such. I just hope I don't have to be hearin' about that every night." Artie said.

"Sorry 'bout that Buddy. I miss working with you out there I just don't miss the weather." Bill said. "You can always come in and talk to me on your breaks."

"I just might take you up on that." Artie said. "Well, I've got to get back out there. Have a good one." He tipped his hat and walked back down the hall to the big steel exit door to go back to his post outside.

"You too." Bill said as he rolled his chair back to the Formica covered ledge that was mounted on the wall in the small room. His show was over on the radio and there wasn't much to listen to after that, so he pulled a book out of his bag and decided to read a little. *The Godfather* was a new Fiction book that came out earlier in the year and he hadn't read it yet. When he was patrolling outside, there wasn't any light to read. He made it a point not let the book distract him from the monitors too much so he would look up after he read a paragraph to check the monitors. There wasn't anything going on in there anyway, and if he stared at a grainy monitor all night, he just might go crazy. He could read and watch for whatever he was supposed to be looking out for at the same time.

The hours passed and the evening of surveillance proved uneventful. It was a few minutes after 3:00 am and Bill needed a bathroom break, so he left the room for a few minutes. When he returned, there was a red light flashing on the control board indicating that there was a problem with one of the cameras. There were four screens to watch, one for each camera mounted in each corner of the lab. The monitor that faced the South East corner was black. "What the Hell?" Bill mumbled to himself. "I guess we've got a camera out." Not sure what he was supposed to do about this, he reached for the control room manual to see if there was a protocol for failed equipment. Other than '*Write up a work ticket and call a technician*' it didn't say much.

Apparently they didn't want him troubleshooting the problem or messing with the equipment. Who was he going to call at 3 am in the morning? He didn't think that failed equipment qualified as an emergency to have to call Lieutenant Colonel Kawalski at home, so he decided to go down to the Lab and take a look. Maybe it was something easy to fix like pushing a reset button or something. There was just one problem: He didn't have a key to Lab 2C.

In fact, it was his first week on the job and he didn't have any keys other than his pass to open the back door and the key to the surveillance room where he was sitting all night. He thought about this for a while and decided that there were three other cameras in the Lab that covered most of the area to watch over. There wasn't anything going on in there previously, it was just an empty room. If anyone had broken in the alarms would sound and Artie would have come bursting in to warn him of the breech.

A short while later, the North East camera went out. The corresponding monitor to that camera went completely black and another red light began flashing on the control board. "Son of a Bitch!" Bill said to himself. One camera was an inconvenience. A small technical glitch that didn't require sounding the alarms, but two cameras? Bill picked up the phone and called the Guard House at the front gate. "Ahh, yeah, this is Bill Wilcox in the Surveillance room. I have an issue here and I need someone with a key to Laboratory 2C."

Martin Reese showed up a few minutes later with a large jailhouse type key ring and offered to go inspect the Lab in question. "Which lab is it?" Martin asked as he looked at the grainy images of an empty lab room on the remaining two monitors.

"It's 2C. The South East camera went out first, then the North East camera went out about 10 minutes later. I'm hoping there's a reset button on the back of the cameras. Easy fix." Bill said.

"Huh. Ok, you want to come down there with me? I've got the key." Martin said.

"Yeah sure." Bill said. At first he didn't know if he should leave his post, but this seemed like a good reason to if there was one. Besides, he would be down there in person and if there was anything going on, he'd see it for himself. The monitors didn't offer a very clear picture anyway.

The two men got into the elevator and went down to the basement where the Laboratories were located. Lab 2C was the largest, and it was located in the far corner of the facility which took a couple of minutes to get to. Martin fumbled with the large key ring that contained over 50 keys on it until he found the key with *2C* stamped on it. He put the key in the door and turned the knob. He opened the door slowly. It was completely silent in there. He stepped in and flipped the light switch on and several fluorescent lightbulbs buzzed and came to life illuminating the sterile white lab. Bill walked over to the South East camera and pulled the rolling ladder over so that he could climb up and take a look. There was no reset button anywhere on it that he could see, and everything seemed to be plugged in properly. He climbed back down and pushed the ladder over to the North East camera. Same thing—no reset button and everything seemed to be securely plugged in.

"Huh." Bill said as he turned to look at Martin. "Everything looks okay from here." He looked around the room to see what was so important that he had to keep watch all night. There was plenty of large equipment and he wasn't really sure what it was called or what it was for. There were a few tables and rolling stools, and a few other scientific instruments. There were no animal cages or fish tanks that one might expect to see in a scientific laboratory. *What was so important that had to be watched all night?* Bill thought to himself.

"Everything looks okay in here. No signs of a break-in." Martin said. "You ready? I need to lock this back up."

"Yeah. We're good. Let's go." Bill said.

As he followed Martin to the door, the hairs stood up on the back of his neck and he got a cold chill all of a sudden. He turned around quickly, but saw nothing. He had a terrible uneasy feeling and he wanted to get out of there as fast as he could. He was being watched.

CHAPTER 29

AUGUST 1, 1970—THE NIGHT OF THE NEW MOON

This was the night everyone had been waiting for—the night when Joey would return. There was an electric energy in the air and even those less sensitive could feel it. Mark thought that it would be best if Officer Clemmons and Officer Rankin were present. They were the officers on the scene when Joey first went missing, and Officer Clemmons knew and respected Edith, so he understood that strange phenomena existed where Human logic and standard science sometimes did not. Mark was also thinking ahead. If Joey returned, the police have to would be involved anyway and it was best to have them there to witness it for themselves because it would be very difficult to explain to the rest of the police force, not to mention the newspapers and the general public.

"Is Stephen coming with us?" Mark asked. Stephen was trying to get as many hours in at the pizza place as he could before school started so Mark assumed that he would be working.

"Yes actually. He asked for tonight off so he could be there." Annie said. "Don't forget, this is our genius son. This is incredibly interesting to him. He wouldn't miss this for the world."

"Good point." Mark said. "So where is he?"

"He's upstairs with Lily. He's helping her prepare the bags with the crucifixes and pieces of Black Tourmaline and Selenite in them. They'll be down shortly." Annie said as she tidied up the house before all of their guests arrived.

It was about 10:30 pm and Annie, Mark, Lily, Vince, Stephen, Edith, Ed, and Barb were in the kitchen assembling the boxes of items they would need to take with them to the pond to get Joey back. Annie had purchased several pillar candles and was looking for a lighter to throw in the box so they could light them. Edith took care of the retriever's elements and she carefully put a piece of Iron, Black Tourmaline, Blue Calcite, Quartz, and Moldavite into a velvet drawstring bag that Ed would carry with him through the portal to rescue Joey Frasier. Mark had two 1 oz. pure Silver bars that his Father had left him each stamped with the Lady Liberty on them. These would be the Silver that Chuck and Cheryl needed to hold.

"Ed, are you nervous about doing this?" Mark asked. "I would be. You don't exactly know where you're going."

"I know, but that's ok. I just have to go in and grab the boy, then go back through the same way I arrived, right Mom?" Ed said as he looked to Edith for confirmation. He was a little nervous. Anyone would be, but he understood that there are strange phenomena in the world and it was necessary to interact with it sometimes. This was one of those times.

"Joey will not be far from the entrance of the portal. You won't have to go look for him." Edith said. "And it's important that you're holding on to him tightly when you come back through. Don't let go of him." Edith made sure that Ed knew exactly what he needed to do. Edith looked over at Barb, who looked terrified, and gave her a warm, reassuring smile.

"How will he know where the portal is to come back? What if he has to go look for Joey and gets lost? How will he find it again?" Barb was starting to panic. This was all so new and made little sense to her. Ed barely knew what the boy looked like so it seemed odd to her that he was supposed to be the guy to go find him and bring him home.

"Well, the New Moon represents birth and resurrection. One of the reasons why we had to wait until the night of the New Moon is because that's when the portals are open and visible to us. They're slightly illuminated. He won't have any trouble finding it." Edith said as she tried to be as reassuring as she could possibly be. "And we are… in a sense, resurrecting Joey back to life in this realm. It all works together."

The doorbell rang and Vince went to answer it. It was Officer Clemmons, Officer Rankin, and the Frasier's. He welcomed them in and led them to the kitchen where everyone else was.

"The Police Officers and the Frasier's are here." Vince said. He looked over at Beth who also looked just as terrified as Barb had, but he could tell that she was also anxious for her brother to be returned home to them.

"Thank you for coming Officers. We're glad you're going to be there. I know that you'll need to document this in your files. It's best if you see it for yourselves." Edith said to them.

"It's a privilege to work with you again Mrs. MacKenzie. We appreciate the call. We want to help in any way we can." Officer Clemmons said.

"Chuck, Cheryl—we were just running through Ed's mission tonight." Annie said.

"You know, I feel like I should be the person to go through the portal and get him. He is my Son." Chuck said.

Edith turned to him and smiled. "I understand Chuck, but it cannot be you. You, Cheryl, and Beth need to be on this side so that you can pull them back through energetically. Everyone here has a very important role to play tonight." She picked up the two Silver bars and handed one to each of them. "This is pure Silver. You need to hold these in your hands. Silver vibrates to the Moon and it awakens and intensifies your unconditional love for Joey. It is the pulling force he will need to come back through the portal."

Chuck was trying to follow that logic. What he knew about Quantum Physics was all very scientific and mathematical of course, but much of it was also quasi unproven theory as well. Everything had a relationship whether molecularly or energetically. In a sense, he understood exactly what Edith was saying and he had no reason to contradict her theory.

Beth sat on the stairs and pet Winnie. She was feeling a little overwhelmed by everything and this was a night that would either be jubilantly triumphant, or devastatingly catastrophic. There was no way to tell. All she could do was put her faith in Annie, Lily, and Edith because it was the only chance that she would ever see her little brother again. Vince sat down next to Beth and put his arm around her. "Nervous?" He asked.

"A little." Beth said as she put her head down and tried to keep from crying. "I miss my Brother. I hope we can get him back."

"We will. You'll see." Vince reassured her. He looked over at Lily who was staring at them from across the room with a concerned look. Vince asked her telepathically to tell him the truth—'Is this going to work?' Lily nodded her head yes to that question and he smiled. "Everything is going to be alright Beth. You'll see." Vince said as he hugged her. Tears began to roll down her cheeks and Winnie propped herself up on her hind legs and very sweetly licked her tears.

Lily approached Chuck and Cheryl to give them a message. "Mr. and Mrs. Frasier? Jon-Jon is here and he wants me to tell you that he loves you very much and he will be at the pond with us." She said.

Tears welled up in Cheryl's eyes, and she bent down to give Lily a hug. "Thank you Lily. We love Jon-Jon too and we miss him very much." She said.

"He knows." Lily said as she smiled at her neighbor.

Annie looked at the clock in the kitchen. It was almost 11:30 pm. Ed needed to go through the portal at exactly 3 minutes before midnight. "We should walk down to the pond now. We'll need a little time to get set up." She said.

"Rankin and I will drive down in the Cruiser. We'll meet you there." Officer Clemmons said.

Mark grabbed the box of candles and Barb and Annie grabbed the flashlights. They all left the house together and walked down the street four blocks to the pond. Although it was a New Moon, it wasn't nearly as bright as a Full Moon, so the flashlights were helpful. It was a warm, Summer night and the Lightning Bugs were flashing their lights all around them like a well-orchestrated light show. The trees were still. As they approached the pond, they could hear the frogs croaking and an owl was hooting in the tree above the rock formation where the portal was. There was an eerie calmness to everything. It was so surreal.

They walked around the pond to the other side of the rock formation to the cave. Mark set the box of candles down on the ground and began to hand them out to everyone but Ed. Annie followed behind him with the lighter and lit each one. The air was still. Each of the flames burned straight up and did not flicker. Lily followed behind and handed each person a blue velvet bag that contained the Black Tourmaline and Selenite crystals and religious talismans.

Edith looked at her watch. It was 11:50 pm. "Please, can I get everyone to stand in a circle and lock elbows with one another." She said as she stood between Ed and Cheryl. "I'm going to do a guided white light meditation. I'd like all of you to take a couple of deep cleansing breaths and exhale. Close your eyes and try to visualize what I say as I guide you through." She said.

As Edith said her meditation, everyone could easily visualize exactly what she said. You could feel a sudden calmness and overall feeling of safety and wellbeing as she spoke. This put everyone at ease. They had a very important task ahead of them and they were all in sync. Lily could feel that Auset was also there. She was all around them and her protection and goodness filled the air.

After the meditation, Edith walked Ed closer to the rock cave. It was exactly 4 minutes to Midnight. She made sure he was holding the black velvet bag in his hand and gave him exact instructions about what to do. "You will need to run into the portal." Edith said as she pointed to the slightly illuminated oval shaped swirl that was forming inside the cave. There was a slight buzzing sound emanating from it that could now be heard. "You will feel like you are weightless and floating. You will not need run when you get in there. Just relax and let it take you. You also must say Joey's name three times—*Joey Frasier, Joey Frasier, Joey Frasier*. Then you will be brought to the exact space in time where he is." She explained. "Call him to you, hold the boy tight and run back into the portal again." Then she looked Ed in the eye and told him that she was proud of him and that she loved him very much.

Ed hugged Edith tightly and said: "I love you too Mom." As Ed finished his hug and stepped away from Edith to prepare to run into the portal, he glanced back at Barb who had a tear run down her cheek.

All of a sudden, a swift unseen force blew past Ed and he fell to the ground. The velvet bag containing the iron and crystals had been ripped from his hand. Ed raised his head just in time to see Vince run into the portal.

CHAPTER 30

The buzzing sound became louder and Vince found himself being pulled faster and faster through an illuminated tunnel that was the most amazing color of light blue. He felt weightless and powerless to move. He tried to keep his eyes open so he could see what was happening but the speed at which he was traveling was so fast that it made him dizzy when he tried to focus his eyes. He closed his eyes tightly and hoped it would end soon. He said Joey's name three times out loud as Edith had instructed Ed to do. He could hear various voices whizzing by his head in different languages. He struggled to pull his knees to his chest and held them tightly with his head down like a cannon ball and he picked up speed until he was tossed out the other end of the tunnel. He rolled as he landed on the sandy ground and the sun was bright and blazing hot.

Vince took a moment to orient himself and slowly rose to his feet. He turned to see where he had come from and there was a small tunnel in the side of a large rock against a rocky hill of dirt and sand. He could see the faintly illuminated oval doorway he had just come out of and made a note of his surroundings so he could find it again. He looked down, and he was still clutching the black velvet bag that contained the elements from his realm and time period. He slipped his hand through the drawstring loops and held the bag in his hand so he wouldn't drop it. He looked all around and saw nothing but vast desert with rocks and sand. "Joey!" He yelled at the top of his lungs as he looked around. He stood still to listen. Silence. He decided to climb up on top of the rocks to see if he could get a better view. When he got to the top, he saw two tall obelisks off in the distance with brightly colored pictures all over them and the tips of the obelisks were covered in gold that were gleaming in the sunlight. There was a large stone complex with tall columns also decorated in bright colors. It was next to a river and the grounds were lush and dotted with Palm trees. It looked like a palace or temple of some sort. He also saw several Sphinx-like statues carved out of stone that lined a long stone road leading up to the obelisks. *I'm in Egypt?* He thought to himself.

As he turned around facing the direction of the portal below him, he saw two figures, a tall man and a boy walking toward him. The tall man had black hair and a large golden shielded collar around his shoulders with gold bands around his upper arms. He was wearing a white pleated skirt with a golden belt with blue and red stones on it. The boy wore a similar skirt and he was very tan and his hair was bleached blonde from the sun. "Joey Frasier!" Vince called out to them.

The boy and the man began running towards him. "Vince!" The boy said. It was Joey. Vince climbed down from the rocks and ran towards the boy. He picked him up off the ground and hugged him tightly.

"I'm so glad I found you!" Vince said. Then he set Joey back down on the ground, and bowed his head to the man with him. "Thank you."

"I am Heru. Come, you must take the boy back to your realm. The doorway closes soon." The man said as he led them up to what was left of the illuminated portal. It was starting to fade which meant that Vince had to get back through with Joey immediately.

Vince picked up Joey and said: "Hold on to me very tightly and don't let go!" Joey did exactly what he asked and Vince held on to Joey as tight as he could and ran straight into the portal.

Mark and Barb ran to Ed to help him up off the ground. Annie and Beth were horrified by what they just saw. Edith stood and watched as the illumination circling inside the cave was beginning to fade. Lily walked up next to Edith and looked up at her. "The doorway is starting to close." Edith said as she looked down at Lily with a look of worry on her face.

"They are on their way back now. Vince has Joey." Lily said. "Everybody stand back!" She yelled as loud as she could.

All of a sudden the buzzing grew louder and louder, and a burst of white light came out of the cave. There was a giant splash in the pond. Within seconds, two heads came up out of the water gasping for air. It was Vince and Joey. They swam to the shore and stood up to see everyone standing around cheering. Chuck and Cheryl ran to Joey and scooped him up and hugged him tightly. Annie and Mark ran to Vince and hugged him. Beth ran to give her little Brother a big hug then turned to look at Vince and mouthed the words *'thank you'* to him as tears came streaming down her cheeks.

"Well son of a bitch." Officer Rankin said. "How the Hell are we going to write this in our report?"

"Just as we witnessed it." Officer Clemmons said.

Stephen, Lily, and Edith stood back and watched this beautiful moment. They had never seen such happiness before. There were tears of joy streaming down everyone's cheeks and this was one of those moments in time that would forever leave a residual footprint. Edith glanced over at the portal, which was no longer illuminated. It was closed, but not sealed. "Come Lily." Edith said. "I'm going to show you how to seal a portal."

Edith lit her sage stick and blew on it until thick white smoke bellowed up from the end of it. She walked over to the portal and made a big circle out of the white smoke with an X through it then she made a tiny swirl in the center of the X and pressed her index finger through it. She made her declaration that it was forever sealed never to be opened again, and at the end, she said: "And so it is." Then she removed the pieces of Black Tourmaline and Moldavite from her velvet bag and buried them in the dirt at the mouth of the cave where the portal was. Then she extinguished her sage stick, wrapped it in plastic and returned it to her bag.

"We don't have to be too descript with what Mrs. MacKenzie just did in our report Rankin." Officer Clemmons said. "Some things need to be left as, shall we say, *'trade secrets'* to Mrs. MacKenzie. You know?"

Officer Rankin nodded in agreement. This was by far the most unusual thing he had ever witnessed and it was something that he would never forget. He looked at his watch, it was 12:17 am. This wrapped up much faster than he had expected and they were technically off duty now. "Let's get these folks home before someone calls another squad out here. It's getting late." He said.

They walked home together and before parting, Chuck and Cheryl thanked everyone for everything they did to help them bring Joey back. Cheryl invited everyone over for a BBQ the next day and they all agreed they'd be there. Then the Frasier's said good-night and went inside their home, feeling a little more complete now that Joey had returned.

"Thank you Edith. We could not have done this without you." Annie said. "And Ed—Thank you for volunteering to be the retriever...Even though SOMEONE pushed you out of the way and did it himself without permission!" Annie said angrily as she glared at Vince.

"I had to Mom. Joey wouldn't have recognized Ed and there wasn't enough time. You saw how fast the portal closed." Vince said in his defense. Which was probably true and everybody knew it. "Lily knew I was coming back."

Annie looked over at Lily who was standing there twisting back and forth and smiling sweetly. "Oh yes…The Telepath thing." She said with one eyebrow raised.

"Well that was incredibly foolish…But incredibly brave of you Son." Mark said. "Now why don't you go in and take a hot shower. You smell like a turtle." He said as he rubbed the top of Vince's head to mess his hair up worse than it already was having been baptized in a muddy pond. "You go too Lily. It's way past your bedtime." Then he kissed Lily on the head and sent her in the house with Stephen and Vince.

"You know, Vince was right." Ed said. "I don't know what went on when he reached the other side, but it took a few minutes to get back through the portal and it closed immediately after they came back through. What if Joey didn't recognize me and got scared and hid or ran away? I might have been stuck there." Ed spoke the truth and everyone knew it. They were thankful that Vince made such a bold move, although Annie wished that they could have discussed it before he went and actually did it.

"Well thank you for volunteering Ed. That was brave of you." Annie said as she gave him a hug. "We'll see you all tomorrow at the BBQ, huh?"

"Oh you betcha!" Barb said. "I am dying to hear more about where Joey was. I have a sneaking suspicion that it was a time and place that I know a lot about given how he was dressed."

Everyone slept in until almost noon. The intensity of the events the night before had taken its toll and all of the people living in the two households across the street from each other were finally well rested and at peace.

Mark had already gotten up and went downstairs to make some coffee. It didn't matter that it was noon. He woke up and his body wanted a cup of that hot dark brown liquid with just the right amount of caffeine to kick his body into gear. Winnie had waited patiently to be let out but was now pacing by the back door. They slept in much later than usual and she was about four hours overdue to drain her tiny little bladder.

The smell of freshly brewed coffee hung in the air and Annie came down the stairs in her bathrobe inhaling that heavenly aroma she looked forward to every morning. She wrapped her arms around Mark and gave him a kiss. "Good morning Babe." She said.

"Good mornin' Darlin'." Mark said as he handed her a fresh cup of coffee.

"Are the kids up yet?" She asked as she caught a glimpse of the clock—it was 12:08 pm. "Crap! Is it Noon?"

Mark laughed as he sat down at the table with his coffee. "Indeed it is."

Annie ran her hand through her hair. "Well, that explains why I feel so rested I guess."

Stephen and Lily came bouncing down the stairs a few minutes later looking for breakfast. "Hey Mom, can we make waffles?" Stephen asked.

"By 'we' you mean your Mother, right?" Mark said as he took another sip of his coffee and smiled at Annie.

"Uh, yeah I guess." Stephen said. "But I'll clean up afterward, deal?"

Annie looked at her oldest son and smiled proudly. "Deal." She said. Then she got up and fetched the waffle iron out of the pantry. "Is Vince up yet?"

"Yes. He's getting dressed." Lily said. "He's going to tell us all about what happened last night."

"Well I hope so!" Annie said as she mixed the waffle batter in a big bowl.

As Lily predicted, Vince came down the stairs fully dressed and also well rested. He was feeling pretty proud of himself for boldly stepping up and fearlessly jumping into the portal the night before. "Good morning Family!" He said.

"Good morning." Mark said. "Well, do tell! What was it like jumping into the unknown?"

"It was freaky! First of all, I was moving so fast that I had to close my eyes. Things were whizzing past at a very high speed and it made me dizzy to watch it, but it was lit up in this deep light bluish color…It's hard to describe. I pulled my legs up to my chest in a cannonball and I'm glad I did that because when I came out the other side, I was thrown. I'm glad I had some gymnastics training because it helped me roll out of it okay." Vince went to the fridge and poured himself a big glass of orange juice. "Anybody want juice?" He asked.

"I do!" Lily said.

Vince poured a glass of juice for Lily and finished his story. "When I got there, it was daytime and the sun was really bright. I was in the desert and it was SO hot. I looked around but didn't see anyone so I climbed up on the top of the rocks to look around and I saw a couple of tall pointy obelisk things and a huge stone palace or temple or something with a bunch of those sphinx things that lined a stone road... Which by the way, does not look ANYTHING like it does in National Geographic magazine. The obelisks were white and had a bunch of colored pictures on them, and the top points were gold...Probably real gold too. The sphinx things were painted in blue and gold...You know, like the sarcophaguses of the Pharaohs." He stopped talking for a minute so he could take a sip of juice. "And the temple? It was totally white with all these painted things on the sides in bright colors. It was cool looking back then, but it looks like shit now."

"Hey...Language!" Annie said as she poured batter in the waffle iron.

"Sorry. Anyway, I turned around and saw an Egyptian guy walking towards me with Joey. He said his name was Harry or something..."

"Heru. His name is Heru." Lily interjected.

"Heru. Anyway," Vince continued. "Joey yelled my name and came running. Then the Egyptian guy said we had to hurry because the doorway was closing so I grabbed Joey, told him to hang on, and ran back in the portal...Then we went whizzing back through the tunnel and it spit us out into the pond." Vince was pretty proud of himself. He had done something that no one else had ever done before and he couldn't wait to tell everyone at school about it.

"You can't tell anyone about this Vince." Lily said. She knew exactly what he was thinking. "People won't understand. You can't tell."

Vince knew that Lily was right. No one would likely believe him anyway. Annie served the first waffle to Vince—a small reward for bringing Joey back, then she poured more batter into the waffle iron and closed the lid. The Family loved waffles, but they only had one waffle iron. She thought it might make sense to get a second waffle iron for future Family breakfasts because it took too long to make enough for everyone at the same time.

"Did Joey say where he had been or what he'd been doing this whole time?" Annie asked.

"We didn't really have time to talk Mom. You couldn't talk in the tunnel. I think he'll tell everyone about it later when we go over there for the BBQ. One thing is for sure though, Barb is going to shit when she finds out what that stuff really looked like back then." Vince said.

"Language Vince..." Annie couldn't bring herself to take her Mom hat off—even for a story as fantastic as this.

CHAPTER 31

Cheryl was singing to herself in the kitchen as she prepped the BBQ ribs for the grill. Beth was happily shucking sweet corn out on the back patio and after starting the charcoal, Chuck threw the Frisbee to Joey who was thrilled to be able to run barefoot through lush green grass in his own back yard again. The Family was elated to have their son back and aside from the extreme suntan and bleached blonde hair, he seemed healthy and as happy as he'd ever been.

As Cheryl spread the tablecloth out over the picnic table, she watched Joey frolic in the grass. She was so thankful that he was home safe and shuddered to think what today would be like if he hadn't returned. They wouldn't be having a BBQ that was for sure. They didn't really have a chance to hear everything about Joey's experience because it was so late when they got home.

After a hot shower and clean PJs, Joey was out like a light the minute his head hit the pillow. Cheryl wondered who had taken care of him all that time. Someone did, because he looked like he had been eating well and he had a change of clothes. No matter. There was plenty of time to hear about it. The important thing was that he was alive and he had been returned to them.

As soon as the MacKenzie's arrived, Mark, Annie, and the kids walked across the street to the Frasier's house together. Beth answered the door and the doom and gloom that once permeated the house was completely gone. All of the blinds were open, the sunlight streamed through the windows and the house felt welcoming again. Edith and Annie glanced at each other and smiled. They remembered how it was before and this was a remarkable improvement—rightfully so. Joey was back and the Family was together again.

Beth led everyone outside where Cheryl had set the long picnic table and a large round patio table and chairs for dinner. "Hello! We're having BBQ baby back ribs and corn on the cob. I hope everyone is hungry!" Cheryl said with an '*all is wonderful in the world*' kind of enthusiasm. "There are beers, sodas, and some white wine on ice in the barrel over there. Help yourselves!" She said.

Joey ran up to Vince and gave him a giant hug. "Whoa Buddy! Good to see you too!" Vince said.

"Cheryl? What can I do to help?" Annie asked as she poured a glass of wine.

"You can pour me a glass of that wine, but other than that, not a darn thing." Cheryl said. Annie handed her the glass and poured three more for herself, Edith, and Barb…Who was dying to hear Joey's story about Egypt.

"The ribs have just a few more minutes to go, so I'm going to go put the sweet corn in the pot on the stove. Everything should be done at the same time." Chery announced. "Beth? Can you please grab some extra napkins and put them out? Ribs and corn are kind of messy." Beth nodded and went inside to get napkins.

As Chuck was turning the ribs over on the grill, Mark asked if Joey was doing okay.

"I've never seen a kid so happy to take a shower!" Chuck laughed. "We didn't get a chance to talk much. The minute his head hit the pillow, he was out like a light."

"I'll bet!" Mark said. "Where exactly was he? Does he remember much?" Mark asked as he took a big gulp of his beer.

"Oh yeah. He remembers everything. He says he was in Ancient Egypt but doesn't know what year it was, and that the Pharaoh took him in and he lived in the palace. He says they treated him very well." Chuck said as he finished turning the ribs and put the lid back on the grill.

"I don't know if you know this or not, but Barb is a Curator at the Field Museum for the Ancient Egypt exhibit." Mark said.

"Really? I did not know that." Chuck raised his eyebrows in surprise. "Well then, she will be fascinated by Joey's story. We only heard a little about it this morning. He's fully prepared to tell all after dinner tonight."

"We can't wait. Vince was only there for a few minutes but he said the structures looked a lot different than they do now." Mark explained.

Cheryl brought two large platters out for the ribs, and a second tray of ribs to put on the grill when Chuck took the cooked ribs off. Similar to Annie's waffle iron situation earlier that morning, Cheryl was wishing she had two grills to work with. The Smoky Joe just wasn't big enough for a party crowd. She set the platters down so Chuck could rotate the ribs, and she went back into the kitchen to fetch the sweet corn. Beth followed with two large bowls of salad and went back in to grab another big bowl with fruit. There was plenty of food to go around.

After dinner, Annie and Barb cleared the plates and took them inside to rinse and load in the dishwasher. With everyone helping with something, both tables were cleaned up in about 5 minutes and they were ready to settle in and hear about Joey's experience…Especially Barb. It was absolute torture for her to sit through dinner without hearing a word about something she spent her entire adult life studying.

Once everything was cleaned up, Cheryl and Chuck stood at the end of the table and made a toast to everyone for standing by them and for helping them bring Joey home. "We thank you all from the bottom of our hearts. You've all been such good friends and we cherish your love, friendship, and support." Chuck said. "Now I'm going to let Joey tell you where he was and how he survived."

Joey jumped right in and shared every little detail about falling into the portal, what it felt like going through the tunnel, and where he came out. "It was dark when I got there. It was the middle of the night. I couldn't see anything and I didn't know where I was so I just sat on the sand until the sun came up." Joey started. "All of a sudden, this man came walking towards me out of the desert and said his name was Heru and that he was going to help me."

Annie, Edith, Lily, and of course Barb knew exactly who Heru was—He was also known as Horus, and Egyptian God, and he was also a Seraphim Angel just like Auset. They sat quietly listening to Joey's story, but Barb was bubbling over with questions.

"Did Heru speak to you in English or Egyptian?" Barb asked.

"English." Joey said. "I was glad too because no one else there spoke any English and I couldn't understand their language at all, but they write in pictures so I could figure some of it out. Heru took me to the Palace and the Lady Pharaoh let me stay there…"

"Wait, you said *Lady Pharaoh?* Do you remember her name?" Barb asked. She was trying to figure out exactly what time period he went back to. Judging from the pleated linen skirt he was wearing when he came out of the portal last night, it was during the New Kingdom period—Between 1570 BC and 1544 BC.

"Her name was Hatshepsut. She had a boy my age. His name was Thutmose, and she treated me like her own Son. She thought my clothes were funny, but Heru asked her to dress me like them so people wouldn't be afraid. They made me wear a skirt." Joey said as he scrunched up his nose and blushed a little.

Barb nearly fell off of her chair and was on the verge of hyperventilating. She was actually speaking to someone who had not only met and Ancient Egyptian Queen, but who had lived with her. She had a million questions but she thought she would just try be quiet and let Joey tell his story before she asked any more. "Oh my goodness Joey! I'm fascinated beyond words! How did you spend your time there? What was it like?" *So much for not asking any questions* Barb thought to herself. Then she turned to Cheryl and said: "Please don't throw away Joey's skirt. I'd like to borrow it and take a closer look at how it was made."

"Glad to save it for you Barb." Cheryl said. "Joey, please finish your story." She prompted. Barb slumped in her chair feeling a little embarrassed that she kept interrupting. Ed put his arm around her and hugged her tight.

"It was very hot." Joey continued. "That's probably why they all wore skirts. But it wasn't bad—we went swimming in the river, we would race each other and threw spears to see who could throw the farthest, and we played board games. One game we played a lot was called Senet.

Hatshepsut liked to play it a lot. Another game I liked was called Hounds and Jackals. You had to have a special table to play it and tall sticks that had dog heads or jackal heads. It was kind of like checkers except you weren't allowed to double or triple jump." Joey explained. Everyone was transfixed by his story. To be able to go back in time and experience the forgotten details of the past was astounding to hear about…Especially for Barb, who was trying her best to keep quiet and listen.

"What was the food like Joey? Any pizza?" Stephen said as he laughed.

"Hahaha! There was no pizza." Joey laughed. "We ate duck and fish. Sometimes we had roasted meat. We had lots of bread and honey. And for dessert there were lots of fruits and nuts that were sometimes mixed in the honey and it was sooooo good." Joey turned to Cheryl and smiled. "And I found out that I like dates. They're sweet like candy. Can we get some next time we go to the store Mom?" Cheryl seemed surprised by that. She had never bought dates when she went grocery shopping before but she was open to try some new recipes.

"We can." Cheryl said.

"Joey, do you know where you were?" Barb asked.

"In Egypt." Joey said.

Barb laughed. "No silly, I mean do you know the name of the place in Egypt. You said that you stayed at Hatshepsut's Palace, so it must have been the Palace of Ma'at." She said.

Joey thought for a minute. "I guess I heard them say that…But I also heard everybody call it Karnak. I don't know if it's the same place and it has two different names or if Ma'at was inside of Karnak."

"I know right where you were." Barb said as she smiled. "You were on the Nile River just north of Thebes—which they would have called *Waset*. Now it's known as Luxor…Anyway, Karnak was a magnificent Temple to the Gods and Pharaohs, and Hatshepsut built a huge addition onto the Karnak Temple. She erected Obelisks in honor of her Father and her Husband. She also constructed other Temples such as Deir el-Bahari, and she constructed tombs in the Valley of the Kings…" Barb loved to talk about all things Egyptian, but she was starting to get carried away and had to pull back a little. "Sorry Joey, I didn't mean to interrupt. Please continue."

"Oh no, don't worry about that Barb. You know so much about the subject and it's nice to have someone fill in the blanks. It's good for Joey to understand where he was and who he was with." Chuck said.

Joey nodded in agreement. "Yeah. I was there, but I don't really know exactly where I was or who I was with." He said. "Now I'm kinda interested in learning about Ancient Egypt."

"So, did anyone wonder where you came from Joey? You don't exactly look Egyptian and when you got there you were wearing clothes from our time…" Vince asked.

"They knew I was from somewhere else, but they didn't care. I heard Heru talk to them in their language so I don't know what he said, but after that, they were very nice to me. Everybody was nice." Joey explained. Then he put his head down as he recalled a low point. "One night I was laying in my bed and I was…*Very* sad because I missed my home. And Hatshepsut came in and sat with me and sang a song until I fell asleep."

Cheryl put her hands up to her heart. She was so touched that another Mother from another time and place who didn't speak the same language that her son did instinctively knew how to comfort a frightened little boy. It was proof to her that nurturing truly transcends time.

"And, every day was about the same. We ate, we swam, we played games, and we slept. And then one morning Heru came and said that it was time for me to go. I said good-bye to Thutmose and Hatshepsut and then we walked out to the desert. Then I heard Vince call my name and Heru said we had to go before the doorway closed, then Vince picked me up and told me to hold on…And then we got thrown in the pond. And here I am." Joey said. He was clearly glad to be home.

"Fascinating!" Barb said. "You know Joey, I could use some help down at the museum figuring some things out. You might be able to help us solve the mysteries about what some of the items we have were used for. Would you like to come to the museum?" She asked.

"Oh, it's REALLY interesting." Annie said. "You guys should go!"

Joey was nodding his head enthusiastically to that suggestion. "I would like that. Can Lily come too?" He asked.

"You can all come!" Barb said.

"That would be terrific Barb, thank you for the invite. We'd really enjoy that." Said Chuck.

"One more question Joey…" Barb said. "I'm sure your bed was kind of a wooden cot with rope strung across the bottom of it, but what was your mattress like?"

Joey thought about it for a minute because it wasn't a detail that he really noticed. "It was a soft white cloth that was stuffed with feathers and stuff. It was comfortable to sleep on." He said.

For some reason all of the curators thought that the mattresses would have been stuffed with straw. Feathers made much more sense since they ate quite a bit of duck and other water fowl. Just another detail that someone like Joey could assist them in understanding the real truth about ancient history.

The phone rang and Beth went into the house to answer it. "Dad? It's for you." She said.

Chuck looked at his watch. 7:12 pm. "Who is it?" He asked.

"I think it's your work." Beth said.

"Huh. Well, if you'll all excuse me for a moment…" Chuck said as he stood up to go into the house to take the call.

Edith looked over at Lily and they were thinking the same thing. This was a portal issue and this was the part that Edith knew she would have to help them deal with eventually. She sat quietly and sipped her wine as she waited for Chuck to return.

Chuck emerged a few minutes later and his face was white. "Chuck? What is it Honey?" Cheryl asked.

"One of our security guards was killed a short while ago. He was thrown against the concrete wall in our lab…" Chuck looked over at Edith who knew that this had to do with what came through the portal. The battle had begun.

CHAPTER 32

Chuck drove as fast as he could to Argon National Laboratories. Even though she didn't have security clearance to enter the facility, Edith came along with him. She knew much more about portals than any of the scientists at Argon did and he was glad she was eager to come along. As he pulled up to the security gate, the parking lot was flooded with police cars. There were so many flashing blue and red lights it was practically blinding to look at. Chuck rolled down the window as the Security Guard approached. "Good evening Dr. Frasier. Did they call you in?" The Security Guard asked as he glanced over at Edith in the passenger seat.

"Yeah they did Larry…Ahh, this is Edith MacKenzie. She's been assisting us with this project off site." Chuck said as he turned to Edith and winked. She leaned forward and smiled at the Security Guard as he flipped the pages of paper on his clipboard.

"I'm sorry sir. I don't see her name here." The Security Guard said. "MacKenzie, is it?"

"Well…We weren't expecting to come in tonight Larry. She may not be on there. This is a *very* unexpected circumstance." Chuck said. "I can assure you that…" Just then a police officer walked in front of the car and shined a flashlight through the windshield as he approached.

"Mrs. MacKenzie? Is that you?" The Officer said as he switched his flashlight off. "Officer Rankin. Hi—Yes, it's me. I was asked to come and assist." Edith said.

The Security Officer scratched his head. He was in a quandary about what to do. It's true that this was a very unique circumstance, but it was his job to keep anyone without clearance or who wasn't an approved visitor on his list out of the complex.

"You can let her through. She's working with us on this crime scene." Officer Rankin said. And with that, Larry pressed the button and lifted the gate so Chuck and Edith could drive through. "Clemmons is already in there. He'll be glad to see you."

Chuck carefully maneuvered through the police cars as he drove toward the back entrance of the building. The Coroner's van was there and they were wheeling Martin Reese's body out on the gurney to load it in the back of the van. There were Officers and Argon Security Guards standing outside of the door blocking their entry as they walked up to the building. "Hello Dr. Frasier—Lt. Colonel Kawalski is in the lab sir. He's waiting for you" The Security Guard said.

"Thank you Wes." Chuck said as he escorted Edith inside the building. The fluorescent lighting in the hallway buzzed and flickered as they walked down the hall. There were Security Guards, Police, and Military personnel scattered about throughout the building. They got in the elevator and Chuck pressed the button to take them down to Lab 2C. When the doors closed, he wondered how he was going to explain Edith to Lenny Kawalski. This was a top secret project and only a handful of people had clearance to go anywhere near Lab 2C. When the elevator doors opened, they got out and turned left to walk toward the lab. A familiar face saw them coming and a solution to the big dilemma Chuck was mentally working through had just presented itself.

"Mrs. MacKenzie! I'm so glad you're here." Officer Clemmons said. He was expecting them. "Dr. Frasier, there's a Lt. Colonel Kawalski in the lab waiting for you."

"What the Hell happened here?" Chuck asked.

"This is one of the damnedest crime scenes I've ever processed." Officer Clemmons explained. "Come on. You've got to see it to believe it." He said as he turned to Edith and put his hand on her shoulder. "It's kind of gory Mrs. MacKenzie. I just want to forewarn you of what you're about to see."

Edith nodded. "Thank you for the warning. Murder scenes are never pretty. I'll be ok." She said.

"Oh, and if Kawalski asks? Edith is with the Police Department." Chuck said as he held up his ID badge showing his clearance and tapped it with his finger.

"Gotcha." Officer Clemmons said.

They walked down to the end of the hall and the Officers standing in the hallway parted to let them through. Chuck entered the lab first and was immediately greeted by a visibly shaken Lt. Colonel Leonard Kawalski. Lab tables were turned on their sides, chairs had been thrown about, and lab equipment and monitors had been smashed to pieces. As Chuck scanned the chaos in the room he saw it—The wall where Marty Reese was thrown so hard that it crushed the back his skull and killed him instantly. There was blood everywhere, in fact, there was so much blood that Chuck wondered if there was a drop of blood left in Marty's broken body. "Good Lord!" He gasped.

Edith walked in behind Chuck and looked around. It was a horrific scene and she did her very best to keep calm. She looked at the bloody wall where the security guard was thrown. The blood spatter started almost up to the ceiling, then smeared straight down the wall to the floor where a large pool of coagulated blood lay on the ground. You could see where his body laid on the floor by the thinned and smeared areas of partially dried blood. The mineral smell of copper hung in the stale air of the room. It was the smell of blood. Something Edith had smelled before. As Edith directed her attention back up to the top of the wall where the blood splatter started, Officer Clemmons walked up next to her.

"We're trying to figure out how the hell his blood got all the way up there. There's no ladder around and no scaffolding that he could have fallen from." Officer Clemmons said. The ceilings were at least 16 ft. high. The walls were cinderblock with a thick coat of glossy white paint on them.

Edith turned to look at the opposite corner of the room. In her mind's eye she could see the dark swirling cloud of the portal that the scientists had opened. Whatever came through there was dark. Evil. She got the feeling that it was still there…hiding. She turned and looked at Officer Clemmons and very calmly said: "He was thrown."

"Thrown? But, how is that possible?" Officer Clemmons asked as he looked up at the height of the wall. He lifted his hat slightly, scratched above his left ear then adjusted his hat firmly back on his head.

"He was thrown from here." Edith pointed to the tipped lab chair in the corner of the room near where the portal was. Both Chuck and Lenny Kawalski were listening as Edith described what she was seeing. "He tried to run, but he tripped here on this chair…And he fell, but he was picked up and thrown against the wall." Edith walked them through the scene she was seeing play out in her mind's eye. She closed her eyes and tapped into the residual energy in the room for a minute. Officer Clemmons looked down on the floor and saw Martin Reese's 9mm pistol laying there not far from where Edith said that he fell.

Just then, one of the Military Police Officers entered the room and saluted to Lt. Colonel Kawalski. "Sir—You need to see this."

"What is it Sargent?" Lenny asked.

"We reviewed the security video sir. There's something you should see." The Sargent said.

Lenny, Chuck, Edith and Officer Clemmons got off the elevator and followed Sargent Foster down the hall to the video surveillance room where two other Military Officers were reviewing the footage. When Lt. Colonel Kawalski entered the room, both of the Officers rose to their feet and saluted. "At ease gentleman." Lenny said. "What have you got?"

When the Military Officers played the tape back, they could not believe what they saw. You could see a tall black mass manifest in the corner where Edith indicated the portal was. It moved about the room slowly for a few minutes, then tipped over a heavy stainless steel lab table and knocked the chair on its side. A few minutes later, you could hear the rattle of keys and the lab door slowly opened revealing Security Guard Martin Reese entering the room with his pistol drawn. *"Security! Who's in here?"* Marty said on the tape. No one answered. Marty stepped into the lab to investigate. He saw the table and chair knocked over and swiftly swayed back and forth with his pistol, scanning the room. *"Who's in here!?!"* He yelled again. No answer. Then he heard something and he turned toward the corner of the room where the portal is and he saw the big black mass. *"Who's there? Identify yourself or I'll shoot!"* He said. Seconds later, the black mass rushed at him. Marty fired one shot as he fell, then the black mass appears to have picked him up like a rag doll and threw him across the room with tremendous force. He flew several feet in the air and smashed into the cinderblock wall so hard that you could hear his skull shatter when his head hit the wall. Then Marty's lifeless body fell to the floor and landed in a contorted, mangled way then slumped on the floor in a large pool of blood. After a few short seconds, all four cameras in the lab went black and the audio became static.

"Sweet Jesus." Officer Clemmons said under his breath.

"What the Hell is that thing?" Lenny Kawalski asked as he stood there with his arms folded in a very authoritarian manner, even though he was completely unnerved by what he just saw. No one knew quite how to answer that question, so they all just stood there and said nothing.

"Pure evil." Edith said as she looked at Lenny. "You brought it here. It came through your portal."

Lenny turned to Edith and squinted one eye. "And, who might *you* be?" He said.

"This is Edith MacKenzie. She works with us to solve difficult and unusual cases, and I think you have to admit, this one is definitely difficult and unusual." Officer Clemmons said. "Mrs. MacKenzie is a Psychic Medium. She can see and hear things that the rest of us can't. I'd listen to what she has to say if I were you Lt. Colonel. This is by NO means, an ordinary crime scene."

Lenny stared at the little old lady with skepticism. "A Psychic, huh?" He said in a slightly condescending way.

"Ah, Lenny?" Chuck said. "She's the real deal... She helped me find my Son."

Everything that Edith had previously described in the lab about how the killing happened had now been proven on the video surveillance tape they just saw. Lenny acknowledged Chuck's validation and quickly reconsidered his opinion of having a Psychic Medium involved in the investigation. "My apologies Mrs. MacKenzie. I meant no disrespect." Lenny said as he bowed ever so slightly as a gesture to ask for forgiveness.

"Thank you." Edith said as she nodded in acceptance of his apology. "Lenny? May I call you Lenny?" She asked.

"Please." Lenny said as he gestured with his hand for her to continue.

"Lenny, you have what Psychic Mediums refer to as...A VERY serious problem." Edith said. The other Officers in the room choked as they stifled their surprise at her response. This little old lady just put the big bad Lieutenant Colonel in his place and this was something they had never seen before. Almost immediately, everyone including Edith, quickly regained their composure and brought themselves back to the present seriousness of the situation. "I don't know what experiment you're conducting here, but you are dealing with something extremely dangerous and you have no business messing with things that you know nothing about." She scolded. "You have opened a doorway from another dimension and you now have absolutely no control over what is coming through there...I think you have a pretty good idea that it has no friendly intentions judging from what you just witnessed on that tape."

Lenny swallowed hard. She made a good point. Perhaps they were playing with fire, but it was all in the name of research. He had a project to manage. A theory to prove. It was going to make him famous...But this was not supposed to happen. No one was supposed to get hurt. No one was supposed to die. Lenny briefly looked down at his feet before speaking. "Mrs. MacKenzie. I'm sorry but I cannot discuss the project with you. You do not have the proper clearance." He defaulted to his comfort zone which was to be the authoritarian.

"I see…" Edith said. "Well then, if you wish to proceed, I suggest you do it VERY carefully." She turned to face Lt. Colonel Kawalski straight on and looked him in the eye. "Or you may find yourself face to face with what you fear most—Death." She pivoted slightly and walked past him as she left the small surveillance room.

"Lenny, I hate to tell you this, but she's right. You've either got to shut this down now, or you need to get her the proper clearance and bring her in as an advisor." Chuck said. "We are clearly in over our heads on this one."

CHAPTER 33

As Chuck and Edith drove home they were both silently processing what they had just witnessed. Although portals were naturally occurring phenomena, Edith now understood Auset's extreme concern over the portals being opened by the Argon Scientists. This was no ordinary portal. This certainly was not a portal that a human being would ever travel through to get to another time and place. This was different and much more serious. *'Danger! Danger! Danger! Death and destruction to everything in its path. The military man summoned it here.'* Edith heard in her ear.

"Chuck? How many portals have you opened at that facility?" Edith asked.

"Only one that I am aware of. Why do you ask?" Chuck responded. "I've only joined the project a couple of weeks ago. The project is supposed to prove the theory of time travel, but I haven't been able to fully discern Kawalski's true motives yet."

"Well, you *know* that time travel is possible. Your Son experienced that firsthand." Edith said. "Have you shared that with them yet?"

Chuck sat quietly for a moment. "No, I have not." He said. He wasn't sure he would ever share that with anyone, even though he was a highly respected Quantum Physicist and this would be a perfectly viable theory for him to prove and share with the world. He was holding back because he didn't trust Lt. Colonel Leonard Kawalski. Not that he was worried about Lenny taking credit for his work, everyone assumed that he would, but because he genuinely did not trust him. He was up to no good and there was another agenda hiding behind the time travel research, but Chuck couldn't put his finger on it.

"Time travel is not what he's interested in." Edith said.

Chuck was a bit surprised by that statement at first, then he reminded himself that Edith was a Psychic Medium...And a damn good one too. "I think that too. It's just a front for something else that he's working on, but I don't know what." Chuck said.

"You can't go back in that lab Chuck. It's still in there and it will kill you." Edith warned. Chuck swallowed hard because he knew she was right.

When they arrived back at the house, everyone was still on the back patio where they had left them. They were all sitting around the fire pit that Chuck built the summer before and everyone was still talking about Joey's trip to Egypt.

"Honey, you're back!" Cheryl said as she stood up to greet them. "What happened down there?" She said.

"There was a terrible accident." Chuck said as he glanced at Edith. He didn't want to go into any more detail than that with the kids there. "Martin was locking up the lab and he tripped and fell on some equipment and hit his head." Plausible story he thought…for now.

"Yes, it was very sad. Officer Clemmons was there. He said to tell you all Hello." Edith said. Annie could tell that there was much more to the story— It wasn't an accident at all, but she understood why they were conveying it that way given the present company. She would have to find out the details another time.

"Joey was just describing what Karnak looked like. We knew that it was painted in bright colored hieroglyphs, but we did not know that the exterior of the structures were also painted white. That makes complete sense since white would reflect the desert heat and the rooms would be much cooler." Barb explained. Her enthusiasm for Ancient Egyptology was the perfect way to change the subject from details about the gory crime scene that Chuck and Edith had just witnessed.

"So Barb…" Annie started, "How are you going to explain to your colleagues just *how* you know all of these things?" She could tell by the look on Barb's face that that small detail had never entered her mind.

"Um…Gee. I hadn't thought of that." Barb said. She got all caught up in the excitement of finally getting answers to things they only had the ability to surmise from the small fragments of tiny preserved evidence they were able to find. She had not considered the obvious fact that it would be tremendously more difficult to explain how a little boy was able to go back in time through a portal to an Ancient Egyptian Civilization and live in the palace of a Pharaoh, then return back home again to talk about it.

"I think you're going to have to keep your source to yourself Honey. You could maybe say *'what if'* to things you already know the answer to. You know? Kind of like it just dawned on you or something." Ed suggested. "You'll have to present the information as if it were your own opinion."

Barb slumped in her chair as if the wind just got knocked out of her. Here she had a credible source—someone who had *actually* been there and who had all of the correct answers to every Archaeologist's unanswered questions and she couldn't tell anybody. She glanced over at Annie and looked as if she was about to cry.

"I'm so sorry Barb." Annie said. "But, look at it this way—You'll be so much smarter than anyone else at the museum...Or than any other expert on Ancient Egypt in the entire world for that matter!" Annie did her best to cheer her up but couldn't tell if her strategy was working or not. Barb shrugged her shoulders and managed to crack a slight semi-forced smile.

"Crap is it 11:00 already? We'd better get going." Mark said as he looked at his watch. "I've got things to do in the morning."

"Oh my gosh yes! Vince and Stephen have appointments with the Dentist in the morning." Annie said as she tipped back the last sip of wine in her glass.

"We *do?*" Vince and Stephen said in perfect unison.

"Yes, you do. I thought it would be a good idea to get you in to get your teeth cleaned and any other dental work you might need before school starts." Annie said. "Thank you Cheryl for a wonderful evening. The ribs were great and the company was even better."

"Yes thank you Cheryl. We're so glad that Joey's back!" Barb said as she gave Cheryl a hug good-bye.

As the adults were saying good-night, Vince and Beth were standing back in the shadows holding hands. "Thank you for bringing my little Brother back Vince. That was very brave of you to run into the portal like that." Beth said.

"No thank you necessary. It just made more sense for me to go in than Ed. Joey wouldn't know who he was and there wasn't much time to find him and get back before the portal closed. Besides, that portal spit you out fast and I was able to pull my knees up so I could roll out of it. Ed probably would have broken his leg or something." Vince said as he winced a little at the visual image in his mind of Ed being hurled through the air and landing in a crumpled slump.

"Well, thank you Vince. I'll never forget it." Beth said, then she leaned in and gave him a big kiss on the lips which took him completely by surprise.

"Vince! Let's go Bud." Mark bellowed.

Vince and Beth broke away from their first kiss and they both looked around to see if anyone had seen what they were doing. "Um…I'll see you tomorrow?" Beth said.

"Um, yeah. For sure. After I get back from the Dentist." Vince said. "See you tomorrow." He squeezed her hand one last time and walked toward the sliding glass door. Beth followed closely behind.

After the Campbell's and MacKenzie's left the house, Beth took Joey to get PJs on and brush their teeth before bed. Cheryl led Chuck back out to the patio to help her drain the barrel that held the iced beverages. "So, how bad was it Chuck?" She asked.

"Oh Cher, it was one of the most gruesome things I have ever seen." Chuck said. "And they caught the entire thing on tape." He had to sit down, and Cheryl sat next to him and held his hand. "He was thrown across the lab, at least 15 ft. in the air and slammed against a concrete wall Cheryl. You could hear his skull shatter on the video tape."

"Oh God." Cheryl gasped. "Who could throw him like that?"

Chuck lifted his head and looked her right in the eye. "Whatever Lenny brought through that portal he opened up. On tape it looked like a 12 ft. tall solid black mass. It's bad Cheryl. It's so bad." He said as he pulled her close to him.

Across the street, Annie sent Stephen, Vince, and Lily inside to get ready for bed while she and Mark stayed back in the driveway to talk to the MacKenzie's before they left to go home. "So Edith, what really happened to that Security Guard?" Annie asked.

Edith leaned against the car and folded her arms as she took a couple of deep breaths. "It's unlike anything I've ever seen. That poor man was thrown across the room with such force that his skull shattered when he hit the wall. I wouldn't be surprised if he broke every bone in his body. It was violent." She said. "All of it was captured on the surveillance tape. It's not a Shadow Person. It's much worse."

"Worse? Is there a more vicious alien being than a Shadow Person?" Annie asked. The experience she had with Shadow People who dragged Lily from her bed and had pressed Winnie to the wall while holding Mark back with an invisible force field was pretty bad, yet she knew that Edith had seen and experienced much worse.

Edith looked her in the eye and paused for a minute as if she were trying to communicate telepathically. "It's very, VERY old. It has NEVER been human, and it's a manifestation of an entire legion of Demons. Hundreds of them—who all converged into a giant solid black mass of pure evil. This is something that is way beyond my ability to handle. They've opened a portal alright…A portal straight to Hell." Edith said.

"Oh God." Annie gasped as she covered her mouth with her hand to catch her breath. "What can we do?"

"I don't know." Edith replied. "I need to see Auset immediately. The beast has been unleashed."

It was almost 12:30 am and everyone was tucked in their beds asleep. The house was quiet. Winnie was curled up at the foot of Lily's bed and she was sleeping soundly. Lily was too tired to help the Dead this evening, so she turned the *'open for business'* sign off and she laid quietly and comfortably in her bed. *Lily! Come to the window!* She heard in her head. It wasn't the Dead speaking to her, this was a telepathic message. It wasn't Vince. Her window was next to his. If he wanted to talk to her, he could just come into her room. Lily got up out of bed and pulled the cord to raise the blinds on her window. She looked out across the front yard, and a flash of light caught her eye from a window across the street. *'Can you hear me Lily?'*

Lily looked at the window where the light was coming from and it was the window in Joey's room. *'I can here you.'* She said with her thoughts.

'I thought so. Jon-Jon told me you could.' Joey said with his thoughts. Joey was telepathic! But even more incredible was that he's also psychic because he can communicate with Jon-Jon.

'You've awakened Joey. The time travel has opened you.' Lily said with her thoughts.

'This is SO cool! I've never been able to do this before.' Joey said telepathically.

Lily and Joey continued their telepathic conversation for about a half hour until Winnie got up and gave Lily a firm nudge with her nose to push her back to bed. They said goodnight and Lily pulled the cord to lower the blinds in her room. Now that Joey had awakened to his abilities, she felt like she should show him the ropes. It's not something that they could talk about when they went back to school, but they had their own little inner circle now and they shared some unique experiences that you couldn't speak about to anyone else. Lily had always had a crush on Joey and their abilities would bring them even closer. She knew that they would be close friends for life, and that made her smile.

After she crawled back in bed, Winnie jerked and put her head up as she stared toward the door that was now opening slowly. "Lil? Are you awake?" Vince whispered.

"I'm up." Lily said as she rolled over on her side to face the door. "What is it Vince?"

He came in and sat on the edge of her bed. "I don't know. I just feel like something's really wrong. I don't know how to explain it." He said.

"I know." Lily said. "I feel it too. Something very, very bad has come. It's going to kill people."

"Do you know what it is?" Vince asked as he sat quietly in the dark trying to hone in on the energy he was picking up.

"Not exactly, but I know that it is very, very, very baaaaaad." Lily said. "I was going to ask Auset what it is."

"Auset? You mean the Egyptian Goddess that bought our old house?" Vince had a way of being very obvious in his speech with a twist of bluntness.

"Ah, yeah. Who else would I ask about this?" Lily said.

"I don't know…Edith? She knows a lot about the paranormal." Vince said.

Lily laid flat on her back and sighed. "Mrs. MacKenzie knows what's going on…But she can't do this by herself. It's too powerful. It will kill her." Lily put her arms up and tucked her hands behind her head. "Auset will know what to do. We have to go see her."

"Can I go with you? I feel like I should meet her." Vince said. His trip back to Ancient Egypt and his interaction with Heru had brought him into the energetic web that Lily and Edith were a part of.

"Sure. I'll tell Momma that you should come with us." Lily said.

"Good." Vince said. "Well, goodnight Lil." He hugged her and stood up to walk toward the door to go back to his room.

"Hey Vince?" Lily said.

Vince stopped and turned back to face his baby sister. "Yeah?" He said. "Joey has abilities. The time travel awakened him." Lily said.

"No shit? That is SO cool! When did you find this out?" Vince asked.

"He spoke to me telepathically and we've been talking through the window tonight. He's also psychic. He can talk to Jon-Jon." Lily said.

Vince nodded his head up and down as if he was grooving to music. "That's so cool…Well, 'night Lil. Love you little sis." Vince said before heading back to his room.

"I love you to big bro." Lily whispered.

CHAPTER 34

The traffic was backed up on I-55 on the way to Argon. Monday mornings were often like this and Chuck felt as if he should have left a half hour earlier, but he couldn't tear himself away from having breakfast with his loving Family. He thought about what might happen next with the lab and how Martin's murder would impact the project, possibly the whole facility.

As he pulled up to the gate, Stan was on duty and he lifted the gate and waived him in. The parking lot was not as full as it was the night before. Chuck parked in his designated parking spot, grabbed his briefcase from the back seat and walked toward the door. He slid his pass key through the slot and the door clicked so he could open it. The hallway looked the same, but the fluorescent lighting on the ceiling didn't seem to flicker and buzz as it had the night before. All of the offices were dark. Chuck checked his watch—8:06 am. Usually this place was teeming with people by now. He was sure that several people were told not to come into work today after what had happened last night. Chuck walked straight to his office, turned on the light, and was startled to see that his drawers were slightly open. He hadn't left them that way, but maybe this was part of processing a crime scene? He wasn't sure. It was just an odd thing to see. He sat down and took inventory of the files to see if anything was missing. Nothing was taken from what he could tell, but he specifically remembered locking his desk drawers on Friday…So someone had to have a key to open them. Who would have done that? And the bigger question was why? He was only involved with the project in Lab 2C for less than two weeks. What could anyone possibly be looking for? As he sat there pondering those questions, Lenny Kawalski was heading down the hall towards him.

"Frasier! Good, you're here. Grab some coffee and meet me in my office." Lenny said. He turned around and headed back down the hall from where he came.

"Yes, I'm here. I'll be right there." Chuck said. He grabbed a notebook and a pen, then went into the break room to grab a cup of coffee. As he headed down the hall to Lenny Kawalski's office, he passed the surveillance room. It was dark, which was peculiar. If there was a murder the night before by an alien black mass that came through a portal that they opened, it would make sense that they would double down on the surveillance wouldn't it? This was a question he would be sure to ask Kawalski about.

Chuck approached Lt. Colonel Kawalski's office and saw him sitting at his desk with his head down reading something intently. Chuck knocked on the doorjamb to get his attention. He thought that would be more appropriate than just barging in…Even though he was ordered to meet Lenny in his office just a few minutes before.

"Ah Frasier. Come in. Have a seat." Lenny said as he looked up from his reading.

Chuck sat down in one of the chairs in front of Lenny's desk and set his notebook on his lap, crossed his legs in a very confident manner, and took a sip of his coffee. "Do we have any more information about what happened last night?" Chuck asked.

"Well, that's what I wanted to discuss with you." Lenny said. "I managed to get Mrs. MacKenzie a Consultant's Pass for the duration of our project. It seems that she is highly regarded at the DGPD and also with the Illinois State Police. They feel that she is credible and she may be able to assist us with a few things." He said as he slid the laminated pass across the desk to Chuck.

"Oh, that's great! I agree—I think that she will be invaluable to the project. You know, in Quantum Physics we can make calculations and assumptions on just about everything, but there are some things we just don't know, and worse, there are a lot of things that we don't know that we don't know." Chuck was referring to the portal they opened without fully understanding what might come through there. "Edith has special abilities that will most certainly help us bridge those gaps in our understanding." Chuck said. He was glad that Lenny saw the value in bringing Edith into the project, but he was also certain that Lenny had another agenda and he wasn't sure what it was.

"Good. Please tell her to register at the Security Gate the first time she comes through. They'll take her photo and keep it there for verification for future access." Lenny said.

"I will." Chuck said. "So, I'm wondering why the surveillance room is dark today. Shouldn't we be beefing up surveillance after last night?" There was a long pause as Lenny stared Chuck straight in the eye with a suspicious look on his face.

"Cameras were damaged in the lab last night so there's no point until we replace them." Lenny said. Chuck shrugged his shoulders. He supposed that it made sense, but still, he would think that they would have been out fixing them first thing this morning after a murder.

"So, what's next for the PDTT project? Are we scrapping it? I would think we can expect our funding to be pulled." Chuck said as he took another big gulp of his coffee.

"No, no. We're NOT scrapping it. This is important research! Even MORE important now. I've got this under control. Once they clear the crime scene this afternoon, we're getting back to it. I suspect that they will be finished by 15:00 hours." Lenny said. His military side was emerging now and Chuck took that as a hint to back off a little.

"Was there any damage to the Hadron Collider? I was a little distracted by the horrible scene in the lab I didn't really notice if it had been damaged or not." Chuck asked. The Hadron Collider was a prototype that was built specifically for the Parallel Dimension Time Travel project to open portals to other dimensions by accelerating particles thus creating a higher vibrational energy. It had taken several years and millions of dollars to construct, and only 10 people in the entire US Government had ever seen it. Knowledge of the existence of this machine was Top Secret. If the HC was damaged, the whole project would be scrapped and Edith may no longer need to be involved.

"The Collider is fine. It's like a colossal tank. We'll be able to fire it up again as soon as we clear the incident reports." Lenny said rather aggressively.

"I see. Okay, well, I guess there's not much we can do until then except run some more assumptions through our models. I'll get back to that then." Chuck said as she stood up and turned to leave. He understood that Lenny was the leader of the top secret PDTT project, but he was rather upset that Martin Reese's brutal murder was just being dismissed and swept away with an incident report. "Any information about the funeral?"

"Funeral? Oh, yeah, Security Guard Reese." Lenny said without any hint of remorse or sadness over an employee's death. "I haven't heard but I'll let you know."

"Thanks." Chuck said as he got up and left Lenny's office. *What an asshole!* He thought to himself as he walked down the hall back to his own office. Lenny clearly didn't care about anything but the project and the notoriety that would be generated from it. If Joey hadn't gone missing as a result of going through the portal by the pond, Chuck would be working on other technology that would benefit the greater good of innocent people and the safety of the U.S. Military. But, he made a promise to Edith and Annie that he would help them close the portals that Lenny was opening and he was committed to keep his promise. He'd just have to hold his nose and keep working on the PDTT project until Edith could help him shut the dangerous portal.

The phone on Chuck's desk was ringing by the time he got back to his office and he picked up as quickly as he could, hoping the caller hadn't hung up yet. "Hello?" Chuck said.

"Chuck—It's Cheryl. How is everything there?" Cheryl asked.

"Very odd. Lenny doesn't seem to be the least bit concerned about what happened here last night. He just wants the incident reports to finish up so he can get back to the project. I see absolutely no empathy regarding Martin's violent death." Chuck said as he tried to keep his voice down. Lenny was known for appearing out of nowhere unexpectedly and he didn't want to get caught saying something he shouldn't.

"Nice." Cheryl replied sarcastically. "What kind of a man is he?" She asked.

"One that doesn't give a shit about anyone but himself. It's going to take a lot for me to keep working with him." Chuck said. "Anyway, is everything okay? You rarely call me here. Is everyone all right?"

"Yeah. I got called into work because they have two nurses out sick. Annie offered to keep an eye on Joey and Beth. I should be home by 3:30." Cheryl said. "I wanted to tell you something I heard from my friend at the Coroner's office."

"What did you hear?" Chuck asked as he sat down. The thought of Martin's brutal murder sickened him.

"Well, they X-rayed Martin's body and the Coroner counted 247 breaks." Chery said. Chuck sat there silently. He could not imagine how painful that would be and he hoped that Martin's death was swift so he didn't have to suffer. "So, he basically broke damn near every bone in his body?"

"No Chuck—There are only 206 bones in the adult human body so he DID break every bone in his body, some several times. He was basically pulverized. They've never seen anything like it. He was thrown hard." Cheryl whispered. She was using the phone in the Nursery and she was trying to keep from waking the sleeping babies she was taking care of.

"Oh my God." Chuck said. He could not fathom what had happened to Martin.

"My friend also said that the FBI has been called in. The lab is about to be shut down." Cheryl whispered. There was a long pause of silence. "Chuck? Are you there?"

"Yeah Cher, I'm here. I'm…I'm just processing all of this." Chuck sat back and brushed his hair back with his other hand. "Well, Lenny thinks that we'll be back in the lab continuing the project later this afternoon. I guess he's got a big surprise coming."

"Um, I wouldn't tell him where you heard this…*If* you decide to tell him. I don't want my friend to get in trouble. He knows that you work there so he was letting me know what's going on. I thought I should call you right away." Cheryl said.

"No, no. I won't say a word about where I heard it. I'll let the FBI do their thing and Lenny can find out that way. I'll probably be reassigned if they're shutting the lab down. I'm not sure where I'll be going but the commute will be a whole lot longer that's for sure." Chuck said. Argon was a very convenient 15 minute drive from home which is why they bought the house in Brookridge. The nearest facility that he would likely be reassigned to was in La Grange, a 2-3 hour minimum round trip daily commute.

"Okay. We'll talk more tonight. I just wanted to let you know." Cheryl said. "I love you."

"I love you too. I'll see you tonight." Chuck said as he hung up the phone. A few minutes later, he could hear Lenny arguing with someone down the hall and he sounded upset. As he was trying to listen to what was being said, two guys came walking down the hall toward him. They flashed their badges as they approached.

"Dr. Frasier? I'm Special Agent Dietrich and this is Special Agent Hanson. We're with the FBI. Can we have a word with you?" The FBI Agent said.

Chuck stood and motioned them in. "Of course, please come in." He said. "I guess you're here about the incident that occurred last night…"

"Yes sir. Were you in the building last night before the incident occurred?" Dietrich asked.

"No. I generally don't work in the lab on weekends. I was at home. We had some friends over for a barbeque and I got a call from Lt. Colonel Kawalski. He said that there had been an accident in the lab and he asked me to come down right away." Chuck said.

"And what time was that?" Dietrich asked. "It was a little after 7 pm." Chuck answered.

"Can you tell me about the project you were working on in Lab 2C?" Dietrich asked as he scribbled some notes in his notebook.

"We're researching the possibility of time travel through particle acceleration. It's top secret and I'm not sure I should be discussing any details." Chuck explained.

"And what is your role in the project Dr. Frasier?" Dietrich asked.

"I validate data." Chuck said. "I've only been brought on to the project a couple of weeks ago. I'm not directly involved in conducting the experiment. My expertise is Quantum Physics so I more or less just confirm the accuracy of their data in their models and make assumptions about things that may or may not be feasible during the course of the experiments. I really don't go down to Lab 2C while they're working down there, I just sit in on the weekly briefings and make adjustments to the data they provide for me. Last night was only the second time I've ever set foot in there." He said. Even though Chuck hadn't done anything wrong, he was nervous about having two FBI officers sitting in front of him taking copious notes.

"How long have you worked in this facility Dr. Frasier?" Hanson asked.

"I've been here for about 8 years now. I was working at NASA before that." Chuck said. "And how long have you known Lt. Colonel Kawalski?" Hanson asked.

"Since he came here. He started a couple of years after me, so probably 6 years." Chuck answered. "But I've never worked with him on a specific project until two weeks ago when he invited me to become more involved in the PDTT Project. Before that, I would review data collected for Military projects and verify the feasibility of their project assumptions."

"So you graded their homework?" Hanson said.

"Yeah, something like that." Chuck laughed.

"And what does PDTT stand for Dr. Frasier?" Dietrich asked.

"Ah, Parallel Dimension Time Travel." Chuck said. "It's very hush-hush. I had to obtain special clearance to work on it."

"Dr. Frasier, have you ever heard Lt. Colonel Kawalski mention the name John Andham?" Hanson asked.

Chuck thought for a moment. "No, not that I can recall. Who is John Andham?" He asked.

"He's a British Scientist. He designed some special equipment similar to what you have downstairs in the lab." Hanson said. "He doesn't think very much of Leonard Kawalski. We just wondered if you ever heard his name mentioned around here."

Chuck shrugged his shoulders and nodded his head no. "I really hadn't spoken to Lenny Kawalski much prior to two weeks ago, but I can say that I've never heard him mention that name before."

Dietrich scribbled a few more notes and then closed his notebook. He looked over at his partner to confirm that they didn't have any more questions. "I think that's it Dr. Frasier. Thank you for your time." He said as they stood up and shook Chuck's hand. "Could I ask you to write your home telephone number and address down here for me?" He opened the notebook again and turned the page, then he handed it to Chuck with his pen.

"Sure." Chuck took the notebook and wrote the information down. "You can always reach me here as well." Chuck said as he handed a business card to both FBI Agents, who looked at each other before taking his cards.

"We'll be in touch if we have any further questions. And, here are our cards in case you remember anything else." Dietrich and Hanson handed their business cards to Chuck then turned and left his office.

About 20 minutes later, Lenny Kawalski came into Chuck's office and sat down in front of his desk. "We've been shut down Frasier! The Feds have padlocked the lab." He said. Chuck could tell that he wasn't happy about it. Lenny could usually make a phone call and get his way with just about anything. Apparently he didn't have anyone to call to help with this.

"Why?" Chuck asked. "Two agents were just in here and asked a few questions but they didn't say anything about shutting us down."

Lenny looked at Chuck and raised an eyebrow. "You had two agents in here talking to you just now? What did they say?"

"They just asked how long I'd been working here and how long I've been working on the PDTT project. I told them I've been on board only a couple of weeks so I really didn't have much to say." Chuck said. Lenny looked a little relieved but slightly suspicious that Chuck might have said something he shouldn't have.

"Did they ask you about the lab equipment?" Lenny asked.

"No, no questions about that." Chuck said noting that Lenny was concerned about questions regarding the lab equipment in particular. "But they did ask me if I'd ever heard you mention the name John Andham." Both of Lenny's eyebrows shot up. He was clearly shocked to hear that.

"Really?" Lenny said.

"I said that I'd never heard the name before. Then they said that he was a British Scientist but that was all that was said." Chuck said.

"Well, I guess they're just doing their job." Lenny said as he shifted in his seat a little. "So Frasier, since they've locked us out of the lab, we're going to have to put the project on pause for a while. I just wanted to let you know that you and all the other members of my team will be assigned to other projects for a while. They'll probably send you to Oak Lawn or La Grange for a couple of months…Its temporary. Just until they finish their investigation."

Chuck tried to act a little surprised, even though he had already been forewarned of this by Cheryl a little earlier. Then he remembered what Edith had told him about the entity that came through the portal and murdered Martin Reese. He leaned forward and looked Lenny right in the eye. "We have an open portal down there Lenny and something very dark and dangerous has come through. You heard what Edith said. It's still in there. What are we going to do about that?"

Lenny leaned forward to mirror Chuck's posture. "We're locked out Frasier. We can't do anything about that right now." He said as he stared back at Chuck. "You didn't mention the Psychic to the FBI did you?"

Chuck sat back in his chair and confidently folded his hands. "I did not." He said. "But I'm sure they're going to see her name on the visitors log at the gate and I'm sure they'll be calling me to ask more questions about that. She came in with *me* last night Lenny." Chuck put his head down for a second to collect his thoughts. He knew Lenny was up to something but he didn't think pushing back would be helpful at that moment. He decided to approach the conversation a little differently. "Look, Edith was very clear about the danger in opening that portal. That's already done. It's open. It's open and the thing that came through killed Martin. Did you know that the Coroner X-rayed his body and found 247 breaks in his bones? The whole human body only has 206 bones Lenny!"

Lenny looked very surprised by that. "Who told you that?" He asked.

"I just heard it today from someone at the Coroner's office. There's no way another human being could do that to a person without using a steam roller. This thing down there is dangerous. I'm not sure it can be contained in the lab either. For all we know, it could be up here on this floor somewhere right now."

CHAPTER 35

Edith sat in the tall wingback chair and took a sip of her apple tea as she glanced out the tall window overlooking Auset's back yard. The landscaping was full of colorful blooms and lush green plants. It reminded Edith of her own flower beds at home. The sun was shining and it was a beautiful summer day outside, but Edith was focused on the dark death and destructive forces that had taken the life of an innocent Security Guard in such a violent manner just two days before. She was there to get some answers.

"You are correct in your observation Edith. There is not one Demon. It is a manifestation of an army of hundreds of Demons. A legion." Auset said.

"And I am only a single old woman. I cannot combat this alone. I am only human and this powerful thing has never been human. We need an army of Angels Auset. A strong army of Angels to drive this thing back to where it came from." Edith said. She was confident in her abilities, but she was also realistic about her limitations as a single vulnerable human being.

"We know this. We are ready for battle. We must wait for the right time." Auset said. "When the doorway is open and when he who summoned the Beast is slain by the Beast."

Edith thought about this for a few minutes. Sometimes Auset spoke cryptically and she wanted to make sure that she fully understood her meaning. She's obviously speaking of Lt. Colonel Kawalski. He opened the portal, and therefore summoned the beast. Now she had to wait for the Beast to kill Kawalski? When would that be happening?

"So, the trigger is the death of the man who opened the portal and summoned this thing here. Is that correct?" Edith said.

"Yes. It has come for him, but it wants to take many… And it will take many before it takes he who summoned it." Auset said.

"How will we know when it's the right time to act?" Edith asked.

"You will know Edith. Lily will know too. Until then you must stay away from the portal or you will become one of the many it takes." Auset said.

"Well, we don't want that." Edith said as she took another sip of the delicious apple tea. She glanced out the window for a moment and noticed three white doves perched on the branch of an apple tree. This is not something you would expect to see in the back yard of a residence in suburban Chicago… Perhaps if it was a magician's home, maybe. But this was Auset who was not human, but a higher light being. Edith would not be surprised to see a full grown Bengal Tiger somewhere out there along with Panda Bear. Edith dropped her eyes down to ground level and saw a Peacock with his feathers fanned out staring at her. *'Of course there's a Peacock!'* Edith mumbled to herself in amusement as she took another sip of tea.

"The boy's Father holds the key. He knows the scientific process that reverses the vortex within the portal. It will pull the beast back through so the doorway can be sealed forever." Auset said. Edith knew she was talking about Chuck but she wasn't sure if Chuck would actually know what Auset was speaking of.

"Does the boy's Father know that he knows how to do this?" Edith asked. Auset smiled as she sat back in the high wingback chair she was sitting in across from Edith. She was pleased that Edith honed in on that small detail. It proved that she was the right person for this very important task.

"No, he does not… Not yet." Auset said.

"Can you tell me *when* all of this will take place? A week, a month?" Edith asked. She wanted to know how much time she had to prepare and she was sure that Auset would be able to define a timeline like she did with Joey Frasier's window to return under the next New Moon.

Auset sat back and looked out over her lush back yard with exotic wild life. "As I said, the Beast will take many before it takes he who summoned it. It has left the confines of the laboratory and is now roaming the Earth causing chaos. The time draws near *after* the Beast slays the summoner, then Bhola comes. Only then will you send it back from where it came." She said.

"What or who is Bhola?" Edith asked.

"Pay attention to world events. You will know as the time draws near." Auset said as she stood up. This was Edith's queue to leave so she set her tea cup down and bid Auset farewell.

Lily and Joey were jumping on the trampoline non-stop for almost a half hour and decided to take a break and rest. They sat on the trampoline mat breathing heavy trying to cool down and catch their breath.

"I think it's really cool that you have abilities now Joey. You just have to keep it to yourself. People don't understand and they will treat you different if you tell anyone." Lily said.

"I know. That's what my Mom and Dad said too. Do you think Beth has abilities?" Joey asked. This was all new to him and he had a million questions.

"She probably does, but she's not open yet. It runs in Families. You opened when you went through the portal." Lily said.

"When did you open Lily?" Joey asked.

"I think that I was always open, but I started to understand I was different than most people about three years ago. Mrs. MacKenzie has been helping me learn to control my abilities and keep myself grounded." Lily explained. "Hey—Do you wanna do some Tai Chi with me?"

"What's Tai Chi?" Joey asked.

"It's a bunch of movements and breathing exercises that align your Chakras and it helps you stay grounded. C'mon. I'll show you! My Mom and Vince do it with me every morning." Lily said as she hopped off of the trampoline and stood in the part of the yard where she routinely did her Tai Chi exercises.

Joey hopped off the trampoline and followed her. "What's a Cha-Kra?" He asked.

"Mrs. MacKenzie says they're energy centers in the human body. There are seven of them. You'll learn about that later. Watch what I do and try to follow along. The breathing is very important." Lily said as she stood straight and tall and took a couple of deep cleansing breaths. Joey mimicked Lily's movements and after a few minutes, he caught on to the concept. Beth and Vince came out of the house and headed toward the trampoline as they watched Lily teach Joey the Tai Chi movements.

"What are you guys doing?" Beth asked.

"Tai Chi!" Lily said.

"Tai what?" Beth asked.

"It's an ancient Chinese exercise routine that helps align your Chakras and grounds you. It's very important for people with abilities to do it all the time." Vince explained.

"Okay, what is a Chakra and why do you need to align them?" Beth asked.

"They're the seven points in your body believed to be energy centers that sort of help your organ functions work as they should. You want to keep your energy centers aligned because it helps you keep psychologically, emotionally, physically, and spiritually balanced." Vince explained as he hopped on to the trampoline and then extended a hand to help Beth get on.

As Beth and Vince were laughing and jumping on the trampoline together, Chuck came walking around the corner from the driveway. Joey was focused on watching Lily's Tai Chi movements so he didn't notice his Father, but Beth noticed and immediately stopped jumping.

"Hi Dad! What are you doing home so early?" Beth said.

Joey turned around. "Hi Dad!" He said.

"Hi guys! What's going on here?" Chuck asked as he watched as Lily moved one arm slowly in a wide circular motion.

"It's called Tai Chi. It's fun. Wanna try?" Joey said.

"Naw, you go ahead. Looks like fun though." Chuck said. "Is your Mom inside Lily?"

As Lily nodded her head, Annie saw Chuck through the kitchen window and came out through the sliding glass door. "Hi Chuck! I didn't expect to see you. I thought Cheryl would be home first." Annie said as she dried her hands with a dish towel.

"Yeah, well, the lab is still shut down so there's not a whole lot to do there. I thought I'd just knock off early." Chuck said.

"Well, come on in. It's much cooler inside." Annie said as she invited him in. "I just made some lemonade, would you like a glass?"

"Sure, that sounds great." Chuck said as he followed her into the kitchen and sat down at the table. Annie poured two glasses of lemonade and sat down across the table from him.

"I get the feeling that there's more to it than just knocking off early because the lab is closed." Annie said.

"You're right. The FBI shut the lab down. We're locked out. It's not just because of Martin Reese's death, there's something else going on there. Kawalski did something and they're after him but I'm not sure why." Chuck said as he took a big gulp of his lemonade.

"You mean something other than opening the portal from Hell?" Annie asked.

"Yes. There's more to it than I originally thought. The FBI doesn't run down and throw a padlock on a government research lab because a Security Guard was murdered. No, there's something bigger that they're interested in but I don't know what it is." Chuck said.

The doorbell rang and Annie excused herself to go answer it. A few seconds later Annie emerged with Edith following behind her. "Look who's here?" She said.

"Hello Chuck." Edith said with a smile.

"Have a seat Edith. I'll get you some lemonade. Chuck was just telling me that the FBI came in today and shut the lab down." Annie said as she opened the cabinet to get a glass.

"Is that so?" Edith said with a surprised look on her face as she turned to Chuck.

"Yes. I didn't expect that." Chuck said. "I'm told it will be shut down for a while. I might have to work out of the La Grange or Oak Lawn facilities for a while. Oh, and Lenny gave me a Visitor's Pass for you. You've got clearance now…Although the project is suspended so you won't be needing it anymore."

"Well, this is probably a good thing. We shouldn't be going anywhere near the lab for a while. I've just come from meeting with Auset…" Edith said. She went on to explain everything that Auset had told her. She told them about the Black Mass that killed Martin Reese and what it really is. She explained that it will take the lives of many, many people before ultimately kills Lt. Colonel Kawalski. And that there would be a world event called *Bhola* that would occur when the time was right to send the Beast back through the portal.

"And there's something else." Edith said as she looked at Chuck. "You hold the key that reverses the vortex to send the Beast back through."

Chuck looked very surprised to hear this. "Me?" He said. "I have absolutely NO idea what that means. What key?"

"It's the scientific process or something. Auset speaks very vaguely. I couldn't get anything more specific out of her than that." Edith said.

"Well, how much time do I have to figure it out? I'm locked out of the lab so I can't get in there to even calibrate the Hadron Collider. I can find out what their coordinates were set at when they pulled the Black Mass through. I just have to look a little harder for it because they didn't run that data past me before they did it, but I can find it." Chuck said as he scratched his head.

"I'm not sure exactly. She told me it would be after the 'summoner' was killed by the Beast when Bhola appeared…Whatever that is." Edith said.

"What could she mean by that?" Annie asked.

Edith looked at Annie with that *does that surprise you?* Look. "It's Auset, dear. She doesn't speak in terms of our calendar. There will apparently be a world event that will occur with the name Bhola relating to it and that will be our queue to deal with the Beast." She said. "And Chuck?" Edith continued. "You can't go anywhere near that lab until we draw closer to that time. It will kill you, so you must stay away. It sounds like the FBI shutting everything down was to your benefit."

Chuck nodded as he took a sip of lemonade. He wasn't sure what *"key"* he was supposed to be responsible for but he was a smart guy and he'd do his best to figure it out. The three of them brainstormed around the kitchen table as to what Auset could have meant about Chuck having the "key" and what Bhola could possibly mean when the phone rang. It was Cheryl calling from the hospital.

"Annie? I think you'd better come down here right now." Cheryl said. "There's been a terrible accident. Mark was just brought in."

Annie dropped the phone.

CHAPTER 36

When Annie arrived at the hospital, she was numb. She knew that driving a truck for a living would subject Mark to risks of a serious accident on the road, but she always thought that if it did happen, it would happen during bad weather. Mark was a good truck driver. One of the best. On a sunny, dry, Summer afternoon things like this rarely happened…Although, this was an unusual accident. There was a 16 car pile-up on I-55 that started with a mysterious explosion in a vacant garage along the side of the highway. There was a piggy back semi-trailer passing the garage at the precise moment the explosion occurred. Both trailers were tossed in the air and landed on 7 cars on the highway, then the others smashed into them. Mark was on his way home from the terminal when his Suburban was one of the 7 cars who suffered the impact of the airborne tractor trailers that were filled with cargo.

Cheryl and another nurse came to get Annie after she had checked in with the ER Nurse manning the front desk. Cheryl took her by the hand and led her down the hall, stopping after they cleared the double doors to the emergency unit. "Annie, look at me." Cheryl said as she firmly grabbed her by the shoulders. Annie looked at her with a blank stare. She was in shock. "Annie, he looks bad. But you have to be strong. Dr. Luccetti is in there with him now and he's the best ER Doc on staff tonight. Don't overreact. Sometimes things look much worse than they really are. Do you understand?" All of Cheryl's words were a string of mumbles to her. She nodded her head in acknowledgement but did not really register everything that Cheryl actually said to her.

"I think maybe we should find a chair until Dr. Luccetti comes out of the room." The other Nurse said.

"Yes, good idea." Cheryl said as she found a spare chair in an empty room and helped Annie sit down.

"I'll get some water." The other Nurse said.

"Thank you Linda." Cheryl said as she squatted down in front of Annie and held her hands. "Annie? Look at me." She said.

Annie looked at Cheryl. "I'm…I'm okay." She said. "I just…What happened to him Cheryl? Is he going to be alright?" She asked. She was trembling.

"He's in the best of hands my friend. I'll take you in to see him as soon as the Doctor says it's okay. I just didn't want to leave you out in the waiting room with all of the chaos." Chery said.

Nurse Linda returned with a cup of water and Annie took a sip. "Linda? Can you stay with her for a moment? I need to go talk to the rest of the Family in the waiting room for a second." Cheryl said.

"Of course. We'll be right here." Linda assured her.

Cheryl walked back through the double doors and saw Chuck sitting in the waiting room with Vince and Lily. "Hi." She said as she gave him a big hug.

"Is Mark going to be okay?" Chuck asked.

Cheryl glanced down at Lily and Vince and gave them a warm reassuring smile. "I think everything will be okay. It's just *not* so okay right now." She said as she hugged the Campbell children. "Where are Beth and Joey?"

"Edith was at the house so I left them with her. I wasn't sure what was happening so I brought Vince and Lily down with Annie. I thought they should all be together." Chuck said.

Cheryl gave him a smile confirming that he made a good decision. She bent down to Lily's level to talk to them. "Your dad was in a bad accident on the highway, but he's here now and the best Doctor we have here tonight is taking care of him. As soon as he says it's alright, I'll take you back to see him, okay?" Cheryl was trying her best not to scare them but they knew better.

"My Daddy is hurt bad isn't he?" Lily said with tears welling up in her eyes.

"Yes Honey. He's hurt bad. But we're doing everything we can to help him. Don't you worry—We're going to take extra good care of him." Cheryl said as sincerely as she could. She didn't want to give them false hope, but there was no sense in scaring them until they knew how bad it was for sure.

Vince put his arm around Lily and hugged her. "It's okay Lil. Dad's going to be okay." He said. Vince was very good at showing how brave he was but inside he was terrified that his Father might not survive.

"Chuck, could you please take the kids down to the cafeteria and get them something to eat or drink? I'm going to go back and sit with Annie. I'll come and find you when I know more." Cheryl said. "Has anyone told Stephen?"

"Edith was calling him at the pizza place when we left. I'm sure he's on his way." Chuck said.

"Ok good." Cheryl kissed her husband lightly on the cheek and went back down the hall through the double doors where she had left Annie sitting in the hallway with Linda.

Dr. Luccetti came out of the room and told them they were going to take Mark to surgery. He had some internal bleeding and they needed to attend to that right away. Seconds later, a team of people swiftly wheeled the gurney that Mark was laying on out of the room and down the hall to surgery. Annie got a quick look at him. He had a big gash on his head and he was covered in blood. He had a cervical collar on, his arm was in a splint and he didn't appear conscious. All she could think about was '*why? Why did this have to happen to him?*' She lowered her head and started praying to God to please let him live. After the gurney carrying Mark disappeared through the next set of double doors down the hall, Cheryl escorted Annie to the cafeteria so she could wait with the kids.

Lily and Vince were sitting at a table in the corner of the cafeteria with their Cokes when Annie and Cheryl walked in. Lily ran to her Mother and hugged her tightly. It was all Annie could do to keep from sobbing. She had to be strong for the kids. "Daddy was taken to surgery. He has some internal injuries that they have to fix." She said.

"What happened to him Momma?" Lily said.

"He was on his way home and there was an accident involving a lot of cars. Your Dad was hurt in the accident." That was all Annie could say. She really didn't know much more than that.

"Is he going to be okay Mom?" Vince asked.

"I'm sure he will Sweetheart. The Doctors are doing everything they can for him. We just have to wait." Annie said.

Cheryl heard her name paged overhead and went to the nearest phone. It was Dr. Luccetti giving her an update. She hung up and returned to the table with Chuck, Annie, and the kids.

"That was the Doctor who evaluated Mark when he came in. The surgeon said that he'll be in surgery for a couple of hours so let's just make ourselves comfortable here for a while." She explained.

"I'm going to run down to the gift shop and see if they have a deck of cards or something. Is there anything else I can get for you Annie?" Chuck asked.

"Not that I can think of right now Chuck, thank you." Annie said as she held Lily on her lap.

"I'll come with you." Vince said. He was upset but found the trip to the gift shop to be an opportunity to break away from the sadness of his Mother and Sister for a few minutes.

Lily sat quietly and asked her Guides and Guardian Angels for help. She was scared and it was hard for her to quiet her mind. Hospitals were full of residual energy of terrible pain and death, all of which she was picking up on at that moment. The room was filled with dead people—some were there to console her, and others were stuck and needed her help. Lily very politely asked them not to seek her help right now and asked for them to help her understand what was happening to her Father. Lily desperately tried to quiet the chatter in her mind so she could connect with her Guides, but she could hear nothing. There were so many dead people in the room that it was almost suffocating, yet she could not hear their voices. She sat quietly holding on tightly to her Mother.

A few minutes later Chuck returned with some candy bars, a deck of cards, and some coloring books and crayons for Lily. "This was all they had, but this will help pass the time while we wait." He said. "Would anyone like a candy bar?" Chuck handed Lily a Mars Bar—Her favorite candy bar that Mark would bring home for her after his long monthly trip. She reached out for it but suddenly lost her appetite. It wouldn't taste the same if she ate it now, and she didn't feel much like eating anything anyway.

"Thank you Mr. Frasier." Lily said sweetly.

Annie looked toward the door as Stephen and Ed came into the room. Stephen ran to his Mother and hugged her. Ed pulled up a couple of chairs and they sat down. "How's Mark? Is he okay?" Ed asked.

"He's in surgery right now. They said it will be a couple of hours. There's some internal bleeding but that's all I know." Annie said.

Ed lowered his head and said a prayer silently to himself. "There are a few Police Officers in the waiting room talking to the families. I'm going to go see if I can find out any more details about what happened. I'll be right back." He said as he rose from his chair and left the cafeteria.

Chuck played Gin Rummy with Vince, Stephen, and Annie for a while and it was a nice distraction for a few minutes. About 40 minutes later, Ed returned with more news about the accident.

"It appears that there were 22 people involved in the accident and there are 8 fatalities so far. Mark was in one of the 7 cars that were crushed by the trailers. It's a miracle that he's alive. The other 8 fatalities were the truck driver and the drivers of the other crushed cars, and also a passenger in one of them. Mark is the only survivor of all of the cars crushed by the trailers. All of the other people involved were injured in the crash but otherwise okay." Ed explained.

"What happened? I heard there was an explosion but do they know what caused it?" Annie asked.

"Well, one Officer said that there were reports of a large cloud of black smoke that hovered over the garage right before the explosion, so it appeared that something was on fire, but they don't know what actually caused it yet. The Fire Marshall is investigating that now." Ed said. "And Annie, the Officers wanted to speak with you directly. I'll walk you out there now if you'd like. I'm sure the kids will be fine here."

"Yeah Annie, go ahead. We'll stay with the kids." Cheryl said.

Annie set Lily down and she instantly crawled up into Stephen's lap. She needed the extra reassurance of human touch in the room full of dead people right now and Stephen gladly obliged. As they walked down the hall, Ed filled her in on some of the other details that he didn't want to share in front of the kids.

"So, the police showed me some Polaroids of the Suburban. I'm amazed that Mark survived." Ed said. "It's a twisted mess. They had to cut him out of it."

"Dear God. I'm not sure I want to see that." Annie said.

"The Police will need Mark's driver's license. I don't suppose they gave you Mark's wallet?" Ed said as he tried to prepare her for things they would need from her.

"No, they didn't…And quite frankly I didn't even think to ask." Annie said. She stopped for a minute and Ed stopped with her in the hallway.

"Are you alright Annie?" Ed asked.

"Yeah, I just…I just had an image flash in my head of my Father standing next to Mark in the Operating Room…Weird." She said. "Ed, did the police say anything about whether or not Mark was conscious when they removed him from the car?"

Ed thought for a minute. "No. No one mentioned it either way. Why do you ask?"

"I just wonder if he realized what happened to him. He didn't look conscious when they wheeled him off to surgery earlier." Annie said. Her biggest fear was that he would never make it out of surgery alive. She couldn't bear the thought of losing him, but she had to trust that the Doctors knew what they were doing and that he would be able to come home soon. She looked at her watch and nearly an hour and a half had passed since he went to surgery but it seemed like an eternity.

As they came out into the waiting room of the ER, there were about six Officers there speaking to the family members of the other victims in the accident. One of the Officers recognized Ed and broke away from the family he was talking to, leaving his partner to answer their questions. Ed saw him and waved him over.

"Hi Officer Jenkins. This is Annie Campbell. Her husband is Mark Campbell—The driver of the Suburban." Ed said as he introduced them.

"Hello." Annie said as she shook the officer's hand.

"It's nice to meet you Mrs. Campbell, and just let me say, I'm sorry to have to meet you under these circumstances. Please, have a seat. I just need to ask you a couple of questions and let you know what we know about the accident so far." Officer Jenkins said as he pulled a chair up in front of where Ed and Annie had just seated themselves.

"Um, I don't have Mark's wallet or anything. They whisked him off to surgery right away and I didn't even get a chance to see him..." Annie said.

"Not to worry Mrs. Campbell, we can get that information later. Was your husband driving for work at the time?" Officer Jenkins asked.

"He's a truck driver but he was finished with his route for the day and was headed home from the terminal when this happened. He was only three exits away from home actually." Annie explained.

"I see. So he was not working at the time." Officer Jenkins said.

"No, he was done for the day and heading home." Annie said. "The Suburban is our personal vehicle."

Officer Jenkins scribbled a few notes in his notebook. "Okay. Well, we'll need to take a statement from your husband at some point and we will be conducting a thorough investigation of the explosion. We're tracking down the owners of the building and we'll determine who was at fault eventually. Your husband being a truck driver for a living tells me that he's a far more experienced driver than most, and judging by the damage to the vehicle, I'd say he was a damn good defensive driver at that. That's probably what saved his life." He said. Annie nodded her head in acknowledgment.

"I told Annie that you had some photos of the wreckage." Ed said. "Do you want to see them Annie?"

Annie wasn't sure she did, but she knew that it would be nagging at her if she did not. "Yes, I'd like to see the photographs if you have them." She said as she braced herself for the images she was about to be shown.

"Yes M'am. Here they are." Officer Jenkins flipped to the back pocket in his notebook and presented Annie with five photographs of the wreckage showing all sides of the vehicle.

Annie took the photographs in her hands and gasped. The Suburban was almost completely crushed on the driver's side and the whole front end was smashed. The tractor trailer was laying on its side next to the driver's side and you could see where it had landed across the front left side of the hood and left side of the windshield and roof. All of the glass in the car was shattered and there was blood all over the front seat and what was left of the dash. One photo showed the fire department cutting Mark out of the tangled wreckage. It was devastating to see. Tears began to well up in Annie's eyes and Ed put his arm around her to comfort her. He could have easily died in this accident. It was truly a miracle that he survived.

"I'm so sorry M'am. I'm not sure what kind of insurance he has at work, but some drivers are covered under Workman's Comp going to and from work in his profession. You might want to check that out." Officer Jenkins said. "Either way, we are required to provide all insurance companies involved with a full report. Once we are able to formally rule the explosion as the cause, and I believe we will, you can file a suit against the owner of the property for damages. I advise you to keep good notes of everything your husband remembers and everyone you talk to about this going forward. It will be very helpful to your case."

"Unfortunately, Briggs Transportation does not cover accidents to or from the terminal. Its great coverage, but only while we're behind the wheel of their company owned trucks." Ed said. "I work for the same company so I already looked into that for Mark."

"Thank you for doing that Ed. I really appreciate it." Annie said as she handed the photographs back to Officer Jenkins. "So, what's next? Are there any forms or anything that you need me to fill out?" Annie was a little anxious to get back to the kids, especially after seeing the photographs of the wreckage that caused Mark to be rushed into emergency surgery.

"No forms Mrs. Campbell, but if you could give me your home address, phone number, and your husband's date of birth I can finish the police report. Do you happen to know the extent of your husband's injuries?" Officer Jenkins said.

"No, not yet. They know that he has some broken bones and internal injuries, but they won't know the extent of it until he's out of surgery. I can call you with that information later." Annie said as she wrote down their address and phone number for the Officer.

"Here's my card. Please give me a call when you know more. I'll keep you informed of our investigation." Officer Jenkins said. "I'm very sorry about your husband Mrs. Campbell. I hope he comes out of this okay."

"Thank you." Annie said as she rose to walk back to the cafeteria. Ed shook the Officer's hand and thanked him again for his help, then he put his arm around Annie and walked her down the hall.

When they got back to the cafeteria, the Gin Rummy game was still going on and Lily was sitting quietly coloring in the coloring book that Chuck got for her in the gift shop, while Cheryl sat next to her looking on. Annie sat down on the other side of Lily and kissed her on the head. "Beautiful picture Lily." She said as she stroked her Daughter's hair.

"Did they have any new information for you Annie?" Cheryl asked.

"Not really. They're still investigating." Annie said as she looked at her watch. 2 ½ hours had passed since Mark went to surgery and she was beginning to worry. She glanced at Cheryl who knew right away what she was thinking.

"I let the recovery room staff know where we are. They said that Dr. Ryerson will be out to talk to you when he's finished." Cheryl assured her.

Nearly another whole hour had passed before a tall skinny Doctor appeared in scrubs, a paper hat, and paper shoe coverings. Cheryl waved him over as soon as he saw her. When he approached the table, he introduced himself and pulled up a chair. The Gin Rummy game halted and Lily set her crayons down so they could listen to what the Doctor said. He was smiling, so that was a good sign.

"Well, your husband is one tough cookie for sure." Dr. Ryerson started. "His spleen was ruptured, so we had to remove it. His left kidney was split in half so we did our best to salvage the half still attached to the renal artery. The left side of his clavicle, or collarbone is broken, as were four of his ribs on the left side. His left humerus was broken in three places and his left femur was broken. We had to call an Orthopedic Surgeon in to put a couple of plates in his arm to stabilize it. He fractured his mandible, or jaw bone, but it's remarkably intact. He broke a couple of teeth on the left side from the impact, and he also has a concussion. On the right side, he's got some cuts and bruises and his right wrist is broken. He's got some deep cuts on his head, arms, and his face, so we cleaned them up and closed those with sutures, but I think he's going to be okay. He's got several weeks of healing time and several months of physical therapy ahead of him, but we expect that he will recover." He said as he paused for a moment to let everyone digest what he had just told them.

"So, my Daddy is going to be okay?" Lily asked in her sweet little voice.

"Yes Honey. I think your Daddy is going to be okay." Dr. Ryerson said. "He's in recovery now and they'll be keeping an eye on him until he comes out of his anesthesia, but the recovery Nurse will come out and bring you back to see him very soon. We want to keep him in the hospital for a couple of weeks just to make sure that kidney functions as it should and that he's stabilized so his bones can start to knit back together properly, but he will be able to go home shortly after that. It's going to take a while, but he should heal up and be almost as good as new."

Annie let out a huge sigh of relief. "Oh thank you Dr. Ryerson. That's such good news!" She said.

"Okay. I'll look in on him a little later once they move him to a room, and then I'll check on him again in the morning when I come in. They'll put a cast on his wrist, arm, and his leg later tomorrow. They have stiff splints on him now, but they need to let the swelling come down a little more before they put the cast on. Everything went well, now we just need to give him a little time heal." Dr. Ryerson stood up as they all thanked him and he walked back out of the cafeteria.

It was like a heavy weight had just been lifted off of them and the whole room felt much lighter. Mark was alive and he was going to be okay. He was one tough cookie indeed.

CHAPTER 37

After discovering that Joey had abilities, Edith seized the opportunity to work with him and explained the basics about setting boundaries with the Dead who would be around him all the time. Beth was fascinated by all of it and felt a little left out because she couldn't relate to what Lily, Vince, and now her little Brother experienced on a regular basis. Edith encouraged her to pay attention as she worked with Joey and assured her that it was very possible to develop her own abilities because everyone has them, it's just that most people are closed to them. Afterward, Edith ordered pizza to be delivered so that the kids would be fed by the time their Parents came back home. She hadn't heard anything from the hospital, but that was okay. She was assured that Mark was going to be fine through other channels.

"Our pizza will arrive any minute now, but do either of you know where they keep Winnie's dog food? Her bowl is empty and she looks like she's ready for dinner." Edith said.

"I'll feed her Mrs. MacKenzie. I know where it is." Beth said as she walked into the kitchen with a very hungry Cocker Spaniel following close behind her.

"Mrs. MacKenzie? Why are there portals, I mean, where do they come from?" Joey asked.

"Well, they're doorways to other dimensions. Sometimes they're opened by humans, and sometimes they're opened by other beings in another dimension." Edith explained.

"So there could be other people walking around from the past or the future and we wouldn't even know it?" Joey asked. He remembered his own experience traveling back in time to Ancient Egypt. Hatshepsut knew he was from the future because Heru had told her. It didn't seem to concern her, in fact, it didn't seem to surprise her at all. Was she used to people traveling through time and showing up in her palace? He wondered about that.

"It's possible, yes." Edith said. "But sometimes there aren't just human time travelers coming through portals. Sometimes they are alien beings. Shadow People and other entities that are not so nice." She explained as the doorbell rang. "That must be our pizza."

Edith went to the door and paid the pizza delivery boy, then she brought the pizza box out to the kitchen. Beth got some paper plates and napkins out of the pantry and the three of them sat down to eat.

"Mrs. MacKenzie? I'm worried about my Dad. I heard him talking to my Mom about a portal at his work and a bad thing that came through and it killed that man." Joey said.

Edith wasn't sure she should be talking to the kids about the portal at Chuck's lab, but Joey was asking a direct question and he deserved some kind of honest answer. "Well, your Dad was invited to work on a project having to do with time travel through a portal. Since it happened to you he became very interested in knowing more about it. But, the portal that was opened at your Dad's lab is different. It's the kind of portal that bad things come out of. He's helping me find a way to seal it shut." She explained.

"Is my Dad in danger?" Beth asked.

"I don't think so dear. Besides, the project was shut down for a while so your Father doesn't have to go in that lab anymore." Edith said as she took a small bite of her pizza. "Your Father is very smart. He'll be fine."

"I hope that Mr. Campbell will be alright. It's getting late and no one has called." Beth said with sincere concern in her voice.

"Mark is going to be okay. Don't you worry." Edith said.

The recovery Nurse came into the cafeteria and recognized Cheryl sitting in the corner of the room with the Campbell Family. "Mrs. Campbell?" She asked.

Annie stood up. "Yes? Can we see my Husband now?" She asked.

"Yes, he's awake and he's asking for you. Follow me and I'll take you to him." The Nurse said.

"Annie, you and the kids go with Shirley. We'll clean up here and we'll wait for you in the hall outside of recovery." Cheryl said.

Annie nodded and gathered her Children. They followed Nurse Shirley through a labyrinth of hallways and doorways until they reached a large room with beds separated by large curtains. Shirley pulled the curtain back and there was Mark, all bandaged up and looking miserable.

Annie and the kids circled around his bed and a small tear rand down his cheek. "Hi Fahh-nly." Mark said in a raspy, slurry voice. "I yuv you ahh tho musch."

Tears welled up in Annie's eyes at the sight of him. She bent over and gave him a soft kiss on his forehead. "I'm so sorry Honey. We were so worried." She said.

"I love you Daddy. Does it hurt really bad?" Lily said.

"I yuv you too punkin. Yessh, it hurts reedy bad but I be okay." Mark mumbled. His mouth was swollen and his jaw and a few of his teeth were broken so it was difficult to talk.

"We're glad you're going to be okay Dad." Stephen said. "Don't worry about anything at home, Vince and I can help Mom with whatever she needs." Vince stood next to him and nodded in agreement.

"I appreeescheate dat schun." Mark slurred.

Dr. Ryerson walked in holding a chart in his hand. "How are you feeling there Mark? Any pain?" He asked.

"A yiddle schooore but not too bad." Mark mumbled.

"Good. I ordered a good dose of morphine for you a little while ago, so Shirley should be bringing that in soon. We want to keep you as comfortable and still as we can for the first few days." Dr. Ryerson said. "We're going to move you upstairs in a few minutes and get you tucked into a semi-private room. No one is in the other bed right now, so you'll have the room all to yourself. Tonight we just want to keep you out of pain so you can rest. Tomorrow, the Orthopedic Doctor will come in and put a full cast on your leg, your arm, and your wrist. We only splinted it for now because we want that swelling to go down." He explained. "Do you have any questions for me?"

"Not dat I can ssink of." Mark mumbled.

"Dr. Ryerson? Now that I've seen him, how is he going to be getting around? With a broken left arm and a broken right wrist he can't use crutches." Annie asked. She was already trying to figure out how they were going to manage things once he got home.

"Wheelchair. He's not a candidate for crutches. That's why we'll probably keep him here for two or three weeks. We're better equipped to take care of him in the early stages of healing. We'll have the discharge planner go through everything with you before he leaves here so you can manage his care at home after that." Dr. Ryerson said. "I'll check in on you in the morning, okay?"

"Sannk you." Mark slurred.

Nurse Shirley came in with a syringe and administered the morphine through his IV. "Ok Mr. Campbell, this is going to make you very sleepy, but you will be feeling no pain." She said.

Within a minute Mark's eyes got heavy and he started to doze. Two large orderlies came in after the Doctor left and prepared to move him up to his room. They released the locking mechanism on the gurney and started wheeling his bed out of recovery.

"We're taking him upstairs to room 318. You can follow us up if you'd like." One of the orderlies said.

"Lead the way." Annie said as she put her arm around Lily and followed the gurney carrying her badly broken Husband down the hall. She turned to Stephen and asked if he would tell Cheryl, Ed, and Chuck what room they were headed to.

Stephen walked down through the double doors outside of recovery where the rest of the posse was waiting and told them what room Mark was being moved to.

"Great! That's a nice corner room." Cheryl said. "Let's go this way— There's another elevator over here."

By the time Stephen, Cheryl, Chuck, and Ed arrived on the 3rd floor, the orderlies who had brought Mark up to his room were standing at the elevator when the doors opened. They recognized Stephen and gave him directions how to get to Mark's room.

"Thank you." Stephen said as Cheryl led them down the hall to room 318. By the time they got there, Mark was all tucked in to a regular hospital bed and his IV was hanging on the stand next to him. The EKG monitor was sitting on a cart next to his bed and electrode wires were coming out of his hospital gown into the machine. Annie and Lily were standing next to him, not sure if it was okay to touch him since hand holding was obviously out of the question. Lily saw Grandpa Tom standing on the other side of Mark's bed watching over him. Lily looked up at Annie and noticed that she was looking directly at Grandpa Tom.

"Momma? Can you see him?" Lily whispered.

Without taking her eyes off of the spirit of her Father standing in front of her, she turned her head slightly toward Lily. "I can." She said softly as if speaking in her normal tone of voice would frighten him away. Her Father appeared to her in transparent form, but solid enough for her to see his face clearly. He smiled warmly at her, looked down at Mark and placed his hand gently on his battered shoulder, then winked at her as he did when she was younger as if to say *'Everything is going to be okay.'* Then he turned and walked out of the room, disappearing before reaching the door.

"Mom? Is everything okay?" Stephen asked. He was confused by the look on Annie's face.

Annie snapped out of her trance. "Huh? Um, yes, yes. Everything is fine Honey." She said as she shook her head a little and walked around the bed to give her son a hug. "We probably shouldn't stay much later. Your Dad has had a big day and he needs his rest."

"He got a healthy dose of medication so he's going to be sleepy. It's probably better if we let him rest. You can come back and see him tomorrow." Cheryl said.

Ed walked around to the side of the bed and leaned over to speak quietly to Mark. "Don't you worry about Annie and the kids, Buddy. We'll take care of anything they need. You just get better." He said. Mark fluttered his eyes a little and let out a slight moan in acknowledgment. Ed gave Annie a hug and told her not to worry about Briggs. He would let everyone know what happened and they'll get Mark's route covered while he recovers.

Annie smiled and thanked Ed for everything. "Who should I call at the office to find out about Mark's disability insurance?" She asked.

"Probably Christine. I'll go in early tomorrow and sort that out for you. She'll give you a call in the morning. Don't worry about a thing, Annie. We'll getcha taken care of." Ed reassured her.

"Thank you Ed. I really appreciate it." Annie said.

Everyone said their goodbyes as Mark slept soundly and comfortably thanks to a healthy dose of morphine. A Nurse came in and introduced herself as Mary, then she checked the IV line and the EKG monitor.

"I'll be taking care of Mr. Campbell tonight." Mary said. "Everything looks good. I'm going to turn the lights out and let him get some sleep. I'll call you if there are any changes, but he should be fine."

"Thank you." Annie said as she waited for the kids to say good night to their Father.

"Annie, since Chuck and I both have our cars here, why don't you and Lily ride home with me? The boys can drive home with Chuck." Cheryl said as she looked to Chuck for confirmation.

"Yeah, that sounds good. Come on boys, I'll take you home." Chuck said.

"I just have to stop by my locker on the 4th floor and get my purse. We'll see you back home." Cheryl said as she gave Chuck a kiss. "Lily? Would you like to go see the newborn babies in the nursery?" She asked.

Lily's eyes light up. "Yeah I would!" She said then she turned and blew a kiss to Mark. "Night night Daddy. We'll be back tomorrow."

In the dusky summer evening light, Edith sat in a chair on the deck sipping her tea as she watched Beth and Joey jump on the trampoline. *'It roams the Earth now Edith. It is responsible for the accident.'* Edith heard in her ear. She took a deep breath and closed her eyes as she focused on the messages she was receiving from her Guides. When she opened her eyes, she noticed headlights illuminating the garage door to her right.

"Hello Edith." Chuck said as he got out of the car. Vince jumped out of the back seat and ran towards Beth on the trampoline. Stephen said *Hello* and went inside to change his clothes. He was walking around smelling like a pizzeria at the hospital and he was getting a little sick of it.

"Hi Chuck. Come, sit. Would you like some tea?" Edith asked.

"No, no thank you. Cheryl, Lily and Annie are following behind us. They'll be here soon." Chuck said as he sat down.

"How is Mark?" Edith asked, even though she already knew the answer to that question.

Chuck looked down at his feet and sighed. "He's hurt pretty bad, but they say his prognosis is good. He's got several broken bones, broke some of his teeth, his jaw, and ruptured his spleen. One of his kidneys was split in half, but they saved the half that was still attached." Chuck looked up at Edith before continuing. The warmth of her face was soothing. "He's a mess."

"Well thank God he survived." She said as she took a sip of her tea before continuing. "Do they know how the accident happened?"

"The Police said that there was an explosion in a vacant storage garage next to the highway. There was a big truck pulling two trailers full of cargo that passed the garage at the exact time of the explosion. That blew the trailers into the air and one of them landed on top of Mark's Suburban. I guess there were 8 fatalities and several injured." Chuck explained.

"That had to be a very powerful explosion." Edith set her tea cup down on the table next to her chair. "Chuck? You're a Scientist. Don't you find it strange that an explosion powerful enough to toss a tractor trailer with two containers of heavy cargo into the air from 50 yards away would come from an empty storage garage? I mean, if it was empty, then the source could only be from a furnace or something…Don't you think?" Edith asked.

Chuck sat back and thought about that for a moment. "It does sound unlikely." He said as he stared at the kids on the trampoline together trying to catch the lightning bugs that were flickering around them as they jumped. "I suppose it's possible for a gas main to blow. That might produce enough force. Why do you ask?" He said.

"Well, something tells me that this wasn't a random accident." Edith said as she looked at Chuck. "I think this was the handiwork of the Dark Entity that came through your portal in the lab."

CHAPTER 38

Two weeks had gone by and Mark's injuries were beginning to heal. Still confined to his hospital bed, the Nurse came in with a tray of food for him. She carefully raised the back of his bed and raised the tray table a little higher so that he could sit up to eat his lunch. She unwrapped a couple of straws and put one in his mug of soup, and one in his cranberry juice. As Mark sipped his soup through a straw, Annie came into the room with Lily in tow, both carrying books and magazines to help him pass the time.

"Hi Daddy!" Lily said as she skipped into the room.

"Hi Punkin! What are you up to today?" Mark said as he pushed the straw out of his mouth with his tongue.

"I'm coming to see you. We brought you the new Elmo Leopard book." Lily said proudly as she held up the *Valdez is Coming* paperback. "I know you can't hold it yourself, but we can read it to you."

Mark laughed. "You mean Elmore Leonard." He said.

"That's what I said. Elmo Leopard." Lily said very matter-of-factly.

The Nurse looked over Annie's shoulder at the books she brought. "Oh, I've heard that's a good one. I wanted to read that myself. I'm sure you'll have no trouble getting the nurses to read a few chapters to you Mr. Campbell." The nurse said. "Is there anything else I can bring for you right now?"

"Ah, no. I think I'm fine right now. Annie can help me with the mashed potatoes and pudding." Mark said.

"Good. Okay, I'll leave you to spend some time with your Family and I'll come back and take your tray in a little bit." The Nurse said as she smiled and left the room.

"How are you feeling Honey? You look better today." Annie said as she pulled up a chair for herself and another one for Lily.

"Eh, a little better but still terribly uncomfortable." Mark explained. "They come in every couple of hours and pack pillows around me and adjust the bed up and down. The part I don't particularly like is when I get help to go to the bathroom...I'd really like to be able to wipe my own ass." He whispered.

Annie laughed. "I'll bet! Don't worry Honey, you'll get there." She stood up to spoon a bite of mashed potatoes and gravy into his mouth. "At least you're getting semi-solid food now. These potatoes smell pretty good."

"Yeah. I was getting tired of broth, Jello, and milkshakes." Mark said. "How's everything at home? Kids being good?"

"Great. Everyone has been great." She said. "The Boys have been very helpful. Vince mows the lawn and takes care of the trash. Stephen bought a few groceries when he got paid last week.

You'd be proud of them." Annie said as she spooned more mashed potatoes into his mouth. With Mark in the hospital and unable to work, the household income came to a complete halt. Annie was extremely worried about their finances. She knew that Mark wouldn't be able to return to work for several months and they didn't have much left in savings. The move to their new home took a large chunk of the cash they had available and Annie knew the reserves were dangerously low. She could make next month's house payment, but she was unsure how she was going to make ends meet after that.

"I start school next week Daddy. Joey is in my class this time so that will be fun!" Lily said. She sensed her Mother's sadness setting in and wanted to change the subject.

"That will be fun!" Mark said. "You'll have someone to do homework with."

"After the kids are back in school, I thought I would go find a part-time job...Although, you're going to need help after they let you come home so I'm not sure how to juggle that, but we'll figure something out." Annie said as she scraped the last of the mashed potatoes and gravy from the sides of the bowl. She did her very best to conceal how worried she was.

"I'm supposed to be getting a disability check. Haven't you seen one yet?" Mark asked. He was a proud man and it hurt him deeply to be so helpless and unable to take care of his Family.

"Not yet." Annie said as she fed the last of the mashed potatoes to her husband. "Mmmmm. Chocolate pudding for dessert!" Annie pulled the plastic wrap off of the bowl and dipped the spoon into it.

Just then, a familiar face peeked around the corner. "Hey there Buddy! How are you feeling today?" Ed appeared in the doorway wearing his usual attire—A baseball cap, white T-shirt, faded blue jeans and cowboy boots. Even in the hot, humid Chicago summers, Ed was rarely seen without cowboy boots.

'Hey hey! Edward. Good to see you!" Mark said. "Just having lunch. I'm up to mashed potatoes and pudding now—big improvement!"

Ed walked around to the side of the bed and gave Annie a big hug. "How are you doing, Annie?"

"I'm hanging in there. We're getting along okay." Annie said as she fed Mark another spoonful of pudding.

"Well, I think I can help you feel a little better about things. Everybody at work feels terrible about what happened, and well…The folks at the terminal all pitched in a little to help you guys out." Ed said as he reached around to his back pocket and pulled out a fat white envelope and handed it to Annie. She opened it and gasped.

"Oh, my gosh Ed!" Tears were welling up in her eyes as she pulled a large wad of cash out of the envelope.

"There's about $1,350 in there. That should help you guys keep the bills paid and food on the table for a little while." Ed said as he blushed.

"I don't know what to say." Mark said as he choked up by this very unexpected display of unselfish generosity by his co-workers. "Thank you. Thank you so much!"

Annie threw her arms around Ed and began to cry. "Thank you so much Ed! This is so helpful… More than you know! Please tell everyone that we are so grateful for their generosity. We appreciate this so much!"

"Well, everybody just feels terrible and they all wanted to do something for you. We figured you could use cash more than anything else." Ed said. Ed's timing was perfect. Annie had expected to discuss their dwindling finances with Mark that afternoon, but now she didn't have to. She was grateful for his friendship and all of the good people Mark worked with.

"And I have some news about the accident." Ed continued. "The Fire Marshall has completed his investigation. They couldn't find the source of the explosion. There just wasn't anything combustible in the garage and the gas lines to the area are still intact."

"Then how did it happen?" Mark asked.

"They don't know." Ed said. "There were several witnesses who said that they saw a cloud of black smoke hovering over the building before the blast."

Lily stood up from the chair she was sitting on and closed her Highlights magazine. She walked around to the opposite side of Mark's bed so she could look straight at her Parents and Ed. "It wasn't a fire. It was something really bad. It's the bad thing that killed the man at Mr. Frasier's work." Lily said in a very serious voice. "*IT* caused that explosion that hurt you Daddy."

Ed knew what Lily was talking about. He had spoken to Edith the day before and she expressed her concerns about the Dark Entity that had escaped the Lab and was now roaming the area causing chaos and destruction.

As they were talking, Mark noticed a news story on the television set on the wall. The volume was down but there was a collapsed bridge and police cars and fire trucks were everywhere. "What the hell is this?" Mark said. "Annie can you turn this up please?"

Ed and Annie turned their attention to the television set as she walked over and turned up the volume.

'The Hwy 55 Bridge over the Mississippi River in Memphis has collapsed and there are multiple casualties. Rescue boats and divers are pulling bodies from automobiles that have fallen into the river. The death count so far is 32. Officials say they are unsure why the bridge collapsed because it just passed a safety inspection earlier this Summer. It's early afternoon and had this occurred two hours from now, the casualty count would have been much higher during the peak commuter hours. Fire and Rescue is searching for any survivors, but there doesn't appear to be much hope left to find anyone alive. This is Jim Parker reporting…Channel 4 news, Memphis.'

"Oh my gosh! How horrible!" Annie said.

Ed turned to Mark. He had a peculiar feeling about what he just watched on TV. "There's something that just doesn't seem right about that. Bridges just don't collapse without a major earthquake or something…Especially bridges that pass an inspection just two months ago." Ed said.

"Do you think there was foul play?" Annie asked as she spooned more pudding into Mark's mouth.

"I don't know. It just feels wrong." Ed said.

"I know what you mean. Something just ain't right there. Bridges just don't collapse like that." Mark said.

"Daddy? How far away is Memphis?" Lily asked.

"It's about 500 miles south of here. Why do you ask?" Mark said.

"Just wondering. It's very sad." Lily said quietly. She knew that there was something strange about this accident—just like the accident that severely injured her Father. Ed knew it too.

The nurse came back into the room to check Mark's blood pressure and take away his lunch tray. "Well Mr. Campbell, your blood pressure is right where we want it—110/78." She said as she unwrapped the blood pressure cuff and hung it back on the wall. "Are you all finished with your lunch?"

"Yes, thank you." Mark said as he tried to shift himself slightly in his bed.

"The Doctor will be in to see you shortly. I think he's planning on sending you home in a couple of days. Mrs. Campbell, can you stick around for a little while? I'm sure he'll want to talk to you about how to manage things at home." The Nurse said.

Lily heard this and squealed a little as she jumped up and down clapping her hands. "Yay! You get to come home Daddy! Winnie will be so excited!" She said.

"Well as nice as you all have been to me these past couple of weeks, I have to say I'm really looking forward to going back home." Mark said. The Nurse smiled and left the room with the lunch tray. Annie smiled. She was thrilled that Mark would get to come home but she realized how immobile he actually was and she was wondering how she was going to manage it. There were stairs everywhere and Mark would be in a wheelchair for at least four more weeks. Before she could say what she was thinking, the Doctor entered the room.

"Hey there Mark—How are you doing today?" Dr. Ryerson said as he flipped the cover of Mark's medical chart. "Your labs look terrific. How's your pain?"

"Not too bad. I'm a little sore after getting out of bed to go to the bathroom, but otherwise I'm felling okay." Mark said. "I heard a rumor that you might be sending me home in a couple of days. Is that true?"

Dr. Ryerson smiled. "I was thinking about it. How do you all feel about that?" He said as he looked at Annie. She looked pleased to hear the news, but the anxiety was written all over her face and there was nothing she could do to hide it.

"Well…" Annie started. "We have a tri-level house and, well, I'm not sure how we're going to move Mark around in a wheelchair…" She didn't want Mark to think that she wasn't happy to have him back home, but she was afraid that he might fall and reinjure himself somehow.

"Annie? I've got some ideas. Don't worry. I'll help you get the house ready for him." Ed said.

"Well there you go. He's going to need someone to help him with a few things, but he's healing up quite well and it shouldn't be too long before he's able to get around on his own again." Dr. Ryerson flipped through a few pages in the chart and made some notes. "I'm going to have the Physical Therapist come in and chat with you before you leave here, and I'd like her to accompany you home on the first day to make some recommendations that will be helpful to manage things.

Annie let out a sign of relief. "That would be really nice, thank you." She said as she turned to Ed and smiled.

"Ok then. I'll be back to look in on you tomorrow." Dr. Ryerson smiled and left the room with Mark's chart tucked under his arm.

"How are we going to get you upstairs to our bedroom?" Annie asked as she adjusted Mark's pillows.

"You're not." Mark said. "I think you should just park me on the couch in the family room. I can come in through the garage—no stairs—and there's a bathroom down there, and its right next to the kitchen…I'll be fine."

"Mark, you are not going to be comfortable sleeping on the family room couch!" Annie said.

"Actually, I think you can rent a hospital bed like the one you're in. You'll be able to raise and lower the back of it. It will be much easier. I can mount a bar on the wall next to the toilet.

There's a few things that we can do to make it work. Don't sweat it Annie. I'll take care of the bathroom. You look into the hospital bed rental. We can do this." Ed said. He had a way of putting tasks into a check list that made things workable. And like Mark, Ed could fix or modify anything. This was very reassuring to Annie.

"There you go—problem solved!" Mark said as he smiled and winked at Lily who stood quietly at the side of his bed.

Lily smiled and turned her attention back to the television set. There was an update on the bridge collapse in Memphis. *"This just in from our CBS affiliate in Memphis…The confirmed death toll has risen to 52…There are no survivors. This is one of the worst structural failures in this country in several decades. The Army Corps of Engineers have been called in to assist with the reconstruction of the bridge. It is unclear at this point why the bridge failed, but inspectors at City Hall insist that the bridge was structurally sound just two months ago and have no explanation as to why it failed. The City is denying responsibility and police are investigating the possibility of foul play…"* It was the Dark Entity that came through the portal at Chuck Frasier's Lab. Lily knew it, and she knew this wouldn't be the last disaster it would cause.

CHAPTER 39

OCTOBER 1970

The kids were back in school and it had been six weeks since Mark's accident. His casts were removed and he was getting around pretty well on his own with a leg brace and a cane. He wasn't cleared to go back to work just yet, but between the disability insurance payments and the cash donation by his co-workers, they managed to keep the bills paid, the lights on, and groceries in the fridge.

"Lily's birthday is next Saturday…" Annie said as she put the last of the groceries away and folded the last paper grocery bag.

"I know. Can't believe she's 7 already. Are we doing a kid party or family thing?" Mark asked as he sat at the table and read the paper.

"Lily doesn't have a lot of friends. She's…*different* and she doesn't seem to have any interest in playing with the other little girls at school. She spends most of her time with Joey. The two of them have really grown rather close after Joey's time travel experience last Summer." Annie said. "I think she'd really enjoy just celebrating with the Frasier's and maybe Edith, Ed, and Barbara. What do you think?"

"That sounds fine. We've got to watch our money a little while longer, so I think celebrating at home is a good idea. We can get pizza or something… Stephen gets a discount." Mark said. He wanted his Daughter's birthday to be special but he was also sensitive to the reality of the limitations of their bank account.

"I can make her favorite Birthday cake—white cake with white frosting. We'll get some balloons. We'll make it fun." Annie said as she jotted down a few things she needed to get the next time she went to the store.

"What does she want this year?" Mark asked.

Annie threw him a *'you've got to be kidding me'* look. "You seriously have to ask? Mark! Where have you been? All she talks about is an Easy Bake Oven." Annie said.

"Oh yeah. The little plastic thing that cooks stuff with a light bulb. How expensive are they?" Mark asked.

"I saw it advertised at K-Mart for $8.99 this week. Maybe we should go get one." Annie said.

"Good idea. I could get out of the house for a little while. Let's go before the kids get home from school." Mark said as he stood up and reached for his cane. "Have you seen my shoes?"

"Sit back down and I'll bring them to you." Annie said as she retrieved his tennis shoes from the front closet and helped him put them on. She put him in the passenger seat of the Toronado, a seat he hated to be in when Annie was in the car. Not that she was a bad driver, she just wasn't as good as he was and he found himself tensing up as she braked at a stop light.

Annie was very skilled at spending on a tight budget. K-Mart was the store of choice when she wanted to stretch a dollar and today was no exception. She managed to get the Easy Bake Oven, wrapping paper, a card, birthday candles, balloons, crepe paper, festive paper plates and napkins, laundry detergent, dog food, and a Malibu Barbie for only $31. Mark was impressed. "Wow! I can't believe we got all this stuff for $31. Good job Babe." Mark complemented her.

"All it takes is shopping the sales and clipping a few coupons. All in a days' work my dear." Annie said proudly as she loaded her purchases in to the trunk of the car. "I'll make Lily's cake on Friday.

Remind me to ask Stephen about the pizza. I think he gets 20% off, but I want to make sure he can do that on a large order."

When they pulled in the driveway, Cheryl was knocking on the front door and waved when she saw them. "Hi! I was just coming over to see how you're getting along Mark." Cheryl said as she walked toward the car.

Cheryl and Chuck were wonderful neighbors and had become very good friends. Cheryl looked in on Mark nearly every day when he first got home, and Chuck assisted when Annie needed a little help lifting Mark out of his wheelchair. Chuck still hadn't returned back to Argon National Laboratories since the brutal murder of the Security Guard, and they hadn't had any further incidents there since the lab was shut down. This was a topic that Annie was itching to inquire about but she was always pre-occupied with Mark's care at home.

"I'm doing well Cheryl, thank you." Mark said.

"Here Annie, let me help you carry this stuff in." Cheryl said as she grabbed a bag out of the trunk.

"Thanks!" Annie said. "Are you just heading out or coming home from work?"

"I just got home. I went in early today." Cheryl said. "The kids seem to like their classes this year."

"Yeah, I haven't heard anything negative at all from any of them. Usually there's something, you know, this teacher sucks, or I have annoying so-and-so in my class, or something like that." Annie said. "I think the friendships that have sprouted between Lily and Joey and with Beth and Vince have made a big difference. They share classes together and that makes school this year much more fun."

"Definitely. My kids are very fortunate to have their best friends in their classes, AND living right across the street." Cheryl said as she laughed. "It just doesn't get much better than that."

"Say, Lily's birthday is next Saturday. We're just going to keep it low key this year. We'd love it if you guys could join us for pizza and Birthday cake. Are you available?" Annie asked.

"Of course! We'd love to come over. What can I help you with?" Cheryl asked. "Chuck and I can pick up the pizza." She knew money was tight and she wanted to help. This seemed like the perfect opportunity. Before Annie could open her mouth, Cheryl said: "And I won't take no for an answer Annie, please. Let us take care of the pizza. We're happy to do that."

"Oh, um, okay. Thank you Cheryl. That's very sweet of you." Annie knew there was no use in arguing. Cheryl was going to do it anyway regardless. "Stephen gets a discount on pizza, so we were thinking it might be a good idea to order from his pizza place. We'll figure out what everyone wants and let him place the order."

"Sounds perfect." Cheryl said. "And we'll go pick it up."

"Any news about the portal in the lab? I know that Chuck hasn't been there in a while. We were just wondering if he was able to figure out what actually came through there. Edith thinks the Dark Entity has escaped the lab and that it actually caused Mark's accident…And then there's the bridge collapse in Memphis. They haven't found the cause for that either." Annie said. She figured this was as good a time as any to ask about it.

"He said that the lab and all of the time travel research has completely stopped. They have him working on another Military project now. He doesn't think Kawalski's project will ever be allowed to continue again." Cheryl explained.

"Oh, but they have to! They can't leave that portal open!" Annie said. She knew that the Dark Entity was free to roam the Earth and it had to be sent back from where it came from…Somehow.

Edith sat comfortably in the wingback chair and gazed out the tall windows at the color displayed by the deciduous trees in Auset's back yard. Summer was over and the leaves were turning all of the glorious Fall colors. The perennial plants had withered away and began to prepare themselves for the dormant Winter season so that they could bloom once more in the Spring. The birds were chirping happily as if they were bidding farewell to friends and neighbors before they prepared themselves for their annual migration south. Auset returned with a tray of her Egyptian apple tea and cookies made from dates and nuts and set them on the marble table between them. She carefully poured two cups of tea and sat down across from Edith.

"You are correct about the accident Edith. It was caused by the Dark Entity but the investigators will not confirm that." Auset said. "It is moving to the southwest. There will be another terrible event in a faraway land. A crossing will collapse. Many people will die."

"Well, that will be the second major bridge collapse…I'm sure you heard about what happened in Memphis, Tennessee last month… It seems to really like causing accidents and destroying bridges." Edith said as she sipped her apple tea.

"Yes, but that will be the last. It grows more powerful. There will be two more disasters after that. Bigger. More devastating…But it will not be disguised as Human construction failure as the others." Auset explained.

"Can we prevent these events?" Edith asked.

"You cannot. It is predestined to occur." Auset said. She paused for a moment as she gazed out the tall windows before continuing. "I am telling you this because the second disaster, Bhola, is the sign. When this occurs, it is time to send it back from which it came." She directed her attention back to

Edith and looked deeply into her eyes. "On the date of two master numbers, you must be prepared. The equipment at the Argon Lab is what you need."

"Well, that *is* going to be a problem. That lab was shut down and locked up since the security guard was killed. It is my understanding that the whole time travel project has been cancelled. I don't even know if the equipment is still there." Edith explained.

Auset got up from the table and left the room. A minute later, she returned with a piece of paper and a pencil. She sat back down and quickly jotted down a note, folded it, and handed it to Edith. "Give this to your Scientist friend. He will know what to do."

Edith stood and took the note from Auset. She open it to look at it. It looked like some sort of coordinates to her and she didn't understand it. She just knew that it was important. "Will he know what this means?" Edith asked.

"He will figure it out." Auset said as she stood up and walked Edith to the door. "He knows what he must do and this information is what he needs to send the Beast back from where it came."

Edith nodded and thanked Auset, then bid her goodbye. She had to meet with Chuck Frasier right away.

Cheryl assisted Mark with his leg brace. She had come over to check on him and saw that he was a little stiff because he had missed his last physical therapy appointment. Knowing that Mark was a bit stubborn, she knew that he was over it—Completely done with being a patient. He had had enough intense medical care to last a lifetime. In his mind he was healed and he just wanted to get back to normal. He wanted to go back to work and assume all of the ordinary things he did in his life before the accident.

"You've got to keep up with the physical therapy Mark. You'll be able to get back to normal much faster if you do." Cheryl reminded him.

"Yeah, yeah." Mark said as he secured the strap around his thigh. "I've got too much to take care of Cheryl. I can't keep sitting around like this."

"I know, but you'll set yourself back if you don't keep up with the physical therapy. Rest helps, but you also have to build the strength back in your muscles and stretch out the scar tissue that has formed. You're doing terrific, just don't miss another PT appointment or I'll have to come back over here and wrench you around again!" Cheryl said as she laughed and lightly slapped him up the back side of his head in jest.

"Welcome to my world Cheryl." Annie laughed.

"I've got to go. The bus will be dropping the kids off in a few minutes and I have to get dinner started. You let me know if he refuses to go to his physical therapy. I can come over and do it." Cheryl said as she walked out the front door.

Annie followed her out and closed the door behind her. "Thanks for doing that. He's a bear sometimes."

"Not a problem. I spent a couple of years working with physical therapists before transferring to maternity. It's kind of like riding a bike—you never forget how to do it. Besides, it keeps my PT skills polished." Cheryl said with a wink.

"Cheryl…Does Chuck still have access to Argon or is he no longer affiliated there?" Annie asked.

"Oh he's still very much an Argon government employee. In fact, he may be transferring back to the Argon Lab in a couple of weeks. As you might have guessed, the commute to La Grange is really getting to him. Normally he'd be home by 5:30 every night, but now he gets home closer to 7:00. He hates it. Why do you ask?" Cheryl asked as she paused in the driveway.

"I'm just trying to figure out how we're supposed to close the portal. I spoke to Edith and she wasn't sure what to do next. I think she went to see Auset at our old house today to speak to her about it." Annie said.

"Hmmm. I'll ask Chuck about that tonight. I know it's been in the back of his mind too, although, the paranormal is not really his area of expertise. He was waiting for some direction from Edith I think." Cheryl said.

"I think we all are. Lily is terribly afraid of this Dark thing roaming around out there. She wakes up in the middle of the night all the time, and that's not like her." Annie said.

Just then, Edith drove up in her new Buick Skylark with all four kids in the car. "Hi there!" She said as she got out of the car and tipped the back of her seat forward so that Beth, Lily, and Joey could get out of the car. "I saw them walking up the hill from the bus stop and decided to give them a lift."

"Nice!" Cheryl said. "Edith? Did you get a new car?"

"I did. My old Chevrolet was getting too expensive to repair and Ed thought this would be a nice upgrade. We got a pretty good deal." Edith said proudly as everyone gathered around the car to peek inside.

"It's beautiful." Annie commented.

"Mom, can I go over to Beth's for a little while? We have a science project due in a couple of weeks and we have to get started on it." Vince asked.

"Sure Honey, go ahead. I'll come get you when dinner is ready." Annie said.

"Momma? Joey and I do not have any homework. Can we go jump on the trampoline for a while?" Lily asked sweetly.

Annie looked at Cheryl to see what she thought about that. After receiving an approving nod, she said: "Sure, go ahead...Just take your books inside first—Last time you left them outside papers were flying around all over the yard."

"Well Edith, what brings you over this way?" Annie asked.

"I just came from Auset's. I was hoping to catch Chuck, but I guess it's a bit too early yet..." Edith said as she looked at her watch.

"Oh, he won't be home until about 7:00. But, you're welcome to come for dinner. That would be the best idea if you want to discuss anything with him. He's pretty burnt out by the time he gets home. The traffic is really getting to him." Cheryl said.

"That would be lovely Cheryl, thank you. I think I'll take you up on that offer." Edith said.

"Well, I'm going to go over and get dinner started then. Edith—just come over around 7 and we'll talk more." Cheryl said as she waved goodbye.

"I'll be there in a few minutes to help you with dinner, how's that? I just want to talk to Annie for a few minutes." Edith said.

"Deal! See you in a few." Cheryl said as she walked across the street carrying Joey's jacket and his backpack.

"So...What did Auset have to say?" Annie asked as she invited Edith inside for a cup of tea.

"We've got quite a bit of work to do. This thing is going to cause more chaos and there's nothing we can do about it. We have to prepare to send it back and she gave me very specific information about how to do that." Edith said.

"Oh? And how exactly are we going to do that?" Annie asked as she filled the tea kettle with water and set it on the stove.

"Well? We have to get back into the lab and use the Hadron Collider. That's how we're sending it back." Edith said. "Chuck has to figure out how to do it. It's way beyond my comprehension. I'm good at the psychic things, but Quantum Physics? Not on your life!"

"I guess I don't understand. Are we supposed to lure it back to the lab again?" Annie asked. This wasn't making much sense to her, but then, the things that Auset says really never did.

"No, Heavens no! We're not bringing it back. It will be on another continent wreaking havoc. We have to create a new doorway and create kind of a vacuum that pulls it through into a vortex to send it back to its dimension of origin." Edith said.

"Sounds complicated." Annie said as she poured two cups of tea and sat down at the table.

"Very. This is why I need to speak to Chuck." Edith said as she sipped her tea. "I only hope that they haven't transferred that Hadron Collider to another facility. We're going to need it to send the Beast back."

CHAPTER 40

After dinner, the kids went to clean up and get ready for bed and Cheryl went to the kitchen to do the dishes. Chuck and Edith moved to the living room where they could talk privately. Chuck studied the piece of paper Edith had handed to him:

On the date of 2 master numbers – 23.71° N
90.41° E
Eltanin – Right Ascension 17h 56m 36.38
Declination +51° 29' 20.2

Well, I'm not sure what "*On the date of 2 master numbers*" means, but the coordinates are a location. The other information is an astral location of some sort. I'm not sure what Eltanin is..." Chuck said. "Give me a day or two to research this."

"The date of 2 master numbers, I believe, is November 11—11/11. In Numerology, eleven is a master number." Edith said.

"Ok, so we're supposed to send this thing back through a new portal on November 11th? That doesn't give us much time." Chuck said as he ran his left hand through his hair. He was looking frustrated and tired. "Edith, I haven't been to Argon since they shut the project down. I don't even know if the Hadron Collider is still there or if they removed it…Although, it's so damn big it would be a tremendous about of trouble to take it apart and move it. I can't imagine that the Federal Government would ever do that. It's a very intricate piece of equipment. The calibration process alone is extremely complicated."

"Well, I have a feeling that it's still there. But the lab is locked down. Do you think you can access the lab?" Edith asked.

"I don't have a key—never did. It all depends on who is still working at the facility. Most of us got transferred to other labs, but I don't see why the Security Guards would have moved. They're job is to secure the facility and whether Scientists are working there or not, they still have a responsibility to safeguard the equipment." Chuck explained as he thought about how to get back in there.

"Are you able to transfer back to that location?" Edith asked.

"Actually? I'm supposed to be transferred back in a couple of weeks when the current project I am working on is complete. I'm almost finished with it. Maybe if I go in early and stay late for the next few days, I'll be able to transfer back to Argon sooner." Chuck said. "If we have to be ready by November 11th that only gives us about 3 weeks to prepare after I get transferred back. Give me a week to finish up the military project, then I'll dive straight into this." Chuck said.

Lily brushed her teeth, put her pajamas on, and crawled into bed. She was physically tired from jumping on the trampoline with Joey after school, but she was also emotionally weary. She had been waking up in the middle of the night every night since her Father's accident—Not because the Dead needed her help, but because she was terrified of the Dark Entity that was now roaming the earth. She could see what it was…How evil it was. It was calling to her and she was terrified. She remembered what Auset had forewarned her about—Being 'hunted by the Dark Ones' and she was worried that they were trying to take her over in her dreams. As she lay in her bed trying to calm her fears, Winnie pushed her bedroom door open with her nose and jumped up on the bed. She licked Lily's face then spun around in circles a couple of times before plopping on the bed, all curled up in a ball, then she let out a big sigh as she always did before going to sleep. Having Winnie in her room made Lily feel somewhat protected, but Winnie was no match for the evil entities that sought to possess Lily.

Annie stuck her head in to say goodnight. "Good night Lil. Sweet dreams baby girl." She said as she slowly closed the door.

"Momma?" Lily said. "Can you come sit with me for a while?"

Annie opened the door a little wider and stepped inside the room. "Sure Lil, what's bothering you Sweetie?" Annie said as she sat down on the edge of Lily's bed.

"I'm scared." Lily whimpered. She was on the edge of tears. "Auset said I had to be careful because I was going to be hunted by the Dark Ones, and Mom? I think that's what they're doing. They wake me up in the middle of the night and I don't know how to make them stop."

"Aw, Lily." Annie's heart was breaking to hear her Daughter say that. She always viewed Lily as a little girl who was much wiser beyond her years. It's what made her so exceptional and strong. But now she was a frightened little girl who needed love and protection. "I won't let anything happen to you Lil. Where is Grandpa Tom? Isn't he here watching over you?" Annie asked.

"Yes, he's here. He's sitting on the chair right there." Lily said as she pointed.

"Well, he's here to protect you Lily." Annie said as she pet Winnie. "And Winnie is right here too." Annie looked out the window and saw that Edith was leaving the Frasier's and getting into her car. "Wait right here Lil—I'll be right back."

Annie ran down the stairs and out the front door. She called to Edith as she crossed the street. Edith had gotten in the car and started it, but heard Annie so she rolled down the window. "Annie? What is it dear?" Edith said.

"I'm so glad you're still here. Um, could you please come and talk to Lily? She just crawled into bed but she's terrified of dark things coming to her in her dreams and I'm just not sure what to say to her. Do you mind?" Annie asked.

"Of course I don't mind. I'd be glad to talk to her." Edith said as she got out of the car and walked across the street with Annie. Once they reached Lily's bedroom, the lights were on and Lily was sitting up in bed petting Winnie.

Annie stepped into the room first. "Lil? Look who's here to see you." Annie said as Edith popped around the corner.

"Hello Lily. Your Mom tells me you're having some bad dreams. What are you seeing that upsets you so?" Edith asked as she sat on the edge of Lily's bed.

"Oh Mrs. MacKenzie, it's awful! They're evil things that look like dragons and monsters. They want me to join them. They keep showing me pictures in my mind of people getting crushed and they're bleeding. People are screaming for help and no one comes. They laugh and keep causing things like buildings and bridges to fall down and crush people. It's just awful." Lily said as she held back her tears. "They call themselves 'Legion' and they want me because I can do things other people can't do."

"Hmmm. I see." Edith said. "They are taunting you Lily. You must be strong and realize that you are more powerful than they are. You must reject them and stand firm." She gently held both of Lily's hands and Lily could feel a tremendous warmth radiating through Edith's small, wrinkled grandmotherly hands. "Let me get into your energy and together we will build a protective barrier around you with white light and your Guardian Angels."

Edith and Lily held hands and closed their eyes. They both took a couple of deep cleansing breaths and began to relax into a meditative state. Annie sat on the floor next to them and closed her eyes and synced her breathing with them. Edith spoke softly and calmly as she walked them through the meditation. Annie visualized everything that Edith had said, and she was beginning to become aware of her Father's presence in the room which gave her great comfort. After a few moments of visualizing the room filled with bright, white, Divine healing light, Edith slowly brought them back into the present and gently squeezed Lily's hands to ground her.

"There my dear. It is done. We have built a wall of protection around you and the whole neighborhood. They won't bother you tonight." Edith reassured her.

Lilly could feel that the room felt lighter and all of the tension was gone. Grandpa Tom was sitting next to Annie on the floor, assuring her that he was there to protect her and all would be well. "Thank you Mrs. MacKenzie. I feel so much better now." Lily said as she leaned forward to give her a hug.

"Remember Lily—You are much more powerful. Never forget that. This is your realm. You have all of the power here." Edith told her. "Now, keep up with your Tai Chi and do this meditation that we just did before you go to bed. You'll be safe."

"I will." Lily said as she snuggled back down into her bed.

Edith got up and Annie bent down to cover up Lily and kissed her on the forehead. "Good night Honey. I'll see you in the morning." She said.

Annie walked Edith back to her car and they chatted on the way. "Thank you so much for that Edith. That meditation was amazing! I should start doing that with Lily every night." Annie said.

"You should! It certainly won't hurt." Edith said. "Lily is learning and she will be able to overcome anything thrown down in her path. She has many gifts and she is only beginning to realize them. I am not at all worried about her and you shouldn't be either." She said.

"Thank you. She is a very special little girl." Annie said. "So…What did Chuck have to say tonight about the lab?"

Edith sighed. "I gave him the note from Auset and he seemed to understand it. He said that he was finishing a project and he would be transferred back to Argon afterward. He also believes that the Hadron Collider is still there. He says it's a big deal to move it and there's no reason that he can think of why they would. He said to give him a week and we can get to work on sending the Beast back to where it came from." She said.

"Does it have to be brought back to the lab in order to send it back?" Annie asked. She had no idea how they were going to pull that off if that's what they had to do.

"No. We just have to wait for something called *Bhola*…And we haven't figured out what that is yet." Edith said as she rubbed her chin.

"Bhola?" Annie asked. "Bhola…Why does that sound familiar?"

"Probably because that was what Auset told us about after the Security Guard was killed. Remember?" Edith asked.

"Oh yes. I remember. She said it was some sort of sign. Is it the name of a place that this thing will show up at? What do you think it is?" Annie asked.

"I'm not sure. Auset just said that we would know when the time was right. We have to trust her. We've got nothing else to go on." Edith said.

All around them the lightning bugs were flashing and it was like a well-choreographed dance. It felt like they were surrounded by tiny fairies welcoming them to their whimsical faraway land. It was after 9:30 and Edith began to yawn.

"You're tired. I'd better let you go home." Annie said.

"It's been a very long day and I have a little research to do myself." Edith said. "Let's talk again in a couple of days. Maybe we'll figure out what this Bhola is and we'll be able to send that evil mass back to Hell."

Annie laughed. "Very well. Good night Edith. Drive carefully!" She gave Edith a hug and walked back across the street to go inside and get ready for bed. As soon as Annie got inside the door, she heard Stephen drive up. She walked back outside to greet him.

"You're home early. I thought you were closing tonight?" Annie asked.

"I was, but it was really slow and I was able to get everything cleaned up early so Marco let me go home." Stephen said. "Why are you out here? I thought you'd be getting ready for bed…Is Dad ok?" Stephen thought maybe

Annie was just coming back from the Frasier's because his Father had fallen or something.

"Your Dad is fine. Feisty as ever." Annie said. "Edith was at the Frasier's tonight and I just walked over to speak to her for a minute. You just passed her on the street as she was driving away."

"That snazzy red Skylark was Edith? When did she get that car?" Stephen asked.

"Just a couple of days ago. I think Ed and Barb picked it out for her. Besides, she looks rather cute in it, don't you think?" Annie said.

"I guess. I didn't really see her. It's dark, Mom." He said as he walked up to the front door. "Oh, Stephen—Before I forget, we're celebrating Lily's birthday at home this year. We thought we'd get some pizza, have the Frasier's and the MacKenzies over, have some cake, etc… Would you get into trouble if we used your employee discount for a big pizza order? The Frasier's are buying the pizza. I thought I'd ask you first." Annie said as she walked in the house with her arm around her son.

"Um, I know it's okay if I'm buying a pizza to bring home, but I'm not sure about a big order. I'll ask Marco when I go into work on Thursday. He's a nice guy and maybe he'll be cool with it if I tell him it's for Lily's birthday… He thinks she's really cute." Stephen said. "I'll let you know Mom."

"Ok, great. Thanks Honey." Annie said.

When they walked in the house, they could hear Mark laughing in the family room. He was watching something on the television that he found amusing. It was good to hear him laugh again—just like old times. Annie thought about how fortunate they were that he survived the accident.

"What are you watching?" Annie asked.

Mark tried to regain his composure from laughing so he could speak. "They're advertising this new sitcom called 'The Odd Couple' and it looks hilarious. It's about two guys who are sharing an apartment and one is a fussy neat freak and the other is a cigar smoking slob. It comes on Thursday night at 7:00. It looks really funny. We have to watch it." He said.

"That does sound funny. I'll make sure dinner is all cleaned up by then so I can watch it with you." Annie said.

"Hey, was that Edith who was here earlier? I was in the bathroom and I could hear you talking to someone but I wasn't sure who it was." Mark asked.

"Yes it was." Annie said. "Lily was feeling a little scared about things she was seeing in her dreams and I noticed that Edith was just leaving the Frasier's house, so I asked her to come and talk to Lily for a bit. She has an extraordinary ability to get things under control."

"I thought that was her voice. Is Lily okay?" Mark asked.

"Now she is, I think. It's so hard to tell. I can't tune in to what she and Edith experience but I can tell you that the room definitely felt more calm and serene after Edith left." Annie said.

Edith always amazed her. She always seemed to be able to hone in on whatever the problem was and she always had an explanation and solution to make things better. Annie knew that Lily would also be that way and it warmed her heart. She was incredibly grateful for her friendship and thanked her lucky stars every day that Edith was in their lives. She couldn't imagine what they would do about the Dark Entity that brutally murdered the Security Guard, caused the accident that nearly killed Mark, then caused a recently inspected bridge to collapse in Memphis, TN. Edith seemed to be the key person involved in fighting this thing and she shuttered to think what life would be like without her insight. According to Edith, there would be two more events—terrible, catastrophic events that had to occur before this thing could be sent back to Hell or wherever it came from. There was nothing that anyone could do about them. Auset said that they were pre-destined to occur and no human intervention could change the course of events.

"Did you remember to invite Edith over on Saturday for Lily's birthday?" Mark asked. "I need to call Ed and Barb and invite them…I probably should do that now while I'm thinking about it." He said as he grabbed his cane and slowly stood up on his good leg and walked toward the short stairway leading to the kitchen.

"I did, yes. She said she'd be here." Annie said. "I also checked with Stephen about his pizza discount. He's going to confirm with Marco that it's okay for a large order and let us know on Thursday when he goes back in to work. The Fraiser's are buying the pizza so it would be really nice to be able to extend a discount if it's possible."

While Mark was on the phone with Ed, Annie noticed a flash of light through the window in the back yard. She walked toward the patio door and watched. There it was again! It was much too big and too bright to be a lightning bug, and it was in a spot where it would be impossible to come from the headlights of a car. The back yard was at least ¾ of an acre and it was completely dark. They backed up to their neighbor's back yard who also had a deep lot. Could it be one of the neighbors out there with a flashlight looking for something? Annie slowly opened the patio door and stepped out onto the deck. She sat quietly in one of their patio deck chairs and watched. There were the usual sounds of chirping crickets, but nothing more. No dogs barking. No people talking. Lightning bugs were randomly glowing here and there, but they were not the source of the bright light she saw. It would take a million of them together in a jar all lit up at once to compare with it. After a few minutes, the light presented itself again. It was a bright white ball of light that seemed to subtly pulse in brightness. It was hanging in the big willow tree at the far corner of their property. *"What the hell is that?"* Annie said to herself. She got up from her chair and cautiously walked out to the yard toward the willow tree. The wind was perfectly still. There was no breeze at all. The air was cool and crisp and Annie had wished that she had worn her sweater, but she was so intrigued by the ball of light, she didn't want to go back in for a sweater for fear that it would disappear before she could return.

As she approached the tree, the ball of light looked bigger and brighter to her. It was white with what seemed like a thin blue outline, and the center of it seemed to be swirling in a clockwise motion. Annie was captivated. It did not feel menacing, it felt inviting and safe. She stood beneath the tree and stared at it, allowing herself to be drawn in to its energy.

"Annie? What are you doing? What is that?" Mark was calling to her from the deck.

As she broke her stare, she looked back at Mark leaning against the railing of the deck trying to get a better look. "Do you see it?" Annie said in a calm voice almost as if she were trying not to scare it away. When she turned back toward the ball of light, it was gone. *"Hey! Where did you go?"* She said to herself.

"Annie? What was that!?!" Mark called to her.

Annie ran back up to the deck. "I'm not sure. It was this beautiful ball of light that just hung there in the tree. Did you see it Mark?" She asked.

CHAPTER 41

OCTOBER 10, 1970

Today started off like any other Saturday at the Campbell household, but today was different. It was Lily's Birthday and that's what made it even more special. To any school aged child, having a Birthday was a big deal. But to have your Birthday land on a Saturday was the BEST! As was the usual birthday protocol at the Campbell's, Lily got to name what they had for breakfast, which was of course, pancakes. Then she got to wear whatever she wanted, which of course was her favorite pair of blue jeans and a pink sweatshirt with an *I dream of Jeannie* iron on decal across the front. Lily thought Barbara Eden was the most beautiful woman in the world, and although *I dream of Jeannie* was recently canceled after only 5 seasons, it was still Lily's favorite TV show. Lily would often pretend that she was Jeannie when practicing her telekinesis exercises. At 7 Lily could move objects at will, but did not make this known to anyone because she found it was far more entertaining to keep that particular ability to herself. At school she would move things on her teacher's desk when she wasn't looking. Once when she was being teased by Brian Hardy, she moved his chair back when he went to sit down and he fell on the floor. All of the kids laughed at him and he was terribly embarrassed because he was always the tough guy who pulled pranks on everyone else. So no, Lily was not about to let anyone know about this ability just yet. She would keep this one to herself for a little longer.

It was a sunny, cool, crisp October afternoon. The leaves had turned into beautiful Fall colors of red, orange, and yellow, and some leaves were beginning to fall off of the trees. Summer had long been over, and Lily grew very fond of this time of year. There was something very calm and serene about it. The northern hemisphere was preparing for Winter hibernation, and things started to slow down long enough for people to take it all in and really enjoy the calmness about it. As Lily came downstairs, Winnie ran from the kitchen to greet her with her usual dog smile and full body wiggle.

"Hello Winnie Pooh!" Lily said as she snuggled the wiggly Cocker Spaniel.

Annie was in the kitchen putting the finishing touches on Lily's Birthday cake of choice—White cake with white frosting. No coloring of any kind was allowed on the cake and all of the writing had to be done in white as well. Just like snow. "Almost done Lil." Annie said. "What do you think?"

"It looks perfect Mom. Thank you!" Lily said.

"It looks like a Wedding cake." Annie said as she admired her work.

"Kinda." Lily said as she shrugged her shoulders. "But at my wedding, my cake is going to look like something else…And it won't be white."

"Oh?" This took Annie a bit by surprise since Lily had never much cared for any other type of cake. "What will your cake look like?"

"It will look like suitcases stacked on top of each other with stickers on them from different cities in the world." Lily said. "I'm going to marry a man who likes to travel the world because that's what I want to do too."

"Well, that sounds very exciting!" Annie said as licked the frosting off her fingers. "Here, do you want to lick the frosting off the spatula?" Annie handed the spatula to Lily.

"Yummy!" Lily said as she licked the cake decorating tool clean.

"Where's Vince? I haven't seen him in a while." Annie asked.

"He's in his room playing records." Lily said. "Do you need him to do something?"

"Yes, I was hoping he would help me blow up balloons. Would you run up and ask him to come down and help us?" Annie asked.

"Sure." Lily said as she ran up the stairs to get her Brother.

"Did you get all of the presents wrapped for Lily?" Mark asked from the family room. He was deeply engrossed in a football game, but was acutely aware that it was Lily's birthday and there were things that needed to be done.

"They're all wrapped." Annie said. "What time are Barb and Ed coming?"

"They said they'd be here by 5:00. Barb had to work today but she was going to bug out a little early." Mark said.

As Annie hung the giant paper *Happy Birthday* sign on the wall above the sliding glass door in the kitchen area, her attention was drawn towards the big Weeping Willow tree in the far corner of the back yard. The very same place she stood in the dark just a few days ago and observed the most magnificent glowing white orb. She had not seen it since, and had never mentioned it to anyone but Mark, who also saw it for a brief moment before it disappeared. It was absolutely mesmerizing and she secretly hoped that she would have the opportunity to see it again, even though, she really wasn't exactly sure what it was. Annie's fugue was interrupted when Vince came down the stairs with Lily and asked where the bag of balloons were.

"They're sitting next to your Dad on the couch." She said as she pointed to the family room where Mark was comfortably sitting on the couch with his feet up on a cushion placed on the coffee table as he watched the NFL football game. On the floor next to him were two halfway inflated balloons bobbing pathetically from the breeze created by Mark's excited arm waiving over a touchdown. "He's been blowing them up for the last hour. You can see he hasn't made much progress, so I'd appreciate your help with that." Annie said.

"Sure thing Mom." Vince said as he laughed at the lack of progress made by his Father, and from the looks of the finished balloons, he wasn't exactly into it.

Annie smiled at Lily and asked her to follow her outside as she opened the sliding glass door and stepped out onto the deck. "Lil? I wanted to show you something. Follow me." She said as she led Lily out to the big Weeping Willow tree in the back yard.

"What is it Momma?" Lily asked.

"Remember when Edith was here and she helped us with that protection meditation the other night?" Annie said.

"Yes." Lily replied.

"Well, after she left your Dad and I saw something remarkable out here in this tree." Annie said as she pointed to the spot where she saw the giant glowing orb. "It was a big ball of light. About the size of a basketball and it was just hanging in the tree—right there. It was bright white with a glowing blue outline and it looked like it was swirling in the middle of it. Do you have any idea what that was?"

Lily looked up into the tree and mentally stepped into its energy to see if she could get a read on it. "It was a spirit Mom. A protective one. We called upon my guardians and spirit energies for the protective barrier. Remember?" She said very matter-of-factly. This was all a part of Lily's normal life but Annie was still trying to figure much of it out. Lily had to remind her of that from time to time. "How did it *feel* to you when you saw it Mom?" Lily asked.

"Well, it felt protective and safe really. Why do you ask?" Annie asked.

"Because you're starting to open Momma. Not everyone can see them. If you can see them, then that means your abilities are getting stronger." Lily explained.

"Huh." Annie said. "Well, I could also feel Grandpa Tom in your room that night. I think he was sitting next to me on the floor."

"He was! I saw him there too." Lily said with excitement. "See? You have it too Momma. Don't doubt yourself. Spirits are all around us all the time. Like Edith always says: You just have to be open to acknowledging that they're there." She explained.

"Fascinating." Annie said under her breath. "Well, shall we go finish getting things ready for your party?"

"Oh yes! Let's go!" Lily giggled as she grabbed her Mother's hand and led her back up to the house.

Vince and Mark had managed to blow up the entire big bag of balloons and they were both sprawled out on the couch to catch their breath. "All done Mom." Vince said. "Is there anything else that you want me to do?"

Annie laughed at the small sea of balloons bobbing freely across the family room floor. "I see that. Well, we can't leave them on the floor. Winnie will come along and pop them all." She said as she tossed a roll of thin white ribbon down the stairs to Vince. "Here—please tie them together in bundles of five and we'll hang them around the house and outside."

Mark held the balloons as Vince tied the ends with the ribbon and bundled them together as he was asked. As the bundles were complete, Annie picked them up and tied a few outside on the front porch. She carefully hung the others around the house in the areas where the party would be—The kitchen, family room, and dining room. After that, she and Lily spread out the festive *Happy Birthday* table cloth and set a matching paper plate and napkin in front of each chair. "Party on a budget." Annie whispered to herself.

It was 5:00 and the doorbell rang. "Mark? Can you please tidy up the family room? Our guests are here." Annie said.

Mark and Vince scurried around picking up the remnants of the balloon assignment, turned off the TV, and fluffed all of the pillows on the back of the couch. "Done!" Mark answered as he carefully walked up the short five stairs to the kitchen.

"Hello Edith!" Annie said as she opened the door.

"Hello! And where's our Birthday Girl?" Edith asked.

"Here I am Mrs. MacKenzie!" Lily said as she appeared from behind her Mother and gave Edith a big hug around her waist.

"Well Happy Birthday my dear!" Edith said as she handed Lily a present. "Thank you." Lily said as she took the gift.

"Lil, why don't you go put that on the coffee table with the other gifts." Annie said as she peeked out the door to the driveway. "Are you alone Edith? I thought you might be coming with Ed and Barb?"

"Oh heavens no. Ed's been staying at Barb's apartment in the city. No need for them to backtrack to pick me up." Edith said. "Besides, I find that I'm looking for reasons to take a drive in the new Skylark these days. It's very fun to drive you know."

"I'll bet." Annie said. "Let me take your coat. Can I offer you something to drink?"

"White wine would be lovely if you have it." Edith said.

Annie threw her one of her famous *'you've got to be kidding me'* looks. "Of course we have it. Remember where you are Edith!" Annie laughed.

"The house looks so festive!" Edith said as she walked in.

"Hello Edith, how are you?" Mark said as he limped around the corner with his cane to greet her. "You look fantastic!"

"Oh I couldn't be better. The real question is: How are you?" Edith asked.

"Getting better every day." Mark said with a smile as he hugged her.

Ed and Barb arrived a short while later, along with Cheryl and Joey. Although she was the reason for the party, Lily wanted nothing more than to go out and jump on the trampoline with Joey. After a very short debate about whether or not it was polite to leave her guests, Annie acquiesced to Lily's request making it clear that they had to come right back in as soon as Chuck and Beth arrived with the pizza.

"So, Barb…How are things going at the museum?" Cheryl asked.

"Funny you should ask! Something very strange happened this past week…" Barb started. "We received a few new artifacts like pottery, jewelry, canopic jars, figurines, and tools, but things were moved around and no one seems to know who did it. I must say, the new displays are fantastic and make much more sense now that I think about it, but still…You would think someone would want to take credit for it and no one seems to know who did it."

This made Edith smile, and Annie knew exactly what she was smiling about. "I know who did it." She said quietly.

"What? Who? I mean, how would you know who rearranged the displays Edith?" Barb asked.

Both Edith and Annie answered in unison: *"Auset!"*

"Auset? You mean Isis the Egyptian Goddess? The Eye of Ra? Are we talking about *that* Auset?" Barb asked.

Edith laughed. "We are indeed!" She said. "I'm sorry Barb, I suppose that I should probably fill you in a little more about that. You see, Auset came to assist in closing the portals that have been opened and we have been consulting with her about how we should do that."

Barb took a giant, very unladylike, gulp of her wine as she sat there completely transfixed by the notion that Edith would be engaged in regular conversation with one of the most famous Ancient Egyptian Goddesses who existed over 3,000 years ago.

"Yeah, and she lives in our old house!" Annie said. "And I must say, it has been renovated to look like a palace…Quite befitting of a Goddess, don't you think Edith?"

"Umm Hmmm. And, she knows that you're the curator of the Ancient Egyptian Exhibit at the Field Museum Barb. I'm sure she wanted to help you out a little." Edith said. "Perhaps you'd like to meet her sometime?"

Barb sprayed wine out of her mouth the moment that Edith asked if she'd like to meet her. "Oh, excuse me! I'm so sorry! It's just that…Did you say *meet* her?" Barb said as she wiped the wine off of the front of her blouse with a napkin.

"Why sure! I'm sure she'd love to meet you. I'll be speaking with her again in a couple of days. I'd be very happy to have you come along." Edith said knowing full well that she just blew Barb's mind in an enormous way.

"And she makes the most interesting Apple Tea. It's really unlike anything I've ever tasted before." Annie said further adding to Barb's astonishment.

"Wait—What? You had *tea* with her?" Barb asked.

"Uh huh. What would you say Edith, 3 maybe 4 times?" Annie asked as she directed her attention to Edith who was clearly entertained by teasing Barb.

"Oh yes, at least that." Edith said as she took a sip of wine. "And those Pistachio date cookies! Those are delicious. I really must ask her for the recipe…"

Poor Barb was in that very awkward place caught between wonder, bewilderment, and pure green envy. Never in her wildest dreams could she ever imagine having the opportunity to meet, let alone drink tea and eat cookies with an Ancient Egyptian Goddess. Ed could tell that Barb needed a break from the casual but shameless teasing put forth by his Mother and he quickly changed the subject.

"So Mark, everybody at the terminal has been asking about you. They're all wondering when you'll be back to work. Has the Doctor cleared you to come back yet?" Ed asked.

"I'm afraid it will be a few more weeks yet Ed. My physical therapy for my shoulder is coming along pretty well, but my leg is going to take a little more work. I'm going to need to operate the clutch before they'll give me clearance…And I'm not quite there yet." Mark explained as he slowly extended his left leg and rotated his ankle a bit.

Annie saw Chuck drive up. "Pizza's here!" She said as she went to the door. "Cheryl? Can you call Lily and Joey back in please?"

"Yes I will." Cheryl said as she went to the kitchen slider to call them in.

Stephen drove up right behind Chuck and parked along-side him. He got out of the car and helped with the pizza boxes. "Hi Mom!" He said.

"Stephen? I thought you were closing tonight?" Annie was surprised but very happy to see him.

"It wasn't that busy so Marco told me I could come home and celebrate Lily's birthday with her." Stephen said.

"That was nice of him. Lily will be very happy that you're here." Annie said as she ushered everyone in. "Let's put the pizza on the kitchen counter, and we'll eat in the dining room. Chuck what would you like to drink?"

"Ahhh, beer would be nice. Gotta have a beer with pizza." Chuck said.

"Beer it is! Coming right up." Annie said.

Cheryl got drinks for all of the kids and everyone got a slice of pizza and sat down in the dining room. They ate their pizza and chatted about all the latest neighborhood gossip, Lily and Joey's classes at school, and Barb's new pieces in the exhibit at the museum. After most of the pizza had been eaten, Beth and Vince cleared everyone's dirty pizza plates and collected the dirty silverware and napkins. A few minutes later, Annie walked into Dining Room carrying a white layer cake with white frosting with 7 lit candles on it. She set it down in front of Lily and everyone began to sing *Happy Birthday.* Lily smiled sweetly as she closed her eyes, made her wish, and blew out her candles being very careful not to spray any spit. Annie removed the candles and started to cut the cake.

"Would anyone like ice cream? We have Chocolate and Mint Chocolate Chip." Annie said as she passed slices of cake out to everyone.

"What did you wish for Lily?" Joey asked.

"I can't tell you cuz if I do, it won't come true." Lily said very matter-of-factly as she quietly slid her hand under the table to let Winnie lick the frosting from her fingers.

"Lily…Don't feed Winnie under the table." Annie reminded her without even looking her way. This was a talent that all Moms possessed and it was truly an unexplainable phenomenon to every kid alive.

After cake, everyone moved to the family room where Lily very excitedly ripped the wrapping paper from each one of her presents. A Malibu Barbie, a Skipper doll, a new Sorry! game, a giant pink teddy bear, fuzzy pink slippers, and an Easy Bake Oven…Which caused Lily to gasp when she opened it. "Thank you! Thank you! Thank you all!" Lily squealed.

Annie noticed a small wooden box sitting on the coffee table that wasn't there earlier. "What's this?" She said as she picked it up. She carefully opened the hinged lid to peek inside, where she saw a small piece of paper that read 'For Lily.'

"What's that?" Mark asked.

"I think it's another gift for Lily. Here Honey—open it and see what's inside." Annie said as she handed the wooden box to the Birthday Girl.

Lily took the box and opened it. Inside were two things: A tiny papyrus scroll, and a small white linen bag with a golden cord tied around it. Lily set the box down on the floor and carefully opened the scroll. It read:

> Lily,
>
> This stone represents the Eye of the Falcon, the Eye of Ra.
>
> The Falcon can see all. One eye is the Sun and the other is the Moon.
>
> When he opens his eyes he fills the Universe with light, and when he shuts them darkness appears. Keep the Falcon's eye with you for protection and guidance always. Love and light be with you Little Bird.
>
> Auset

Lily handed the scroll to Edith who read it aloud as she carefully untied the golden cord around the bag. Inside was a gold necklace with a single black polished cabochon stone mounted in the center. "Ohhh!" Lily gasped as she held it up for everyone to see.

"Wow! That's an expensive gift." Mark said.

"That is beautiful!" Cheryl remarked.

"Lily? Bring your necklace and come with me. I want to show you something." Edith said as she stood up and held Lily's hand. They walked over to the big lamp in the corner of the room. "May I show you?"

Lily nodded enthusiastically and handed her necklace to Edith, who laid the stone flat in her hand under the light. When the light hit the center of the stone, 12 golden rays burst from the center and radiated out toward the edges of the stone. "You see? This is what Auset means by *'his open eye fills the Universe with light.'* Edith said. "And when you move the stone away from the light into the darkness? It becomes black and the rays go away, but they are always there when you need them."

"Ohhhh! It's so pretty!" Lily said. "What kind of stone is it? Is it magic?"

Edith chuckled. "Well, yes, it is kind of magical. It's called a black star sapphire. They are very special—and the 12 ray sapphires are very rare. Most have only 4 rays." She explained. "Auset has given you a very special gift. Would you like to put it on?"

"Yes please!" Lily said as she turned her back to Edith and lifted her hair off of her neck.

"Lily, that is gorgeous! You'll have to thank Auset for such a beautiful gift when you see her." Annie said.

The necklace fit Lily perfectly, but not too tight that she couldn't grow into it. This was a very special gift that she knew she would treasure for a lifetime. Lily would thank Auset tonight in her dreams since that was the very best way for her to communicate with the Egyptian Goddess without going over to her house and thanking her in person…Which she planned to do as soon as she could anyway.

"May I see your pretty necklace Lily?" Barb asked as she bent down to take a closer look. She was completely blown away by this very close relationship Lily, Annie, and Edith had with the infamous Ancient Egyptian Goddess. As Barb examined the necklace, she was stunned by the quality craftsmanship of the piece. This was not machine made, and it had to be made of 24K gold as were all Ancient Egyptian gold pieces. The stone was exquisite. Barb had not noticed black star sapphires in any Ancient Egyptian collections, but she would be sure to study it further since this was a genuine gift from Isis herself.

After cleaning up the shreds of wrapping paper and ribbon of the floor, Lily, Joey, Vince, and Beth sat on the floor playing the new *Sorry!* game, and all of the adults migrated back to the living room to chat. "So Mark, have the police ever determined what caused the accident?" Cheryl asked.

"No, they haven't." Mark said. "At first they thought it was a fire, then they suspected a gas leak, but both have been debunked. They have no idea what caused the explosion."

"Since they can't determine the cause, they can't name a responsible party." Annie said. "Luckily, our insurance has been very good about covering all of Mark's medical costs and the disability insurance has been very helpful too…" Annie paused for a moment before continuing. "There were a few reports from witnesses who said that they saw a big black cloud of smoke over the building just seconds before it blew up. I personally believe it was the Dark Entity that escaped from the Argon lab." There. She said it.

Edith nodded her head in agreement. "I also believe that's true." She said.

Chuck looked down at his feet. "You might be right." He said. "I heard a rumor that a Security Guard saw a dense black mist seep out of a vent on the side of the building where the lab is just shortly after Marty Reese was killed."

CHAPTER 42

Annie woke up to the sound of the doorbell. She rolled over and looked at the clock—8:15 am. "Shit!" She jumped out of bed, grabbed her bathrobe, and went downstairs to find Cheryl at the front door.

"Hi Annie—I guess our power went off last night and we overslept. By the looks of it, it looks like you did too. I'll be late for work, but I'm happy to drop the kids off at school on the way." Cheryl said.

"Oh Cheryl, go ahead and go to work. I'll throw some sweats on and drive the kids. Are Beth and Joey ready to go?" Annie said.

"Yes, they're in the car. Are you sure you don't mind? I called the hospital, and they said they're pretty busy this morning, so I know they want me to get there A.S.A.P." Cheryl said.

"Tell the kids to come over, I'll go get Lily and Vince up and I'll run them to school. It'll take me 5 minutes. You go ahead." Annie ran upstairs and woke Lily and Vince. "Kids! We overslept. Throw some clothes on and I'll run you to school. Pronto!"

Vince and Lily jumped out of bed and got dressed, quickly brushed their teeth and combed their hair, and off they went. Beth and Joey were already in the car.

"Here Lily, here's breakfast." Vince said as he handed Lily a Chocolate Peanut Butter Space Food Stick he grabbed out of the pantry.

As Annie pulled out of the driveway, she had to decide who was going to school first. The High School and Elementary Schools were at opposite ends of town. While waiting at the stop light, she decided to let the kids make that decision.

"Ok, decision time. Two of you are going to be slightly late, and two of you are going to be very late. Who gets dropped off first?" Annie asked them.

Lily hated to be late for anything and this was creating a bit of anxiety for her, but she knew that Vince had to give a speech this morning in his English class and he had been working very hard on it all week. There was a moment of silence that was finally broken by Joey.

"You can take Beth and Vince first Mrs. Campbell. We're just doing regular stuff in our class. It won't matter if we're late." Joey said. He wasn't the least bit bothered if he was tardy or not.

Annie threw a look to Lily in the back seat through the rear view mirror and saw that she was nodding in agreement. "Ok. Downers South it is." Annie said as she made a left at the light. "Vince, you have English, but what about you Beth? What's your first class?"

"I have ceramics. I've already finished my project on Friday so today is just a catch-up day for people who need more time to finish. I won't be missing anything important." Beth said.

As Annie pulled up to the front door of the school, she got out to walk in to the office with Vince and Beth to explain why they were late and to get their tardiness excused. After signing the parent excuse form, she said goodbye, wished Vince luck with his speech, and got back into the car to take Joey and Lilly to their school. "Jeez! What a morning." She said.

"It's okay Mom. It's not your fault." Lily said. "Why did our power go off last night?"

"I'm not sure Lil. Sometimes it just happens." Annie said.

As she pulled into the Elementary School driveway, she found a nice spot right up front. They all got out of the car, and as she did at the High School, Annie escorted Joey and Lily to the office to sign an excuse form for them. As she walked up to the desk in the attendance office, she saw a familiar face standing behind the counter. "Good morning Patsy! I'm sorry the kids are late—Our power went off during the night and our alarm clocks didn't go off this morning." She said.

"Annie! It's been a while! How are you?" Patsy said. They hadn't seen each other since the 4th of July, but it was nice to see that neither one of them were the least bit upset about it. Patsy looked at the clock and wrote out two passes, one for Joey and one for Lily so that they could go to class. "Here you go." Patsy said as she handed the passes to the children. "Now get to class because those passes expire in 5 minutes!" Joey and Lily took the passes, said '*thank you,*' and ran off to the classroom.

"So Annie, I've been meaning to call you. I have some news…" Patsy said very seriously.

"Oh? What's that?" Annie said. She wasn't sure if this was old neighborhood gossip or something serious that Annie should be concerned about.

"Well," Patsy started as she quickly looked over her shoulder to see if anyone else was listening. "We're moving." She whispered. "Don got a job offer that he just couldn't refuse, and well, he took it! We have to be in Redmond, WA by January 1st."

"Washington? Wow!" Annie said. "Is Don staying with the same company or making a change?"

"Same company. Don was asked to head the Pacific Northwest Division and that's where their offices are located." Patsy said rather proudly.

"January, well, that's not very far off. Are you pulling the kids from school?" Annie asked.

"Yes, actually, we're putting our house up for sale next week, so they'll probably have to transfer halfway through the school year. Isn't that exciting?" Patsy said gleefully. "I've always wanted to live in the Pacific Northwest somewhere, you know, surrounded by mountains and all of the big pine trees."

"That sounds amazing Patsy. Congratulations!" Annie said. "I feel bad that we haven't seen much of each other lately. With Mark's accident and all, it's been rather chaotic at our house."

"No, no, I should be the one who feels bad! I haven't been a very good friend. I should have been over there helping you out. I'm only working here part-time now anyway." Patsy said.

"Oh, that's very sweet of you Patsy. We're getting along okay. Mark is in physical therapy and doing quite well. He should be back to work in a few weeks." Annie said. As much as Patsy had the ability to annoy her with her gossipy busybody tendencies, she realized how much she was going to miss her when she moved away. They were good neighbors for a long time and it was Patsy who actually saved her and Edith from the Shadow People in the old house.

"Oh, and the other bit of good news? Your old house has really pumped up the neighborhood values. Our house is worth about 25% more since the Middle Eastern folks renovated your old house." Patsy was very happy to be able to capitalize on the efforts of her strange and mysterious neighbors.

"How do the kids feel about transferring to a new school?" Annie asked. She knew her kids wouldn't be very happy about it, and she couldn't imagine that the Sunderland kids would be either.

"Hmmm…Well? The truth is, they're not happy about it at all. But, with the extra income Don will be earning, we told them that we would take them to Europe next Summer for a nice vacation. You know, it will give them a little incentive to get on board with the move." Patsy said. "If we could have postponed at least until school was out we would, but employers don't always care about that."

"Well, we'll have to make sure we spend some time with you before you go. We'll have to have you over for dinner." Annie said. "Listen Patsy, I've got to run. I left the house in a rush and didn't even get to take a shower. Give me a call if you need help with packing or anything. I'm not working right now and I'd love to help."

"I will! Thank you Annie—It's good to see you!" Patsy said as she waved goodbye and answered the office phone that was now ringing.

When Annie got back to the house, Mark was sitting at the kitchen table talking to someone on the phone.

"Uh huh. Yeah, that sounds terrific! Tell me more." Mark said. Annie wondered who he could be talking too because he never sounds that excited about anything. The tone of the conversation piqued her interest so much that she decided to sit down at the table for a minute rather than running up the stairs to take a shower.

"Oh that sounds fantastic!" Mark said as he winked at Annie.

"Who is that?" Annie whispered.

"Uh huh. So, can I ask you one question?" Mark said as the person on the other line paused so he could ask his question. "How are you going to put aluminum siding on my brick house?" Mark started to laugh uncontrollably as he pulled the phone away from his ear. "Can you believe that? I've been talking to this guy for over 20 minutes. I ask a simple question and hangs up!" He laughed.

"Have you been talking to a salesman this whole time?" Annie asked. Mark was notorious for being a smartass with phone solicitors. He was very good at reeling them in then taking them down with one simple question when he was done playing with them. It was nice to see that he was starting to get back to his *old self.*

"Hey—Those people call you at home, interrupt whatever you're doing, and waste a bunch of your time. Why can't I waste a little bit of their time? Turnabout is fair play." Mark said.

"Yep, you're back." Annie said. "I'm going to go take a shower. I'm glad the power is back on."

"Yeah, it came on about 10 minutes after you left. I made some coffee, do you want some?" Mark asked.

"That sounds good actually. Yes, thank you." Annie said. "OH! I saw Patsy at the school this morning. They're moving to Washington."

"State or DC?" Mark asked as he poured his wife a cup of coffee and brought it back to the table.

"State." Annie said as she took a sip of hot coffee. "Don got a big promotion with his company and he has to be out there by January 1st. They're putting their house on the market next week."

"Wow. Good for Don! It's nice when you can move up in the ranks." Mark said as he sat back down. "I'm sure the neighborhood is going to miss Patsy. She seemed to keep everything and everybody in check."

"That she did." Annie said. "Oh, that reminds me! Edith wanted to go over to see Auset this afternoon and I thought I'd wait until Lily go home so she could come along. What time is your physical therapy appointment today?"

"At 11:00. We'll be back before Lily gets home." Mark said.

"Perfect." Annie said. "I'm going to go take a shower."

Annie went upstairs and Mark went downstairs to the family room to turn on the television and watch the last part of the morning news... *The devastation from the collapse of the West Gate Bridge this morning is breathtaking. The 10 lane dual carriageway is completely destroyed and with it, the lives of 35 people and 18 more injured. This is Australia's worst industrial accident ever recorded... This is Mick Sherman, SkyNews, Melbourne, Australia.*'

"Holy shit!" Mark said under his breath. "Another bridge collapse? What's going on?"

Annie came down the stairs a short while later with Winnie following close behind her. She was drying her hair with a towel as she walked downstairs to the laundry room just off the family room to throw a load of laundry in the washer.

"Another bridge collapse in Australia this morning." Mark said when he saw her.

"What? That's terrible." Annie said as she paused to watch what was left of the news cast. "35 dead and 18 severely injured." Mark said. "What is happening in the world these days?"

"I have a sneaking suspicion we know what it is. In fact, we've experienced it firsthand...Remember?" Annie said.

"You think it's the Black Mass that caused my accident?" Mark asked.

"Yes, I do." Annie said confidently. "Auset warned that there would be much more chaos and devastation. I'll be sure to ask her about that this afternoon when we see her. Now let's get you ready to go to physical therapy."

As soon as Lily was home from school, Edith came by to pick them up so they could drive over to see Auset together. Lily was very excited to see her as she played with the black star sapphire hanging around her neck. When Auset came to the door, she saw Lily and smiled. Auset never smiled. She was probably the most serious person Annie had ever met, but when she smiled her face shone brightly like the sun and it bathed all those around her in golden healing light. Auset greeted them and held her hand out to Lily, who gladly took it and followed her inside.

"Did you enjoy the celebration of the day of your birth Lily?" Auset asked.

"Yes I did! Very much!" Lily said as she gazed up at the radiant Egyptian woman. "And I want to thank you so very much for my necklace. It's very special and I will always wear it forever and ever." She said.

"I am pleased that you are fond of it Little Bird. It will protect you and show you things that are difficult to see." Auset said as she led them into the room with the tall windows where they usually got together to talk. They all took a seat in the tall wing-backed chairs and felt instantly relaxed. Auset poured her usual apple tea in everyone's cup and there were dried fruits, nuts, and pistachio date cookies on the plate in the center of the table. The view to the back yard was an explosion of Autumn color that seemed to have an aura of golden light around each leaf on the trees.

"My soon to be Daughter-in-Law, Barb, was very surprised by the new arrangement of her Ancient Egypt displays at the museum. She said that it makes so much more sense now. She wanted to come and thank you for your help with that, but she was not able to come with us today." Edith said.

"Barbara is a very intelligent woman, but truths are often lost over time. I was very happy to make a few corrections to her display. I am grateful for the respect she has shown to our history." Auset said.

"I will be sure to tell her. She will be honored and pleased." Edith said as she took a sip of her apple tea.

"I wanted to speak with all of you today because the time draws near to open the Stargate." Auset said.

"Stargate? Wait, what are we talking about?" Annie asked. This was the first she had heard about opening anything. She was under the impression that they were supposed to be *closing* a portal, not opening a new Stargate portal.

Auset looked at Edith and spoke to her telepathically. *'You know of what I speak do you not?'*

"Um, Annie, this has to do with what Chuck and I are working on… When Chuck gets back to Argon." Edith said.

"Oh. I guess I haven't been clued in on that." Annie said.

"But there is more you should know." Auset continued as she turned her attention to Lily. "There is a young boy in a city in the Satavahana Kingdom who can help you. He too has the gifts you possess, Little Bird. He will make himself known to you and you will work with him to send the Beast through the Stargate." She said as she then turned her attention back to Edith. "And Edith, the young boy's Father possesses knowledge of the science you will need for the Quantum Physicist."

"How will I find him?" Edith asked.

"He has already made contact with Dr. Frasier. See that he understands the importance of this connection." Auset said.

"What is this man's name?" Annie asked. Although completely fascinated by Auset's knowledge, the way she communicated was a bit too cryptic for Annie's brain to process. She thought that keeping it simple was always the best way to go.

"They have the surname of *Chadha.*" Auset said. She paused for a sip of apple tea before continuing. "Four days from now, there will be the last event before the final act of the Dark Beast. Today was the destruction of a man-made crossing. The next will be a nature event. On Mindanao hundreds will perish. After that, the final act will occur on the date of 2 master numbers."

'There she goes getting all cryptic again! What's Mindanao?' Annie thought to herself. She needed to write this down. Why didn't she think about bring-

ing a note pad with her this time? "Hundreds? That's so many. We have to do something to stop it!" Annie said.

"You cannot. You should not. It is their time. It must play out as it is written in their Akashic records." Auset said.

"I'm sorry to be so dense, but what are Akashic records?" Annie asked.

"The Akashic records are a compendia or written compilation of all human thoughts, actions, emotions, intentions, and events to have ever happened past, present, and future. There is an Akashic record for every single soul in the Universe." Edith explained, although she knew that she would be revisiting this explanation with Annie later because it was such an ethereal and mysterious topic. Auset smiled at Edith's explanation and nodded her head in agreement.

"Auset?" Lily asked in her quiet little girl voice. "Is the boy's name Reyansh?" She asked.

Auset turned her attention back to Lily. "Yes it is." She said.

"I talked to a boy last night in my dreams. He said that his name was Reyansh and that he would talk to me again soon." Lily answered. "I thought he was a dead person but his energy felt different...Then my Mom woke me up because we overslept."

"He is very much among the living Little Bird. Keep speaking to him. He will be your greatest ally in this most important task you must do." Auset said.

CHAPTER 43

Chuck arrived at the gate at Argon National Laboratories and was pleased to see Stan there at his usual post. "Good morning Stan!" He said with a smile.

"Good morning Dr. Frasier! It's very nice to have you back sir." The Security Guard answered as he leaned over to grab a lanyard out of his drawer. "Here's your security pass Dr. Frasier. We've updated your codes. You have full access as ordered." He said.

"Great! Thank you Stan." Chuck said as he reached for the lanyard with his ID badge and keycard hanging off of it. "Say, is Lt. Col. Kawalski still around?"

"No sir. You haven't heard?" Stan said as he looked around to see if anyone was within earshot before he shared the news. "Lt. Col. Kawalski was shit canned right after the lab shut down. He's facing Federal Espionage charges. I think he's sitting in the brig at the Great Lakes Naval Station right now awaiting trial."

"Espionage? What did he do?" Chuck was taken aback by this. He knew Kawalski was a conniving jerk, but espionage was beyond anything Chuck had considered.

"It seems that he stole some top secret information from the British Military and was conspiring with the Soviet Union to create some sort of satellite weapon system against Europe. The Feds collected him in handcuffs." Stan said. "I never much cared for the guy myself."

"Yeah, he wasn't my favorite guy either. What a jerk!" Chuck said. "So, Stan, did the information he stole have anything to do with the Hadron Collider equipment in there?"

"I'm not sure. The lab is still locked down as far as I know. I don't think they removed any of the equipment." Stan said as he pushed the button to raise the security gate. "Have a nice day Dr. Frasier. Glad to have you back!" He said.

"Thanks Stan, you have a nice day as well!" Chuck said as he drove through the gate. As Chuck parked his car, he sat quietly in the car for a minute to collect his thoughts. He was back at the old facility again, and he needed to figure out what his next steps were going to be so that they could use the Hadron Collider to return the destructive Dark Entity back to its Hell hole in outer space. As he walked in the back door, he was greeted by his old secretary, Dorothy James.

"Hello Dr. Frasier! So glad to have you back sir." She said cheerfully as she handed him a file. "You've been assigned to a new project sir. Here is your brief. There is a meeting in the front conference room at 10:00." She said. "Oh, and they've moved you to Lt. Col. Kawalski's old office. I took the liberty of moving your things in for you. You might want to rearrange things the way you want them."

"Well thank you Dorothy. Kawalski's office huh?" Chuck rubbed his chin. This was a surprise. "Have I been promoted and someone forgot to tell me?" He asked.

Dorothy laughed. "I'm not sure what's going on anymore sir. I was just told to show you to that office this morning." She said. "That happens to be the only office in this wing that is wired for satellite calls, so that may have something to do with it. It's my understanding that this project will be collaborated with various scientific communities in India and Japan."

"Huh. Okay, well I hope they speak English because I don't know any Japanese." Chuck said.

"I believe they do sir. If not, there are always translators. The US Military is full of translators." Dorothy said. "Let me know if you need anything. I'm sitting at the same desk as always."

Chuck sat at Kawalski's old desk and gazed around the room. There were two narrow windows to the outside in the corner of the room behind him that let a little sunlight shine through. In front of his desk were two leather barrel chairs and there were bookcases on both sides of the room, and above the console behind him. There was a tall window on the interior wall on either side of the door so he could see people passing by if his door was closed. '*This will do rather nicely*'. He thought to himself as he rearranged a few things on his desk to settle in. After retrieving a hot cup of coffee from the breakroom around the corner, Chuck settled into his chair and opened the file briefing that Dorothy handed to him earlier. "*Space weather*?" He said to himself. "My next project is predicting weather in space?" It sounded a bit boring, but it piqued his interest so he kept reading since it was not a project he would normally be assigned to, but may prove to be more interesting that he had originally thought.

As Chuck was reading the end of his brief, Dorothy stuck her head in his office to remind him of the 10:00 meeting. "They're waiting for you in the front conference room sir." She said.

"Oh, right. Is it 10:00 already?" Chuck said as he looked at his watch. "Who is leading this meeting?"

"Dr. Theodore Wurmser sir." Dorothy said.

"Ted is here? I haven't seen him in ages." Chuck said as he put his jacket on. "Who else is working on this?" He asked.

"I believe Jeff Larson, Jeremy Camas, Pete Schroeder, and Dr. Connie Deutsch…She's new. She just started here this morning as well sir." Dorothy said as she walked briskly down the hall with Chuck toward the conference room.

Annie rushed into the Principal's office only to find that Cheryl was already sitting in a chair outside the office door waiting to go in and have a chat with Principal Ellis herself. "Cheryl? You too?" Annie said in surprise.

"I guess Joey and Lily got into a bit of trouble, although they wouldn't tell me anything over the phone." Cheryl said.

"Where are they?" Annie asked as she looked around the office.

"They're sitting in a classroom with one of the Hall Monitors doing their homework. I guess the Principal wanted to speak with us first." Cheryl said.

"What do you suppose they did?" Annie asked.

"I'm not really sure. They didn't tell me anything over the phone either. I guess we'll find out." Annie said.

A short, chubby woman came around the corner and asked them to follow her to the Principal's office. "This way please." The lady said to them as she motioned them down the hall. Principal Ellis stood up from behind his desk when they entered the room.

"Ah, Mrs. Frasier and Mrs. Campbell. Please, sit down." The Principal said as they took their seats before the scolding that they felt was about to be cast upon them began.

"I'm sorry Mr. Ellis, but, why are we here?" Cheryl asked. "Neither of us has been told anything."

"Well, Mrs. Streuber asked me to have a chat with the two of you regarding Joey and Lily. She suspects that they have been cheating on tests. I've asked her to join us so she'll be here in a minute." Principal Ellis said as he shuffled some papers on his desk in an effort to keep from talking further until the teacher arrived.

"Cheating? That doesn't sound like Lily or Joey. I'll be very interested to hear the details about this." Annie said as Mrs. Streuber came into the room.

"Ah, Martha, please come in." The Principal said as he stood and pulled a chair closer to his desk so she could sit down.

"Hello Mrs. Frasier, Mrs. Campbell. I'm so sorry to have to call you in like this but I am very concerned about what's been going on in my classroom and I'm not sure how they're doing it, but one is definitely copying off of the other's paper. I've even separated them but this last test indicates that they are sharing the same answers to test questions somehow." Martha said.

Annie and Cheryl looked at each other. They knew about the telepathy between the two children, but it never occurred to them that it would be put to use to pass a test. They were both very smart children and there would be no reason to cheat. They could easily pass any test on their own merit.

"Well, we do live right across the street from each other and the kids do their homework together just about every day…" Cheryl said.

"Yes, perhaps that's why they're answering test questions the same way?" Annie proposed. It sounded like a perfectly well reasoned explanation as to why they were giving the same answers.

"Well, I would agree with that possibility, except we just completed our annual standardized testing last week and there are a lot of critical thinking questions on there that students are unable to study for. The questions are quite random and the teachers don't even see them until the day the exams are given." Martha said. "And Joey and Lily have given the exact same answers. Now, either they have some kind of ESP going on or one is clearly copying from the other's test paper." She said rather sternly.

Annie nearly choked when she mentioned ESP, and she glanced over at Cheryl to help her with an explanation to that one. "Perhaps it's just a coincidence?" Annie said for lack of a better thing to say.

"Highly unlikely." Martha said curtly in her rigid schoolmarm sort of tone.

"Well, we're very sorry that you feel that our children are cheating. If you've separated them, then I don't see how one could possibly copy off the other one's paper. Do you have any explanation as to how that might happen? Are you in the classroom supervising at all times?" Cheryl asked.

'Good one Cheryl! Let's see how miss smarty pants answers that one.' Annie thought as she threw a questioning look to the now nervous teacher who didn't seem to have an answer for that.

"Well of course I'm supervising my classroom!" Martha said with a defensive tone.

"Then how is it possible that one is copying answers from the other one?" Cheryl asked. "I assume that you've moved them pretty far apart…"

"Yes Martha, Mrs. Frasier has a point there. How far apart have you separated them?" Principal Ellis asked.

"As far apart as they can possibly be! I moved Lily to the front right desk and Joey to the farthest back on the left. There is at least 15 feet between them!" Martha protested.

"Then how is it possible to copy from that distance?" Annie asked. All eyes were on Mrs. Streuber who was now beginning to perspire as she struggled to offer a good answer to this very obvious question.

"Well I don't know, but something suspicious is going on I tell you!" Martha said.

"If I may just interrupt here for a second." Principal Ellis said as he calmly folded his hands on his desk. "I think that this may be one of those uncanny coincidences like Mrs. Campbell said. Let's just keep an eye on future test results and see if the pattern continues. If their answers are always the same going forward, we'll reconvene and perhaps move one of them to a different classroom. Agreed?" He said as he took full control of the conversation and ended it before it got too out of hand.

"Agreed." Cheryl and Annie said in unison as they looked to Martha Streuber for her acknowledgement that this would be an acceptable solution to the matter.

"Alright then." Martha said as she closed her folder and stood up. "I'll be paying very close attention to the two of them. I sincerely hope that we do not have to have this conversation again in the future. In the meantime, I would appreciate it very much if you would speak to your children about the very serious problem of cheating." She said as she dismissed herself from the meeting and left the room.

Cheryl and Annie also stood, and Cheryl saluted the disgruntled teacher as she left the room.

"Okay then." Principal Ellis stood. "Please, let me walk you out." After following Cheryl and Annie out of his office, he turned to his secretary and asked her to bring the children out so they could go home with their Mothers. "I'm sorry you had to come down. Hopefully, this was just a fluke and not an incident of cheating." He said as he bid them good afternoon and turned to go back to his office.

"Of course. Thank you Mr. Ellis." Annie said.

"If they're helping each other telepathically they're going to have to be a lot more clever about it." Cheryl whispered.

"I just hope they haven't told anyone they can do that. That's the last thing we need!" Annie whispered back.

A few minutes later, Lily and Joey emerged from the double doors leading to the open classroom wing of the school. They smiled when they saw their Mothers, but said nothing until they were well outside of the building. When they got to the parking lot, they stood by Cheryl's car and had a quick chat about what just happened in there.

"Okay, come clean you two. Are you communicating telepathically and sharing your answers on test questions?" Cheryl asked.

Lily and Joey's eyes were big and they looked at each other looking slightly surprised, but seriously guilty. "Well…" Lily said quietly as she scrunched up her nose. "Maybe a little."

"Lily!" Annie gasped as she tried to look casual in case Mrs. Streuber or Principal Ellis were watching them from the window. "You don't need to cheat. You're both very smart." She said.

"But we don't really do it that often, just when we get really stuck." Joey said.

"Ok, well this is not the place to be having this discussion. Let's talk about it when we get home." Cheryl said. "We'll see you back home Annie."

Annie and Lily got in their car, as did Cheryl and Joey, and they drove out of the school parking lot onto Plainfield Rd. towards home. Both children were informed of their teacher's suspicions and what the consequences were going to be if they were caught doing it again. They both promised not to do it ever again, but telepathy was not the kind of thing that could be ignored.

"Momma?" Lily said sweetly.

"Yes Lily?" Annie answered.

"Are you mad?" Lily asked.

"No, I'm not mad Baby Girl." Annie said. "But I am interested in knowing how often you and Joey have done this. I hope you're not doing it all the time, are you?"

"Not all the time Mom. Just when one of us needs a little help." Lily explained. "But I'll be more careful about it Mom. I don't want to get in trouble." She said.

"Have you told anyone that you have this ability Lil?" Annie asked.

"Nuh uh. No one." She said.

"Do you think Joey has told anyone?" Annie asked. "Because that would be a big problem if people knew about that."

"I don't think so, no. He knows that we can't talk about it to anyone. I don't think he would tell." Lily said.

"Ok, good. Never tell anyone, okay?" Annie said. "Because you would instantly become a circus attraction if people ever found out about that, understand?"

"I know." Lily said as she cast her head down to stare at her feet. She often forgot about what her life would be like if anyone knew about her abilities. She knew that she must guard against any of it becoming public knowledge. She hoped that Joey understood that too, but she would talk to him about it after they got back home to make sure.

After returning home, Cheryl, Annie and the kids stood in the Frasier's driveway and talked about using telepathy while at school and to avoid doing it all together. Both children acknowledged the potential consequences and agreed that they would not communicate telepathically while taking tests. After a brief discussion about it, the conversation quickly turned to Annie and Lily's recent visit with Auset and what she expected the next steps to be in order to slay the Dark Beast.

"There will be another catastrophic event that kills hundreds of people, let's see, she said in 4 days…" Annie said as she counted forward since she visited Auset and had that conversation. "Oh my gosh! It's going to happen tomorrow! Four days past would be October 19th!"

"Did she say what was going to happen?" Cheryl asked.

"No. Just that it was a nature event, so, maybe a storm or an earthquake or something. She called it *Mindanao* or something like that." Annie said.

"Mindanao? Hmmm. I have no idea what that is." Cheryl said.

"She didn't tell us either. I guess we'll just have to be on the lookout for it." Annie said as she said good night to Cheryl and went inside to make dinner.

"Everything okay at school Lily?" Mark asked as she came inside with her school books and set them on the table.

"Joey and I got in trouble today. The teacher says we were copying each other's papers, but we didn't." Lily said as she went downstairs to the family room and snuggled up next to her Father to watch the News.

"Oh, I see." Mark said as he pulled her close and kissed her on the top of her head.

"Hi Honey!" Annie said as she walked into the kitchen and called down to Mark sitting on the couch in front of the television set. "I'm going to make some spaghetti for dinner. That okay with you?"

"Yes!" Lily squealed. She loved spaghetti…Almost as much as she loved pancakes.

"Sounds good Hun." Mark said as he flipped the channels with the remote control.

"…*Typhoon Kate, a full Category 4 Typhoon, now referred to as a Super Typhoon barreled down on the island of Mindanao just hours ago. Although we cannot confirm the number of people dead at this time, the damage is catastrophic and the death toll is said to be great…*"

Annie dropped a pan on the floor. "Did they just say *Mindanao?*" She was speechless.

CHAPTER 44

C huck carefully studied the new project protocols. Everything seemed to be pretty straight forward. The project was essentially to study how cosmic rays can affect the Earth and how those affects might be causing changes in our weather. Galactic cosmic rays can cause clouds to form in our upper atmosphere. When the particles collide with other various atmospheric particles in our troposphere, the particles in our atmosphere disintegrate into smaller pions, or muons, which produces a phenomenon known as a *cosmic ray shower*. The project is to study how the primary cosmic ray particles interact with the atmosphere to generate secondaries, which are the particles that reach the surface of the earth and affect our weather. A necessary part of the project was to first build a cosmic ray neutron monitor suitable for this experiment so that they can accurately measure the cosmic ray levels reaching the Earth's surface. This has been done before, but there are always new possibilities for experimentation with new detection techniques. They would not necessarily need the Hadron Collider for this project, but they would need the lab where it currently resides since it is the only lab in the facility equipped with the proper lead shielding they'll need for an experiment like this. *'That's my ticket in.'* Chuck thought to himself. As he resumed studying the material, Dorothy came in to let him know that he was wanted on the phone.

"I have a satellite call for you sir. It's an Astro Physicist in Cochin, India. His name is Dr. Baljeet Chadha. Shall I patch him through?" Dorothy asked.

"Yes, Dorothy. Thank you." Chuck said. "Oh, wait—Dorothy?"

"Yes sir?" She answered.

"This Dr. Chadha, he speaks English, correct?" Chuck asked. There was nothing more frustrating to him than trying to communicate about scientific topics when both people were speaking a different language. He had encountered this at several international symposiums he had attended in the past and he hated it. It was awkward and he was always worried that he would offend someone somehow when he became frustrated, which he was prone to do in those situations.

"He's fluent sir." Dorothy replied with a reassuring smile. "I'll patch him through."

Chuck picked up the phone when the satellite line button lit up. "Hello? Dr. Chadha? This is Dr. Charles Frasier."

'Hello Dr. Frasier! You can call me Baljeet. May I also call you Charles?' Dr. Chadha said in a cheerful voice.

"Actually, no one ever calls me Charles. Please call me Chuck." Chuck said.

'Oh fine then. Chuck.' Dr. Chadha replied cheerfully. *'I just wanted to give you a jingle to introduce myself since we will be working on the cosmic ray project together. I have heard many great things about you and I am honored to have the privilege to be working with you.'*

"Well thank you!" Chuck replied. "I've been reading your resume and it's very impressive. I'm looking forward to working with you as well. I'm sure you'll teach me a lot."

'I know that it is not outlined in the project protocol document directly, but I am particularly interested in researching one of my recent findings. I hope you will agree that we should investigate this...' Dr. Chadha said.

"Sure. Which findings specifically? Everything in this dossier seems rather...Ordinary in scope." Chuck replied.

'It's not in the dossier Chuck. Recently, I have recorded a burst of galactic cosmic rays that indicates a crack in the Earth's magnetic shield. The burst seems to have occurred when a giant cloud of plasma ejected from the solar corona and struck Earth at a very high speed causing massive compression of the Earth's magnetosphere and triggered, in my opinion, a severe geomagnetic storm.' Dr. Chadha explained with a sense of urgency in his voice. *'I haven't actually told anybody about it yet. I was hoping we would have the opportunity to investigate this together. You see, and this might sound strange... my young son insists that you and I must investigate this together. He says the world depends on it.'*

Any other Quantum Physicist collaborating on a project with a foreign scientist whom they have never met might think what Dr. Chadha just said was just plain nuts, but Chuck felt differently. Perhaps it was because he was surrounded by extraordinary people in his home life who had extra sensory abilities, and he had come to understand that they just know what they know and they're usually correct. No, he didn't think Dr. Chadha was nuts at all.

This was a match being made for a divine purpose and Chuck was going to embrace it.

"Actually Baljeet? What your son says does not sound strange to me at all. I have a feeling that he might be right and I am very interested in investigating this phenomena with you. I actually have something that I would like to propose to you as well, but it's too difficult to discuss over the phone. It says here that you will be joining us here at Argon to work on this project, is that true?" Chuck asked.

'Yes, yes it is. I will be leaving here at the end of this week and I will join you at Argon on Monday morning. I look forward to meeting you in person Chuck, we have a lot to discuss.' Dr. Chadha said.

"That's perfect. I look forward to meeting you. Have a safe trip and I'll see you next week!" Chuck said as he hung up the phone. This was good. Chuck now found himself with another scientific mind to collaborate with on the monumental task of sending the Dark Entity back to the darkness from where it came. Edith will be pleased.

Typhoon Kate had proven to be the disaster that Auset forewarned them about. Mindanao Island, in the Philippines, took a direct hit by a super typhoon and 130 people died in one day. But it didn't stop there. As predicted, it weakened slightly going over the mountainous terrain of the Philippine archipelago, but quickly regained strength as it headed toward the Indochina coastline. In the end, it claimed the lives of 631 people and 284 people were missing. This was the deadliest typhoon ever to hit the Philippines on record. The next catastrophic event, Auset warned, would be even deadlier yet. On the date of 2 master numbers: 11/11. November 11th.

Annie sat at the kitchen table with Mark, as they did twice per month, and paid their bills. The donation money from the terminal employees held things together at a pretty normal level, but that was being spent bit by bit and there wasn't going to be much of it left after next month, right in time for the Holidays. Annie sat there silently making a list in her head of things she could do without for the next few weeks so that Christmas wouldn't feel like they were poor.

"Do you have any idea how much longer it will be before you can go back to work?" Annie asked.

Mark knew what she was worried about and did his best calm her fears, as he always did. "I'm actually doing better than they expected. I have a follow-up appointment with the doctor at the end of next week. We'll see what he says." Mark said as he wrote out the biggest check of the month—the house payment. "I'm going to ask if he'd clear me to do some short local routes. The local fleet has automatic transmissions. They'll be easier to drive. If he'll give me the green light next week, I'm sure I can pick up a couple of local routes each week until I'm ready to go back to driving a long haul big rig."

Annie smiled. She knew he really didn't want to run the local routes. They didn't pay all that well and the traffic was awful. But Mark was a man who would do whatever it took to take care of his family and she knew there'd be no talking him out of it. "You know, right after Halloween the stores start hiring extra help for Christmas. I saw an ad for JC Penny's out at Yorktown. And there was also a job posting for the stock room at Marshall Field's in Oakbrook. I could apply there." She said.

"You could." Mark said. He appreciated that she was willing to help with the financial burden, but he also kind of liked having her home so she can be there for the kids when he was away. He finished balancing the checkbook and put everything away in the designated bill pay box and looked at Annie over his glasses resting on his nose. "Honey, you do whatever makes you happy. I'm not worried about it. We'll get by. We always do." He said as he smiled at her and winked.

"Well, I want to do something. I have the time." Annie said. "I'll go apply for short term Christmas help and see if I can work part-time at least. Just while the kids are at school all day."

"Sounds like a plan." Mark said as he rose to his feet, grabbed his cane, and tucked the bill pay box under his other arm. "Oh, I forgot to tell you—Edith called earlier while you were out walking Winnie. She wanted you to call her back." He said.

"Oh, okay. I'll give her a ring." Annie said as she grabbed the phone and dialed Edith's number. "Hi Edith, It's Annie…Yes, Mark said that you called. What's up?"

'Hi Annie. I just wondered if you had spoken to Chuck since he went back to Argon. He said he would be starting back there this past Monday, but I haven't heard from him.' Edith said.

"No, no I haven't. But I'm surprised that he hasn't been checking in with you. Should I run over there and see what I can find out?" Annie asked.

'No, that's okay. You don't have to do that. I'm sure he's probably just getting settled in back at the old office. I'm just getting a little concerned because November 11th is right around the corner and I want to make sure we're prepared.' Edith explained.

"Well, you could always call him at home this evening. It probably wouldn't hurt to check in." Annie said.

'That's a good idea. I think I will…Say, why don't we just plan on getting together this weekend and talk about it a little more. I've had quite a few new revelations from my spirit guides that might be helpful for all of us to know.' Edith said.

"That sounds great. We can get together over here on Friday night. I can make a pot of Chili. How does that sound?" Annie suggested.

'That would be lovely, thank you for the invite Annie.' Edith replied. They said good-bye and Edith hung up the phone so she could try to get a hold of Chuck. They had a lot to do and she wanted to make sure everyone was on the same page.

Upstairs, Lily sat quietly on the floor in her bedroom meditating with gratitude. This was an important ritual for her to stick too since it was her central source to balance her energy and connect with her higher power. As she sat quietly, she began to see visions of future events. Her guides revealed a strong kinship and bond with a young boy from India. She was shown that his father would also play an important role in the events that would stop the destruction caused by the Dark Entity and remove it from the Earth plane and this realm. Lily knew that she must stay centered, calm, clear, and balanced to be able to assist Edith and Chuck, in fact, it would take several people together focusing on the task at the same time. The more intuitives the better! But even less intuitive people were going to be needed. After all, everyone has abilities. Most don't even realize that they have them. Lily knew that it was going to take the intentions of many people willing the Beast to be removed at the same time to get the job done. This was a monumental task for a 7 year old, but Lily was no ordinary 7 year old and she felt that she was up for the task.

As she started to close her meditation, Auset appeared to her surrounded in golden healing light. *'You are ready Little Bird. Have confidence and rely on your instincts. It will be done as you will it.'* She said to her. This gave Lily the feeling of power that she wasn't entirely sure she possessed before. She was grounded, centered, and all of her Chakras were aligned. She was ready.

As she finished her meditation, Annie knocked on her door. "Lil? May I come in?" Annie asked.

"Sure Mom." Lily replied as she got up off the floor.

"I wanted to see if anything in particular sounded good to you for dinner." Annie asked. "Whatcha doing up here?"

"Just meditating." Lily replied. "Auset says I'm ready and I think that I am now."

"Ready for what?" Annie asked.

"Ready to get rid of the Dark Entity Mom, what do you think?" Lily said.

"Oh yes, that." Annie said. "I just spoke to Edith on the phone and it sounds like she's getting ready too. I invited everyone to come over on Friday night so we could make sure we're all on the same page."

"So, Mom?" Lily asked. "Do you feel like you're ready too?"

It had never occurred to Annie that she needed to be *ready* for something that seemed to be incredibly scientific or that involved advanced psychic abilities in order to be helpful. She just thought of herself as sort of an observer ready to assist in more mundane ways if needed. "Well, I guess I haven't really thought about it." She said as she sat on the edge of Lily's bed. "I'm not sure how I can be of any help with this."

"Oh but you can! We need you Momma." Lily said with concern. "We are going to need lots of people to send it away. We need your help, and Daddy's, and Vince, Stephen, Beth, Joey, and Mrs. Frasier too." She said.

"Not all of us have your abilities Lil. How can somebody like me help you?" Annie asked.

"It's very simple Mom. You get quiet, ground yourself to the Earth, and sort of visualize it being carried up into the Vortex that Dr. Frasier is going to create. That's all there is to it. You have to help!" Lily said.

"Well, I can certainly do that!" Annie said.

"Remember Mom, this is OUR world and we have all the power against it. Since it's not from our world, we can push it away just by commanding it to go." Lily explained.

Annie had never thought about it like that. Was that really all there was to this intuitive stuff? Just setting your mind to something to make it happen? Annie had never considered the simplicity of it all. "Well, you can count on me Lily. I will do whatever I need to do. You might have to walk us through the process, but Daddy, Vince, Stephen, and everyone else will help in any way you need us too." She said. "Now, what shall we make for dinner?"

CHAPTER 45

It was Friday, October 23rd. Less than a month until the date with 2 master numbers. The day the world would be spared from further destruction and chaos. Annie dropped Mark off at the Doctor's office while she made a quick run to the grocery store to get what she needed for a large batch of Chili and Cornbread for the get-together that evening. When she returned to the medical office building, Mark was sitting on the bench just outside the front doors.

"I'm sorry Honey. I didn't know you'd be so quick." Annie said as Mark walked around to the driver's side of the car.

"That's okay. I wasn't waiting long." Mark said. "Let me drive."

"What? Wait, what did the Doctor say?" She asked.

Mark held up the piece of paper in his hand. "He says I can go back to work." He said proudly. "My reflexes and range of motion required to do my job are in satisfactory order."

"Oh that's great!" Annie said as she threw her arms around her husband. "I'll bet you're relieved."

"Very. He still recommends continuing my exercises at home for a few weeks, but I'm good to go back to work and that's what matters." Mark said as he moved his left ankle in a circular motion. "So, don't feel like you have to run off and get a job if you don't want to…Or maybe you want to. That's okay too. Whatever you want to do is fine with me Honey."

"Well, it's always nice *not* to have to do anything. But I kind of think I might like the stock room job at Marshall Fields. A little extra money at Christmas time wouldn't be a bad thing." Annie said.

"Your call." Mark replied as he put the car into Drive and drove home.

Chuck, Jeremy Camas, and Pete Schroeder got into the Elevator that took them down to Lab 2C. This was the first time anyone other than the police or the FBI have been allowed down there, and Chuck and his team needed to inspect the facility to make sure it was properly set up for the cosmic ray project. As they got off the elevator, the stark white concrete walls with flickering fluorescent lighting gave them the feeling they were entering a depressing insane asylum. They walked down the hall to the double doors labeled "LAB 2C" and Chuck used his key card to unlock the door. The lab no longer resembled a crime scene. It was cleaned up, repainted, and it looked shiny and new. The Hadron Collider was still there, sitting in the center of the room facing the corner where the portal was. You couldn't see the portal, but Chuck knew it was there and it was still open.

"So, this is where it all happened, huh?" Jeremy said as he gazed around the room cautiously.

"Yes it is." Chuck said remembering for a brief moment how it looked the night of the murder.

"Whoa! Is this what I think it is?" Pete asked as he walked toward the Hadron Collider.

"If you're thinking that it's a Hadron Collider, then you'd be correct." Chuck said.

"Can we use it?" Pete asked.

"I plan to." Said Chuck, even though he wasn't sure they would be using it for their cosmic ray project, but he would definitely be using it on November 11th.

"I've read so much about this." Pete said. "I heard that this is what Kawalski is partially being prosecuted for. I guess he stole the blueprints to build this from the British Government. I'm surprised that it's still in here. I would have guessed that it would have been confiscated."

"Pete, it's the size of a dump truck! I'm sure it will be removed at some point, but they're going to finish prosecuting Kawalski for the crime first." Jeremy said. "And cosmic rays are known to have energies exceeding 10^{20} eV—far more than I've heard the Hadron Collider produces. I don't think we'll need it."

Chuck quickly tried to change the subject. "Guys? These walls are leaded, but do you think we will need additional shielding for the Neutron Monitor or will this be sufficient?" He asked.

"Well that depends." Jeremy said. "How thick is the lead? Terrestrial radio-active sources can be very penetrative. Natural Cobalt-60 gammas can have energies up to 1.3 MeV, so that can easily penetrate up to 10mm of lead."

"I'm not sure how thick it is, but you're right. If we don't have adequate radiation shielding it will cause a substantial number of false detections." Chuck replied. He smiled to himself after that exchange because it really didn't take much to distract a nerdy Scientist, which is exactly what these two guys were in every way imaginable. Pocket protectors to them were like Chanel handbags to high society women. "I'll notify the construction crew of our shielding needs." He said as he made a note in his notebook.

"Chuck, I don't see any of the components we need to build the Neutron Monitor here. Are they stored somewhere else?" Pete asked.

"That's why we're down here today gentlemen. I wanted to see if there was anything here that we could use before I submit our requisition order." Chuck explained. "Let's see, we're going to need a boron coated cathode corona pulse neutron tube, a moderator and reflector, preferably ultra-high molecular weight polyethylene, a producer, and all of the electronics we need…" He said as he made a list of items.

"Hey Chuck, here's a Geiger Counter. I can modify the circuit with an adjustable high voltage regulated DC supply pretty easily. Can we use this?" Jeremy asked.

"Yes, of course. That's why I wanted to bring you down here. I'd rather use what we have and save money in the budget for something we might need later." Chuck said. "How long do you think it will take you to build this?"

Jeremy and Pete discussed the process and decided upon a time frame. "About 3 days, and that's if we have everything we need on hand." Jeremy said.

"Good. I'll put this requisition request in today and hopefully we'll have everything we need by Wednesday at the latest." Chuck said. "Let's go back upstairs and draw out the design on the whiteboard so we're clear on specs and what we need."

As the three men were leaving the lab, Chuck caught a fast moving black shadow out of the corner of his right eye and it gave him an icy chill up his spine. At that same moment, Jeremy turned his head in the same direction. "Did you see that?" Jeremy asked.

"See what?" Chuck said. He knew, but he didn't want to alarm his team in case they did not know the exact details of Martin Reese's murder.

Jeremy stood silently staring in the corner of the lab where the portal was for a moment, then he turned to head out the door. "Huh. It must have just been your shadow behind me Chuck." He said.

As the Chili was simmering on the stove, Annie put 2 large pans of cornbread batter in the oven and set the timer for 35 minutes. "There." She said. "Now for the honey butter." She had set out a pound of butter on the counter to soften and now it was exactly the right temperature to work with. As she whisked honey into the softened butter with the hand mixer, Lily came down the stairs with Winnie who immediately ran to the kitchen to see if anything edible had fallen on the floor.

"Is that honey butter Mom?" Lily asked.

"It sure is. We can't have cornbread without honey butter." Annie said.

"Mom? I've been meditating in my room after I finished my homework, and Auset knows that we're all meeting tonight. She says that we have to make a triangle energy field to get rid of the Dark Entity." Lily said.

"Well, that's interesting." Annie paused for a moment as she said that. "I wonder how we're going to do that?"

"She didn't tell me but she said that Chuck and Edith will know. I'm only supposed to work with Reyansh to help form the base part of the energy triangle." Lily said.

"That name sounds familiar. Who's Reyansh again?" Annie asked.

"He's a boy with abilities like me. He lives in India. I've been communicating with him every night." Lily said. "Auset and Heru have been visiting him too…But mostly Heru."

"Well, we will be sure to talk about all of this tonight when Edith and Chuck arrive." Annie said. "But right now, Winnie would like to be fed. Would you mind feeding her Lil?"

"Sure Mom. Are you hungry Winnie Pooh?" Lily said as she looked down at Winnie who was in full body wiggle mode expressing that yes, she would like to be fed.

After all of their guests had arrived, Annie set the pot of Chili out on the kitchen counter along with a bowl of shredded cheddar cheese, a bowl of tortilla chips, a plate of warm cornbread, and a bowl of honey butter for everyone to help themselves buffet style. After eating the delicious comfort food meal, which was perfect on a crisp mid-October Friday night, everyone got comfortable in the living room to talk about the upcoming task of sending the Dark Entity out of this realm.

"I had access to the lab where the Hadron Collider is today. It's still there and we can use it." Chuck said. "Now, I can't get everybody in there, but Edith, I checked on your visitors pass and it's still valid. I can bring you in with me, but everyone else will have to work remotely."

"That's perfect." Edith said. "Everyone else can do their part from right here."

"It's interesting. There's another Scientist who will be joining my team on Monday. He made a remarkable discovery last week and it is directly related to what we need to do on 11/11. His name is Dr. Baljeet Chadha." Chuck said.

"Oh!" Lily said. "I know who that is. That's Reyansh's Father. He told me that he would be helping you."

Chuck looked at Lily with an expression of confusion and bewilderment. "I'm not even going to ask how you know that because your abilities are beyond my comprehension. But yes, he did tell me that he had a son who insisted that he had to help us with this project, so I assume we're talking about Reyansh." Chuck said. He was amazed at how powerful psychic abilities could be. This was something that wasn't within his field of study, but he wouldn't be opposed to researching psychic phenomena at some point in the future.

Lily shrugged her shoulders and very innocently said: "It's a gift." Which made everybody laugh.

"That it is!" Chuck laughed. "But seriously…" He continued as he turned to Edith. "I'm not exactly sure what everyone's part is or how we will be collaborating to make this work."

"Well, the Hadron Collider is definitely your part Chuck. We'll do everything else." Edith said. She went on to explain that there is a planetary collective and polarized forces are battling for control. On November 11th, the Stargate and hidden portals on Earth and in space will be revealed, and energy will be ramping up in intensity. All of the intuitives, or Light Workers as their sometimes called, on Earth will be instinctively drawn to the ascension gateway, where the dimensional veil will be the thinnest. At that point, their spiritual invocations and intentions will become more effective while the veil comes down for a brief time. "So, many of us must use our energy to work

with higher octave vibrations of light all at the same time, to harmonize reso-
nance with the Earth."

"So, while I'm accelerating energy particles with the Hadron Collider
aimed at the coordinates that Auset provided me with, we'll punch through
the Crystalline Grid 147.59 light years away to Eltanin, the brightest star in
the Draco Constellation in the Milky Way…And all of the intuitives here on
Earth will create a linear energy stream to where the Dark Entity is, and it
in turn, it will force it up into the vortex that we've created and will be gone
forever. Is that how we're doing this?" Chuck was scribbling notes in his notebook to make sure he wasn't forgetting any important details.

"In theory, yes." Edith said. "It will form a perfect energy triangle, which
is important to forming the gateway to get rid of this thing."

Mark, Annie, and Cheryl sat quietly without knowing what to say. This
was so far beyond their ability to comprehend that they were utterly speechless.
Only Lily, at the young age of 7 had a clue what they were talking about. Still,
they wanted to help in any way they could since the welfare of Humankind
depended on it.

"So what do you need *us* to do?" Annie asked.

Edith turned to them half embarrassed that they'd been left out of the
conversation. "Oh, we need all of you!" She said. "We need your help in man-
ifesting our intentions to banish this Beast from our realm. You all have a very
important role to play here."

Lilly could tell that things weren't quite making sense to her parents, so
she decided to explain in a way that only an enlightened 7 year old could.
"We need you to *wish* it to go away…Very strongly. With all your might!" Lily
explained. A moment of silence lingered as they looked at each other.

"I guess we can do that." Mark said. "What do you think Cheryl?"

"Absolutely! I'm very good at wishing things away!" Cheryl replied.

As Chuck was writing more notes in his notebook, he stopped to think
about what Edith just said about the energy triangle. That was the piece he
was missing. He flipped back through his notes to double check the coordinates on the piece of paper that Auset had given them. "Annie? Do you have a
globe that shows longitude and latitude in the house?" He asked.

"Yes, actually there's one in Stephen's room." Annie said. "Follow me."

Annie led Chuck upstairs to the end of the hall to Stephen's room. There,
sitting on top of his dresser was a 12 inch globe mounted on a polished num-
bered metal meridian. Hanging on the wall above it was a large poster of the

constellations in the sky. "Oh this could not be more perfect!" Chuck said. "I had no idea that Stephen was into this stuff."

"Oh, he's all about anything scientific. In fact, he'd love to take a tour of Argon sometime…That is, if you're allowed to show him." Annie said. She could tell that Chuck was deep in thought and probably didn't hear a word she just said.

"Where did Lily say her friend Reyansh lived?" Chuck asked.

"She says he's from India, but I don't know exactly where." Annie replied.

"His Father is coming out to Argon to work with me on a project. He said on the phone that he lives in Cochin…" Chuck said as he double checked the coordinates that Auset gave to him. "I know where the Dark Entity will be on November 11th." Chuck closed his notebook, picked up the globe, and went back downstairs to join the rest of the group.

"Chuck? What is it?" Cheryl asked.

"I know where the Dark Entity will be on November 11th. It will be in East Pakistan." Chuck said. "It aligns directly on the baseline of our triangle." He said as he drew a line on the globe with his finger from Argon, through East Pakistan, to Cochin, India, then up to approximately where the star known as Eltanin would be above the Earth. "That's it!" He said excitedly as he looked to Edith for confirmation.

"Well, I'll be. Chuck, I do believe you've figured out the missing piece." Edith said.

"And Edith?" Chuck whispered as the others were examining the globe. "That portal in the lab is still open. I saw a shadowy figure dart past me when I was down there today. One of my co-workers saw it, but I didn't admit that I saw it too. Are we safe going back in there?" He asked.

"I can show you how to lay down a protective barrier with salt, herbs, and Holy water while you're working, but do be careful." Edith said. "These entities are evil and they're dangerous. Don't stay in there for very long if you can help it. They know you're working to banish them. They *will* kill you."

THEY. WILL. KILL. YOU. Four words that sent a shiver down Chuck's spine. Going to work just got more terrifying and he would need all of the courage he could muster for the next few weeks.

CHAPTER 46

As Chuck opened the back door to the offices at Argon National Laboratories, Dorothy greeted him in the hallway.

"Good morning Dr. Frasier." She said. "Dr. Chadha is waiting in reception up front. Let me know when you'd like me to bring him back."

"He's here already?" Chuck asked. "Why don't you bring him back and I'll put my stuff down and grab some coffee. Did you offer him some coffee?"

"Yes, but he prefers tea. I've already taken care of it sir." Dorothy said. She was incredibly dependable and efficient and Chuck couldn't imagine how the place would run without her. Moments later, she came around the corner leading Dr. Baljeet Chadha to Chuck's office.

"Baljeet! It's a pleasure to finally meet you." Chuck said as he extended his hand to the short, skinny, Indian gentleman standing before him.

"Yes, Chuck! Very nice to meet you too!" Baljeet said enthusiastically.

"Please, have a seat." Chuck said as he motioned his guest to sit down. "How was your flight? That had to be a long one."

"Oh, yes, very, very long. It was 22 hours I believe." Baljeet said. "But, I had no trouble going to sleep when I reached the hotel. I slept from Saturday night to this morning at 4 am. I'm sure I'll reset my body clock in the next few days." He said cheerfully.

"Well, I've been to Europe many times, but I think my longest flight was only 8 hours. 22 sounds brutal." Chuck said. "Did you bring your family with you?"

"No, not this time. I have 5 children and my wife is taking care of her elderly father. This is a short assignment so it made no sense to uproot them to bring them here." Baljeet explained.

"Hmmm. I suppose you're right." Chuck said as he took a sip of his coffee. "So, I'm sure you've read the brief on our project?"

"Yes, I have. In great detail." Baljeet said. There was a pause for a minute and the two men stared at each other wondering how to brooch the subject of the experiment *outside* of the cosmic ray experiment they would be working on.

"But…I'm actually more interested in talking about your findings about a geomagnetic storm." There. Chuck just got right to the point. "I think I might have a theory about how that happened." He said. "Come with me."

Chuck stood up and let Dorothy know that he was going to give Dr. Chadha a tour of the lab and that he'd be back shortly. He walked with Baljeet to the elevator, got in, and pushed the button to the basement which took them down to Lab 2C.

"There are security cameras everywhere, so I'm going to speak softly at times. Please pay close attention when I do this." Baljeet nodded his head indicating that he understood.

When the elevator doors opened, Chuck led Baljeet down to the steel double doors to Lab 2C and ran his key card through the electronic lock. There was a loud *click* then the doors opened. Chuck stepped in and turned on the lights. He quickly glanced around the room to see if there were any signs of a black shadow lurking anywhere. All clear. As Baljeet stepped in, he looked down at his arms. All of the hair on his arms were raised and he had goosebumps.

"I wanted to bring you down here to show you where we will be conducting the cosmic ray experiment." Chuck said in a loud projecting voice. Then he turned his face away from the surveillance camera and whispered: "This is the room where we were working on a time travel project and we opened a portal to another dimension."

"This will do nicely. Leaded walls I presume?" Baljeet said in a loud voice, then turned his head to whisper back: "I know. My son told me about it. That is really why I am here." Baljeet whispered.

"Yes. There's 50mm of lead shielding down here. That should suffice." Chuck said loudly. "We thought that we could use some of the equipment down here to build the Neutron Monitor. We won't be using the Hadron Collider, obviously, but there are a few things here that we could make good use of." He could tell that Baljeet seemed to be sensitive to whatever was down there and not in a good way. "Let's go back upstairs and run through Phase 1 of this project, shall we?" He said in a loud voice as he led Baljeet out of the room, shut off the lights, and locked the door. He gave one last look through the small window on the door but saw nothing but pitch black. They got back into the elevator and went upstairs to Chuck's office to finish the conversation.

"Dorothy? Dr. Chadha and I are going to dive into the project details. Can you please hold my calls for a little while? I don't want to be interrupted until we finalize our Phase 1 objectives." Chuck said.

"Of course Dr. Frasier." Dorothy said. "Let me know if you need anything."

Chuck and Baljeet went back into Chuck's office and closed the door. *Were there cameras or microphones in his office left over from the FBI takedown of Kawalski?'* He thought to himself. He glanced around the room and pretended to drop a pen on the floor so he could take a look under his desk to make sure. Nothing there that he could see.

"Baljeet, you keep mentioning your son. Is he a Scientist?" Chuck asked.

"Reyansh? No. He's only 8 years old." Baljeet said wondering at the same time how he was going to explain that the boy has psychic abilities and is being guided by an Ancient Egyptian Entity to help save the Earth. "But...He is very special. He has...abilities that other people do not have." He said.

Chuck nodded his head and looked down toward his desk for a brief moment. "You mean like *psychic abilities?*" He asked.

"Yes." Baljeet said, relieved that Chuck seemed to have a level of understanding of this. "He is very gifted and knows things that no one else could possibly know. He has always been right in his predictions and he has never been more strongly insistent about anything before than this."

"I understand, believe me." Chuck said. "My Son and our neighbor, who are both 7 years old have various extra sensory abilities. We also have a friend, Edith MacKenzie, who is a Psychic Medium and she is helping me with this... And you know what else? They are also being guided by an Ancient Egyptian Deity by the name of Auset who is helping us send this evil Dark Entity back to where it came from." Chuck paused for a moment as Dorothy passed the window outside. She didn't knock on the door so he continued. "I was brought on in the late stages of the time travel project where a portal was opened down there in the lab and this evil thing came through. It pulverized, and I literally mean *pulverized* one of our Security Guards down in that room. Edith is working with me to close that portal." He said.

"Reyansh has told me this also. This is why I volunteered to work on this project. He says that I must be here with you to do our part." Baljeet said.

"On November 11th, there will be some sort of catastrophic event called *Bhola* that is the sign for us to engage and create a vortex using that big Hadron

Collider down there in the lab." Chuck said as he reached in his back pocket for his wallet and pulled out a small folded piece of paper. "The Egyptian lady, Auset, wrote this out for me. They're coordinates for an area near the Ganges river in East Pakistan, but I am unsure how this correlates with the astral coordinates here…" He said as he pointed to the part referencing Eltanin. Since Baljeet was an Astro Physicist, he was sure that he could explain that part.

"You are correct. This is an astral location. It is the astral location of the constellation *Draco* in the north sky. Eltanin is the brightest star in that constellation." Baljeet said. "And Chuck? You know that *Draco* means Dragon."

Chuck knew that, but he never made that connection until Baljeet pointed it out. "So, is this a reference to the evil Dark Entity? A Dragon?" Chuck asked.

"It is possible. Rather fitting, don't you think?" Baljeet said as he smiled.

"Hmmm…Yes, I think you might be on to something." Chuck said. Then he made another startling connection. "Baljeet? When did you make the discovery about the geomagnetic storm?"

"It was in July." Baljeet said. "Why do you ask?"

Chuck sat back in his chair and tipped his head back for a second to collect his thoughts. "Because I think that Lt. Col. Leonard Kawalski caused it when he opened the portal in the lab downstairs. I think that's how the crack in the Earth's magnetic shield occurred." Chuck said. It was all starting to make sense now. "I think that this is how the Dark Entity was able to enter our realm, and now it's up to us to get rid of that damn thing."

CHAPTER 47

October 27, 1970 Cochin, India

It was a hot and muggy October evening and Reyansh Chadha gazed out his bedroom window watching the large fruit bats stirring in the mango trees. Everything living served a purpose and contributed to the complex eco system of this wonderful planet called Earth. Reyansh gave thanks for every living thing on the planet and was grateful to be alive and part of this big world. He was even more thankful that he was *aware* of his existence in that, he was a part of all things on Earth and in the Universe. He closed his eyes and took four big cleansing breaths as he focused on the rhythm of his breathing. He opened his awareness to it all—the sounds of the bats rustling through the trees above. The sound of the fruit falling that the bats knocked to the ground. The sound of the Indian Palm Squirrels eating the ripe fruit that had fallen from the trees. Everything was in order. Everything had its place. Everything served an important purpose. As he entered his meditative state, Heru appeared to him as he often had in recent months.

'*Reyansh, you will be called to anchor the energy of the triangle. I will be at your side. In 15 days you must be ready. A young girl with a flower's name will be your conduit in a faraway land.*' Heru said to him.

'*Do you mean Lily, Heru? Is that the girl you speak of?*' Reyansh said telepathically.

'*Yes, young one. She is like you. She will anchor another part of the triangle with my Mother, Auset by her side. Your Father will open the portal and my Father, Ausar will anchor it to the stars. The energy triangle will be strong and it will force the Dark Entity into the portal and will be in this realm no more.*' Heru said to him. '*There is much chaos to come, but fear not. You will be safe here. I will be by your side.*'

"Reyansh! Come and say goodnight to your Grandfather." Reyansh's Mother called.

He thanked Heru for his message and his guidance, and brought himself out of his meditative state. Then he stood up and left his bedroom to bid his Grandfather goodnight as his Mother had asked. As he stood in the doorway of his Grandfather's bedroom, he waited patiently to be invited in.

"Come in Little Tiger!" His Grandfather said as he patted the side of his bed with his hand. "Come, sit here with me." He said.

Reyansh went to his Grandfather's bed and sat down. "How are you feeling Grandfather?" He asked.

"I am old Rey Rey. I feel very old and very tired." The old man said with a smile. "But, I am still alive and here with you. Tell me, what have you seen today?" The old man knew of the boy's abilities and he was an intuitive himself. He was a good source of wisdom for the boy and had taught Reyansh to have a profound respect for all living things.

"I was watching the fruit bats in the mango trees outside. They were knocking the ripe fruit to the ground so the squirrels could eat them. It was as if they were working together in harmony, Grandfather." Reyansh said as he sat in gratitude, as he often did with his elderly Grandfather who was his teacher in the ways of the Universe ever since he could remember.

"Yes Rey Rey. All things work together so that each may benefit from the other." The old man said. "And soon you will work with others far away to benefit this world."

Reyansh lowered his head and closed his eyes for a moment recalling the message he had just received from Heru a few minutes ago. "Am I ready Grandfather?" He asked.

The old man laughed which turned into a spout of coughing. When he caught his breath, he answered. "Yes, my young tiger. You are ready. And you will continue this important work throughout your life. Live with gratitude my young tiger and you will illuminate the world with your happiness."

Reyansh knew what his Grandfather spoke of. He lived each day with gratitude and appreciated the purpose of all living things. He was inspired by the teachings of Ghandi but he knew his life path would be different. He embraced his life, his family, his home, and he had much to be grateful for. His Grandfather coughed a little more and squeezed Reyansh's tiny hand.

"I will not be among the living much longer Rey Rey. I have lived my life and soon it will be time to depart the world of the living." The old man said quietly.

"Don't say such things Grandfather!" Reyansh said. He knew that his Grandfather spoke the truth, but it was hard for him to accept.

"Hush little tiger. There is no reason to upset yourself. This is part of the cycle of life. It is natural and organic. My journey here will be done and I will return home again. BUT, I will always be watching over you, and you…" The old man said as he pointed his finger at Reyansh's chest. "…Will be able to see and speak to me just as you are at this moment." The old man said. "We will never be apart. You know this, do you not?"

These were very painful words for the boy to hear, but he knew that his Grandfather was right and in a way, he was relieved to hear him say it. "Sleep well Grandfather, and we will speak again in the morning." Reyansh said as he kissed the old man's hand and laid it gently on his chest as the old man started to doze off.

It was 7:20 am and Lily was in her room getting dressed for school. As she usually did every morning, she chatted with Grandpa Tom, and some of the other spirits who gave her guidance for the day. As she came down the stairs, Vince, Stephen, and Annie were in the kitchen eating breakfast.

"Oh there you are Lil. I was just about to come up and get you. Would you like some scrambled eggs?" Annie said as she poured herself a second cup of coffee.

"No thanks. I'm kind of in the mood for cereal." Lily said as she went to the pantry to retrieve the box of Rice Krispies.

"We were just talking about the Pythagorean triangle. Stephen did some research about how important that was to the Ancient Egyptians." Annie said as Lily sat up to the table and poured the milk on her cereal.

"Well, the Pythagorean Theorem states that $a^2 + b^2 = c^2$, and that is the basis of trigonometry. BUT, it represented much more to the Ancient Egyptians. Sure, they built the Pyramids with that formula, but it also represented the harmony of opposites, like a child being created by male and female opposites for example…" Stephen explained. "It also represented their connection to the spiritual world. It was a symbol of enlightenment, revelation, and a higher state of being." He said.

"Fascinating how they knew so much so long ago." Annie remarked.

"But here's the most interesting and the most relevant to us right now: Energetically, triangles—all triangles, not just the Pythagorean triangles, direct energy and power in the direction in which they point." Stephen said.

There was a long pause and everyone stopped eating and looked to Lily. Stephen had just explained the purpose of Lily's connection to Reyansh so far away in India, and the coordinates in the stars that was told to Edith by Auset. Chuck had revealed the formation of the triangle when they got together last week, but the significance of that triangle energetically was not considered... Until now.

But Lily already instinctively knew this. She wasn't able to explain it as Stephen just did, but she knew it. She took a bite of her Rice Krispies and smiled at everyone as she chewed. After swallowing she very resolutely replied: "And now you get it." She said proudly.

"Lil?" Vince asked. "Do you think I can do a science project on this? I have to submit an idea for the science fair in February and the power of triangles would be a cool project."

Lily looked at Stephen and they were thinking the same thing. "Which part Vince? The part about the Pythagorean triangle and its significance to the Ancient Egyptians or the energetic significance?" Stephen asked.

"The energetic part of course! That is SO cool!" Vince said.

Annie knew what Stephen and Lily were thinking and she decided to throw her two cents in. "Honey, I'm not sure that would be a wise subject for you to do your project on. Remember, most people don't believe in this stuff. In fact, much of the scientific community regards it as fantasy." Annie said.

"But if it's the truth and we can prove that it is the truth by what is going to happen on November 11th, then why not?" Vince asked. He was always willing to step out of the norm and do things that no one else would be comfortable doing. Unlike most people, Vince had a fearless streak to his personality and he really didn't care what other people thought. He thrived on doing the unique and unusual things that were out of most people's comfort zones.

"I understand Honey, but think of it this way: What if your science teacher is one of those people who does not believe in the paranormal or psychic abilities. What if he gives you a bad grade because he thinks it's not a project about a *real* scientific subject?" Annie said. "Besides, you cannot mention that Lily has abilities or that Edith and the rest of us will be involved in using our energy and intentions to remove a Dark Entity from the Earth. That would ostracize the entire Family…And the Frasier's. There's more to consider here than just an interesting science project theme." She explained.

Vince slumped in his chair. The wind had been taken out of his sails just like that, but he knew his Mother was right. If word got out about Lily, Joey, Edith, and Dr. Frasier using Argon for a purpose like this they would all be ruined. Stephen thought of an equally interesting project idea and spoke up.

"How about this? You can do a project on the Pythagorean Theorem and how significant it was in building the great Pyramids of Giza in Ancient Egyptian times with no modern tools. You can expand on that in several interesting ways…" Stephen said. "I'll help you with it. You'll get an 'A' on it. Easy."

Lily sat quietly and nodded her head in agreement. *You can't tell anyone Vince. We have to keep this a secret at school.'* Lily said telepathically. Vince lifted his head and looked at Lily and nodded in acknowledgement that he agreed with her.

"Ok. Yeah, you're right. That would also be a good project. Thanks Stephen." Vince said as he brought his breakfast dishes to the sink. "Maybe Barb has some cool stuff we can use for the Egyptian part."

"Okay you three—time to head out for school. Vince, are you and Beth riding with Stephen this morning?" Annie asked.

"Um, yeah if that's okay." Vince said as he looked at Stephen.

"Sure. You just have to take the bus home after school because I have to go straight to work from there today." Stephen said.

"Good. And Lily? You've got 15 minutes before the bus comes so I'll get my shoes on and walk you down to the corner while I take Winnie for a walk." Annie said as she cleaned off the table.

After walking Lily and Joey to the bus stop, Annie finished her brisk walk around the neighborhood with Winnie. As she approached their driveway, Chuck was backing his car out of his driveway and stopped to roll his window down.

"Good morning Annie!" He said.

"Good morning Chuck! Headed to work?" Annie said as she bent down to talk to him through the passenger side window.

"Today and every day." He said jovially. "I spoke to Edith this morning and we're going to get together this coming weekend to lay out our plans for the 11th. I've invited an Astro Physicist I'm working with from India to join us. I want you to meet him." Chuck said.

"Sure! We'll be there." Annie said. "You know, Stephen just pointed out something very interesting this morning at breakfast."

"Oh? What's that?" Chuck asked.

"That triangles direct energy and power in the direction that they point. It all fits doesn't it?" Annie said.

Chuck raised his eyebrows. He hadn't thought of it that way, but it made a lot of sense. "I would agree with that. Especially in this case." He said as he glanced in the rear view mirror at the car approaching behind him. "I've got to get to the lab. We'll see you this weekend." He said as he waived and rolled up his passenger window before driving away.

Annie waived goodbye and went back into the house with Winnie.

CHAPTER 48

Edith went out to her garden to trim back her rose bushes before the cold winter months arrived. She was very diligent about tending to her gardens and always had been. It was her way of adding beauty to the world and it often reminded her of her belated husband, Ian. In the little cottage that they lived in just outside of Inverness, they grew their own vegetables in the summer. It was something they loved to do together and she thought of him every time she tended to her garden. *"You're more lovely than the most perfect Rose, Edie…"* He used to say to her. She longed to hear his comforting voice again, but alas, he never came to visit her. Sure, she could talk to the Dead, but usually just her spirit guides, or random dead people who needed her assistance. Ian wasn't among them—probably because he didn't need her help. She liked to think that he was on the other side tending to their cottage and their garden so it was ready when she arrived.

When Edith finished the front flower garden, she walked around to the back of the house to trim the rose bushes planted in her backyard garden. She laid her gardening pad down on the ground and knelt down to start trimming her prized *Princesse Charlene de Monaco* rose bush. As she knelt down, the air grew still and eerily silent. The crows that had been cawing to each other in the trees above ceased. The slight rustling of leaves falling to the ground from the trees as the breeze blew through the branches halted, and the unmistakable feeling that you were being watched rushed over Edith. She turned to see who or *what* was staring at her, and she saw it. Out at the edge of her yard where it met the tree line to the woods was a tall, dark, Shadow Person with red glowing eyes. Edith dropped her pruning tools and stood up. She turned to the direction of the Shadow Person and stared back at it, trying hard not to turn and run. "Why are you here?" She said forcefully. She was standing her ground. This was her property. Her world.

The Dark Entity growled as it stared back at her. She began calling upon her Spirit Guides and Guardian Angels to surround her with protection. As she began to fill herself with the Divine white light showered upon her, a familiar voice broke the trance.

"Mom? Everything okay out here?" Ed said.

Edith turned to see her son walking toward her with a box of tools. "Oh Edward! I am so happy to see you son!" She said.

"What's wrong?" Ed said as he set the box down and hugged his mother.

Edith turned back to the edge of the yard and the tall, dark, Shadow Person had disappeared. "The Shadow Person is back." She said. "It was growling at me from the edge of the yard back there just now. I don't suppose you saw it?"

"No, sorry Mom. I didn't see anything but you standing there looking like you were being showered in rainbows." Ed said.

"Yes, well, I asked for a little protective back up. I wasn't sure what it was going to do. It was growling, so I'm not so sure it was an actual Shadow Person, but it wanted me to *think* that it was." Edith explained. "What brings you over this way Edward?"

"I'm cleaning out my garage and I found these extra tools. I thought maybe I'd bring them over in case we need to fix something over here." Ed said as he stared off towards the tree line looking for the shadowy figure his mother just described.

"Oh, thank you. I was actually looking for a pair of vice grips yesterday. I couldn't unscrew the hose from the hose bib. Do you have any vice grips in there?" Edith asked as she bent down to dig through the box.

"You shouldn't need vice grips to unscrew a hose Mom. Show me which garden hose is stuck and I'll take care of it for you." Ed said.

"It's the one right there next to rain gutter spout. I wanted to put it away before it snows." Edith said as she pointed to the garden hose at the far corner of the house.

"Got it." Ed said as he walked over, unscrewed the hose, and rolled it up. "Where do you want this?"

"Oh, there's a gardening cabinet in the corner of the garage. Just put it on the bottom shelf." Edith said as she knelt back down to finish trimming her prized rose bush.

Ed put the hose away and walked back to see if Edith needed any help with anything else. She was fiercely independent and unless he specifically asked her, she would not tell him when something was broken and just attempted to repair it herself. Edith was handy, but she was getting older and injuries were a concern. "Do you need anything repaired Mom? I might as well fix it if you do." Ed said.

"No, everything is working fine Son. Thank you for unscrewing that hose for me. It was on there pretty tight!" Edith said as she smiled.

"Well, can I take you out for dinner then? We can go to White Fence Farm. We haven't been there in a while." Ed said.

White Fence Farm was a local family owned restaurant that served the best fried chicken Ed had ever tasted. The owners were a local farm family and everything was made fresh from ingredients grown on their farm. It was all served family style, and the atmosphere was warm and delightful. The family owned a sprawling ranch house on a frontage road near I-55 that was converted into a restaurant. Each room of the house was decorated in a farm house theme with tables scattered throughout the rooms. Ed and Edith had been going there for years, and Ed was convinced that it was absolutely impossible to get a bad meal there.

"You know? That sounds perfect. Just let me finish cutting back this rose bush and we can go." Edith said.

As they stood in the hostess line at the restaurant waiting to be seated, Edith noticed a shy little boy peering at her from behind his Father's leg. Edith smiled at the boy and his grin grew bigger until he burst into a chuckle. She took great delight in the innocent nature of children. They were so limitless in their possibilities and she thought about how the world had a way of destroying a child's innocence and belief that all things were possible. *'You can do anything you want to do and don't let the world tell you different. Dream big!'* Edith said to the boy telepathically. The boy said nothing, but he looked her in the eye as if he'd heard what she said and smiled.

"Good evening Mr. MacKenzie! How are you? I haven't seen you in a while." The hostess said as she greeted Ed. "Just you and your Mom tonight?"

"Hi Linda. Yes, table for two please." Ed said as he held his arm out to escort Edith to the table.

The hostess led them to a table in the corner of the grand living room right next to the big stone fireplace with a crackling fire. "How is this table?" The Hostess asked.

"Best seat in the house!" Ed said as he pulled the chair out for Edith to sit down. "Thank you."

"Great! Pam will be your waitress and she will be with you soon. Here are the menus. I highly recommend the butternut squash soup, and for sides, the twice baked potatoes are delicious tonight. They're whipped with a touch of sour cream for extra creaminess. You'll love them" Linda said.

"Oh, that does sound good!" Edith said as she look her menu. "Thank you Linda."

Edith and Ed enjoyed their dinner together and talked about several things: The change in Ed's routes at the trucking company and how Mark's return to work allowed Ed to go back to his old schedule again, Ed and Barb's wedding plans next Spring, and where they planned to live afterward. Barb's apartment on Fullerton Avenue was convenient for her being a curator at the Field Museum, but Ed's hobbies and interests involved acquiring and restoring old cars and he needed a large garage space with specific tools and equipment for that. An apartment in the city was not going to work for him.

"Maybe you can find a nice place between here and the city that gives you the garage space you need, but offers a reasonable commute for Barb?" Edith suggested.

"We discussed that. Barb REALLY loves her apartment and she loves living in the city. She's not really a suburb kind of person, but that would be a great compromise." Ed said.

"I'm sure you two will find something that you're both happy with. You have plenty of time." Edith said. "Besides, Barb has a very bright future ahead of her at the museum. In just a few years she's going to get the one thing that she desires most—She will be curating one of the most famous Ancient Egyptian collections in the world." She said as she sipped her tea and nibbled on the small slice of German Chocolate Cake she ordered for dessert.

Ed smiled as he heard that. He knew exactly what Edith was talking about. Barb's dream was to curate an exhibit featuring the treasures of King Tutankhamun. It was currently on display at the Museum of Egyptian Antiquities in Cairo, Egypt and there was talk that it might become a traveling exhibit, although no official plans have been announced. "That's her dream." He said.

Ed payed the bill and drove his mother back home. They said their goodbyes and Ed waited until she was safely inside and the lights were turned on. She walked to the front window and waved goodbye, which was her signal that all was well and he could leave. Once inside, Edith settled into her usual nighttime routine. She went around to all of the doors to make sure every-hing was properly locked. She prepared her coffee pot and measured the right amount of ground coffee into the percolator so that all she had to do in the morning was turn the pot on to start brewing.

She went to her bedroom, changed into her nightgown, and brushed her teeth and washed her face. Then she crawled into bed with a good book to do a little reading before she went to sleep. She found this to be very relaxing and t was a great way to unwind from the day. After about 45 minutes of reading, Edith found her eyelids growing heavy and she was getting sleepy. She placed a bookmark on the page she just finished, closed her book, and set it on her nightstand. Then she fluffed her pillows, and turned off her lamp. Edith was warm, relaxed, and she very easily dozed off to sleep.

At 3:02 am, Edith was awakened by a deep feeling of fear. She opened her eyes and could see the faint glow of the nightlight in her Master Bathroom, but otherwise she was surrounded by darkness. The hair on her arms stood straight up and she could feel the presence of something dark and evil in the room with her. The air in the room changed. It became very dense as if something heavy was right in front of her face making it hard to breathe. She could hear a faint growl coming from the corner of the room not far from the corner of her bed. She tried to focus her eyes but could only see darkness as she sat up in her bed.

"What do you want?" Edith said. The response was more growling. As strong and intuitive as Edith was, this thing instilled fear that was difficult to resist. Edith very slowly reached over to open the drawer of her nightstand with her right hand to retrieve a bag of salt and special herbs she kept there. She needed to sprinkle salt around her bed to create a barrier of protection and she needed to do it quickly, but she could not move any faster than a sloth. The fear was heavy and immobilizing. The moment she had the bag of salt in her hand, her entire bed was flipped over and Edith was tossed on the floor. Everything on her nightstand toppled on top of her and she hit the floor hard. There was a bright flash, and Edith blacked out.

A few minutes later, Edith regained consciousness to the fast busy signal sound from the phone being off the hook for a while. She felt intense pain in her shoulder, hip and right arm. Her head was throbbing in pain and she could barely move. She managed to free her left arm and grabbed the phone cord so she could pull it closer to her. She pushed the button to hang up the phone and held it for a moment until she could get the dial tone back. When she heard the dial tone, she dialed "0" and an operator came on the line.

"Operator, how may I help you?" The voice on the phone said. *"Hello? This is the Operator."* Edith moaned and took a deep breath so that she could speak up. "I...I...need help." She said. *"Do you need the Police or an Ambulance Ma'am?"* The Operator said.

"Amb-ul-ance please." Edith muttered. "1-2-5-2 Ranch Rd...Please h-hurry."

"They're on their way Ma'am. Stay with me on the phone until they get there." The Operator said. *"The Police are on their way now—They're just down the street from you."*

"Ohhhhh-kay." Edith muttered. As she lay on the floor, she could hear a car drive up. It was the Police. They were knocking on the door.

"Ma'am the Police are at your front door. Is there a way for them to get in?" The Operator said. *"Shall I instruct them to go through another door?"*

"B—back door. Do what-e-ver they need t—to do." Edith said.

Soon she heard the Police break the small pane of glass on the back door in the laundry room. "Police!" The Policeman said as they burst through the door and entered the house.

"In h—here!" Edith yelled as loudly as she could.

Seconds later, two Police Officers came into the bedroom and lifted the bed off of Edith. She was laying on her side, and the Officers gently rolled her onto her back. "The ambulance is on its way Ma'am. Try to stay still." The Officer said. "How did your bed get tipped over?"

"Something picked it up." Edith said knowing that the Police Officers would not understand if she went into detail about the Dark Entity in her room.

"Brian! Let's search the rest of the house. This woman was attacked and the perp may still be here." The Officer said as he stood up and drew his gun from his holster. The Officers went room to room but found no one there, and no sign of forced entry other than the window they had just broken on the back door to get in.

The paramedics arrived and were let in through the front door. They put a cervical collar on Edith, slid a lift board underneath her, and lifted her up onto a gurney. They stabilized her arm with a splint, and rolled her out the front door and loaded her gurney onto the ambulance, where she was whisked off to the hospital. A second squad car arrived, and Officer Clemmons and Officer Rankin got out of their car. They walked in through the front door and met Officer Brian in the hallway.

"Clemmons, Rankin, glad you're here. This is very strange. There's no sign of a break-in, but we found this lady in her 70s laying on the floor. This was not a little old lady who fell getting out of bed. Her whole bed had been flipped upside down and it was on top of her. Somebody picked it up and flipped it." Officer Brian said.

Officer Clemmons looked around the room. "I know this lady. This is Edith MacKenzie. This wasn't a person who did this, it was something else." He said.

"What do you mean...*Something else?*" Officer Brian asked.

Officer Clemmons looked at Officer Rankin who simply put his head down and looked at his feet. "Edith MacKenzie is a well-respected Psychic Medium whom I have worked with on several difficult cases for many years. I don't know what your belief in the paranormal is, but I can tell you that I have personally seen shit that was not caused by any Human Being." Officer Clemmons said. "Just look around Brian—Who violently flips a queen sized bed over with a little old lady sleeping in it in the middle of the night and damages nothing else—All without a trace of forced entry?"

Officer Brian scanned the room then removed his hat as he scratched his head. "Uhhhh...I don't have an answer for that." He said.

"Well, I do. This is a paranormal attack on Mrs. MacKenzie. This is something that we probably can't even see and we are certainly not going to be able to track it down and arrest it for assault." Clemmons said. "You can write up the report as you see everything. You can say that the victim was found on the floor and that her bed was flipped over and that after a thorough search of the premises, no suspect was found and there was no leading evidence to pursue. We'll leave it at that."

Brian nodded his head and agreed to write the report exactly that way. After a few photographs, the Officers taped off the bedroom door and the back door, secured the property and left.

Officers Clemmons and Rankin returned to their vehicle and sat in the circular driveway for a while.

"Are you thinking what I'm thinking?" Officer Rankin said.

"That this is somehow related to the Argon Lab incident?" Officer Clemmons asked. "Yeah. That's exactly what I'm thinking."

CHAPTER 49

At 5:20 a.m., Ed rushed through the Emergency Room doors at Hinsdale Hospital. He stopped at the front desk to see where his mother was.

"Mrs. MacKenzie is through these doors and down the hall to the left. She's in exam room 14." The Nurse at the registration desk told him. Ed rushed down the hall to exam room 14 and there she was. Edith was battered and bruised but she looked like she was comfortable and not in any pain.

"Mom, what happened?" Ed said as he rushed to her side.

"Oh Edward! I'm so glad you're here Son. I had a little run in with an uninvited guest." Edith said. Although this would be absolutely terrifying and traumatizing for any other person, Edith seemed to take it all in stride as if it was just a bad day at the office. "I'll be okay." She said.

Dr. Lucchetti, the same ER Physician who was on duty when Mark was brought in after his accident stood in the doorway of the room holding some x-rays in hand. "Knock-knock." The Doctor said. "May I come in?"

"Hi Doc, yes, of course. I'm Ed, Edith's Son." Ed said as he extended his hand to the Doctor.

"It's very nice to meet you. I'm Dr. Lucchetti." The Doctor said as he shook Ed's hand. "Edith, I have some x-rays I'd like to show you." He said as he flipped the switch on the light box mounted on the wall next to her bed and clipped the x-rays on the front of it. "The good news is that you did not break your hip. The pelvis, your femur, and all of your lumbar and sacral vertebrae are intact. You'll be badly bruised and sore for a while, but nothing's broken." He said as he turned and smiled at her before yanking those x-rays off the light box and clipping on the other two he had. "But, I'm afraid, you broke your arm."

"Oh my!" Edith said.

"You can't really see the break on the film, but see here?" Dr. Lucchetti explained as he pointed to a small dark area near her elbow. "There's a blood pad forming here. Your body starts pooling blood around a fracture. The break will show up after it heals, but I've seen this a million times and I really believe it's broken, so, I'd like to put you in a cast for a few weeks until it heals." He explained. "And you also have a mild concussion. That gash on your head is going to need a couple of stitches, so let me wash up and grab some sutures and I'll get you stitched up." He said as he turned the light box off and went to the cabinet to retrieve a suture pack and a syringe of Lidocaine before scrubbing his hands.

"Does she need to stay here in the hospital or can I take her home today?" Ed asked.

"I think you can take her home a little later. I want to keep the ice pack on her arm for a little longer to keep the swelling down then we'll put a plaster cast on her arm. She'll be good to go home before noon." Dr. Lucchetti said as he removed the gauze bandage from the cut on her head so he could clean it. "I'm going to inject a little something to numb this up. You'll feel a little pinch…"

Edith winced a little as he injected the Lidocaine, but it started numbing almost immediately and she was able to relax. The Nurse came in to assist the Doctor with the sutures and she smiled warmly at Edith. "You're in great shape Mrs. MacKenzie." The nurse said. "Most women your age would break a hip with a fall like that." She said.

"Well, I think I owe that to good, healthy living…And my Scottish heritage." Edith said proudly as she winked at Ed. "The Scots are a tough breed you know."

The Nurse smiled. "That's very good to know! My boyfriend's Family is from Scotland." She said.

"Oh? What clan is he from dear?" Edith asked. "His last name is MacCleod." The Nurse said.

"Ahhh, the MacCleod clan of the Outer Hebrides. The northern islands. Well then, he's a Northerner too. The MacKenzies are from Northern Scotland just west of Inverness." Edith said. The conversation of her homeland was a nice distraction, but it made it difficult for her to hold still because Edith was a very expressive talker.

"Hold still Mrs. MacKenzie. I'm almost finished here." Dr. Lucchetti said.

After receiving four perfectly spaced sutures, Dr. Lucchetti put a little anti-biotic ointment over the sutures and covered it with a clean bandage. "There. We'll leave those in for about 10 days, and you'll have to come back so we can remove them." The Doctor said. "I'll be back in a little while and we'll set your arm in a cast." He said then he turned to the Nurse. "Lynn? Can you please get another ice pack for her arm?" The Nurse nodded and left the room to get another ice pack out of the freezer down the hall. "I'll be back—you sit tight." He said as he peeled off his gloves and left the room.

"Mom, what exactly happened?" Ed asked now that they were alone.

"Well, I was just sleeping and I woke up suddenly around 3 a.m. I could feel that there was a dark presence in the room with me. I sat up and I couldn't see anything, but I knew right where it was standing. I asked it what it wanted but it just growled at me. This was NOT a Shadow Person, Ed…" Edith explained. Just then, the Nurse returned with the ice pack.

"There you are. How is your pain Edith?" The Nurse asked.

"Oh fine dear. It hurts a little, but I don't think you need to give me anything more. That first dose of whatever you gave me when I arrived is still working pretty well." Edith said.

"Good. You let me know if it starts hurting again. It's best to stay ahead of it. Would you like anything to drink or maybe a snack? I have some graham crackers, pudding, and I think there's some applesauce in the fridge." The Nurse asked.

"Oh I don't need anything dear. Thank you." Edith replied.

The Nurse smiled and left the room, and Ed continued his conversation. "What happened after it growled?" He asked.

"Well, I knew right then that I needed to protect myself. I keep some black salt in my nightstand drawer, and I reached for that because I was going to toss some at it and surround my bed with the salt…But before I could reach my hand in the bag, it flipped my entire bed over and I went tumbling down onto the floor. When I fell, the salt scattered all around me so it created a pro-tective barrier. There was nothing more it could do I guess, so it left." Edith said. "But it will be back. It came to kill me. It knows we're planning to send the Dark Entity back on November 11th, and this was a fragmented part of it sent to take me out to try to prevent that from happening."

"Thank God for that salt!" Ed said. "Listen Mom, I don't want you to go back there until this is all over. I'll run over there and get some of your things, but I want you to stay at my house until it's safe to go back home. Right now, t's not safe. Besides, you're going to need someone to take care of you for a while and you shouldn't be alone." He said as he gently held her other hand. "Mark is back at work so I'll be able to take a few days off."

"That sounds like a good idea. Thank you dear." Edith said.

'Lily...Wake up Little Bird...Edith has been attacked and she needs us...' Lily slowly opened her eyes and was surprised to see Auset standing there in her room.

"Auset? What are you doing here?" Lily asked as she sat up and rubbed her eyes. It was early morning, but still dark outside.

"I've come to tell you about Edith Little Bird. She was attacked by the Dark Entity in the night. She's at the hospital." Auset said.

"Oh no! Is she alright?" Lily asked.

"She is. But, she will need our healing energy to be sent out to her." Auset said. "I am also here because I need to watch over you. The Dark Entity will come for you next but it will not if I am here with you." She said.

"Auset, I'm frightened. I'm just a little girl. I don't know what to do to protect myself." Lily said as she started to cry.

"Shhhhhh. Fear not Little Bird. This is why I am here." Auset said. Then, she stood straight up, held her head high, and put her arms out wide. In that moment, a golden light began to swirl around her. Golden wings covered her arms and a golden helmet in the shape of a Falcon's head appeared on her head. She knelt down and wrapped her wings around Lily as a Mother bird would wrap her wings around her chicks in her nest. In that moment, Lily felt pure and complete protection. She had never felt anything like it before in her life. The black star sapphire necklace around her neck began to gently vibrate and Lily could hear the hum of a higher frequency in her ears. When Lily finally stopped crying and opened her eyes, Auset was gone and Lily felt awake, alive, and empowered. She leaped out of bed, stood tall holding her head high, and stretched her arms out above her head. She could see a glowing aura of golden light energy outlining her entire body as she looked at herself in the mirror above her dresser. Something was different. *She* was different. Lily was ready to do battle and she wasn't waiting a minute longer. She ran out of her room and across the hall where her parents were sleeping. She stood quietly next to Annie, giving her a gentle nudge. "Momma? Wake up." She whispered.

Annie opened her eyes. "What is it Lil? Is everything alright?" Annie asked as she rubbed her eyes. "What time is it?" She looked at her clock—6:25 a.m. "Why are you up so early?" Mark stirred in the bed next to her half listening to the conversation.

"We hafta get up. Mrs. MacKenzie got hurt. She's at the hospital." Lily said.

"Whaaat? How do you know?" Annie asked, then realized she knew how Lily knew but had to ask the question anyway.

"Where'd you hear that Lil?" Mark asked.

"Auset just told me. C'mon. We hafta go!" Lily said as she tugged on her Mother's hand.

Annie rolled out of bed and went to the bathroom, then slipped into her bathrobe and sat back down on the edge of the bed. She reached down to grab the phone book from under the night stand and looked up the telephone number for Hinsdale Hospital. She picked up the phone and dialed the number. "Hello, yes, can you please check and see if you have a patient by the name of Edith MacKenzie there?" Annie asked. "Okay, thank you." Annie dropped the phone below her chin. "You're right Lil. She's there."

The phone rang in Edith's room while the Doctor was in the middle of putting Edith's plaster cast on. Ed picked up the phone. "Hello?" He said. He was a little surprised that anyone would be calling since he hadn't had a chance to tell anyone what happened yet.

"Ed? It's Annie. How's Edith?" She said.

"Annie? How did you know we were here?" Ed was puzzled.

"Lily told me…You know, psychics…" Annie said.

Ed laughed a little. "I keep forgetting about that connection. She's doing well. There was an incident last night and she fell and broke her arm, but she's all right. They're putting her cast on right now." He said.

"What happened?" Annie asked.

"Long story. I'll tell you about it later." Ed said. "I'm going to take her to my house in a little while. Is Mark awake by chance?"

"Yes, he's right here." Annie said as she passed the phone to Mark who was still half asleep lying next to her. "It's Ed. He wants to talk to you."

"Hey Ed. What happened? Is Edith okay?" Mark asked. He was starting to wake up a little more.

"She fell and broke her arm, but she's okay. Nothing serious." Ed said. "I think I'm going to call Briggs this morning and ask for a few days off. Mom's going to need someone to look after her for a while." He said.

"Sure Ed. I can pick up an extra trip or two for you. I have a lot to make up for. Glad to do it." Mark said.

"I was supposed to run some farm equipment out to DeKalb this morning before the Quad City turn route this evening. I know you're doing the Quad City run, but do you think you can handle the DeKalb trip for me? It's going to be hard for Christine to plug anybody in this late. I was scheduled to leave the terminal at 7:30 this morning." Ed explained.

Mark rolled over and looked at the clock. "Sure Buddy, I'll get up now and get to the terminal. Don't worry—I'll run the cargo. Just do me a favor and let Christine know that I'm covering for you this morning. I'll head out now." Mark said.

"Thanks Buddy." Ed said.

Mark handed the phone back to Annie then got up to get in the shower. "Ed?" Annie said when she grabbed the phone. "Lily has a message for Edith, so I'm going to hand the phone to her now, but I'll come over later to see how Edith's doing. I'll see you soon."

"Okay, thanks Annie." Ed said.

Annie handed the phone to Lily. "Mr. MacKenzie? Please tell Mrs. MacKenzie that Auset protected her and she's watching over us." Lily said. "Please tell her that, okay?"

"Will do Lily." Ed said. "Don't worry about a thing, she'll be fine. We'll see you later."

"Ok. Bye." Lily said as she hung up the phone. "Momma? Can I stay home from school today? I want to go see Mrs. MacKenzie."

"Well, Mrs. MacKenzie will be at the hospital for most of the morning." Annie said. "But I have an idea. We'll go straight over to Ed's house to see Edith after I pick you up from school. Deal?"

Lily had hoped to skip school today, but since Edith was not going to be home for several hours, her Mother's offer made more sense. "Okay, deal." She said.

"Why don't you go and get dressed." Annie said. "And since we have a little extra time this morning, how about if I make French Toast for breakfast?"

Lilly jumped up and down while clapping her hands in delight. French Toast sounded like a perfect way to follow the illuminating high frequency energy hug she received from Auset this morning. This was Lily's *Breakfast of Champions*. "Yummy! I'm going to go wake up Stephen and Vince. They like French Toast too!" She said as she ran out of the room.

The Doctor was finished with Edith's cast and told her to stay still for a little while it dried. When he left the room to prepare her discharge papers and write her a prescription for Tylenol 3 for pain, Ed delivered Lily's message to Edith.

"Lily asked me to tell you that Auset is watching over you and protecting you." Ed said. Edith smiled and it made her think of something that she hadn't immediately recalled before.

Right before she fell to the floor, she remembered a bright flash of light in the room. *'Was that Auset chasing the Dark Entity away?'* Possibly, she thought. Edith didn't really know for sure because she was knocked unconscious for a few minutes. She couldn't recall exactly what happened after she fell to the floor. She thought it was the salt scattered about that protected her, but now she wasn't so sure.

"You know Ed, Lily might be right. I think it was Auset who came and drove the Dark Entity away. This thing has the power to kill me." Edith said as she reflected on what Lily said. "Sure, the salt creates a barrier that cannot be crossed, but that certainly wouldn't stop it from throwing the dresser on my head." She paused for a moment and looked at Ed. "It really *should* have killed me."

"Mom, don't say things like that." Ed shuddered to think what he would be feeling right now if the Dark Entity had killed her last night.

"No dear, it's true." Edith continued. "I remember a bright flash of light in the room before I landed on the floor. Unfortunately, I blacked out after that..." She said as she lightly touched the gash on her head that was just stitched up. "But I have no explanation as to why I'm not dead right now. It had to be Auset."

"Well, Thank God for time traveling Egyptian Gods!" Ed said.

CHAPTER 50

Chuck and his team finished building their Neutron Monitor and were ready to set everything up in Lab 2C for their cosmic ray project. No one had spent much time in Lab 2C lately, mainly because they needed to use another lab that was amply equipped with the workbench and the soldering tools they needed to build the monitor, but also because Chuck had reservations about letting anyone set foot in the lab with the portal still open. He didn't have a choice though. Lab 2C was the only lab constructed with the required leaded shielding in the walls for the project. If they used any other lab, there would be too many false readings and the entire project would have to be scrapped. As he sat in his office contemplating how he could stall the project until after November 11th, Dorothy popped in.

"Dr. Frasier? Can I speak to you for a minute?" Dorothy said as she stepped inside the office door.

"Sure Dorothy. Have a seat." Chuck said as he motioned for her to sit down. "What's up?"

"Well sir, I'm not quite sure how to say this, but should anybody ever be going back into Lab 2C?" She asked.

Chuck sat back in his chair. It was interesting that Dorothy brought this up. He was just wondering that very same thing himself. "What makes you say that Dort? Has there been another incident that I'm not aware of?" Chuck said.

"Well, I was in the surveillance room getting a signature for a delivery, and, well, I was watching one of the monitors…" Dorothy hesitated for a moment. She wasn't sure how Chuck would react, but thought she'd better say something since he and his team would be spending the next few weeks down there.

"And?" Chuck said.

"And…I saw something." Dorothy said.

"What did you see?" Chuck asked. "It's okay Dorothy. You can tell me." He paused for a moment. "To be honest? I don't really want to go back down there." This put Dorothy at ease a little bit.

"I saw a solid black figure moving about the lab. Only the night lights were on, but you could clearly see it. It was tall and so densely black you couldn't see anything behind it." She said.

"Hmmm." Chuck said as he thought for a minute. Dorothy had been an employee at Argon for several years and she was here when Martin Reese was murdered. He was sure that she knew about the project, that Lenny Kawalski had opened a portal that let this thing in, that it brutally murdered a Security Guard, and that Lenny was now being held in a nearby military holding cell awaiting trial for stealing British Military secrets to conspire with the Russians to take over Europe. All of this was common knowledge around here, and Dorothy was in a position to know everything there was to know about everything.

"So, you know about the time travel project then?" Chuck asked. He figured that was a good place to start to see how much she really knew.

"Yes sir. Remember, it was me who typed out the protocol manuals for the project." Dorothy said.

"Mmm. Yes, right." Chuck said. "Well, I've got to level with you then Dort. Yes, we need to conduct the cosmic ray project in Lab 2C because of the lead shielding, but I really want to have access for another reason…" He paused and looked her in the eye. "I'm going to send it back Dorothy, and I'm going to close the portal. Dr. Chadha really came over here to help me with that. The cosmic ray project was just an excuse to bring him here."

"I figured that sir." Dorothy said. "That's why I'm sitting here telling you what I saw. You need to be careful sir."

This came as no surprise to Chuck that she knew what their real intentions were. What's more, he was just reassured that he could trust her. "As a matter of fact, right before you came in here to talk to me, I was trying to think of a way that I could stall the cosmic ray project until after November 11th." He said.

"November 11th sir?" Dorothy asked.

"Yes. That's the appointed day that we have to do this. I'm going to need the Hadron Collider to open a new vortex that aligns with a specific astral location, then I can reverse the particles on the open portal and close it. I'll have to have some assistance from another associate to seal it shut once we do that…And she's not an employee of Argon so I'm going to have to make sure she has a visitor's pass that day…Perhaps you can help us with that." Chuck explained.

"Of course sir. Whatever you need." Dorothy said.

"Great. I appreciate your help Dorothy." Chuck said.

"And what is the woman's name sir? I want to get her logged in so we have plenty of time to get clearance for her." Dorothy said as she flipped the cover of her notebook to write down the woman's name.

"It's Edith MacKenzie." Chuck said.

"The Psychic?" Dorothy asked.

"You've heard of her?" Chuck was surprised.

"Who hasn't? She's amazing! I once dated a Police Officer who was working cold cases. He raved about her. These were cases that were left unsolved for years, decades even. I guess they brought Edith MacKenzie in and she was able to piece together the missing information that lead to arrests and convictions." Dorothy replied as she wrote Edith's name down in her notebook. "Actually sir, we've already done a background check on her at the request of the County Sheriff after the lab incident, and I believe that her clearance is still valid, but I'll make sure." She said.

"Great. One less thing to worry about." Chuck said. "Now, any ideas how we can stall the cosmic ray project?"

"I'll come up with something, sir." Dorothy said. As she stood up to leave the room, she turned back to tell Chuck one more thing. "Oh, and sir? Lt. Col. Kawalski was found dead in his cell this morning. Cause of death is unknown."

Ed stopped off at Edith's house on the way back home from the hospital to pick up some of her things. As they drove up the long driveway, a feeling of foreboding washed over Edith.

"Do you want to come in and tell me what you want to pack or should I just go in a get the essentials and a few things out of your closet?" Ed asked. He wasn't sure if she should go back into the house again. No telling if there might be something in there waiting for her.

"I'll come in." Edith said as she took a deep breath. She was nervous about going back to the scene of the incident, but her guides assured her that the Dark Entity was not inside any longer. "Let's make it quick though, okay?" She said.

"That's my plan Mom. Quick and easy." Ed said.

Ed put his key in the lock on the front door, turned it, and slowly opened the door. The house was quiet. Edith liked the natural sunlight to fill the rooms of her house, so all of the windows were open. She paused before stepping across the threshold making sure that she wasn't picking up any negative energies. She was battered and tired and she didn't feel like she had the strength to protect herself if confronted again. Ed held his Mother's good arm to steady her as she stepped up into the house.

"Are you okay? I can put you back in the truck if you're not feeling up to this." Ed sensed that she was a little wobbly.

"I'm fine. I think I'm just tired and the medication is making me a little unsteady, but I'm okay." Edith said as she leaned in to Ed a little more.

"Well, let's go pack a bag Mom." Ed said as he walked her down the hall to her bedroom. When he reached the doorway, he gasped. "My God Mom! You could have been killed!" Ed knew that her bed had been turned upside down, but seeing it with his own eyes was an unexpected shock.

He pulled an upholstered arm chair from the corner behind the door and positioned it in front of Edith's dresser and closet. He guided her to the chair so she could sit and tell him which items she wanted him to pack for her. Ed retrieved a small suitcase from the back of the closet and laid it open on the floor.

"Ok Mom, I'll paw through your closet and you tell me what you want to put in your suitcase." Ed said as he started pulling outfits out that he had seen her wear frequently. "How about this?"

"I won't be able to put that on with this cast dear." Edith said.

"Oh yeah, right. See? It was a good thing you came in with me or I would have packed things you wouldn't be able to wear." Ed said as he grabbed knit items that were more generous in the arms and a bit stretchy. "How about this?"

"Yes, that's good." Edith said. "Just look for stretchy knit things dear. And would you please grab my slippers? I took them off when I got into bed last night, so they're under the bed there somewhere…" She said. "And my shawl. Please don't forget my shawl."

Ed gathered clothes that she would likely be able to wear, then went into the bathroom to get her toothbrush and toiletries. He packed everything neatly in her suitcase and snapped it shut. He noticed a canvas tote bag hanging over the back of the chair she was sitting in and thought he might fill it with a few books and other things to keep her entertained. "I guess you won't be crocheting much, huh?" He said jokingly.

"That's not very likely." She said.

"Is there anything else that you can think of?" Ed asked.

"Not in here, but I have some perishables in the refrigerator that we should probably bring over to your house. They'll just go bad if we leave them." Edith said.

"Ok I'll clean out the fridge, but what about clothing, things from the bathroom, you know…" Ed said.

"I think we've got enough. I can't think of anything else right now." Edith was starting to get tired and her pain was getting more intense. She just wanted to go lay down for a while.

"Here Mom, let's get you back to the truck. We still have to pick up your prescription, so let's get going. I can come back and clean out the fridge later." Ed said as he threw the canvas book bag over his shoulder and helped her stand up. After getting her prescription filled, Ed took Edith back to his house and tucked her into the guest room so she could take a nap. Once she fell asleep, he picked up the phone to call Annie.

"Hi Annie, Its Ed." He said. "Can I ask you for a favor?"

"Of course Ed, what do you need?" Annie asked.

"I just gave Mom another dose of pain medication and she's taking a nap. I need to run back over to her place and get some things. Do you think you can come over for an hour or so? I just don't want to leave her here alone in case she wakes up and needs something." Ed explained.

"Sure thing. I'll be there in 15 minutes." Annie said as she hung up the phone and grabbed her purse and her car keys.

When Annie arrived, Ed greeted her at the door. "Thanks for coming over. Mom's sleeping in the guest room. She didn't get much rest last night." Ed said.

"Happy to do it Ed." Annie said quietly. "What exactly happened to her?"

Ed took a deep breath as he recalled the scene in Edith's bedroom. "She says a Dark Entity appeared in her bedroom around 3 am and it completely flipped her bed over…With her still in it. She hit the floor pretty hard, broke her arm, and was trapped under the bed. Luckily the phone on her nightstand landed right next to her, so she was able to call for help when she came to." Ed explained.

Annie gasped. "Oh Ed, that's horrible!"

"It was. But, you know how my Mom is—She's a fighter and she's dealt with this kind of phenomena before. If it were anyone else, they might not have survived." Ed said as he reached in his pocket for the keys to his truck. "I need to run back over to her house and get a few more things. I shouldn't be long. I just gave her a dose of her pain medication about an half hour ago, and she went right to sleep. Make yourself comfortable and I'll be back as soon as I can."

"No rush. I'll be here if she needs anything." Annie said.

After Ed left, Annie looked in on Edith. She was resting comfortably, laying on her back with a pillow tucked under her broken arm and there was a thick blanket thrown over her. Although battered and bruised, Edith slept soundly and she radiated a certain strength that assured Annie that she would be okay. Annie left the door ajar and crept away quietly. She went out to the kitchen and decided to help Ed tidy up a bit. He lived alone so things weren't too messy, but there were a few dishes in the sink that needed to be washed and it was something helpful that Annie could do while she was there.

About an hour later, Ed returned with a couple of boxes full of food. "How is she?" He asked as he set the boxes on the kitchen counter.

"She's still asleep. I didn't want to wake her so I came out here and did your dishes." Annie said.

"Oh, thank you. You didn't have to do that." Ed said.

"No problem. I couldn't just sit with nothing to do." Annie replied. "What's all this?" She asked as she helped Ed put the food items in the refrigerator.

"Mom had some perishables at the house and she didn't want them to go to waste, so I thought I'd bring it over here." Ed said.

"Hmmm, well, it looks like you've got all the ingredients for Beef Vegetable Soup." Annie said. "How about if I make that for you, and you and Edith can have it for dinner later?"

"That sounds great Annie, thank you." Ed said. "I can grill, but I'm not much of a cook. You can tell that my stove doesn't get used much."

Annie laughed. She did notice that his stove was in pristine condition and it wasn't because he meticulously cleaned it. "No worries. Do you happen to have any barley? That's really good in this soup." She asked.

Ed walked over to the pantry and pulled out a bag of barley. "Will this do?" He asked.

"Perfect!" Annie said. "I'm surprised you have some. I thought you didn't cook?"

"I don't, but Barb does. Lucky for us, she made a salad with barley in it the last time she was here." Ed said.

As Annie browned the stewing beef and chopped vegetables, Ed finished putting all of the food away that he brought back from Edith's house. From down the hall, they could hear Edith calling for Ed. They both quit what they were doing and went to see what she needed.

"Everything okay Mom?" Ed said as he peered in through the doorway with Annie standing close behind him.

"Hi Edith." Annie said. "How are you feeling?"

Edith tried to sit up. "Oh Annie! I'm glad to see you." She said.

"Don't sit up Mom. Let me help you." Ed said as he grabbed another pillow and tucked it in behind her shoulders. "How's that?"

"Oh that's good, thank you dear." Edith said. "Could I have a glass of water? My mouth is kind of dry from this medicine."

"I'll go get you one." Ed said as he left the room.

Annie sat down on the opposite side of the bed so that she didn't accidentally bump Edith's injured arm. "I heard what happened." She said. "You are one tough lady Edith MacKenzie."

Edith laughed. "Oh, well, it was not a pleasant experience to be sure. I know that it could have been much worse, but I'll be okay." She said.

"What was it that tipped your bed over like that?" Annie asked.

"It was a Dark Entity Annie. It was a fractured part of the Beast that we're sending back on November 11th. It came to kill me off to try to prevent it." Edith explained. "And I can't be sure, but I think Auset came at that moment and put a stop to it. I owe her my life."

"Did you see her?" Annie asked.

"No, but I remember a bright flash of white light in the room right before I hit the ground. Dark Entities don't generate white light. It was her, I just know it was her." Edith explained.

Ed returned with a glass of cold water and helped Edith take a sip. "I went and cleaned out your fridge. Annie's making some Vegetable Beef Barley soup for us. You had all the ingredients she needed—fancy that!" He said.

"Oh that does sound good! I haven't really eaten anything since yesterday. Thank you for making soup Annie." Edith said trying to stay cheerful even though she was hurting and exhausted.

"It needs to simmer on the stove for a little bit, so I'll go finish chopping veggies and get that going. I just wanted to see you." Annie said as she gently squeezed Edith's hand before heading back to the kitchen.

Ed stayed and made sure his mother was comfortable. He pulled up a chair next to her bed and needed to talk to her. "Mom? Today is Nov. 5th. That means the 11th is only 6 days away. Are you going to be able to help with this?" He asked.

Edith sat quietly for a moment and assessed her physical injuries. "Edward. I'm not going to battle with weapons that require two hands to handle." She said with a slightly disapproving look. "I'm going to battle with my psychic abilities and those have not been injured. I will absolutely be ready to do this…The world depends on it!"

CHAPTER 51

SATURDAY, NOVEMBER 7, 1970

Cheryl rushed home from the day shift at the hospital so that she could get organized before everyone came over that evening. This would be the first time that they would meet Dr. Baljeet Chadha and run through the specific roles everyone would play on November 11th. Food was always a requirement whenever people got together, and given Cheryl's busy work week, she had no time or energy to prepare a big meal for 13 people. Pizza was a terrific option so she called in an order and arranged for Mark to pick it up on his way home from the terminal that evening. All she had to worry about was beverages, so she ducked into the local IGA to pick up some beer and soda on the way home. As she pulled in the driveway and opened the garage door, Beth came out of the house to greet her.

"Hi Mom!" Beth said. "Mr. Campbell called and said he should be here with the pizza by 6:00."

"Hi sweetie! That's perfect, thank you." Cheryl replied. "Can you please give me a hand with the beer and sodas? I want to get them in the fridge right away so they're cold by the time everyone gets here."

"Sure Mom." Beth said as she opened the trunk.

"Have you heard from your Dad?" Cheryl asked.

"He called an hour ago and said that he and Dr. Chadha should be here by 5:30. He sounded frustrated. I hope everything is okay." Beth said as she carried a case of root beer into the house.

"I do too." Cheryl said. "He normally doesn't work on Saturdays, so I hope there's not a serious problem. I guess we'll hear about it when he gets here."

Cheryl closed the garage door and went inside to change out of her scrubs while Beth finished loading the beverages into the spare refrigerator in the basement. Joey and Lily were in the finished basement family room watching their favorite TV show, *Dark Shadows*. After putting the beverages in the fridge, Beth sat down to watch the show with them.

"What's Barnabas Collins up to today?" Beth asked.

"It's dawn so he has to get back to the mausoleum before the sun comes up. He's very far away from it and he might not make it back in time." Joey said as he turned to Lily sitting right beside him. "Lily? Do you think Vampires really exist?"

"I don't know. I've never seen one." Lily said. "I know that Shadow People exist. They're really bad, but they don't suck your blood."

"What are Shadow People?" Beth asked. She had only been exposed to the paranormal since the Campbell's moved in across the street a few months ago and this was all still very new to her.

Lily got up of the floor in front of the TV and crawled up onto the couch next to Beth. "Nobody really knows. Mrs. MacKenzie says that she thinks they are alien beings from another dimension. They're really tall and they are very, very solid black. You can't see through them. Sometimes they have red glowing eyes." Lily explained.

"Have you ever seen one?" Beth asked.

Lily sat silently for a moment recalling her experience with Shadow People in her bedroom in the old house. She turned to Beth and began to tell her about it. Beth had never heard the story before and she was shocked to hear what Lily went through. The more she learned about other dimensions and the creepy stuff that seeps into our world, the more fearful she was to ever be alone by herself.

"Has Vince ever seen one?" Beth asked.

"I don't think so, but my Mom, Dad, and Edith MacKenzie sure have." Lily said. "Beth, you don't want to see those things. They're really, REALLY bad."

"How can you get rid of them?" Beth asked. She was growing concerned that Shadow People could be anywhere at any time and she wanted to know what to if, God forbid, she ever came across one.

"You can't." Lily said matter of factly. "They go in and out through their portal as they please. Mrs. MacKenzie says that you can do things to keep them at bay for a while, but they're very smart and they figure out how to get around it. Nothing works for long."

Beth was frightened to hear this. She couldn't imagine that these things actually existed, but she had no reason to doubt what Lily was saying. The television show was over and Joey stood up and turned off the TV.

"What time is everybody coming over tonight?" Joey asked.

"Dad and his work friend will be here around 5:30, but I think everybody else is coming over at 6:00." Beth said. "We should go upstairs and see if Mom needs help with anything."

"Hold on—Beth?" Lily said as she grabbed Beth's arm. Something in the far corner of the room caught her eye. Joey also saw it too and he froze. "Do you see that?" She asked.

"See what?" Beth asked as she scanned the corner of the room. "I don't see anything."

"You see it, don't you Joey?" Lily asked.

"Yeah, I see it." Joey said as he slowly stepped closer to Lily. The hair on his arms stood straight up and a cold shiver ran down his spine. "Lily, what is that?" He asked.

There in the corner of the basement was a large black mass with glowing red eyes. It was as tall as the ceiling and so densely black that you couldn't even see the glow of the dusky evening light streaming through the high window behind it. *'Who are you?'* Lily asked telepathically. It did not answer. All she heard was a low guttural growl that emerged from the corner where the tall black mass was standing.

Beth took a step back. She heard the growl, and like Joey, the hair on the back of her neck stood up and she had goosebumps on her arms. This was a growl that sounded neither animal nor human and it was terrifying to hear. "Ahh, guys? Let's go back upstairs...Now." Beth said. She put her arms around Lily and her little Brother, and all three of them walked slowly to the stairway, none taking their eyes off of the dark mass in the corner. When they reached the stairway, they ran up the stairs as fast as they could, slamming the door when they reached the top.

Cheryl was startled to hear the door slam, and went to see what was going on. "Hey! Go easy on the door there." She said, then she noticed that the kids looked terrified as if they just out ran a giant poisonous snake trying to bite them. "What's wrong?"

"There's a dark thing down there growling at us Mom!" Joey said. "It's NOT good! I'm never going down there again!"

"A *what?*" Cheryl asked as she looked to Lily for some kind of explanation since Joey was new to this phenomena.

Lily took a deep breath "It's evil...And Mrs. Frasier? It's here because it's trying to stop us. It knows everyone is coming over and it wants to stop us from sending it back." Lily explained. "I can't get rid of it by myself. I need help." She said in a quivery voice. Cheryl hugged her tightly just as the doorbell rang.

Beth ran to the door and opened it. Ed, Barb, and Edith MacKenzie were standing there smiling, but their smiles quickly drained from their faces and changed to a look of concern. Beth hadn't heard about Edith's accident so she was shocked to see that she was in a cast. "Mrs. MacKenzie! What happened? Are you alright?" She asked.

Edith felt the wave of negative energy wash over her the minute Beth opened the door. She knew what had come and why it was there. "I'm fine dear." She said in her usual reassuring voice. "But it seems *you* have an unwanted guest in the house." She said. They stepped inside, and Edith felt pure evil. She knew that if she allowed herself to be afraid it would give the Dark Entity the upper hand so she did her best to stay calm and strong.

Beth's eyes grew bigger as she nodded acknowledging that Edith was right. "In the basement. It growled at us!" She said.

Lily heard Edith's voice and came running to the door. "Oh Mrs. MacKenzie! I'm so glad to see you!" She said as she hugged her waist being careful not to bump the cast. "I'm so sorry you got hurt!" Lily said.

"I'm fine honey. You don't need to worry about me." Edith said as she hugged the little girl clinging to her side. Edith looked up at Ed and said: "It's here Edward. It's trying to stop us, but we're going to put a stop to it right now!"

"Mom, you got badly hurt the last time you ran into this thing. Shouldn't we just leave?" Ed asked.

"No. We can't leave." Edith said. "*It* has to leave." Edith looked down at Lily and they connected telepathically. *'We need Auset.'* She communicated. Lily nodded, and she stepped away from Edith so that she could hold her hand.

They entered the house and Cheryl greeted them. "Oh Edith, the kids just had a terrifying encounter downstairs!"

"Everyone, listen to me please." Edith said as she walked over to the basement door. "We're going to open the door, and when we do, I need all of you to join hands with me and help Lily and I summon Auset." She explained.

"How do we do that Mrs. MacKenzie?" Beth asked.

"All you have to do is close your eyes and imagine yourself surrounded in Divine, white light. Lily and I will summon Auset." Edith explained. "And whatever you do, DO NOT let fear take over you...No matter what! Trust that you are safe and protected. Do you understand?" She asked as she made eye contact with everyone to confirm that they understood.

Once everyone was standing in a circle, hand in hand, Lily opened the basement door, then wrapped her left arm around Edith, and tightly held Cheryl's hand to her right. The basement was pitch black and a terrible odor of sulfur bellowed up the stairway. Lily and Edith transmitted the same message out to the Universe telepathically: *'Auset! Auset! Auset! We call upon you for protection from the Dark One in this house. We ask that you join us now and banish this evil from the basement!'* The black star sapphire necklace around Lily's neck began to warm and vibrate, and she knew at that moment that Auset had come.

All of a sudden, a mighty wind was stirred throughout the house. Beth slowly peeked through one eye and she saw that the whole room was filled with bright white light and golden sparks were swirling around them. Then, all at once, the golden sparks rushed down the stairway and there was a bright flash of light. The wind ceased, and the room grew still and quiet. Edith opened her eyes and looked down the stairway to the basement. The Dark Entity was gone. She turned to look out the window to see a Falcon perched on the window sill looking back at her. Edith smiled at the bird with gratitude before it flew away.

"We did it!" Edith said as everyone opened their eyes. "It's gone." The whole house felt lighter. The positive energy that was generated by everyone filled the house and restored the peace.

Chuck came through the garage door to the house with Dr. Chadha in tow to see everyone standing in a circle holding hands. "What'd I miss?" A very perplexed Chuck asked.

Cheryl ran to him and threw her arms around him. Chuck hugged her as he looked around for anyone willing to give him an explanation. "What just happened here?" He asked.

"The Dark Entity was here to stop our efforts Chuck." Edith said. "It's gone now, but we need to create a barrier of protection around your home to keep you safe for a few more days." She said as she looked toward the kitchen. "Cheryl? How much salt do you have on hand dear?"

Cheryl peeled herself away from Chuck and walked to the kitchen to see how much salt she had. She had what was in the salt shaker, and a partially full cylindrical carton of Morton's Salt in the spice cabinet. "This is all I have

Edith." She said as she set it on the counter shaking the container to indicate that it was not full.

"Hmmmm…That's not going to be enough. What I need is enough salt to pour around the perimeter of the house." Edith said.

"I have a solution." Chuck said as he descended down the stairs to the basement. A minute later, he came back up with a 50 lb. bag of salt pellets. "I bought this the other day for the water softener. Will this do?" He asked.

"Salt is salt! Yes, that will do nicely." Edith said as she gave instructions for Chuck and Ed to sprinkle a barrier of the salt pellets around the perimeter of the house.

"Oh, and everyone? I'd like you to meet Dr. Baljeet Chadha." Chuck said. "Dr. Chadha? This is Ed, Barb, Edith, Lily, and my Wife Cheryl, and my Children Beth and Joey."

"Please, call me Baljeet." Dr. Chadha said as he bowed in gratitude to make their acquaintance.

"I especially want you to get to know Edith. She's the Psychic Medium I told you about who will be helping us." Chuck said.

"It's a pleasure to make your acquaintance Miss Edith." Baljeet said warmly, then he turned his attention to the small girl standing next to her. "And you must be Lily." He said. "I have heard many good things about you."

Lily blushed. "You're Reyansh's Father aren't you?" She said.

"Yes, yes I am." Baljeet said.

"He told me you would be coming." Lily said. "It's very nice to meet you."

As Ed and Chuck sprinkled the salt pellets around the front of the house, Mark, Annie, Stephen, and Vince approached carrying the pizza. "Hey Buddy, what's all this?" Mark asked.

Ed stood up and proceeded to explain what just happened inside the house and that Edith had instructed them to lay down a salt barrier for protection. The Campbells went inside with the pizza while Ed and Chuck finished laying the barrier.

After introductions were made to the newest member of the team, Dr. Chadha, everyone enjoyed their pizza and chatted about the experience they just had. Beth, who had witnessed the presence of the Divine white light and swirling golden sparks herself, asked Edith to explain what she saw.

"I know I wasn't supposed to peek, but I couldn't help it." Beth admitted. "Where did the bright light and golden sparkles come from?"

"Well," Edith started, "that was Auset. We summoned her to come and help us do battle. She is very powerful and we could not have done this without her." She said.

"I'm confused. Isn't Auset the Egyptian lady who bought the Campbells old house? The lady who gave Lily the pretty necklace for her birthday?" Beth asked.

"The very same." Edith said. "But she is not human dear. She is what we call a Seraphim Angel. She is from the highest order of Angels and she's extremely powerful. She can project herself in any image she wishes, and for some reason, she chose to come to us as the Ancient Egyptian Goddess, Isis, which is pronounced *Auset* in Ancient Egyptian." She explained.

"Yes, and my son, Reyansh is working with Heru, or Horus in Ancient Egyptian. He is back in India and will be anchoring the second point in the energy triangle there." Baljeet interjected.

"Heru is in India?" Joey asked. "He was with me when I went through the portal back in time. He helped take care of me until I could come back." Joey was now feeling more like he was an important part of this than he had before and it inspired him to give every bit of effort toward the cause.

"Yes Joey, that's the same Heru." Edith said jovially. She could tell that he was proud to have had that experience and felt very important and special. "Let's review what needs to take place on the 11th." She said as she turned her attention to the task at hand.

"Yes, thank you Edith." Chuck said as he proceeded to explain what he and Baljeet would be doing in the lab at Argon with the Hadron Collider to open a new vortex and reverse the particle flow on the open portal that brought the Dark Entity through. Edith would be with Baljeet and Chuck in the lab to assist in closing and sealing the portal shut. At the same time, Lily will be leading the energy circle at home with Mark, Annie, Stephen, Vince, Cheryl, Beth, Joey, Ed, and Barb. Edith explained that a group of eight or more people focusing their energy on the same thing was much more powerful than a lesser number.

"Lily, your group will be anchored to Auset's power. She will be with us in the Lab, but you are connected to her through the black star sapphire around your neck." Edith said with a smile. Lily smiled back as she placed her right hand over the precious stone. "Make sure it is exposed and not hidden under a sweater." She said. Lily nodded in acknowledgement.

"And while we are doing our part here, Reyansh will be with Heru and his Grandfather in Cochin anchoring the second point of the triangle." Baljeet said. "But, who then, is anchoring the third point on Eltanin?" He asked. This was a detail that Chuck did not have an answer to.

"Well, that's where we receive help from the 3rd Ancient Egyptian God— Osiris. Correct?" Barb said. She had been silent through most of the discussion, but being the expert in the room on anything having to do with Ancient Egyptians, it all made perfect sense to her. Osiris, or *Auser*, was Heru's Father. He was known as Ra or *Re* the all-powerful Sun God.

"Yes Barb—That's correct!" Edith said. She was glad to see that her soon-to-be Daughter-in-Law was becoming an enthusiastic participant. "This is precisely why the trio has come to us. We need their Divine power, but they also need our human energy as well. This is a great battle we are about to engage in, make no mistake about that!" Edith said.

CHAPTER 52

On Monday morning, Chuck arrived at the entry gate at Argon. He waved to Stan, the usual security guard on duty in the morning, and drove through the lifted gate. When he parked his car, he sat quietly for a moment and contemplated what he was going to do. The cosmic ray project was scheduled to start this morning and there was nothing he could do to prevent it. Government funded projects were carefully scheduled and precisely planned. The top brass did not tolerate changes in scheduled projects very well. Any disruption or delay would be regarded as the failure of the project lead, which in this case was Chuck. It could cost him his reputation and he would never be asked to lead a project ever again. He was deeply concerned for the safety of his team, and himself. Especially after hearing about what happened to Edith in the middle of the night in her home, and what his own children had encountered in their own basement on Saturday. He pulled himself together and realized that he would just have to be extra vigilant while they were in Lab 2C and try to protect his team as best he could. He brought a bag of salt with him in his briefcase so that he could sneak in before the team arrived and lay a protective barrier in the lab. He got out of the car and went into the building to prepare for the pre-experiment meeting.

As he walked into the front conference room to review the objectives of the experiment for the day, the entire team was already seated at the table anxiously awaiting his arrival. "Good morning Dr. Frasier." Jeremy said. "The day has finally arrived!" He said as he briskly rubbed his hands together in anticipatory delight.

"I've confirmed the atmospheric conditions this morning with Dr. Wurmser at the Pentagon, and conditions are ideal." Said Dr. Connie Deutsch.

"Oh? That's great to hear!" Chuck said as he tried very hard to keep an acceptable level of enthusiasm for the project while in front of his team. Deep down, he was struggling with an undeniable feeling of foreboding. He glanced around the room, and saw nothing but smiling, jubilant faces, until he set his eyes upon Baljeet at the end of the table. They knew what they were up against, and Baljeet was also doing his best to hide his fear. Chuck proceeded to outline the objectives for the day on the white board and addressed each participant's role in the project as they normally would before starting an experiment. He purposely took longer than usual in an effort to stall. This wasn't difficult since he was actually dividing his attention between the specific details of the project while still trying to think of a way to delay the project for three more days.

Pete Schroeder grew impatient and spoke up. "I'm sorry Dr. Frasier, but are you okay? You seem a little distracted." He said.

Chuck looked at him with surprise. "Me? Oh, um, I suppose I'm a little off today. I've got a splitting headache and the Aspirin I took an hour ago doesn't seem to be working." That was all he could think to say.

"Maybe you need a little more coffee." Jeff Larson said. "Caffeine can help with morning headaches sometimes."

"Oh—good point Jeff. I'll bet that's it. I haven't had any coffee yet this morning." Chuck responded.

At that moment, Dorothy James entered the room with a stack of papers in her hand. "I'm sorry to interrupt sir, but we have a problem." She said. Everyone cast their attention immediately to Dorothy who stood there with a very concerned look on her face.

"What kind of problem Dorothy?" Chuck asked.

"Well sir, we do not have the Inspector General's approval that all safety protocols have been cleared to use the lab." Dorothy said very seriously. "It seems that the inspection documents after the, um, *incident* a few months ago never reached the Inspector General's office for his signature. I'm sorry, but we cannot set foot in the lab without his authorization to do so." Dorothy turned to Chuck and gave a slight wink with the eye not visible to the rest of the team.

"Damn it!" Chuck said as he dropped his head as if this were the worst thing that could ever happen, when really he was smiling from ear to ear. Dorothy had saved the day and he loved her for that.

"That's terrible!" Baljeet said. "We are all ready to go. How can we resolve this?" He said feeling equally as relieved.

"I'm faxing the document over to the Pentagon now sir, but it's a lengthy document and each page takes several minutes to go through." Dorothy said.

"However, there is one other snag…The Inspector General is out of the office until Thursday."

Chuck turned to the team seated around the conference room table. "Well, there you have it. This project is officially postponed until we have proper clearance." He said. "If you have other things to prepare for at this time, please do. If not, I'll just see you back here again on Thursday." Chuck closed his binder and dismissed everyone.

After all of the greatly disappointed scientists left the conference room, only Chuck, Baljeet and Dorothy remained. "Dort, I could kiss you right now. Thank you for coming up with that. That was brilliant!" Chuck said.

"Thank you sir. I noticed that the document hadn't been signed after we spoke last week. I could have taken care of it then, but saw it as the opportunity we were looking for so I put it off until this morning." Dorothy said. "Administrative oversight sir. I won't be disciplined for it. Besides, how were we supposed to know that the Inspector General would be away this week?" She knew that he would be, but no one else would have known. The circumstances were just too perfect and Dorothy felt it was her duty for the sake of everyone's safety to take advantage of them.

"Well, thank you Dorothy. You saved the day." Chuck said. Dorothy nodded and left the conference room to finish faxing the inspection report.

A short while later, after Chuck and Baljeet had returned to Chuck's office to discuss the details of Wednesday, Dorothy knocked on the door. "Sir? Edith MacKenzie is here to see you. Shall I show her in?" She asked.

Chuck stood up. "Edith's here? Yes, please bring her back." He said.

As Edith entered the office, Baljeet rose to his feet and politely bowed. "A pleasure to see you this morning Mrs. MacKenzie." He said.

"Oh, Baljeet, please call me Edith." She said. "No need to be so formal anymore."

"What brings you out here Edith?" Chuck asked. He really wasn't expecting to see her until Wednesday, so he was hopeful that there wasn't anything wrong. "And, how did you get here? I hope you're not driving."

"Oh heavens no! Not with this cast on my arm. Ed drove me. They let him through the gate but wouldn't let him come in the building so he's waiting in the truck outside." Edith said. "You haven't laid the salt barrier in the lab yet, have you Chuck?" She asked.

Chuck had completely forgotten about that. He was so distracted by how he was going to delay the project that he never gave it a second thought after

Dorothy presented a clever solution. "No, not yet. I'm sorry, I forgot about that after my meeting. The good news is that Dorothy found an authorization technicality that delayed our project until Thursday so no one would need to go in there until we're done anyway." He said.

"Oh good!" She said as she smiled. "I had a feeling that would happen."

Chuck looked surprised, although he really shouldn't have been. Edith *was* a gifted Psychic after all.

"I do think we need to lay a strong protective barrier down for our own protection though. That's why I'm here. After last week, I don't want to risk it. This Entity will do everything in its power to stop us. The barrier may not stop it completely, but it will help." Edith explained. "Can we go down there now?"

"Ah, sure Edith. Let's go." Chuck said as he grabbed his key card from his desk and the bag of salt from his briefcase. He and Baljeet escorted Edith to the elevator leading down to Lab 2C.

When the elevator doors opened, there was an eerie silence in the corridor leading down to the lab. Edith was sensing that the portal was open, but she could not feel a heavy negative presence in the area. Hopefully, this was a window of opportunity that would not entail an unfortunate encounter with anything. As Chuck swiped his key card through the slot, the door clicked and popped open. Chuck slowly entered the room and turned on the light switch right next to the door. As the fluorescent lighting flickered and began to light up the room, Edith scanned the lab for anything that might be in there waiting for them. There was nothing that she could see, hear, or feel. "I think the coast is clear." She said.

Edith reached into her crossbody bag with her left hand and pulled out a sage stick and some matches. "Baljeet? Would you mind lighting this for me?" She asked.

"Yes, yes of course Edith." Baljeet said as he took the sage stick and lit the end of it. Once a flame had started, he blew it out and let the white smoke rise into the room.

"That's good. Now, walk around every inch of the room with that and say: *Only Peace, Love, and Light may enter. All negative energies must leave. You are not welcome here.*" Edith said. Baljeet nodded his head and bowed to her as he proceeded to walk around the room waving the smudge stick and reciting the words Edith had instructed him to say.

"Now Chuck, you and I will follow Baljeet with the salt and Holy water. You walk ahead of me and sprinkle a thin, continuous line of salt on the floor, and I'll follow with the Holy water." Edith said.

"Got it." Chuck said as he opened the bag and grabbed a handful of salt.

Following closely behind Chuck, Edith began sprinkling a small amount of Holy water along the wall as she walked while reciting: "*I lay this salt to purify the negative energies and to create a protective barrier that they may not cross…I bless these walls with Holy water so that no evil may enter this space.*" When they reached the corner of the room where the portal was, Edith doused the area with a little extra Holy water and asked Baljeet to linger there a little longer burning the sage.

Once they had covered the boundaries of the entire room, Baljeet went to the lab sink to extinguish the burning sage stick, wrapped it in a paper towel, and handed it back to Edith. Chuck sealed the plastic bag with the remaining salt and they stood there silently together for a moment, listening.

"Is that it?" Chuck asked.

"Yes. It's all done." Edith said. "This won't hold forever, but it should definitely keep the negative entities out until we can close and seal the portal on Wednesday."

"I hope the janitorial people don't come in and sweep up the salt!" Baljeet said.

"They're not allowed to come in here. There are only three people with key card access to this lab and that's Me, Dorothy, and the night Security Guard. Dorothy won't touch it, and I'll make sure the Security Guard knows not to disturb the salt. I'll tell him that it's part of our experiment. He won't disturb it." Chuck said.

As Chuck was walking to the door to turn out the lights, he noticed Baljeet inspecting the Hadron Collider. "So this is it?" He asked as he rubbed his hands on the cold metal surface of the giant cylinder.

"That's the Collider. Pretty impressive, huh?" Chuck said. "Have you ever worked with one?"

"Never. There are only one or two in the whole world. How would I have the opportunity to do that? We have nothing like this in India." Baljeet said.

"Damn it! I was hoping you knew how to operate it." Chuck said with a serious look on his face.

Baljeet looked at him, slightly terrified. "Are you telling me Mr. Chuck that you do not know how to operate this machinery? What are we going to do!?! We have only two days! Does it have a manual? Where is the power button?" Baljeet panicked as these questions flooded his mind.

Chuck couldn't contain his laughter. "I'm just kidding my friend!" He laughed. "Of course I know how to operate it. I'm just joking with you."

"Ha ha. Not very funny Mr. Chuck. Not very funny at all." Baljeet said as he shook his head and walked briskly towards the door.

"Oh come on!" Chuck said as he turned out the light and shut the door. "It was a little funny. Wasn't it Edith?"

"I thought it was a little funny." She said as they entered the elevator.

"Okay, it was a tiny bit funny." Baljeet admitted as he held up his thumb and his forefinger indicating a very small amount. The three of them shared a bit of much needed laughter over the joke, and Baljeet was grateful that they could manage to maintain their sense of humor despite the raw evil they were charged with disposing of.

By the time the elevator reached the main floor, Dorothy was standing in the hallway waiting for them. "Oh there you are sir!" Dorothy said. "Dr. Wurmser is on the line for you…And he's NOT very happy. Shall I patch him through?"

"Shit." Chuck said under his breath. This was an ass chewing that he was not looking forward to, but was more than willing to take given the circumstances. "Go ahead and put him through." He said. "And Dort?"

"Yes sir?" Dorothy answered.

"Please put a notice out that no one is to enter the area of Lab 2C until Thursday. Call it, an inspection day or something. We have to be down there at 11:00 am on Wednesday, and no one else can be around so whatever you can come up with to keep people away would be great." Chuck said as he walked back to his office to take a call that he was not looking forward to.

Later that evening, Baljeet went home to his furnished apartment that the government provides for visiting project collaborators such as Dr. Chadha. It wasn't the Four Seasons, but it was fully furnished with all of the comforts of a modern home. After preparing some dinner for himself, he decided to check in with his family back home in Cochin just to make sure that everything was in place for November 11th.

"I'm so happy to hear your voice Rey Rey. How is your Grandfather?" Baljeet asked.

"He is old and growing weary Father, but he is cheerful." Reyansh replied.

"And where is your Mother this morning?" Baljeet asked. Although it was 7:00 pm in the Chicago area, it was 7:00 am the following morning in Southern India.

"She is with Harini and Jayanti at the market. She left about 10 minutes ago. I am sorry she missed your call Father." Reyansh said. *"How is America Father? Do you like it there?"*

"Oh, I am sorry I missed her too." Baljeet said. "America is fine Rey Rey. Very different from India. They are very wealthy here. The lab I am working at has very special equipment that no one else has in the world. It is a privilege and an honor to be working here."

"Have you met my friend Lily Father? What is she like?" Reyansh asked. Although he was very interested in their objectives with the energy triangle, he was still a young boy who was beginning to appreciate the wonder and beauty of girls.

Baljeet laughed. "I have met her Rey Rey and she is very smart, very sweet, and more beautiful than you could imagine!" He said. "I think that you and Miss Lily will be great lifelong friends when we are finished with our very important task…Which is why I am calling you today Reyansh. Do you understand what you are to do on Wednesday?"

"Yes Father. Grandfather and everyone in the house will be joining me in the circle and Heru will be with us." Reyansh said.

"Very good Rey Rey. And you know you are 12 hours ahead of us here so you must do this at 10:55 pm on Wednesday, yes?" Baljeet explained. "You will need a few minutes to accelerate the energy intensity before 11:00 so make sure everyone is clear and grounded before then. Do you understand?"

"Yes Father." Reyansh replied respectfully. *"Both Heru and Grandfather have explained the importance of the time to me."*

"Very good then. While you are working there at 11:00 pm on November 11th, we will be working here at 11:00 am on November 11th. The number 11 is very important to fully activate the Stargate." Baljeet explained.

"I am aware of the importance Father. Do not worry. I will do as I have been instructed." Reyansh replied.

"That's fine Rey Rey. Please tell everyone that I send my love and I miss you all very much. I will call again soon. Godspeed Rey Rey." Baljeet said as he said goodbye and hung up the phone.

CHAPTER 53

TUESDAY, NOVEMBER 10, 1970

Annie finished cleaning up the dishes from dinner while Mark and the kids relaxed in the family room to watch TV together. Before joining the family, Annie went to the sliding glass door by the kitchen to let Winnie out, and stood quietly watching her dog through the window as Winnie ran around the back yard sniffing out the perfect spot to pee.

"How are you feeling about tomorrow, Lil? Is there anything else we need to do?" Annie asked as she called down to the family room that was open, but on a split level slightly lower than the kitchen area.

"Good. I know what we need to do Mom…And besides, Auset will be with us to make sure it goes well." Lily explained.

"I thought Auset was going to be in the lab with Edith, Chuck, and Baljeet?" Annie asked.

Lily turned around and stood on her knees on the back of the couch to face Annie standing by the sliding glass door waiting to let Winnie back in. "Remember Mom, Auset can be in many places at once. She *will* be with Edith in the lab, but she will always be with me when I need her." Lily said as she touched the black star sapphire hanging around her neck. "That's why she gave this to me. It is an extension of her. Kind of like Batman and the light in the sky showing a bat when Gotham City needs him."

"Hmmmm. Good analogy Lil. That makes sense." Annie said. "So then that's much more than just a pretty necklace, huh?"

Lily smiled. "MUCH more Momma. It's very special to me. I will always wear it."

Annie smiled at that. She was proud of Lily and she was impressed that even though she was a very young girl, she was incredibly mature for her age and had an understanding of the Universe well beyond the understanding by most adults.

After an evening of *The Mod Squad* followed by the *ABC Movie of the Week*, it was now 10:00 pm which was an hour later than Lily's usual bedtime. Since everyone was taking the day off from school to help with the energy circle, Annie didn't think extending bedtime an hour later would hurt.

"Okay everyone—we have a really big day tomorrow and you all need to be well rested. Time for bed!" Annie announced as she got up and turned off the television.

Surprisingly, everyone did what she asked and marched upstairs to go brush their teeth and go to bed. After tucking the kids in to bed, with the exception of Stephen who usually stayed up late reading, but was consistent getting up early in the morning regardless, Mark and Annie retired to their own bedroom to settle in. Mark turned on the television in their room so he could watch the nightly news while he brushed his teeth.

'A devastating category 4 tropical cyclone referred to as Bhola is bearing down in the Bay of Bengal, heading towards East Pakistan. Sustained winds are expected to hit 240 mph by the time it makes landfall sometime within the next 28-32 hours.' The nightly news anchor reported.

"Mark did you hear that!?! That's the sign! Bhola—That's what Auset said was the sign!" Annie said as her heart was racing and a lump was forming in her throat. "She said it would be one of the worst natural disasters in history."

"Wow! That's remarkable. What does that mean for us tomorrow?" Mark asked.

"It just means that Auset was correct and that tomorrow is the right day to send the Beast out into oblivion. That's what it means." Annie said as she sat on the edge of the bed and watched the satellite images of the storm shown on the television. This storm was a monster and there was absolutely no doubt it was going to be devastating when it hit land. "I wonder how far away Baljeet's family lives?"

"They're just south of Bombay I think Honey, and that's on the other side of India, here." Mark said as he pointed to the approximate location of Bombay on the map shown on the television.

"Oh, that's a relief." Annie said.

"Remember, Edith said that Baljeet's son and his family were anchoring the other energy point of the triangle in India. I'm sure they wouldn't be doing it in the middle of a devastating storm." Mark reminded her.

Annie nodded her head in agreement and crawled into bed and turned out the light. They watched the news just up to the sportscast before turning t off. Mark rolled over to his right side and Annie spooned behind him as they usually did most nights when Mark was home, and they fell fast asleep.

Just shortly after 3:00 am, Annie and Mark were awakened by the sound of screaming and Winnie's panic bark. Mark shot up out of bed. The room was filling with smoke and he began to cough.

"Annie! Wake up! Something is on fire!" He said as he ran to the door and opened it. The entire hallway was filled with smoke and he could hear the crackle of fire and feel the heat of the flames bellowing up the stairway. Mark ran across the hall to Lily's room, where she was sitting in the corner of her smoke filled room screaming with her knees drawn up to her chest on her bed. He wrapped her in a blanket and threw her over his shoulder, and ran down to Stephen's room at the end of the hall where Annie, Vince and Stephen were waiting for him. Winnie was close behind as he entered Stephen's room and he shut the door behind him, rolled up a blanket, and pressed it firmly under the door.

"Open the window Stephen!" Mark yelled as he quickly took inventory to make sure everyone was there in the room.

"Can you see a way to climb down?" Mark asked.

"Yeah, I think I can drop to the flowerbed from here Dad. It's not that high." Stephen said as he crawled backwards out the window, hung from the window sill, and dropped 8 ft. to the empty flower beds below.

"Annie, you go next." Mark said. "Stephen—run across the street and wake the Frasiers! Hurry!" He said as he helped Annie out the window.

Annie stretch out and hung from the window sill before dropping to the ground. "Okay, hand Lily down to me!" She said as she stood below the window with outstretched arms.

Mark unwrapped Lily from the blanket and tossed the blanket down. "Lil? I'm going to hand you down to your Mother. Don't be afraid Honey." He said as he sat her up on the window sill and grabbed her firmly by the arms, lowering her down to where Annie could touch her feet. "I'm going to let go of you Honey, but your Mom is going to catch you. Don't be scared." He said as calmly as he could.

"I'm scared Daddy! Where's Winnie?" Lily cried.

"I'll get Winnie, don't worry." He reassured her. "At the count of three I'm going to let go, okay? One…Two…Three." Mark let loose of his Daughter and she fell into Annie's arms.

Stephen and the Frasier's rushed across the street carrying a ladder that they quickly propped up under Stephen's bedroom window. "Climb down on this! The fire department is on its way!" Chuck yelled.

"Okay Vince—your turn son. Climb down the ladder." Mark said.

"Dad, hand Winnie to me! I can climb down with her." Vince said as he took hold of the frightened Cocker Spaniel under his arm and climbed down the ladder.

The wooden hollow core door to Stephen's bedroom began to burn and the flames were breeching through. Smoke was filling the room at an alarming pace and Mark began to cough violently from the heavy smoke. His arm and shoulder hurt badly from lowering Annie and Lily and he struggled to get himself through the window. He tucked his hurt arm into his side and he climbed down as quickly and carefully as he could with one hand. When he reached the ground, Annie and Lily ran to his side and hugged him.

"Let's get back!" Mark said as he and Chuck ushered everyone across the street to the Frasier's driveway. The fire truck came roaring up the street. The firemen quickly jumped out of the truck, and attached the fire hose to the fire hydrant that happened to be located at the corner of the Campbell's lot.

"Is there anyone inside the house?" The fireman asked them.

"No, no. We all got out." Mark said as he coughed and quickly scanned the area to make sure everyone was accounted for.

"Good! Is everyone okay?" The fireman asked.

"No, I think my husband is hurt." Annie said as she examined his hurt arm. "He was in a terrible car accident a few months ago and he may have reinjured his arm helping us out of the window." Cheryl walked over to take a look to see if he had re-broken anything.

"The paramedics are on their way Ma'am." The fireman said. "Any pets remaining in the house?" They shook their heads *no* as the fireman noticed Winnie sitting dutifully at Lily's feet.

The Campbell Family stood helplessly watching as their home was engulfed in flames. Everyone survived, everyone was safe, but every worldly possession they had was quickly being disintegrated right before their eyes.

"How did this happen?" Annie asked. "We've never even used the fireplaces yet. Faulty wiring? Or, could I have left the stove on after dinner?" She said as she looked up at Mark.

"I don't know Honey. All of that was inspected before we bought the house. They must have missed something if that's what started it." Mark said.

"I know how it happened." Lily said with an absolution in her voice. "It was the Dark Entity. This was its last attempt to stop us before 11:00 on November 11th." At that moment, no one said anything. There was no further discussion to be had. They all had a gut feeling that Lily was right.

The Paramedics arrived and after first checking the Children and Annie, Mark sat on the back of the truck with an oxygen tube as the Paramedics put his arm in a sling. "I think you need to go to the hospital for an x-ray on that arm Mr. Campbell. It's swelling pretty badly." The Paramedic said as he wrapped an ice pack in a hand towel and gently placed it inside the sling.

"Yeah, I'll go in and have the Doctor look at it tomorrow. I just want to stay here with my family tonight." Mark replied.

"I hear ya." The Paramedic said. "Is there anyone else we need to check out before we leave?"

"No, you've seen all of us." Mark said. "Thank you. I appreciate you coming out in the middle of the night to take care of us."

"No thanks necessary. It's what we do." The Paramedic said.

Mark slowly walked away from the EMT vehicle and joined Annie and the kids in the driveway. Cheryl walked up behind them and gave them a hug.

"Annie? I think we should try to make some sleeping arrangements here tonight. Beth has a double bed in her room, so we can put Lily in there with her. Joey has bunk beds, so if Vince doesn't mind sleeping in his room we can put him there. We have a guest room with a queen sized bed for you and Mark, and I'll make the living room couch as comfortable as possible for Stephen if that's okay." Cheryl said.

"That sounds great. Thank you Cheryl." Annie said.

"Annie, why don't you go with Cheryl and get the kids settled in. I'll be along in a few minutes." Mark said.

"Ok." Annie said as she gave him a kiss on the cheek then gathered the kids and followed Cheryl into the house.

Chuck stood in the driveway with Chuck mesmerized by the scene of raging orange flames across the street. Two large pumper trucks arrived and they had two powerful fire hoses spouting water into the flames, but it didn't seem to matter. Flames would reappear in the areas they just watered down as if water didn't faze it.

"I'm so sorry Mark." Chuck said sympathetically. "Do you have any idea what started this?"

"No, but…Lily said rather confidently that it was started by the Dark Entity we're about to get rid of today. She said it was its last attempt to stop us." Mark said.

Chuck put his arm around Mark. "Well, it's about to get its ass kicked."

CHAPTER 54

WEDNESDAY, NOVEMBER 11, 1970

C huck's alarm went off at 7:00 am as it had every other ordinary work day. Chuck rolled out of bed, went to the bathroom and turned on the shower. After getting dressed, he walked down the hallway and was surprised to see Cheryl and Annie sitting at the kitchen table having coffee.

"What are you two doing up so early?" Chuck asked. "I thought you'd sleep for another hour or so."

"I can't say that I ever went to sleep." Annie said. She was in complete shock about what happened last night and was stuck in a surreal fog. She was trying to figure out what they were going to do next. They couldn't impose and move in with the Frasier's. Who knew how long it would take to rebuild their home. Where were they going to go? For God's sake they didn't even have a toothbrush or a change of clothes. Annie was completely devastated as the total loss of everything they owned became a reality.

Chuck poured a cup of coffee and sat down. He reached across the table and held Annie's hands. "Annie? Look at me. You're going to get through this. Cheryl and I will help you—whatever it takes, don't you worry. You are more than welcome to stay here as long as you need to." He said with reassuring sincerity.

"Thank you." Annie said as tears welled up in her eyes.

Chuck gave her hands a gentle squeeze. "I'm not trying to be insensitive, but we all have to pull together and send this damn thing out into oblivion this morning. We'll figure everything else out later. Okay?" He said as he looked into her eyes. "Can you do that?"

"Yes, yes." Annie said as she wiped her tears and straightened up in her chair. "I can do this. Don't worry Chuck, we'll do our part."

"Good." Chuck said as he took a big gulp of coffee and stood up. "I've got to go pick up Edith, so I've gotta run." He said as he kissed Cheryl and then gave Annie a kiss on the cheek. "We've got this!"

As Chuck opened the garage door, the smell of an extinguished fire hit him hard. He looked across the street at what was left of the Campbell's house and gasped. In the dark it was hard to see how bad it was, but now seeing it in the early morning light was shocking. The house had nearly burnt to the ground. All that remained was part of the garage, the front stone pillars that held up the portico, the stone fireplace in the family room, a few charred timbers, and the charred remains of Annie's Oldsmobile Toronado that was parked in the garage. Everything else had been torched. The only structure that remained was the detached garage in the back where the boat was stored, Stephen's car which was parked at the far side of the driveway by the detached garage, and the gym equipment in the back yard. The Fire Marshall and a group of investigators were already out there sifting through the charred remains. Knowing that it was the Dark Entity that did this to his good friends and neighbors infuriated Chuck. He was determined to end its very existence by noon today. That was a promise.

"I smell like an ashtray." Annie said as she sniffed her flannel pajama shirt and a lock of her hair. "I don't know how you can sit next to me Cheryl."

"Hey—You went through quite an ordeal last night. I don't care what you smell like. I'm just happy you and your family are alive!" Cheryl said as she stood up. "Come with me." She took Annie by the hand and led her down the hall to the Master bedroom. "What size do you wear Annie?" She asked as she opened a drawer and pulled out a pair of jeans and a navy blue turtle neck sweater. "These jeans are too tight on me, but they'll probably fit you. We're both the same height so they'll definitely be long enough."

"Thanks Cheryl. I think these will fit just fine." Annie said as she held them up.

Cheryl walked over to the linen closet by the Master bathroom and retrieved a fresh towel and a wash cloth. "Here. There's shampoo and conditioner in the shower. I've got a package of toothbrushes here too." She said as she pulled a new pack of 5 toothbrushes out of the drawer and handed one to Annie.

"Thank you Cheryl." Annie said as she carried the clothes and clean towel into the bathroom.

"You get washed up and I'm going to go see what I can find for Mark and the kids to wear today." Cheryl said as she went back to closet to see what she had that might work.

As Annie stood in the shower with the warm water pouring over her, she started sobbing uncontrollably. She felt completely defeated…Violated even. Everything she and Mark had worked so hard for their entire lives was gone. Cheryl and Chuck had taken them in, but they couldn't stay there long term. Where would they go? They were just starting to get back on their feet financially after Mark's terrible accident, and now they were even worse off than they were then. What were they going to do? As Annie shampooed the smoke and soot out of her hair, she remembered what they had to do today. She had to pull herself together. She needed all of her strength and wisdom to be intact and not destroyed as the Dark Entity had intended by causing the fire. It intended to kill them, but they survived. Everyone was alive and that was what was most important.

Annie got dressed and went to the guest room to see if Mark was awake. The bed was empty, but she heard his voice down the hall towards the kitchen so she walked that way. When she got to the Kitchen, Cheryl had neatly stacked sets of clothes and toothbrushes out on the kitchen table for everyone and she was checking the swelling on Mark's arm.

"The swelling is down quite a bit." Cheryl said. "How high can you raise your arm over your head?"

Mark slowly raised his arm and winced once he raised it just a few inches above his shoulder. "Ouch." He said. "That's about as high as I can go Cheryl. It feels like I pinched a nerve or something."

"You might have." Cheryl said. "I don't think it's broken though. Let's keep the sling on it and if it's still bothering you by tomorrow, you should go get an X-Ray and see what the Doctor says." She said as she reattached the sling.

"Good Morning." Annie said as she walked up behind him and hugged Mark around the waist. "Hi Sweetheart. Did you sleep at all?" Mark asked as he kissed the top of her head.

"Not really. You?" Annie asked.

"Not much at all either." Mark said.

"C'Mon Mark. Let me get you a fresh towel and show you where the shower is." Cheryl said as she handed him a pair of jeans and a flannel shirt. "Here, I think these will fit you."

"Thank you Cheryl. A shower sounds great." Mark said as he took the neatly folded clothing in his good hand and followed Cheryl down the hall.

Stephen was sacked out on the living room couch, but he was stirring a bit so Annie went to check on him. "Are you awake?" She asked.

"Yeah, I'm up Mom. I'm just laying here trying to figure out what happened last night." Stephen said as he put his hands behind his head.

"I'm not sure Honey, but we'll find out. Were you able to sleep?" Annie asked.

"Only for a couple of hours. The fire trucks didn't leave until almost 5:30 this morning. I think I fell asleep after that. What time is it?" Stephen asked.

"It's about 8:30. Cheryl found some clothes for you to change into for today, and she's got a new toothbrush for you too. Your Dad's in the shower now, so you can take one next." Annie said to him as she placed her loving hand on his cheek.

"Oh, thanks Mom. I forgot about that important detail. We have no clothes or anything now. What are we going to do?" Stephen asked as he sat up.

"Well, when we're done with the energy circle, which is VERY important for us to be able to do today…" Annie explained "We will go on a little shopping spree for some new clothes, toiletries, shoes, coats, and other things we're going to need for the time being. The Frasier's are insisting that we stay here for a while, just until we can figure out what to do next." She said.

Beth and Lily came down the hall and went to the kitchen to get some breakfast. Beth got a box of Cheerios out of the cabinet and poured a bowl for herself and Lily. Annie and Stephen joined them.

"Beth? Where's that box of clothes that you've outgrown from when we cleaned out your closet last year?" Cheryl asked. "I meant to take it to Goodwill, but I don't think I ever did. I'm sure there are a few things in there that Lilly might be able to fit into." She said.

"I think it is downstairs in the basement in the storage closet next to the Christmas decorations. I saw it there a couple of months ago when I was looking for my old track sweatshirt." Beth said as she poured the milk over the cereal sitting in front of Lily.

"Ok, I'll run down and take a look." Cheryl said as she noticed Stephen walk into the kitchen. "Good morning Stephen! I hope the couch was okay?" She asked.

"Yes, it was fine Mrs. Frasier. Thank you." Stephen said as Beth passed him a bowl and the box of Cheerios.

"And this stack here is for you. These are a pair of jeans that are too small for Chuck, they might be a little big on you, but they should do for today. Here's a hooded sweatshirt and a toothbrush." Cheryl said as she slid the stack of clothing over next to Stephen.

"Does anyone know if the boys are up?" Annie asked.

"They're up Momma." Lily said. "They're in Joey's room talking."

"Oh and, I have a pair of Chuck's sweats for Vince. He's too tall for anything Joey has but I think these will work." Cheryl said. "And I've got the day off today, so as soon as we're done killing that evil thing, you can use my car to go get some things later if you want to."

"Cheryl? You're the best, thank you." Annie said with gratitude as she walked down the hall to get the boys up.

Annie knocked on the door. "Come in!" Joey yelled.

"Are you boys up?" Annie asked.

"Hi Mom. We've been up for a while. We're just talking." Vince said. He sounded very low.

Annie noticed that he had a clear shot of their house through the window from his bed, and the scene was very devastating. She hadn't seen what it looked like after the fire had been put out and this was her first glance at it. She held her hand up to her mouth and gasped.

"Oh my God." She said.

"It's gone. Nothing left but Stephen's shit car." Vince said.

Annie pulled the blinds closed and pulled herself together. "Okay. Let's not focus on that right now. We all know that the Dark Entity is responsible for that fire. It knows what we're about to do today, and it was trying to stop it from happening…But we survived. We're still here and we are going to defeat that evil piece of shit today!" Annie said in a manner that was strong, forceful, and inspiring. "Let's get out of bed, get cleaned up and eat some breakfast. We have important work to do!"

CHAPTER 55

C huck had picked up Edith that morning and was surprised to find that the infamous Auset was with her. Auset was a tall, lean, absolutely stunning woman with radiant skin and shiny, straight black hair that hung just past her shoulders with blunt bangs framing her beautiful face. Chuck could barely keep his eyes off of her. When they arrived at the gate, Chuck had a visitor's pass in place for Edith, but he did not expect to be bringing Auset along so he was concerned that this would cause a delay. To his surprise, Stan at the gate was so captivated by Auset's beauty that he didn't even ask about her and waived them through anyway without checking the visitor's list.

When they entered the back door of the building, Dorothy rushed toward them with a large bundle of folded white HazMat suits in her hand. "Good morning sir." She said.

"Good morning Dorothy." Chuck said. "You know Edith, and this is Auset. I don't have clearance for her but somehow Stan just lifted the gate without…"

"I know sir." Dorothy said. "I've sent out a memo to everyone in the building alerting them of a surprise Bio Hazard inspection in the labs this morning. I think you should dress the part." She said as she handed everyone a HazMat suit. "The hoods will also mask your identities."

Chuck, Edith and Auset each took a suit. "Dorothy, you are truly amazing!" Chuck said.

"Thank you sir." Dorothy said. "That should keep everyone out of your way for today."

They stepped into Chuck's office quickly and slipped into the HazMat suits. When they were all suited up, they opened up the door and stepped out into the hall. At the elevator, Baljeet was standing there waiting for them, suited up in a HazMat suit as well.

"Ready to go Chuck?" Baljeet asked.

"Readier than I've ever been. Let's go blast this thing." Chuck said as he held the elevator door open so everyone could step in. He pushed the button to take them down to the Lab Level, and the doors closed.

It was 10:50 pm in Cochin, India and Reyansh and his family were sitting on the floor in a circle in the living room of their small house. Reyansh's Grandfather was sitting on the couch, and his Mother was sitting next to him. He set a small timer so that it would ding in exactly 10 minutes, indicating the time they were to accelerate their energy and manifest their intentions to activate their point of the triangle to send the Evil Entity out of the Universe. He instructed everyone to hold hands and he guided them with rhythmic breathing, and a guided meditation. *I am here with you Reyansh. At the appointed time I will elevate your energy to the highest frequency.'* Heru said to him telepathically. They were ready.

Back at the Frasier's house, Lily instructed everyone to sit in a circle. Cheryl set a small cooking timer on the floor next to her to ding at exactly 11:00 am. Everyone joined hands and Lily guided them through a process of rhythmic breathing and meditation, just as Reyansh was doing at the exact same time halfway around the world.

At Argon, Chuck swiped his key card to unlock the door to Lab 2C. As he opened the door and turned on the lights, he stepped in cautiously to make sure they would not be ambushed by the Shadowy being that had been seen in there recently.

"It is safe Dr. Frasier. The barrier of protection you laid has held. We can proceed." Auset said.

Chuck nodded and entered the lab. He walked toward the Hadron Collider and turned it on. A loud humming noise began to emanate from the large machine and Baljeet was in awe. "In about 3 minutes, I can begin the particle reversal after we enter the astral coordinates." Chuck said. "Baljeet? Would you like to do the honors?"

"Yes, yes, it would be my pleasure!" Baljeet said as he reached into his pocket and pulled out the note with the coordinates on it. "I am setting galactic latitude 29.21732278° and galactic longitude 79.05502528°." He said.

This was the most exciting and most important thing he had ever done in his life and he was having a hard time keeping his hands steady.

"Coordinates confirmed." Chuck said as he looked at his watch. 10:57 am. "Three minutes to go."

Edith took a deep breath and looked at Auset. "Shall we join hands?"

Auset placed her hand on Edith's shoulder above her cast and reached for Chuck's hand with her other hand. At that moment, both Chuck and Edith felt a surge of protection, power, and wellbeing unlike anything else they have ever felt before. It was pure blissful contentment. It was strength, safety, confidence, and absolute knowledge that all would be well. Edith reached over and took Baljeet's hand, and he too felt the pure power and protection that was surging though each of them.

At exactly 11:00, Chuck raised the lever and pushed the activation button on the Hadron Collider. A high pitched humming sound emanated from the machine. Chuck grabbed Baljeet's hand and held tightly.

"Close your eyes!" Auset instructed, and in that moment a giant flash of bright, white light filled the room. Golden firey particles filled the air and an enormous surge of pure energy jolted through their bodies.

In the Chadha's living room in India, at precisely 11:00 pm when the timer went off, an enormous surge of energy and bright white light filled the room. Golden embers were swirling around each person in the circle and they could feel a mighty warm wind blow between them. They held each other's hands tightly and held firm on their intentions to send the Beast away.

As the cooking timer on the floor in front of Cheryl went off, Lily yelled: "Close your eyes!" Her necklace began to vibrate. A flash of bright, white light surged through the room, a strong, warm wind began to blow, and golden embers swirled around each person in the circle. All of a sudden, The 12 rays of the Star Sapphire around Lily's neck projected into every direction in the room and everyone could feel an intense vibration surrounding them.

At that moment, the outer bands of the Bhola Cyclone were making landfall in East Pakistan. The Dark Entity was the source of this devastating storm and the intensity of the energy triangle activated by Lily, Reyansh, and the coordinates anchored to the star Eltanin now activated by Chuck and Baljeet, was disrupting the force of the Dark Entity. It was being stripped of its power. As it surged its dark, angry energy into the Cyclone, winds rapidly increased to 240 mph. The vortex was open and it was spinning with vigorous intensity. The Dark Entity fought hard and exerted all of its strength to resist being pulled up into the vortex, but the energy triangle was too strong. The Cyclone raged as it pressed on toward land, spinning faster and expanding wider. The surge of energy activated by Auset, Heru, and Auser in the Galaxy above were greater than the Dark Entity could withstand. Then, all at once, the Beast succumbed to the power of the vortex. A deafening high pitched scream was heard around the world as a blinding flash of light like a magnificent lightning storm illuminated the sky and the vortex swallowed the Dark Entity unto the darkness of the Pakistani night sky.

Outside, the entire world came to a halt at that moment. Cars stopped in the middle of the road. Elevators in buildings came to a stop between floors. Inside peoples' homes the lights flickered. People in their houses went outside to see what was happening. People on the street stopped to look to the sky. For a brief moment, the entire world had an apocalyptic feel. For a brief moment, all of the electricity everywhere across the world shut down. Silence. Not a sound could be heard.

Edith and Chuck slowly opened their eyes. The lights came back on and the only sound that could be heard was the small comfortable hum of the Hadron Collider like that of a kitchen refrigerator. They looked at Baljeet and he was still clutching their hands and his eyes were shut tight. They looked to where Auset had been standing between them and found the crumpled HazMat suit laying empty on the floor.

"It is done." Edith said. "You can open your eyes now Baljeet."

Baljeet slowly opened his eyes, first his right, then his left. He looked around the room and saw Auset's HazMat suit laying on the floor. "Ohhhhh! Ohhhh no! What has happened to the beautiful lady?" He said in a panic.

Edith laughed. "She's fine, trust me." She said as she winked at Chuck. "We have one more thing to do—I have to seal the portal."

"How do you do that?" Chuck asked.

"Like this." Edith said as she walked over to the corner of the room where the portal was. She raised her left hand and pointed with her finger like she was drawing a big circle. Then she motioned like she was finger painting a large X in the center of the circle, then pointed to the center of the X in a tiny circular motion while saying: "I close and seal this doorway forever and ever. It is sealed shut never to be opened again." She said. Then she turned and smiled at Chuck and Baljeet. "Mission accomplished gentlemen."

When it was all over, there was a comforting silence and calmness in the air. Lily opened her eyes and smiled at everyone who was sitting in the circle with her. "It's done." She said.

"We did it?" Joey asked "That was SO cool!"

Mark reached over and gave Lily a big hug. "I'm so proud of you Pumpkin! You saved the world!"

Everyone cheered and praised Lily for leading the charge in their circle. She reached up and held the star sapphire hanging around her neck. She could still feel the intense energy emanating from it and it empowered her. She no longer felt helpless. She felt strong and purposeful. She felt like she could do anything. She turned and smiled sweetly at Annie then turned to Cheryl and asked: "Mrs. Frasier? May I have a glass of juice? I'm kind of thirsty." The whole room broke out in laughter.

"You most certainly can my dear!" Cheryl said. As she stood up and went into the kitchen, the doorbell rang.

"I'll get the door for you Cheryl." Mark said as he went to answer it.

When Mark opened the door, a short balding man with black glasses was standing there with a clipboard. "Hello. Can I help you?" Mark said.

"Oh hello, I'm Henry Blinkman. I'm with Union Mutual Insurance." The balding man said as he handed his card to Mark. "I'm looking for the people who own the property across the street. Do you know where I can find them? Their...ah... telephone is not working." He said awkwardly.

"You found them." Mark said. "I'm Mark Campbell. Our neighbors were kind enough to take us in last night."

The man's eyebrows raised and his eyes lit up. "Oh my! I'm so glad I found you." He said. "I'm so sorry about this. It's a very unfortunate tragedy..." The man said as he lowered his eyes and shook his head. "But, the good news is that you are fully insured. I'm your insurance adjustor and, well, I don't think there's anything else to be said other than I'm noting that it's a total loss on your claim. You'll be paid the full amount you're insured for so that you can rebuild your home." The man said. "Can you walk the site with me for a few minutes? I want to make sure I list everything."

"Sure." Mark said as he stepped outside and closed the door behind him.

Mark walked over to where his house used to stand with the insurance adjustor and they walked around the skeletal remains as Mark pointed out everything that they had lost. "How long before we can rebuild?" He asked.

"Oh, you can start as soon as we cut the check." The man said. "We won't be holding anything up ourselves, but we do need to wait until the Fire Marshall's report comes back. You know, just to make sure you didn't set the fire intentionally yourself for financial gain…That would of course be fraud and it's an exception on your policy."

Mark threw him a sarcastic look as if he would ever set his own house on fire in the middle of the night while his Family was sleeping. The man read Mark's expression, felt badly and replied: "I know, I know. We don't suspect that you did that by any means Mr. Campbell. It's just the law and we have to follow the rules." The man said.

"I understand." Mark said. "How long does that typically take?" He asked.

"It shouldn't be long at all. It's my understanding that the Fire Marshall was out here at 7:00 am this morning." The man said as he flipped the top page on his clip board. "My notes indicate that they're calling it *faulty wiring*. That means we'll cover it."

When Mark returned back to the Frasier's, everyone was jubilantly recounting the experience they just had and there were smiles all around. This made him smile despite the devastating reality that he had just walked away from across the street.

"Who was that Honey?" Annie asked.

"That was our insurance adjustor. He's calling it a total loss. He's going back to his office to process the claim now. He says he can bring a check over to us in a few days." Mark said.

"Wow. Fast service from Union Mutual." Annie said. "So, what are we going to do in the meantime?" She asked.

"Well, I think we should start at the bank. We have no credit cards, no checks, and no money on us. We need to get the kids some clothing, coats, and shoes. We have enough in our account to cover everything we need for now." Mark explained.

Cheryl walked over and handed Mark the keys to her car. "Here Mark. You guys go take care of that. Beth and I will wash your pajamas from last night and tidy up around here. We'll see you when you get back." She said as she hugged them both. "Things are going to work out. Don't worry—You'll see."

Mark thanked Cheryl and took the keys, then he and Annie rounded up their Family and they headed off to the bank, then to do a little shopping. When they walked out to the garage to get in the car, the scene across the street sickened all of them. No one said a word. They all stood there for a minute in sorrow and disbelief before getting into the car.

As Mark approached the stop light at the entrance of the neighborhood, Lily broke the awkward silence. "Daddy? Auset says not to be sad." Lily said. "She says we have a good surprise coming and not to worry. All will be well." Lily's voice was calming and the words were comforting.

"What did she say Lil?" Vince asked as he fidgeted with the drawstring on his sweatpants.

"She says that we did a good job and that we will be rewarded. She says not to worry." Lily said. Annie turned around to talk to Lily from the front seat. "Where is Auset, Lily?" She asked.

Lily stared at her mother and smiled. "She's everywhere Momma. She hasn't left us." She said as she smiled. "Things are going to be okay."

CHAPTER 56

In the early morning hours after the big event, Reyansh was summoned to his Grandfather's bedside. His Grandfather laid there, his labored breathing growing more shallow with each breath. Reyansh knelt down next to the bed and held his Grandfather's frail hand.

"I am here Grandfather. It's me, Rey Rey." Reyansh said as tears welled up in his eyes.

His Grandfather's eyes fluttered as he tried to open them. He licked his dry lips and opened his mouth letting out a faint wheeze as he exhaled. "I am proud of you my little tiger. You fulfilled your obligation to the world well." His Grandfather said in a faint voice as he gasped to catch his breath after every word. "My time is very near Rey Rey. I am ready." He said.

"Oh Grandfather!" Reyansh cried. "Please don't leave me—I love you Grandfather! What will I do without you?"

His Grandfather turned his head to face Reyansh. "Fear not Rey Rey. All things are as they should be…Thanks to you." He said as he lifted his hand to point to Reyansh. "I will not be in this bed any longer, but I will be with you always in spirit my young tiger… And we will meet again when your time here is done. Do not be sad for me, for I am returning home. I love you Rey Rey." He said as he dropped his hand down to his side no longer having the strength to hold it up.

At that moment, the room filled with light and Heru appeared at the foot of the bed. He lifted his arm and extended his hand. *'It is time to go. Come with me…'* Heru said as he held out his hand to his Grandfather. Then something unexpected happened. Heru's image turned in to the image of the Hindu God, Brahma, the Creator. Reyansh saw his Grandfather take his last breath, and then he watched as his Grandfather's spirit separated from his body and rose above it with his arm outstretched as his spirit took Brahma's hand. When they touched, Brahma's image changed into a magnificent Angel with 3 sets of wings that stretched out wide. As the Angel pulled his Grandfather closer, the Angel wrapped all 3 sets of wings around him. Tiny white and golden lights began to elegantly swirl around them as they rose higher and faded into an opening that appeared in the ceiling. Reyansh sat quietly with tears rolling down his cheeks, he felt a mixture of sadness that he just witnessed his Grandfather's passing, but also joy that he was going to a wonderful heavenly place. The room was silent as Reyansh gently placed a blanket over his Grandfather's lifeless body. "Goodbye Grandfather." He whimpered. "I will see you again. I love you."

Mark and Annie were able to go into their bank and arrange for new credit cards and checks to be sent to them using the Frasier's as their temporary address, and Mark was able to withdraw enough cash from their account to buy the things they needed immediately. They had finished shopping and were on their way back to the Frasier's. Lily sat in the back seat of the car admiring her new shoes but she was feeling a bit melancholy. She was still very much attached to her counterpart in India and she was experiencing Reyansh's loss of his Grandfather like it was happening to her.

Mark noticed her sadness in the rear view mirror. "Everything alright Pumpkin?" He asked.

"I'm just sad Daddy." Lily said softly. "Reyansh's Grandfather just died. I feel bad for him."

"I'm sorry." Mark said. "Was he sick?"

Lily took a deep breath and exhaled to gain clarity on that question. "No, he was just very old. He was kind of like my Mrs. MacKenzie. He helped Reyansh manage his abilities." She said with a sigh. "I would be very sad if anything happened to Mrs. MacKenzie. That would be terrible."

"Well, let's not think about that. Aside from her broken arm, Edith is in terrific shape. I don't think we have to be worried about her right now." Annie said as she smiled back at Lily.

When they arrived back at the Frasier's house, they all stared at the skeletal remains of their home across the street. Mark could feel the gloominess that was shrouded over his Family and decided to give them something else to think about. "Well, it may not have been the most pleasant experience, but we survived and we can rebuild it. We can rebuild it even better than it was before, right?" Mark said.

"Yes we can Daddy, and I would like to make my room a little bigger this time." Lily said optimistically.

"And I think we should put a mini fridge and a microwave in my room, and also bigger windows so I can see the planes land better, so my room should be bigger too." Vince piped up.

"And I kind of wish my built-in desk was a little bigger. I barely had room for an open book and a notebook on the other one. It was way too small." Stephen said. "And maybe a second closet to store my Rocketry supplies too."

Annie looked over at Mark and started laughing. "That's the spirit kids! Look at the bright side. We'll rebuild and it will be better than before." She said. "Come on you guys, everybody grab a bag."

Mark opened the trunk of the car and everyone grabbed as many bags as they could carry into the house. They bought quite a few things and the trunk of Cheryl's 1970 Olds Ninety-Eight was packed full. They bought clothes, shoes, snow boots, gloves, hats, scarves, coats, socks, underwear, backpacks, toothbrushes, toiletries, and other things they would need. It wasn't a complete replacement of everything they once had, but it was a decent supply of the things they needed most for now. As they went into the house through the garage door, the smell of chocolate chip cookies in the oven wafted over them.

"Something smells sooooooo good!" Vince said as he dropped his bags and headed for the kitchen.

Beth was just taking a cookie sheet out of the oven with the first batch of chocolate chip cookies she made. "You like chocolate chip?" She asked.

"Who doesn't?" Vince said.

Cheryl heard them come in, and came down the hall to help with the packages. "Wow! Looks like you had a successful shopping trip!" She said. "So, both Joey and Beth cleared some space in their dressers so Vince, you and Lily will have a place to put your clothes. That dresser in the guestroom is empty, so Mark, you and Annie can put your things away in there. And Stephen…" She said as she turned to Stephen who was occupying the living room couch at the moment. "You have a choice."

"I do?" Stephen asked.

"Yes. You can continue to stay up here on the living room couch, or you can take up residence in the family room downstairs. You'll have more privacy downstairs, and that happens to be where the TV and the spare refrigerator are so it's kind of like a mini apartment." Cheryl said as she winked. "I found an empty plastic bin in the garage that we used to store camping stuff in, but I brought it in and washed it so you can use it to store your clean clothes."

"I'm fine either place Mrs. Frasier, although, I might stay out of everybody's way if I'm downstairs." Stephen said.

"Ok. We'll make up the couch for you downstairs then." Cheryl said as she turned to Annie. "So as you've probably noticed, Beth made some chocolate chip cookies."

"How could we not? It smells heavenly!" Annie said.

"I made two pans of lasagna and they're in the refrigerator downstairs. We can pop those in the oven later for dinner." Cheryl said. "I invited Edith and Ed over tonight, but I think Barb has to stay late at the museum so she's staying in the city tonight and won't be joining us."

"Mrs. MacKenzie is coming over?" Lily's ears perked up when she heard this. She was still feeling the loss of Reyansh's Grandfather and she desperately wanted to see Edith.

"She is! And she's very excited to see you Lily. She told me to tell you that you did an excellent job today." Cheryl said.

"We ALL did an excellent job. It took all of us together to do it." Lily said proudly.

"Well that's why we're getting everyone together for dinner tonight. Call it, a little celebration for saving the world." Cheryl said as she smiled.

Later that evening, Ed and Edith came over and they enjoyed a celebratory dinner together. Lily stayed close by Edith's side and actually felt a new bond being formed between them, much stronger than they had before. As they were sitting around the dining room table, Annie noticed an empty seat.

"Where is Baljeet? Isn't he joining us?" Annie asked.

Chuck looked at Edith with a heavy expression before speaking, then he turned back to Annie. "Baljeet will not be joining us tonight. His Father passed away this afternoon and he is heading back to India first thing in the morning." He said.

"Oh, I'm so sorry." Annie said. "Actually, Lily told us that Reyansh's Grandfather had passed away today but I guess I didn't make the connection in my mind." She said as she regretted bringing it up.

"But we are eternally grateful for his help and his family's help today." Edith said as she held up her wine glass to make a toast. "To Baljeet. May he and his family never want for anything and live a long and happy life." She said.

"To Baljeet!" Everyone said in unison as they clinked their glasses together.

The evening continued and Edith and Chuck told everyone what was happening in the lab as everyone else described the events at the Frasier's that day. Lily talked about how she activated her star sapphire to boost the energy intensity and what it felt like to wear it around her neck.

The whole experience was unlike any other and each person around the table felt privileged to be a part of it. They all had a new perspective of the world and the constant battle between good and evil. The Frasier's especially had a new respect for the unknown. Their experience losing Joey for several weeks when he went through the portal and went back in time to Ancient Egypt was something they had never dreamed could ever happen, but they were wrong. Portals and time travel do exist. Vortexes and Shadow People do exist. Paranormal phenomena does exist. And they were all very aware of how thin the veil actually was between dimensions and other worlds.

As the table was being cleared and the plate of fresh chocolate chip cookies that Beth baked earlier was set on the table, someone was knocking on the front door.

"I wonder who that could be?" Chuck said as he stood up to answer it.

It was a courier who had a large brown envelope in one hand, and a clip board in the other. "Good evening." The courier said. "Are you Mr. Mark Campbell?"

"No, but he's here and I'm happy to get him for you. Please come in." Chuck said as he opened the door wider to let the man inside. "I'll be right back." Chuck walked back into the dining room to let Mark know there was someone at the door to see him.

Mark walked to the front door and introduced himself. "I'm Mark Campbell." He said.

"I have an important delivery for you from the law firm of Robertson, Zwerzinsky & Chisholm." The courier said. "Sign here please." He said as he handed the clipboard and a pen to Mark and pointed to where he should sign.

Mark signed the document and the courier handed him the thick envelope. "Thank you. Have a nice evening." He said as he closed the door behind the courier and walked back to the dining room.

"Who was that Honey?" Annie asked. "Surely that's not the check from the insurance company already. The fire just happened yesterday."

"No, but it's from a law firm that I've never heard of before." Mark said. "Maybe it's something about my car accident?" Mark wasn't sure what it was and the only way to find out was to open it. As he took a clean knife from the table and swiped it just under the flap, Lily and Edith smiled at each other. Mark pulled the stack of papers out and began reading the cover letter to himself. "Well, I'll be." He said. He could hardly believe what he was reading.

"What is it? What does it say?" Annie asked as she started to read the letter over his shoulder for herself.

Mark looked up from the letter. "This is the deed to our old house in Bruce Lake. It says that Auset had to return to the Middle East and she left the house to us." Mark was stunned.

"Daddy, I think there's more in there." Lily said as she clasped her hands together in anticipatory delight.

Mark set the papers down and pulled out a smaller envelope that contained 2 sets of new car keys. There was a handwritten note with them. The note said:

> Dear Mark and Annie,
>
> You have been truthful and pure, yet so much has been taken from you. I have no further use for these worldly goods, but your Family does. I leave to you this home with all of the furnishings and the automobiles in the garage. The Universe thanks you. God thanks you. Humanity thanks you. Be well and live long until the day comes when we meet again.
>
> Auset

"Oh my God Mark." Annie said in disbelief. "Auset left us her house!"

As everyone around the table sat silently with their mouths hanging open. Edith giggled and winked at Lily. "She wanted you to have it." Edith said.

"You knew about this?" Mark asked.

"Yes, she told me this morning." Edith said. "She instructed the law firm not to courier it over until she was gone. You've done a great thing for mankind. The Universe is just giving back to you." Edith said as she looked at Lily to pick it up from there.

"That's just how the Universe works Daddy. It gives back what we give of ourselves." Lily said profoundly as she ran to his side and gave him a big hug. "Love conquers all Dad…And you are VERY loved!"

THE END

Made in the USA
Las Vegas, NV
24 January 2021